A Pact of Blood

EVA CHASE

THE ROYAL SPARES - BOOK 2

A Pact of Blood

Book 2 in the Royal Spares series

First Digital Edition, 2024

Cover design: Sanja Balan (Sanja's Covers)

Map design: Fictive Designs

Ebook ISBN: 978-1-998752-97-3

Paperback ISBN: 978-1-998752-98-0

Hardcover ISBN: 978-1-998582-11-2

CHAPTER ONE

Aurelia

I stand next to one monster, watching another laid out on a pyre.

In the sunlight that streaks down over the immense city square, Emperor Tarquin's pale skin looks as if it could be made of wax. The devouts who prepared his body may even have rubbed a little into his flesh. I've heard that's done here in Dariu, for public funerals where they want the deceased to look at his or her best.

His sharp features form a stern expression. It's too easy to imagine him opening his eyes and aiming his piercing gray stare at me.

At his murderer.

None of the medics who've examined him or the guards who were protecting him have expressed any suspicion of foul play. Word has spread through court and presumably the common folk as well that his death was caused by a failure of his heart brought on by old age. Exactly as I intended the potion I concocted to make it appear.

It's been nearly two full days: the first dedicated to inquiry and private rites, the second to this public spectacle of mourning. No one has aimed the slightest accusation at me.

My plan succeeded. As soon as Tarquin's body burns, any remaining chance of uncovering evidence will go up in smoke.

I'll go on unimprisoned for my crime, jailed only in the gilded torture chamber of my own making.

My chief tormentor, the man who's now my husband, steps up to the podium on the broad steps overlooking the crowd. The black silk of Marclinus's suit turns his already pale skin even sallower, but that doesn't diminish the stark magnificence of his chiseled face. The imperial crown gleams a slightly richer gold than the wavy strands of his normally wayward hair, carefully coiffed for this solemn occasion.

A slimmer gold band hugs his right wrist, matching the marriage band fitted around my own. I doubt it feels as much like a manacle to him as it does to me.

He cuts an impressive picture of a new emperor. It's a shame so much beneath that stunning façade is rotten.

He gazes out over the sea of citizens also clothed in black —the color that encompasses all other colors, representing the full host of gods the departed has gone to join. Thousands of civilians have swarmed from the capital city's streets into its largest square to peer at the dead emperor and his grieving heir.

Marclinus has always enjoyed an audience.

The murmurs and sobs dwindle with the recognition that he's about to give his first speech as emperor. He lifts his chin, his well-built frame drawn straight in a commanding posture—every inch his father's son.

His voice rings out through the square, projected by the amplification charm embedded in the top of the podium. "Good citizens of Dariu, you honor me and my father by joining us today to mourn our country's tremendous loss. The great Emperor Tarquin ruled over our empire for nearly thirty years, bringing prosperity and security all across our great realm."

Prosperity and security for those born of Dariu, at least—brought in part by stealing the same from the conquered countries of the empire. How many of my own people back home in Accasy have endured boundless suffering or even given their lives for Emperor Tarquin's grand ideals?

What do all these Darium citizens make of the Accasian princess in their midst, the woman who is now by marriage their empress?

This is the first time I've stood before them as Marclinus's wife. My only previous public appearance was as a spectator of a bloody exhibition in the city's arena, when I was only one of several ladies vying for the imperial heir's hand.

As Marclinus continues heaping praise on his father's shoulders, I let my gaze drift over the crowd. Their attention is mostly fixed on their new emperor, but here and there, eyes flick toward me.

It's hard to read the reactions of the common folk when they're already downcast with mourning. Did that woman's mouth tighten into more of a scowl at the sight of me? Did that man's forehead furrow in possible consternation?

This isn't how I'd have wanted to introduce myself to the people I mean to rule over—however much Marclinus allows me to share in his rule.

Perhaps I can start to earn their good will *and* set a precedent for sharing this very afternoon.

Marclinus finishes his speech to a wave of applause. As he

steps back to our spot in the middle of the gathered nobles and advisors, I touch his arm.

I pitch my voice low. "Do you think I should say a few words to show how committed I am to the empire and to you?"

From what I've seen of my husband over the past few weeks, there's little he likes more than having everyone around him demonstrate their devotion. He never misses a chance to have his ego stroked.

"What a canny idea." He prods me toward the podium with a nudge that manages to also be a subtle grope of my ass and raises his voice again. "My wife and your new empress would speak to you as well!"

I catch a brief mutter behind me as if a few of our noble companions disapprove of this move, but I'm already at the podium. The thousands of gazes settle directly on me.

Taking a measured breath, I gather my words. I don't want to appear too grasping or self-important.

Keep it short, simple, and full of reverence for the man I despised.

I dip my head humbly. The empress serves her people at least as much as the other way around.

The amplification charm flings my voice out across the vast square. "I'm sorry to meet you all under such tragic circumstances. I only got to spend a few weeks in Emperor Tarquin's incredible presence, but I grew up in awe of his leadership and the legacy he was building."

In awe of how any man could contain so much callousness and cruelty. A legacy of subjecting the people of my home country to assaults and enforced labor.

I swallow those silent sentiments and go on. "I was met with the warmest of welcomes when I arrived at the palace. It was immediately obvious how much impact His Imperial Majesty had on all of his court. I have never—"

My gaze flicks to the noble retinue around us on the stairs—and jars on the faces I least need haunting me right now.

Since my wedding, I've been doing my best to avoid the four princes Emperor Tarquin was fostering. As later-born royals from the other conquered countries within the empire, more hostages than adoptive sons, their hatred for him and his empire burns even hotter than my own.

And now they have every reason to hate me as well. I won the three older princes' hearts, dallied with them as if I was giving my own over to them, and then rejected their offer of escape to marry Marclinus instead.

I wasn't paying enough mind to where they'd placed themselves in our assembly, and now I'm faced with their searing gazes unprepared. I can't say what's the worst: Bastien's cold, hard glower, Lorenzo's anguished stare, or the way Raul cuts his fierce gaze away from me as if I'm not even worthy of his attention.

My words muddle on my tongue. I wrench my attention back to the larger mass of spectators in front of me.

What will they make of my stumble?

My chest hitches. I hastily swipe at my eyes as if I'm brushing away tears. Let them think I'm overcome with grief for the fallen emperor.

The emotion isn't difficult to fake. The truth is that my heart does feel wrenched in two—because the princes standing just a few paces away captured it far more than I can afford to let on.

Because I don't know how much they'll prove to be my enemies all over again.

I'd swear Raul suspected that I had a hand in Tarquin's death. The look he gave me right afterward…

None of them have spoken up about it, but that's likely only because I know things about *them* they wouldn't want coming out either. I have no idea how long they'll hold their tongues or what might compel them to accuse me.

I can't let those worries distract me in this moment. With a shaky inhalation that the amplification charm will project as well as it did my words, I allow a quaver to creep into my voice that has nothing to do with the man I'm talking about.

"I have never felt so blessed as I did getting the opportunity to be part of such a brilliant and accomplished family. It saddens me beyond words that I couldn't serve Emperor Tarquin longer or benefit from his sage guidance. I will strive with all I am to see that his legacy continues while I stand with his son, your new emperor, and guide us into the future."

A future filled with much less bloodshed and horror beyond this country's borders, if I have anything to say about it.

I bow my head once more and retreat to Marclinus's side. He rests his fingers briefly against my back with a hum I think is approving.

More than anyone, I need *him* to believe I wholeheartedly support him and his family's vision for the empire. My only chance at swaying him onto a more peaceful, compassionate course will be if he thinks that course will benefit his own ends—and that my priorities are the same as his.

A couple of Tarquin's chief advisors go forward to speak about the wonders of the late emperor's rule, and the cleric from the imperial temple carries out the final rites. As the robed man prepares to light the pyre, Marclinus and I ease down the steps to come closer.

The soldiers guarding us pull tighter around us. I brace myself for the surge of heat.

The flames roar up over the heap of wood, swallowing Tarquin's body.

Through the hiss of the fire, I just make out the low voice

of one of the soldiers behind me. "Seems a bad omen, don't you think, Galen? He dies like that the same night as His Imperial Highness's wedding?"

"His Imperial Majesty to us now," his companion grumbles, equally quiet. "Don't let him hear you making that mistake."

"I just mean—it could be a sign from the godlen that the marriage will bring more problems than good. That *she* is going to be a—"

His voice cuts off with a faint *oof* as if he's been elbowed and a curt response. "Hush."

Even with the crackling heat coursing over my skin, a chill collects in my gut.

How many of the other imperial soldiers are thinking the same way about me? How many of the regular citizens of Dariu or the nobles of its court?

It doesn't matter whether they believe Tarquin's death came about through natural causes. They can still consider it a strike against me.

Should I have waited? My original plan was to settle in for a week or two after the marriage before I made my final move.

But it'd already *been* weeks by the time I was actually married. Tarquin had put me through so much already, I couldn't be sure I'd get another chance.

It might not have made any difference anyway. A death two weeks after a marriage could still be seen as a bad omen by anyone looking for reasons to be wary of the relative stranger in their midst.

Who knows what other incidents they might blame on my presence once they have that idea in their head?

I need to prove I'll be a force for good as quickly as I can.

The fire blazes on. A smoky flavor coats the inside of my mouth. Marclinus is standing even closer to the pyre than I am, the orange light dancing off his sharp features that echo his father's.

I will tame this monster, whatever it takes, however long it takes. This marriage is the most important mission I could have been given. Even Elox—my patron godlen, the divinity who champions peace and healing—has urged me on this path.

I tap my fingers down my front in the gesture that recognizes all nine of our lesser gods with a more emphatic acknowledgment of the one I dedicated myself to. By the fire, Marclinus does the same.

When the blaze has dwindled to embers and nothing but a charred mass remains of the body and the pyre, my husband takes my elbow. We walk along the steps to the imperial carriage that led the funeral procession through the city to the square.

I've only taken a few steps when a dark mass whips through the air from somewhere in the crowd of commoners and splats against the skirt of my dress.

I jerk to the side, my hand instinctively dropping to the spot where I was struck. The blob that hit me has fallen to the stone steps.

The place where it smacked into the black silk is wet. When I lift my fingers, they come away smeared with the reddish-brown of old blood.

"Who threw that?" one of the guards is hollering, pushing toward the edge of the throng. Another flicks the tip of his sword against the projectile, and I see it's some kind of animal organ—a liver, I think.

"Find the culprit and deal with them appropriately!" Marclinus barks, and tugs me onward. "Good thing black doesn't show stains. Let's be on our way before the commoners turn their mourning into a festival of entrails, shall we?"

CHAPTER TWO

Aurelia

The open-top carriage makes a circuit of the square and several of the surrounding streets without any further bloody incident. Marclinus keeps up the same smile through the entire route: steady but subdued in recognition of his loss.

As the citizens we pass call out condolences and well-wishes to their new emperor, a merrier light glints in his eyes. They wouldn't notice it, but I'm far too familiar with my husband's moods.

He's reveling in their adulation, enjoying every moment of this tour of mourning.

I'm sure he feels some grief over his father's death. I've seen hints of it over the past two days, slipping through his unflappable front.

But I wouldn't be surprised if on the whole he counts this turn of events as more of a win than a loss.

When we reach the wide street that leads the last short distance to the palace, a line of soldiers holds the lingering crowd well back from our procession. With a glance around us, I decide it's safe to talk. I didn't intend to bring up the comments I overheard from the one soldier, but it would seem careless to ignore the aggressive act that followed.

I tug at my skirt, where the bloody patch is now only faintly damp. "Some of the people aren't totally happy to see me. I suppose your father's funeral wasn't the most ideal circumstance for an introduction."

Marclinus makes a dismissive sound, swiping his hand past the small scar on his upper lip. "They're upset, and that riles them up."

Does he really think it's reasonable for a civilian to have thrown animal guts at their empress?

"I'm also a stranger to them, from a country they know little about," I venture. Accasy is the farthest flung of the empire's territories, off in what many refer to as the "wild north." I doubt nobles from back home have ventured as far as this city since my great-grandfather's brother came as a hostage decades before most of these people were even born.

"If that worries them, you'll soon cure them of it. You've adapted quickly." Marclinus shoots me a slightly wider smile, though the cool evaluation in his gaze divests it of much comfort. "They didn't really know my mother either, you know. She was Darium but from one of the border provinces, not all that often at court. But she earned so much devotion that less than a year after my father took the throne, the common people created a new festival to celebrate her and present her with gifts."

His gaze turns briefly vague in recollection. "I still have the wreath crown they made for her, woven with leaves from every type of tree throughout the country. I never got to see her wear it, and it's dried and faded now, but it must have been something to watch her presented with it."

I hesitate. Marclinus lost his mother due to complications of his birth. He never knew her at all. As callous as he can be, it feels like sensitive territory to tread into.

He does me the favor of changing the subject himself, adjusting his position so he sprawls in a more typical languid pose on the seat across from me. "In any case, you needn't worry about your safety. Your host of guards is nearly as gifted as my own. If anything hard enough to do damage had been flung at you, they'd have sensed it coming and intervened. And the new clothes commissioned for you are godlen-blessed to deflect any weapon, which will protect most of your vital areas."

His mention of "nearly" reminds me of the other talent I've heard some of the palace guards possess. "What of attacks by magic?"

Marclinus snorts. "I doubt you'll need to worry about that. We don't hire staff with gifts that could pose a significant threat, and anytime you're out in the wider world, you should be with me. A few of my guards can recognize magic the moment it's invoked. They'll shield both of us if you're nearby."

My own guards can't pick up on the working of a magical gift, then. That's good to know, considering I expect to be working my gift quite a bit in the privacy of my chambers. I'd rather not face questions about my activities from the soldiers stationed outside my door.

The carriage pulls through the grand imperial gate and draws to a stop in front of the immense palace's front stairs. As the footmen hustle around to set down a step so we can disembark, Marclinus and I get up.

My husband slides his arm around me and gives my ass a

firmer pat than his brief grope during the funeral. "I have a few things to attend to before dinner, but I look forward to what'll come afterward. We'll finally be able to enjoy our first marital night."

He hops down from the carriage ahead of me and strides off into the palace with a few guards trailing behind him at a discreet distance.

I descend as quickly as my long skirt allows, the contents of my stomach curdling at his reminder.

Between the shock of Emperor Tarquin's death, the hasty funeral preparations, and the private rites, I've managed to avoid the expected activities of my wedding night twice. It'd have been a little much to expect that reprieve to continue.

I need to be prepared.

I hustle through the palace halls to my newly-appointed apartment in the imperial family's section of the palace. My thumb slides over the rippled surface of the gold and sapphire ring I brought with me from Accasy.

It held the concoction that killed Tarquin within its hidden crevice. I had time yesterday to clean it and refill it with a potion of a different nature.

Unfortunately, when I was preparing for my marriage, I had no idea just how much I'd recoil from the thought of enduring Marclinus's intimate attentions. I only brewed a small amount of the concoction that'll give me some grace, in case of extreme circumstances.

How could I have known how extreme even the essentials of palace life would so quickly become?

The very thought of him using my body to take his pleasure makes me want to vomit—gods only know how I'd respond to the reality of it. I don't know if I can convincingly fake the appearance of the sort of eager lover Marclinus will expect.

He clearly thinks highly of his seductive appeal. None of

the court ladies I've watched him fondle have done anything to dissuade his confidence.

There's enough of the drug in my ring to protect me tonight, but there's no telling how frequently he'll want to enjoy full marital relations. If I want to spare myself that awfulness and the chance of revealing my true feelings, I'll need a plentiful supply.

I prod my gift, focusing my mind on my sense of purpose: a "cure" of sorts for carnal urges, in a roundabout way. Images of the ingredients I need rise up with a relieving familiarity.

As much time as I spent perfecting this concoction, it's good to have the confirmation that my memory is correct. I didn't dare write down the recipe.

Technically, the magical gift Elox blessed me with in exchange for my sacrificed spleen is only meant to help me craft actual cures and salves. It just happens that nearly any purpose can be presented as a healing one if you think of it in the right way.

Even the poison that shut down Tarquin's body would have been beneficial to someone in the throes of a contradictory disease.

Of course, I sweep into my bedroom to find my two new maids waiting for me. Jinalle and Eusette dip into matching curtsies.

They're a more welcome sight than the first maid assigned to me at the palace would have been. Melisse let my rivals bribe her so they could ruin my belongings during the trials. As soon as I moved to this apartment yesterday morning, I informed the palace head of staff that I needed a different attendant.

I suppose I shouldn't be surprised that an empress is accorded at least two, but it does mean twice as many curious eyes I need to be wary of.

"Welcome, Your Imperial Highness," Jinalle chirps, pushing her pale hair behind her ears in an anxious gesture. "Is there anything we can do for you?"

I glance down at my soiled dress. Actually, there is. I can change the elaborate imperial outfits much faster with help.

I offer them a quick smile. "I need a new gown. Something we can get on without needing to redo my hair, ideally." The upswept styles expected of married Darium women are a lot more of a hassle to arrange as well.

The two maids spring into action, easing off the black mourning dress and retrieving another from my expansive new wardrobe with only a few innocuous remarks. They're being nothing short of kind and perfectly polite, but as they maneuver me into the gown, an ache wraps around my heart.

For a short time, I had another maid here. A fellow noblewoman I took on in supposed disgrace, but really as a ploy to save her life.

But Emperor Tarquin and his son's sadistic schemes still took Lady Rochelle's life in the end.

I've lost both my only true friend here and the men I was falling for. The bedroom around me glitters with gold and shines with satin, but its vastness only emphasizes how alone I am—far from my real home, in the midst of so much brutality.

A faint burn forms behind my eyes. I blink it away with a determined swallow.

I have to hold tight to my purpose and let it keep me steady as it has so far.

When the new dress is in place, my gaze veers to the trunks brought over from the lovely but not quite as immense room I was given before my marriage. The steps of the needed brewing flit through my mind again.

One downside of being empress: it'd look particularly odd if I marched right into the palace kitchens.

I offer my maids another smile. "Thank you so much. I'd like to take a bit of fresh air and then some rest on my own before dinner. Could one of you bring a pot of boiled water and a bowl of walnuts and leave them on the table? I could use some tea and a snack in my repose."

Eusette bobs her ruddy head with an eager, "Of course, Your Imperial Highness!" and they both scamper out of the room.

As soon as they're gone, I retrieve my tea box. The upper layer with its multitude of dried leaves and herbs lifts to reveal the more potent ingredients for my craft below.

Worrying at my lower lip with my teeth, I check the packets and vials to confirm what I already have on hand. There's a decent amount of the rarest ingredients, but depending on Marclinus's enthusiasm, I may need to make up some excuses to venture into the marketplace before the month is over.

For now, I have everything except for a couple of other common items I expected to find easily at hand should I need them, those best worked with fresh.

Inventing my excuses in my head, I stride out of my room again prepared for the two guards stationed outside to question me. It turns out that the position of empress does come with a few benefits. They simply trail several paces behind me as if assuming whatever I'm up to, it must be for a good reason.

I descend the stairs to the palace gardens. Conveniently, I don't need to look odd poking around in the herb garden around the side of the building. Carnella is a popular garden plant throughout the continent, and I've already seen plenty of its crimson blooms popping up amid the beds. I meander past them, bending to snap off a few of the flowers and tucking them into the pouch on my belt.

The silvervein vine clinging to one of the trellises offers

plenty of leaves for me to pluck. I'm just slipping those away too when I turn and find myself face to face with Vicerine Bianca.

The noblewoman looks me up and down with a bemused expression. Her own mourning clothes cling to the generous curves of her voluptuous body. The black fabric and her equally dark hair set off the creaminess of her brown skin, like tea with a dollop of milk, to impressive effect.

"Whatever are you doing out here on your own, Your Imperial Highness?" she asks in a tart voice.

Of course Bianca would nose her way into my business. She's been a thorn in my side from the moment I stepped into the palace, treating me as an interloper getting in the way of her cousin's claim on Marclinus's hand—and her own role as one of Marclinus's most favored mistresses.

But Lady Fausta, the cousin and friend on whose behalf Bianca has attacked me, died in the horrific trials meant to prove our worth. I've told the vicerine that I won't stand in the way of her relationship with Marclinus. She has no reason to harass me now.

Then again, people like her don't necessarily need a reason.

I keep my own tone even. "I needed a couple of things for a herbal tea—to help settle the spirits after disheartening events."

Bianca gives a sniff as if the idea of making any kind of beverage is beneath her—which it quite possibly might be—and swans off with her head held high.

Well, that encounter could have gone a lot worse.

I hustle back to my chambers, reaching them just as Eusette arrives with my pot and my bowl of walnuts. With a quick murmur of gratitude, I leave her and my guards at the door and head inside.

This potion requires a complex process, steeping one

thing and boiling another, mashing this herb with that pollen for just the right amount of time. As I lay out my apparatus and get to work, the steps unfurl through my head with a tingle of my gift.

Tapping into my magic comes easier the more familiar I already am with a recipe. All the same, I let out a weary sigh by the time I can pour the final mixture of pale pink syrup into a bottle. The top of my skull prickles with a hint of strain.

I cap the bottle and set it among my other supplies in the bottom of the tea box. I'm just gathering my tools when brisk footsteps sound right beyond the door.

My pulse hiccups. I dump the last few pieces into the chest less gently than I'd have preferred and whirl just as my door flings open.

Marclinus strolls into my bedroom as if he has every right to, which by law he does. All things in the empire belong to the emperor—including me.

Thanks to enchantments worked on all relevant surfaces, every lock in the palace will open at the touch of his hand.

I force a smile onto my face to cover the thudding of my heart. "Husband, how good to see you. Are you finished with your business already?"

"It's dinner time," he says, holding out his hand to me. "Let us go preside over our court together."

"It is always a pleasure and an honor to accompany you."

I tuck my hand around his elbow and walk with him into the hall, my nerves still jangling with the awareness of just how little privacy I have from the man I most need it from.

CHAPTER THREE

Bastien

The smile that sent my spirits soaring just a few days ago now leaves my gut in a knot.

I force myself to watch Aurelia where she's sitting at the far end of the long main table in the palace dining room. Naturally, Marclinus has claimed his rightful spot at the head of the table, where his father used to sit. He's placed his new wife beside him.

She joins the nearby nobles in laughter at some joke he made that I didn't catch. Her dark blue eyes shine, and amusement lingers on her lips. A few minutes later, she pats Marclinus's arm with apparent fondness. When he tugs at one of the lower whorls of her bronze-brown hair, pinned up to reflect her married status, she lowers her gaze coyly.

I shove another bite of roast chicken into my mouth. The sugared berry sauce tastes like dirt as I chew and force myself to swallow. My stomach has balled even tighter.

Is her performance as a devoted and loving wife just that —an act? I want to believe it is, to convince myself that not everything she revealed to my foster brothers and me was a lie.

But if she could put on a performance this convincing with our vicious new emperor... how can I say the stalwart, compassionate princess she showed us wasn't the real act? That the vulnerabilities she revealed and the affections she offered weren't every bit as calculated as I'd like to think her current behavior is?

Her dalliance with Lorenzo, Raul, and me did serve her well, after all. If we hadn't cared enough to help her in the trials, she might have died multiple times over. She even won some of our most closely guarded secrets out of us—so she'd have leverage if we ever accused her of disloyalty?

I clearly can't trust my own judgment when it comes to her. She had me so head over heels that I put not only my but all my foster brothers' futures on the line, imagining she'd rather be with us on the fringes of the world than with Marclinus and his imperial riches.

If the palace guards had stumbled on us before we managed to clean up the evidence of our scheme... if my gamble had failed and they'd detected our magic... what punishment would Tarquin have inflicted on his hostages for attempting to flee?

We could all be dead right now—even Neven, when the kid was only following my lead. My ill-advised confidence.

Gods help me, what revenge would the emperor have inflicted on our home countries for our disobedience?

My mind slips back to my last brief visit home, to the strained meetings with my parents and my brother alongside the imperial delegates. I can picture so easily the relief on my mother's face every time I was able to speak up and moderate the empire's demands with careful diplomacy. The tight hug my father gave me when we were given a few moments alone echoes through my chest.

They're depending on me to maintain what peace Cotea has with the empire. My fellow princes are relying on me to be the cool-headed one who steers us wisely.

I risked so much for the woman who's now giggling at the tap of Marclinus's finger against her chin.

How could I have let myself be so careless? So *stupid*?

The tension in my stomach liquifies into pure nausea. I draw my eyes back to my plate, but I don't think I can tolerate another bite.

When dessert arrives, I push around the currant-dappled pudding with my spoon until it looks as if I've had at least a few bites. Finally, the servants clear the dishes.

Marclinus stands, his sharp grin making me tense up. He claps his hands for our attention.

"We've had two days of the bleak blackness of mourning," he says. "My father would have wanted us to honor his life with joy as well as grief. Let us convene in the ballroom for music and a little dancing as the mood takes us."

The last thing I feel like doing is prancing around the ballroom, but I should at least make an appearance on the sidelines for an hour or two. If I avoid the court activities completely, Marclinus might wonder why.

I don't need my behavior to face any more scrutiny than it already would if Aurelia lets a hint of what she knows slip.

We file into the vast room with its high, painted ceilings. The enchanted artwork above us shifts as if the colorful figures are frolicking to the lively tune the court musicians have started playing.

It's one small blessing that Marclinus hasn't called on Lorenzo's musical talents yet. Even if Tarquin's demands over the past couple of weeks hadn't exhausted my friend, Aurelia's betrayal hit him even harder than the rest of us. He's been holding it together, but I'd rather not see him put under any more strain.

I amble along the wall past the glinting mosaics embedded in the plaster surface. Many of the nobles have already coupled up on the dance floor despite the day's solemn events. It's a much more somber spectacle than usual, all the gowns and suits in mourning black spinning across the polished floor. You'd almost think these were serious people who cared about more than fashion and food.

Just moments after I've picked my spot to stand and watch, a willowy woman around my age glides over to my side. My gaze flicks over her reddish-blond hair and pale skin, stirring my recollection.

Lady Betisse. Daughter of Marchion Litius, making her one of the more prominent unattached women of the court. Her parents were wise enough not to complain about Tarquin's choice in filial bride, so she escaped the trials.

She's never spoken to me before other than in passing. I have no idea what she might want now.

I dip my head in acknowledgment. "Good evening, Lady Betisse."

"Good evening, Prince Bastien." She peers over the growing crowd of dancers. "I hope you enjoyed your dinner."

"I did," I lie, still puzzled but maintaining my politeness. "I hope you found it satisfying as well."

"Yes." She darts a glance toward me, and a shy smile curves her lips. "If it's not too forward of me to say, especially given the circumstances, you cut quite a striking figure in black."

For a second, my mind blanks. She's... *flirting* with me?

It isn't as if that's never happened before. I might be a second-born prince from a country under Dariu's thumb, but the title still comes with a certain prestige. It'll only be a few more years before my "fostering" here is complete and I can take on a respectable and somewhat high-ranking role in the governing of the empire.

If you can call it governing when it's always the emperor and his advisors calling the shots.

Still, it doesn't happen often. My slim frame and restrained attitude hardly offer the same appeals as my foster brothers' brawnier builds and skills with music and seduction.

The thought sends another sharp pang through my gut. Even if Aurelia was honestly tempted by the two of them, what are the chances she found *me* equally enticing?

No, even in the best of scenarios, it's most likely she pursued me as well because she could tell Raul and Lorenzo listen to my judgment. I was the one she most needed to sway if she was going to benefit from her dallying beyond a little fleeting pleasure.

It wouldn't have been so different from this noblewoman's interest—driven by pragmatism rather than desire.

In situations where we're both aware of where we stand, I can appreciate pragmatism. I manage to summon a modest smile for Lady Betisse and a reasonably gracious response. "I certainly take no offense to the compliment."

And I look at her with more considering eyes.

I can't recall ever noticing her acting as a particularly keen conversational partner, but I can't say she's ever come across as especially vapid either. She's certainly pretty. A month ago, the overture might have made my heart skip a beat.

A month ago. Before Aurelia.

Now, even as I try to focus only on the woman before me, I find myself cataloguing the ways she falls short. Her coloring is too washed out and wan. Her light brown eyes hold no real vigor. Her decision to focus her compliments on my appearance rather than anything more perceptive shows how little she understands me.

The criticism isn't fair to her. She's a perfectly nice woman. The woman I'm unwillingly comparing her to doesn't even exist beyond my imagination, as far as I can tell.

But I can't dredge up the slightest bit of enthusiasm to invite this lady to join me for a dance, let alone whatever other attentions she might hope I'll bestow.

The imprint of Aurelia's touch lingers on my skin, her kiss on my lips. I don't know how to shake them.

I hold out my hand anyway, making myself extend the invitation. "Join me for a dance?"

Keep up appearances. Don't let on that anything's disturbed me.

I've partnered plenty of ladies on this dance floor without it meaning anything to either of us.

We follow the melody of the next song, stepping and dipping together. I'm careful not to ease closer than I need to, not to make any overtures I don't intend to follow through on, and Lady Betisse doesn't push.

When we part ways and I return to the sidelines, all I feel is relief.

With the dancing figures all garbed in black, they should blend together. Nonetheless, my gaze immediately latches onto Aurelia's hair gleaming under the chandelier light as Marclinus twirls her beneath his outstretched arm.

Neven comes up beside me, his broad shoulders slightly hunched in his black silk shirt. When I glance at the youngest of my foster brothers, he's looking in the same direction I was a moment ago, his tan face tight.

He runs his hand through his white-blond hair and glances at me. For all his teenage recklessness, he has enough sense to keep his voice so low only I'll hear it over the music. "How are we going to handle her now?"

It wasn't long ago that I had a talk with him about treating the Accasian princess as an ally rather than an enemy. I don't think Neven has realized just how intimately entangled the rest of us became with her, but our frustration and pain over recent events won't have escaped his notice. He knows we expected her to run away with us.

The truth is, I don't know how to answer that question yet.

I lift my shoulders in a brief shrug, dragging my attention away from the subject of our conversation. "We obviously can't trust her. She's in this for herself, just as we suspected at the start, and she managed to deceive us into believing better of her for a while. But with how much she knows now about our gifts and plans, we have to be cautious."

His grimace deepens. "If she encourages Marclinus to do anything that hurts our countries…"

"We shouldn't assume she'll go that far," I allow. "We can't really be sure of anything at this point except that she's an unknown threat. We'll wait and see what she does."

As the last words leave my mouth, my throat constricts.

For a short but shining time, I couldn't wait to see what Aurelia would do next. How she would surprise me with her defiance and her subtle strength.

Believing in her felt so damned *good* after everything that's gone wrong in this place. I should have known I couldn't trust that unexpected sense of hope.

I shouldn't miss it now that it's gone and the world looks dim and dreary again.

"This whole situation is fucked up," Neven mutters, as only a seventeen-year-old can.

Raul ambles over to us, his tall, broad body exuding his

usual assurance. I hesitate, but it could be useful to have him weigh in on this subject. To maintain as much plausible deniability as possible if anyone accuses us of conspiring, the four of us have avoided spending time together since our first bewildered conversation as we scrambled to destroy the evidence of our planned escape.

I'm not sure what's been going on in the prince of Lavira's head over the past two days, but he's never shied from a chance at vengeance.

I tap Neven's arm in an attempt at reassurance. "We won't simply stand by. If we have to, we still have ways we can subtly undermine her. It'll be much easier to manipulate our new emperor against her than we could his father, that's for—"

Raul breaks in with a voice that's harsh despite its hush. "What the fuck are you talking about?"

My head jerks toward him. Even though he's one of the few people in this palace I can count on, his massive frame is imposing when he's glowering down at me with his icy blue gaze.

I gather myself before answering. "Only potential problems that might arise. Considering the false loyalties that've been shown—"

Raul snorts with a shake of his head that makes his short ponytail swish against his tawny neck. "False loyalties? In all your 'wisdom,' you didn't even figure out— For fuck's sake. We all need to talk."

I blink at him, thrown by his mood. "That's what we're doing."

"Not like this. Properly." He jabs his thumb toward the doorway. "I'll round up Lorenzo. Meet us in the library."

CHAPTER FOUR

Aurelia

When Marclinus takes my hand for our fourth dance of the night, I don't recoil inwardly quite as much as the first three times. He's refrained from pawing me so far. It seems as if he's come down from the high of the entire city's adulation into one of his more subdued moods.

Which doesn't mean I'm looking forward to the dance or what will follow later tonight any more than I was before, but at least I don't have to hold my instinctive reactions quite so tightly in check.

This particular tune is more lilting than spirited, winding through the room at an almost languid pace. I have room to breathe—and strike up a conversation.

I tilt my head to the side as I gaze up at him. "What's in

store for us from tomorrow onward, husband? You'll have to give me some guidance—I wasn't expecting to find myself empress so soon after arriving."

And perhaps feeling as if he's gotten to guide me will make him more susceptible to a little persuasion from my end.

Marclinus arches an eyebrow at me. "Are you already thinking ahead?"

I give him a placating smile. "I want to make sure I'm as prepared as possible so I can put my best foot forward with your people."

He gives a thoughtful hum. "From what I understand, there's the standard confirmation process to go through. A few ceremonial rites to show I have the favor of the gods before I'm officially emperor in every capacity. Those require a little traveling, but I don't think they'll take long. There won't be much required of you other than appearing at my side."

I'm not familiar with the confirmation rites, but then, the last emperor was instated years before I was even born. It sounds as if we'll have some time in between each to address other matters.

Where can I best begin nudging the empire in the direction I'd like to see it go? I've already observed during the trials how resistant Marclinus is to outside suggestions.

I need to start small, with something innocuous enough that he won't have a strong opinion one way or the other. Something I can handle well enough to earn a little trust so he might be more open to *my* opinions going forward.

He turns me with a flare of my skirt around my legs. My gaze slides over the crowd of nobles around us.

When I'm facing Marclinus again, I offer another winning smile. "I'd like the chance to show your court that I appreciate their welcome, if there'll be time for that. Perhaps I could put together a banquet or a day of entertainments in their honor?"

If the people Marclinus spends the most time around are speaking my praises, some of their good favor might pass on to him.

Marclinus cocks his head, his own smile wry. "I suppose that is the sort of thing they'd like. Although it hasn't seemed their welcome was all that warm on the whole."

Are we not pretending that my first weeks here have been all sunshine and sweetness?

I let my tone turn drier. "They've been warm enough since our wedding. I can understand it took many of them some time to adjust to the foreigner in their midst."

"The whole empire is Dariu's, so technically you're as Darium as any of them. But if it pleases you, I'm sure we can find an opportunity."

As we both swivel around with a shift in the music, a more melancholy cast comes over the new emperor's face. His grip on my fingers tightens. "My father always said it's a careful balance, keeping the court satisfied without letting them get complacent."

The slight roughening of his tone is the first hint of grief I've observed from him all day that's felt genuine.

I have no regrets about Emperor Tarquin's death myself, but it's good to see that somewhere inside, his son has enough capacity for caring to be affected at least by that loss.

And it offers me another opening to establish myself not just as a bauble of a wife but a true companion and confidante.

I stroke my thumb over his where our hands are clasped. "You benefitted from his wisdom for much longer than I did, but I know you couldn't have imagined you'd lose him so suddenly. I'll do whatever I can to make your own work easier."

Marclinus peers at me for a moment with an evaluating glint in his pale gray eyes. I think I might catch a flicker of gratitude, but it's gone so quickly it might have been only wishful thinking.

His voice flattens as if to remove all emotion from the situation. "It is what it is. Death comes as it will, and I won't shy from the honor or the duty I've been granted."

Is he offended that I implied he might need support? I grasp for the best way to recover from a possible misstep, and the song dwindles with the pealing of the city bells beyond the palace walls.

"It's getting late," Marclinus says abruptly as we come to a stop on the dance floor. "We have to leave time for more private activities." His wry smile returns. "Why don't you prepare yourself for our night together with a bath so the experience can be all the more pleasing? I'll join you shortly."

My teeth set on edge. Is he implying that my current state isn't pleasing enough? Is *he* going to take a bath of his own to make himself more pleasing to me?

I can't ask either of those questions, so I simply dip my head in a slight bow. "I'll look forward to your arrival."

Even though I have my reprieve from the worst of what's to come thoroughly plotted, my heart sinks heavy in my chest as I hurry back to my chambers.

Marclinus must have sent word ahead in between dances —my maids have already filled the massive marble tub in my expansive private bathing room with steaming, frothy water that gives off a jasmine scent. I submit myself to their scrubbing and then ask them to take their leave.

Once I have the room to myself, the warm water offers a balm to my nerves. I soak in it for several minutes, centering myself and cultivating my inner calm, before I climb out.

Over by the towels, I discover the robe Marclinus must have instructed the staff to leave for me tonight. The silky garment is shaped much like my previous bathrobes, but other than the embroidered bits along the hem, the fabric is so thin the darker pink at the peaks of my breasts shows through. The bottom hits the middle of my thighs rather than below my knees.

Wearing the garment is only slightly better than being naked. Perhaps worse, given that the design feels like an open invitation to peel it off for one very specific activity.

I do need to appear eager, though. I fasten the robe at the waist so that the V of overlapping cloth shows a little cleavage and return to my bed.

Sitting cross-legged on the soft bedspread, I trace my thumb over my sapphire ring and close my eyes in a brief meditation. Brief because it can't be more than a minute or two before the door swings open without warning.

Marclinus saunters inside with a slyer air than he showed when he sent me off, his lips curved into a wicked smile and his eyes gleaming with anticipation. As his leering gaze travels over me, every inch of my skin crawls.

He doesn't bother to lock the door before prowling over to the bed. He'll have left his guards outside to stop anyone else from intruding—and they'll be monitoring the room with their gifts for any sign of a threat, ready to burst in if they sense unexpected magic or violence.

I force myself to scoot to the edge of the bed to meet him. Before I can get up, he brings his hand to the side of my face, trailing his fingers from my temple to my chin.

"How lucky I am that the woman who bested our trials was also one of the prettiest," he murmurs in a languid, self-satisfied tone. I can't help noticing that he isn't going to pretend he found me the absolute most appealing out of the bunch. "But then, it wouldn't do for the emperor to have a wife who needs a sack over her head before he can do the deed. Let's see all of you."

His comment about the sack sparks a flare of rage deep inside me. He dismissed the only real friend I made in this awful place on the basis that she wasn't stunning enough for his tastes. He'd have *murdered* Rochelle for that supposed failing, and he's never shown the slightest concern over the death she did meet, protecting me in one of the final trials.

Well, he isn't going to get what he wants tonight, not really.

I loosen the robe and let it slide off my shoulders into a silky puddle. Marclinus's attention roves from the swell of my breasts—ample enough if not as impressive as his lover Bianca's—to the apex of my thighs and then over the purple scars that mark my lower arms.

He lifts one of my wrists and skims his fingertips over the blotches left behind by a failed potion that erupted from my cauldron years ago. "Such an adventurous woman. I hope you'll bring that spirit to the bedroom as well."

I peek through my eyelashes with all the coyness I can summon, tamping down my nausea. "Any adventure with you would be nothing but thrilling, husband."

Marclinus apparently sees no need to remove any of his own clothing just yet. He leans in to claim my mouth, fondling one of my breasts at the same time. I hold myself in place through sheer strength of will and kiss him back with as much feigned passion as I'm capable of.

I want to move this encounter along so I can get to the part where I disengage.

I yank his vest off him and tug at the collar of the shirt underneath to loosen the ties. Marclinus chuckles against my mouth. He steps back for long enough to pull the garment over his head.

Muscles ripple all across his sculpted chest. The imperial artists are going to enjoy depicting his form.

The deeper pink lines of the godlen brand in the middle of that chest show he's dedicated to Sabrelle. The godlen of warfare and hunting—appropriate enough. I'd assumed it would be her or Creaden, godlen of rulership.

As Marclinus pushes me farther back on the bed and clambers over me, I flick my thumb across my ring in the way that releases the tiny thorn embedded in its surface. The needle point is crafted to be so short and thin it's nearly invisible—and imperceptible when it grazes the skin to deliver whatever potion the ring's hidden cavity contains.

At the brush of my hand against his bicep, Marclinus shows no more reaction to that gentlest of jabs than his father did two nights ago. I tap the ring again to tuck any sign of its hidden purpose away.

The only problem with this incredibly surreptitious method of delivery is that chemicals penetrating only the upper layers of skin take their time seeping to the bloodstream. With Tarquin, I wanted a significant delay before the effect took hold to avoid suspicion, so I brewed my concoction with that in mind. This one should be more immediately potent… but I still have to endure my husband's unwanted attentions for a little more time.

He's already got his thigh between my legs, his mouth uncomfortably hot against the side of my neck, his hand pawing at my breast. The only sensations he's provoking in me are horror and revulsion.

The easiest way to slow him down is to take the lead myself. I push myself farther upright again and nudge him back onto his ass. Before he can protest, I bring my lips to his shoulder and begin to chart a teasing path down his chest toward his abdomen.

Marclinus makes an approving sound and tangles his

fingers in my hair. "That's right, princess. Worship your emperor."

Ugh. I restrain a grimace and continue acting as if there's nothing I'd rather do than adore him. I draw the process out as long as I can, pecking kisses across the taut plane of his belly and stroking my hands over his outer thighs through his pants.

He braces his hands on the bedcovers behind him and tips back, clearly expecting me to delve into those pants and service every part of him with my mouth. More bile threatens to rise up my throat.

Then a slackness comes over his pose. His arms relax, his shoulders sagging. His head lolls to one side.

When I sit up to look at him, his gaze is hazy, fixed at some point in the vicinity of my ear.

He licks his lips and gives a heated growl. "That's right. Just like that."

I'm not even touching him at this moment, but the hallucinogenic properties of the potion I brewed must be conjuring those impressions. I smile and run my hands down my nude body to add fuel to his fantasies.

Marclinus's hips start to rock, whether he thinks into my mouth or my loins, I have no idea. I do free him from his pants and drawers then, tossing one article after the other onto the floor next to the bed. They'll serve both as proof of our having consummated this interlude and ensure no unexpected stains linger from its culmination.

His pale cock juts rigidly upward. He might be close already.

I ease him down on his back with his head on the pillow and hover over him. He doesn't reach for me, too lost in his deepening delirium, but his mouth twitches with imagined kisses and his ass bucks upward with futile thrusts. A groan escapes his lips.

"You make me feel so good, husband," I say with feigned giddiness.

Even in his daze, one of those arrogant smirks crosses his face.

It only takes another few minutes before his breath hitches. His release spurts across his abdomen.

He slumps into the bedspread, his eyelids already drooping shut. Before I've even finished wiping him clean with one of the bath towels, he's snoring.

Of course he'd be a snorer.

Well, I could have fucked him the way he was aiming for and then he'd probably have left after. I'll take this unpleasantness over that one.

I rinse the towel for caution's sake, re-don my robe, and wriggle under the covers on the opposite side of the bed. If the drug works as my tests suggested it should, he'll be out for a couple of hours. I might as well get my rest while I can.

I snuff out the lantern on the bedside table and burrow my head in my pillow as far as I can in an attempt to mute Marclinus's snores. When I close my eyes, a sudden hot prickle forms behind them. The sensation clogs my throat as well.

It's over now—my wedding night. And it was as far from the sort any woman might dream about as I can imagine.

I knew better than to expect that this moment would be full of love and mutual passion. I never would have asked for that much. But I did sometimes allow myself to picture that it'd be with a man I could grow to appreciate.

I clench my hands against the swell of grief. As Marclinus said of his own situation, it is what it is.

And because of it, I'm in a position to do something incredible.

At least my strategy succeeded. My monster of a husband

can believe he's rutting me every night without subjecting me to more than a little groping.

I do still have a little control over my life.

In the wake of the surge of emotion, exhaustion rolls in. My own eyelids drift down. My breaths even out.

I'm somewhere in the space between waking and sleep when a soft hiss carries from the wall.

CHAPTER FIVE

Raul

The moment we step into the library, I unfurl my gift. My awareness ripples through every shadow that drapes across the bookcases and beneath the tables, confirming that no one else has ventured out this way at this hour of the evening.

Bastien doesn't like being bossed around, since he figures he's the only one of us wise enough to give orders. He keeps scowling the whole way to the small repair room where we can carry out a discreet conversation, but he is at least smart enough to keep his mouth shut.

The second the door clicks shut behind us and Lorenzo has tapped on the magical lantern, my older foster brother whirls on me. His voice is flat but biting. "Why did you need to drag us all the way down here? You know we're trying to avoid drawing suspicion."

I glower right back at him, wrinkling my nose at the

lingering smell of binding glue. "We decided to stay apart because we didn't know what Aurelia was going to do. It's obvious she isn't spilling our secrets. She's on our side."

Bastien lets out an incredulous guffaw at the same time as Lorenzo's face twitches. Neven glances between the three of us, looking more bewildered than anything.

"She could have been *by* our side." Bastien jabs his finger vaguely toward the ballroom. "She decided she'd rather marry that psychopathic prick and sit in the lap of luxurious corruption."

Lorenzo's illusionary voice sounds mournful as it travels into my head. *"She won't even look at us now. We offered her so much…"*

She offered him more than anyone, while he welcomed her with his heart on his sleeve. I can see why her seeming rejection deflated him. But still—

I swipe my hand through the air dismissively. "Don't you see? She's *protecting* us. After everything she was brave enough to do—"

Neven interrupts me. "What are you talking about? She made you all use your gifts when you could have been caught, and then she turned her back on us. She hasn't done anything at all to thank you."

I can't stop a laugh from sputtering out of me. "You don't think so? She did exactly what we always planned to do. She did our dirty work *for* us, all by herself—she saw it was still possible to win even when we gave up ages ago."

Bastien's gaze sharpens into a glare. "Now you just sound insane. What work did she do?"

I have to drop my voice even though I can feel that there's no one remotely nearby to overhear. "She killed Tarquin, you idiots. Did you really think him dying on her own fucking wedding night was a coincidence?"

Lorenzo blinks at me, his brow knitting. *"How could she have killed him? The medics said it was a natural death."*

"I was dancing with her when he fell," Bastien adds. "Had her hands right in mine. I think I'd have noticed if she'd carried out an assassination."

Neven frowns. "Didn't she run right over to see if she could *cure* him?"

"Of course she needed a cover story." I exhale in a rush of exasperation. "Do you really think a woman so stoic she could hide the fact that she's dying from food poisoning couldn't fake a little concern? That a woman who could outsmart every noble lady in the imperial court and cure herself of anything shy of a broken bone couldn't come up with some secret means of offing an old man?"

Bastien studies me for a long moment. When he speaks again, he's more resigned than angry. "I think you're telling yourself stories to make yourself feel better about our epic misjudgment."

My frustration spills out of me in a growl. "I saw her right after she stepped away from Tarquin. There was a moment when she looked as if the whole weight of the world had been taken off her shoulders."

Lorenzo offers me a pained smile. *"Being glad he's gone doesn't mean she murdered him."*

He probably doesn't *want* to believe Aurelia would resort to murder. That's the problem with all of them, isn't it?

I'm the one who sparred with her, who stirred up her hotter emotions. She was mostly soft with them, but I saw how fierce she could be.

Aurelia has every bit as much grit and fire in that gorgeous body as I do when I'm slaughtering opponents in the arena.

Except I've only imagined the bodies I toppled were our

Imperial Eminences. She was brilliant enough to take on the real thing.

I give it one last try, for her. "I *know* it was her. It wouldn't have made any sense for her to stay here after she saw what callous fucks Tarquin and Marclinus were—unless she was sure at least one of them would be out of the way soon. Whatever you can say about her, she was never stupid. She's a fucking hero."

Lorenzo's head droops, as if complimenting the woman who once lit him up brighter than that lantern now pains him.

Bastien only gives me a brief grimace. "You're making the assumptions you want to be true."

Neven's hands ball at his sides, but he stays silent. I couldn't expect anything else from the kid—he's been on the sidelines this whole time. He doesn't know what Aurelia is capable of.

Clenching my jaw, I spin on my heel. "Just wait until she proves it to you. We owe her better than this. We promised her we'd be there for her no matter what."

Since none of my foster brothers seem inclined to get their heads out of their asses tonight, I stalk off to do just that on my own.

Gods above, how alone must Aurelia be feeling right now? She hasn't risked talking to us in two days, and it's not as if she has any other allies, let alone friends, in the entire court. She sure as fuck can't count her husband as one.

Our princess—no, our *empress*—is so strong, she can endure almost anything. She isn't going to let a little loneliness get in the way of her mission. But I saw how she came alive in our arms.

I know she craves so much more, so much *better*, than the jackass now on the throne could ever provide.

She deserves to know I'm still standing with her, that I'm

speaking up on her behalf with the others. That she won't have to see the rest of her brilliant plans through on her own.

There's got to be something useful I can contribute.

I don't have many options for approaching the new empress, of course. Thanks to her heightened status, she's got at least a couple of guards monitoring her everywhere she goes… except the privacy of her own chambers.

So I head straight from the library to the unused bedroom in the same hall as my own.

The secret passages in the walls go all the way up to the imperial apartments on the third floor. Each of the bedrooms up there has its own entrance, from back when the imperial family trusted their staff enough to allow them easier access.

Each of those discreet panels was bolted shut with the closing up of the network. It wouldn't have done us any good to gain access to Marclinus's or Tarquin's chambers anyway, not as soon as it became clear just how well their guards were able to protect them even at a distance from any threat we could present.

I'm not looking to threaten now, only to talk.

I took the little spare time I've had in the past two days working the bolts free and setting aside the metal slabs that secured the sliding panel in the wall of the empress's bedroom. This morning, I peeled off the last of them. When I reach the right branch in the passage, there's nothing left blocking my entrance.

Pausing outside the panel, I hesitate. Is it worth the risk of using my gift? I don't even know if Aurelia has left the ball. If she has, it's possible the guards who'd have followed her have the same gift for detecting magic as some of Marclinus's.

The consequences of a misstep would destroy everything I've come here for.

I waver in indecision and then lean my head close to the edge of the panel, my ear grazing the wood. If I can't "see" what's going on in the shadows beyond, maybe my regular senses will help me out.

For the first few minutes, I pick up nothing at all. Just as impatience digs its claws into me so deep I almost give in, there's a faint rustling sound, like a restless body turning over beneath the sheets.

A smile crosses my lips. I'm about to nudge the panel open when a raspy snore carries through the wall.

My body goes rigid. I don't think that sound is from Aurelia.

In fact, it sounds an awful lot like the snores I remember from various times Marclinus got drunk to the point of passing out on a sofa or a rug somewhere around the palace.

Fuck. I was so focused on her I was hardly thinking straight. They just got married—of course he'll be exerting his marital rights as often and as thoroughly as he can.

A surge of fury rushes through me. My hands ball at my sides with the urge to grasp the nearest swatch of shadow, harden it into a blade, and carve open the prick from throat to gut.

I tense my muscles against the anger with as even a breath as I can draw. No. I can't be an idiot about this and let my temper take over.

As much as a very large part of me would like to storm in there and pummel the imperial asshole to smithereens, I know *his* guard wouldn't fail to notice such an aggressive intrusion. I'd be throwing my own life away and lucky to deal out so much as a scratch in the process.

I grapple with my options, listening the snores carry on. I've definitely never heard a sound like that out of Marclinus when he *wasn't* outright unconscious.

There's a chance Aurelia is still awake. I can give her an opening, whatever she thinks is best to do with the chance.

Bastien would say I'm insane, but I *do* know this woman. If he'd get the stick out of his ass, he'd realize he does too.

I slide my hand through the darkness to the spot that'll release the panel and press firmly.

As the hidden door slides open with the faintest of rasps, my entire body tenses. If Marclinus reacts or his guards outside charge in—I think I can shut the panel again before they'd have the wherewithal to figure out what's going on. Even if they found the hidden doorway afterward, I'd be long gone within the walls.

But I'd have to be awfully fast. And this point of access would be cut off to me forever.

There are no yells or stomping feet, though. Not even a stutter in Marclinus's next snore.

The panel halts at its farthest point. I adjust my position so I can peer toward the bed without stepping out—just as the figure at the end closer to me sits up with a rustle of the sheets.

Only the dimmest light from a lantern outside the palace seeps past the closed curtains, but I'm at ease in the dark even when I can't bring my gift to bear. I recognize the fall of Aurelia's wavy hair, tumbling over her shoulders with the wildness that suits her so much better than the upswept styles of the past two days.

She stares at me, her deep blue eyes turned black by the night. Her voice comes out in a stiff whisper. "What are you—"

I hold up my hand to stop her and pitch my voice equally low. "I only came to talk. But we're safer having a conversation in here."

Aurelia's posture turns even more rigid than her voice. "I'm not slipping away into the wall with you."

Why should she trust me when we were all staring daggers at her two evenings ago throughout her marriage ceremony and the celebrations? When my foster brothers have kept up the glowers ever since?

I've tried to catch her eyes only briefly, to convey that I'm still with her but that I recognize the need for caution, but maybe she took my approach for animosity too.

Fuck.

I hold out my hand. "Please. I swear to you on my own life that I'm not here to do you any harm."

Aurelia's fingers clench around the bedcovers. "You should go before anyone notices. You know what the guards would do to you."

I could take that statement as a threat, but instead my heart leaps with a flicker of hopeful recognition.

She's *warning* me. She's afraid of what would happen to me.

For her own benefit too, Bastien would say, but the knowledge gives me enough confidence to switch the cards I'm playing.

I meet her gaze unwaveringly. "If you don't come with me, I'm going to have to confess to an executable crime right here where the emperor might hear me. Because I'm going to tell you one way or another. It's up to you how."

Aurelia's expression ticks with a brief widening of her eyes. For just an instant, I'm not sure the gambit will be enough.

Then she pushes aside the covers and eases off the bed.

Relief rushes through me, sharp and poignant, at the proof that she cares more about protecting me than whatever fears she has for her own safety. If the others could see this, they'd have to know that she's never faked her feelings for us.

As Aurelia darts around the bedside table to the passage, the filmy fabric of her robe sways with her movements. My relief crumples under a wave of desire.

By all that's holy, she's coming to me practically naked.

The scrap of a garment barely covers her upper thighs; it's so thin I can make out every detail of her perfect breasts.

Wrenching my gaze back to her face, I step back to make room. She was barely willing to speak to me—I'd better discard any lewder thoughts before they take hold.

Even if my dick has already risen to attention.

Aurelia slips into the narrow alcove where the passage ends. The moment she's inside, I press the control to close the panel so our voices will be more muffled.

Then we're alone. The old enchantment that illuminates the passages casts its glow over us, faint as moonlight.

I keep my gaze fixed on Aurelia's face in the dimness. All the same, every particle of my body tingles with the awareness of her body: the ebb and flow of her breath, the silky rustle of her flimsy robe. Her coolly sweet scent fills my lungs.

I still have to speak quietly, but it's easier with the snores muffled. Since I don't know how much time we'll have, I get straight to the point. "I'm sorry. Bastien and Lorenzo are being idiots. I understand why you had to stay. I have no idea how you managed to pull it off, but that just makes the whole thing more incredible. To have toppled Tarquin in front of the whole court—"

Aurelia breaks in, her voice rough but steady. "I don't know what you're talking about. Tarquin was ill. I had nothing to do with it."

Of course she doesn't feel she can admit her own crime. My fingers curl toward my palm against the urge to touch her cheek, to draw her closer, as if my embrace would make it easier to convince her.

Instead, I give her the confession I promised. "Shepherdess, you don't have to pretend with me. Don't you see—you pulled off what we always meant to. You put us to gods-damned shame, getting the job we'd given up on done in a matter of weeks. I'm not accusing you of anything. I'm in awe. If the others don't want to believe it, it's at least as much because of how much we failed as anything to do with you."

Aurelia's pause hangs in the air, her expression carefully blank. "What—what are you saying?"

Even with her, I have to gather myself before I lay it all out. Before I say the things I've never spoken about so baldly with anyone, even my co-conspirators.

"You know how we all felt about Tarquin and everything he stands for. When we were kids, after we'd been through a couple years of his treatment, we started plotting. How we could strike him down without getting caught and seeing our kingdoms razed in punishment. We picked the most powerful gifts we thought we could get away with concealing behind different ones—we came up with the best combination to work together and destroy him. When we were alone, it was almost all we talked about."

When Aurelia speaks again, I think her voice has softened. "But—Bastien told me Pavel lashed out without warning—"

I swallow down the surge of guilt that comes with the memory. "He did. We were supposed to wait until we'd all gotten a good handle on our new powers and then come up with a plan that'd look like an accident. But by the time Lorenzo had his dedication sacrifice, Pavel had already been waiting two and a half years. I'd been grappling with my gift for months and was still shaky with it…"

My shoulders slump with the weight of that admission. "Maybe if I'd gotten a grip on my power faster, Pavel would have felt more confident that we'd manage a coordinated effort. Maybe he wouldn't have snapped. But he must have gotten impatient, and he thought he saw an opening—I don't know how he figured he'd explain the death if he succeeded—but he didn't. You know the rest."

"That was ten years ago," Aurelia says in a tone I can't read.

"Yes. We saw how well protected Tarquin was, how quickly his guards could detect any magic, and no amount of talking got us any closer to figuring out how to murder him without us and our countries going down with him, if we even managed to hurt him in the first place. So we... gave up. We've been stewing in that frustration, being utterly useless, all this time, and then—" I grimace. "Great God smite me, we tried to *run away*. We tried to convince you to come with us, when you were prepared to do exactly what we always wanted."

I step toward her, unable to stop my hand from rising to graze her soft hair. "That would have been the biggest mistake we'd ever made. But you knew better. I can't imagine how much pressure you were under, the danger you knew you were putting yourself in, but you didn't take the easy way out like we would have. So I can't ask for anything except your forgiveness, that we fucked up so badly without even realizing it—that we didn't see just how incredible you actually are."

Aurelia's gaze drops, a flicker of pain crossing her face that snags in my heart with a sharp pang. "You've all seemed so angry with me."

I bow my head toward her, close enough that her warmth emanates over me. "We were at first, when we didn't understand why—and the others are finding it hard to believe that you could have arranged what happened. Lorenzo always takes things hard, and Bastien... He came up with the whole escape plan on his own, you know. I think his ego is wounded that you rejected it. But he cares about you that much. He has to come around."

Her gaze jerks back to mine. "*He* wanted to… I never would have thought—he's always been so cautious—"

I have to smile at the wonder in her voice. Bastien's had quite an effect on her too, and I can't feel jealous of that. "You've inspired a lot of surprising things in all of us, Shepherdess. I'll keep working on them. I just needed you to know that you still have me, whatever you need, however I can help with every amazing thing you do next. Hopefully you'll have all of us again before long."

Her fingers brush my chest as they clutch at the front of my shirt. "Raul."

There's so much need in the way she says my name that I can't rein in my own hunger any longer. I trace the line of her jaw to tip her chin up toward me and capture her mouth with mine.

The kiss is everything I've missed about her, fire and tenderness mingled together. When she leans into me to deepen the embrace, my groin aches.

No small part of my awe of this woman is for the urges she can stir inside me. The cleric who oversaw my sacrifice left enough flesh to avoid totally stunting my physical development, even if I'm completely impotent when it comes to fathering children. Still, it's always taken a certain amount of will and concentrated focus to perform for the ladies I've seduced from their husbands.

I'm not sure how much I could say I was getting off on *them* rather than the idea of carrying out some minor vengeance.

But Aurelia has never wanted a performance from me, only what I can honestly give. Whether it's because of that or the endless challenge she presents or her formidable strength, or some combination of all that's wonderful about her, her touch floods me with more genuine desire than any other woman has come close to.

As I trail my hand down her side, following the curve of her breast and waist, the thought of the other man sprawled in her bed sparks a different sort of heat. I can't keep the growl out of my voice. "Has that prick of a husband even tried to satisfy you?"

Aurelia's breath tickles over my neck with her answer. "I didn't really give him the chance. I— There are ways to 'cure' a man of the idea that we haven't coupled yet without needing to go through the entire act."

Her admission sends a thrill through my veins. I muffle my laugh against her cheek. "You concocted one of your clever potions, did you, my brilliant empress? Such a worthy cause. No wonder he's knocked right out."

She sounds almost abashed. "I didn't think I could manage to pretend—"

"You shouldn't need to." I nudge her back against the wall and claim another kiss. My tongue twines with hers until a whimper works from her throat—and a bolt of inspiration strikes me. "How long will he be out for?"

"At least another hour."

Not as long as this woman deserves, but more than enough to make a decent start on my full apology.

I sink down before her, pressing kisses down her sternum and her belly between my words. "I promised I'd worship you. I owe you nothing less than being down on my knees, venerating you like the goddess you are."

When my lips brush the spot just above her sex, Aurelia's breath catches. She tenses just for a second, but before I can worry that she'll push me away, she runs her fingers into my hair to grip the strands as if settling in for the ride.

And I intend to give her an ecstatic one.

Sweeping the flaps of her robe aside, I plant my mouth right on the slickest, sweetest part of her.

Aurelia clutches at my hair, her other hand stifling a gasp.

I suck on her clit and lap my tongue from it down to the dampened folds of her cunt.

Her hips rock toward me, more of her juices seeping out to flood my mouth. With a groan I can't suppress, I delve deep between her thighs.

I'll give her every shred of pleasure Marclinus wouldn't even bother to consider. I'll leave her with a delicious memory to ward off at least a little of the horrors of her marriage—one I intend to follow with many more, every chance I get.

I don't know what else I'll be able to do for my empress, but this is one service where I'm completely sure of my skills.

It's a shame I can't bring my gift into play tonight, but I've gotten plenty of ladies moaning without it throughout my career as the imperial court's most notorious rake.

That reputation is dead now. No minor revenge or fleeting sense of power could compare to dedicating myself to the woman in front of me now.

I return the attentions of my mouth to Aurelia's clit, teasing the edges of my teeth over it while tracing the lips of her pussy with my fingers. As I stroke one up into her hot channel, her body shivers around a moan.

That's right. Let me erase every bit of awfulness she experienced in that bed while she worked her own subtle craft. Let me replace every kiss, every touch she would have recoiled from if she could.

I add a second finger, working them higher until I find that perfect pliant spot inside that makes her hips buck faster. Her fingernails scrape over my scalp, tugging strands free from my ponytail, but I only suckle her harder. The pricks of pain flare into deeper pleasure.

Aurelia pants for breath, swaying against my mouth, and then clenches up. The force of her climax radiates into me with the spasming of her cunt and her arousal drenching my hand.

I give her sex one more lingering kiss and then grin up at her through the darkness, meaning to make some approving remark. Before I've hit on the right one, she tugs me toward her.

One hand wrenches my face to hers, our lips melding together in a collision of passion. The other yanks at the waist of my trousers.

My pulse hiccups. I wasn't going to ask for this, but I'm sure as shit not going to deny her, not when my erection is throbbing against my drawers.

As our mouths crash into each other again and again, I help her free me from my clothes. She raises one knee against my thigh to urge me on, and I lift her other leg as I line myself up.

I have no doubt about whether she's ready for me, regardless of my size. She's so wet I slide straight into her.

The clamp of her channel around my cock brings me to the verge of release in an instant. I close my eyes and tuck my head against the crook of her shoulder, fighting for control.

"This is how it should always be," I murmur raggedly. "You should never settle for anything less than this, Empress."

With an urgent noise, she tilts her hips toward me. There's nothing I can do but meet her plea, slamming deeper home.

It doesn't matter that I'm already on the edge. She clings to my shoulders and quivers in my embrace, teetering on the verge of her second orgasm already.

I thrust into her hard and fast, every bit of bliss enhanced by the knowledge that I'm bringing her to these heights while her asshole of a husband dozes completely unaware on the other side of the wall.

Marclinus might all but own my life, but he doesn't own her.

Right now, she's only mine.

Aurelia comes with a quake of her body and a nip of my neck that electrifies me. It only takes a couple more thrusts before I'm spilling myself inside her with a groan I can't contain.

I hold her there against the wall, my head tipped next to hers, my arms fitting her tight against my broad frame. She rests her forehead against my shoulder.

Then a sigh slips out of her that sounds unnervingly close to a sob.

I jerk back with a wobble of my nerves, cupping her face. A trail of dampness streaks down her cheek.

She's crying. Gods smite me. This is the opposite of the response I meant to provoke.

"Aurelia?" I ask, my voice barely a croak. My thumb wipes another tear away.

She pulls me back to her, looping her arms behind my neck. "I'm not upset. Just overwhelmed, in a good way. You know *everything*… and you're still here. You still want me."

A startled guffaw tumbles out of me. "I want you *more* because of everything you are. Everything you've proven you're capable of."

"I wanted to go with you all, you know. During that last trial. It sounded like the best of dreams. But there's so much else—"

"I know," I say before she has to justify the only decision I can imagine this woman making. "You had bigger dreams. You made the dream we once had a reality. Nothing could be better than that."

There's so much else I want to say to her, my throat aches with the words. All my practice is with passion and seduction, not gentler emotions.

I don't want to screw up this reconciliation.

I let her lower her feet to the ground and sling my arms around her waist. "You're not in this alone. Anything you need that I can offer, all you have to do is get word to me. And Bastien and Lorenzo too, once they get their heads on straight."

"Thank you." She trails her fingers down the side of my face. "You know… I don't think we can do *this* again. I probably shouldn't have let it happen at all. If I'm going to bring about that dream of a better empire, I need to stay totally focused on Marclinus, earning whatever trust and good will I can… It'll be that much harder the more I'm looking forward to illicit meetings with other men."

She sounds a bit choked up again. As much as I hate the thought of this being the last time I have this kind of intimacy with her, I can't say I don't understand. I have to be grateful I got this one moment at all.

Who knows what the future might bring?

I nuzzle her temple. "All right. After tonight, I'll stick to worshipping you at a distance. But don't you ever forget that you can count on me, no matter what mess you end up tangled in."

CHAPTER SIX

Aurelia

At the end of our lunch, Marclinus leans toward me from his spot at the head of the table. "I have something to show you."

As I smile, apprehension prickles over me. As much as our interlude last night was delusion, it's seemed to have tempered my husband's lustful inclinations for the time being. He'd left my chambers by the time I woke up this morning, presumably unaware of the much more pleasurable interlude I slipped off to while he slept, and he hasn't done more than briefly touch my arm since we met up afterward.

His current statement sounds ominously vague, though. Is he already planning to resume our intimate relations in some unexpected way?

Resisting the urge to glance toward Raul, I get up from my seat. My heart skips a beat remembering the prince's embrace last night, but I meant it when I told him that I have to focus on Marclinus rather than him—for both of our sakes. I can't see what he could do for me right now anyway.

At least I had time to replenish the hallucinatory potion in my ring before my maids arrived to dress me.

Marclinus acts the perfect gentleman, ushering me into the hall with his hand on my back rather than my ass and then extending his elbow for me to take it. I have trouble deciding if that should make me less worried or more.

He leads me down a few halls, up a flight of stairs, and into the third-floor wing opposite the private imperial apartments. I'm not familiar with most of the rooms up here, as the court activities have been mainly restricted to the second floor and the gardens. I glance at the doors we pass, but none of them offer any hint of the contents other than what I might speculate from the etchings of historic events on their surfaces.

We stop at a door holding an image of Sabrelle in full battle armor. The godlen of war stands atop a pile of helms, her spear raised in a triumphant pose.

All right, I'm going to assume my husband isn't leading me into a seduction. I'm not sure I'll like his actual purpose any more.

Marclinus pushes the door wide and strides in so quickly I lose my grasp on his arm, leaving me to trot after him. As at my bed chambers, the guards who trailed behind us remain outside.

A few paces into the room, my steps slow.

The hexagonal space is as large as my opulent imperial bedroom, but the only furniture it holds is a round table so vast that I'd have to stand on a stool to reach even halfway across. It gleams with fine marlwood, but most of its top shimmers in an unnatural way.

The effect is enhanced by the sunlight streaming down from above. The room's walls contain no windows, only a mural of a sprawling landscape with a battle in one nook, a peaceful farm in another. The illumination comes from several glass panes set in the ceiling, forming an enormous skylight.

As I take all that in, most of the room's other occupants move closer around the table. I jerk my gaze from the ceiling to take them in.

All four of the main imperial advisors—who served Emperor Tarquin and who I suppose his son has inherited—were waiting for us. The cleric among them in his purple robes for Creaden bobs his head to me in acknowledgment after a deeper bow to his new emperor. He even offers a small smile.

The two solely political counselors eye me with similar uncertainty despite their nearly opposite physiques. Counsel Etta stands short and sturdily stout, her slate-gray hair pulled into a neat and simple bun that only emphasizes the squareness of her pale face. Counsel Severo has drawn his tall, slim frame even straighter, his pointed jaw working beneath the mussed white curls that contrast with his deep brown skin.

"Your Imperial Eminences," they all murmur in greeting.

A louder voice carries from the far side of the table, which the fourth advisor hasn't bothered to stir from. "Your Imperial Majesty," High Commander Axius calls out with a hint of emphasis on the singular. "There was no need for you to bring your wife to this conference."

Only a handful of soldiers have earned the highest military title in the empire, and from what I understand, Axius has held it the longest. He's dressed in the same sort of airy noble clothes as the other advisors, but there's so much steel in his burly frame and his dark gaze that it's easy to picture him in uniform. His face, rigid and ruddy-brown as fired clay, does nothing to soften my impression of him.

I've only seen him in passing before. I don't think I've given him any reason to dislike me. But who knows what he'd require to earn his respect.

Marclinus matches the other man in height but not in heft, his muscular body somewhat leaner in comparison. He doesn't appear at all intimidated, though, as he steps toward the table with his head high.

"My empress will be accompanying me on the necessary travels. It isn't as if anything we'll discuss here today will be secret from her."

High Commander Axius rubs the slight shadow of a graying beard along his jaw. "She won't be playing any real part in the proceedings."

"She'll be presenting herself as my partner before our people. I'm sure she'll impress them all the more if she's fully prepared."

Marclinus turns to me. "You asked me what to expect from the coming days. This meeting is for us to discuss our initial plans for the confirmation rites."

I dip into a minute curtsy. "I appreciate your including me." Then I shift my gaze to the high commander. "My only concern is supporting our emperor in every way and as well as I'm able."

Axius grunts, but he raises no further protest. He remains on the far side of the table while the rest of us spread out along the nearer curve.

Marclinus aims a brief grin at me as if he really is glad I'm here. "This is one of our greatest treasures, created through several decades of magical work."

He taps the tabletop, and the wooden surface ripples. An image forms on the smooth plane as if swimming up from the depths, the edges of the shapes sharpening by the second.

My breath catches in my throat. "That's the entire continent."

Marclinus's grin returns, broader this time. "Indeed it is."

An enchanted map sprawls across the table like a vibrant painting. In the eastern half, Dariu lies framed by the island of Rione to the south and Cotea, Lavira, and Goric to the north, with my much-missed home of Accasy even farther above. On the western side of the Seafell Channel sprawls the territory lost a century ago, the countries I know little about that managed to heave off the empire's tyranny.

I suspect Marclinus brought me here more to show off than because he cares about how I fit into his plans, but it's an amazing sight all the same.

A quiver runs down the center of me, tingling through my limbs. For a second, as I gaze across the lines of borders and rivers and mountains, a white glow spreads across the eastern territory, from Dariu's capital to every corner of the current empire. Like the light of peace Elox keeps steady inside me.

It's only in my head. Has my patron godlen touched my mind, sent that vision to encourage me in my purpose?

Eventually I could make that peaceful possibility a reality.

The flick of Marclinus's hand demonstrates more of the table's enchantment. With a few quick gestures, he expands the section containing Dariu so its expanse fills most of the table, the other countries fading away around it.

He motions to the capital where we are right now. The city of Vivencia is the largest on the map. "All right. I have four ceremonies to complete. Should we get on with them as quickly as possible?"

Counsel Severo clears his throat. "Many of your citizens are quite stunned by your father's abrupt passing. We feel it would be wisest to... ease them into the transition. You should begin right away to give them confidence in your ascension, but spread the rest of the rites out so you don't appear too hasty to dismiss the impact of his rule."

Axius makes a scoffing sound. "*They* feel. I think we need to show our people—especially those beyond Dariu's borders —that we're still united behind a worthy emperor."

Counsel Etta flicks her gaze toward him. "And we will. The confidence to be patient shows plenty of strength. We won't stretch the process out *too* long."

Marclinus braces his hands against the edge of the table. An air of authoritative focus has come over him, not at all like the leering hedonist who lolls on his throne.

I suppose my husband can rise to the occasion as it demands. Something I'll need to keep in mind for my own plans.

"I can understand both sets of concerns," he says. "What exactly are you thinking, Counsels?"

It's Cleric Pierus who speaks up instead, with a rustle of his robes around his stately frame. "The typical path is to begin with the rite of Estera conducted at the Temple of Boundless Wisdom, which doesn't require uprooting the court from Vivencia." He points out a spot just to the northeast of the capital. "The arrangements can be made in just a few days."

Marclinus nods. "Excellent. And after that would be Prospira, wouldn't it?"

Severo jumps in again. "Yes. The temple that oversees that rite is out by Ubetta." He points the city out on the southeastern side of the map. "With the regular court convoy, it'll take a week traveling there and the same again back, with a short stay in between. I would say you should remain here in the capital for several days before leaving for that length of time. Then afterward, another week or two staying in Vivencia before a similar journey northwest to Rexoran for Creaden's rite."

Etta nods. "Then you return to Vivencia for the final rite under Sabrelle's watch. The entire series could be complete within two months. Not long at all while still giving space to honor your father's twenty-eight-year rule."

I grasp Marclinus's hand in a show of solidarity that seems befitting my role. "And I'll be right by your side for every mile of that journey."

The high commander studies us from across the table with a frown. "Making yourself *too* visible may not be the most strategic option, Your Imperial Highness. Some have taken the emperor's passing on the night of your wedding as a bad omen of sorts. Feelings among the citizenry seem to be somewhat... mixed."

The image flickers through my mind of the bloody organ thrown from the crowd just yesterday. Mixed indeed.

My pulse thumps a little faster, but I lift my chin. "Then it's important that they see how much their emperor and their country mean to me so I can earn their good will."

Marclinus tsks his tongue. "She's made of strong stuff, Axius, or she wouldn't be my wife. We'll set attitudes in order. And I trust my army will take every precaution to ensure no actual harm comes to her?"

With a tick of his jaw, the high commander bows his head. "Of course, Your Imperial Majesty. I'll see that double the usual host of soldiers accompanies each procession."

"Excellent. It sounds as though we have plenty of time to go over the details of each of the rites before I must face them. If I recall correctly, Estera's involves a maze of some sort?"

"That's right," Counsel Etta says quickly. "But none of them will provide any great challenge to you. The imagery is what's most important."

The symbolic indication that the four godlen most revered in Dariu approve of the new emperor. Wisdom, abundance, authority, and might. It's not a surprising combination. Do the other five of our lesser gods feel left out?

Marclinus waves his hand dismissively. "Make the appropriate arrangements for the first rite and check with me before finalizing them. We may as well rejoin the court for the afternoon."

Or perhaps he'll return to speak with his advisors at more length without me, but I can hardly complain about that in my current position.

High Commander Axius's warning has set my mind bubbling with possibilities. As I follow my husband into the hall, I consider the best way to approach the subject without giving away all of my aims.

I slip my hand around Marclinus's elbow again. "Do you think perhaps I should pursue a little combat training in case I need to defend myself? It isn't something I've had much experience in with my dedication to Elox."

That isn't entirely true—my parents ensured that both my sister and I were tutored in every skill we might need, including the basics of self-defense—but I don't think Marclinus will find it difficult to believe. And it wouldn't hurt to brush up on my admittedly limited abilities regardless.

He hums. "I'm sure our soldiers can protect you quite well if any civilian dares to attack you. But a certain amount of martial competency can only be a benefit, if you're inclined to learn. I'm not sure how well you'd get on with the typical military regimens, though."

I produce a light laugh. "Oh, to be sure, I can't see heading down to the barracks for lessons. Is there anyone in the court who's proficient enough to serve as a decent teacher? I'm sure Axius is far too busy with more important matters."

I'm prepared to prod Marclinus farther, but for once his inclination to make use of his foster brothers however he can works in my favor. He snaps his fingers. "Prince Raul is quite a fighter—you might remember his performance during the fighting exhibition a couple of weeks back. I'll have him give you a tutoring session or two."

I make myself hesitate before picking up my pace again. "Do you think he'll agree? He and the other princes have been rather... distant with me. I suppose there's also my guards—"

Marclinus shrugs off my feigned discomfort. "He'll do what I tell him. And he'll know how to handle a lady of your standing better than anyone on staff. Your guards will be standing by to protect you from any outside threat—and to make sure he doesn't get overly familiar. Unless you had someone else in mind?"

At his evaluating look, I shake my head with a sheepish expression. "I was hoping you'd advise me on that, and clearly you have. Prince Raul will be fine."

Better that he thinks I was reluctant rather than eager. And now I'll have an easy opportunity to pass on any messages I want to convey to the prince without risking it more publicly—or relying on him sneaking into my chambers.

"Once he's run you through the basics, I'll test you myself and see if anything's lacking," Marclinus says, a promise that feels more ominous than I like.

I snatch at the opportunity to broach another topic that's been on my mind. "As long as you play fair. I haven't heard tell yet whether you took a dedication gift from Sabrelle or what it might be."

If he made a sacrifice, it isn't an immediately visible one. But it seems unlikely that the heir to the empire would have given up the chance to gain at least a little extra power.

Marclinus simply tsks his tongue at me. "There's no need for you to worry yourself about that either."

Because he hasn't got one or he'd rather keep it secret even from his wife?

Before I can find a way to pry further, we arrive at the hall of entertainments. The several dozen current members of the court are filling the space with their chatter and laughter.

Those nearest the door dip respectfully at their emperor's entrance. Marclinus gives them a brisk nod, his gaze searching farther beyond. "Where are those foster 'brothers' of mine? I can speak to Raul right now."

I can't make out the prince of Lavira's massive frame and cocoa-brown hair anywhere around us, but my gaze quickly snags on Bastien's slim form. His dark green gaze jabs through me from beneath his shaggy auburn hair for the instant before he turns on his heel.

If Raul has talked to the prince of Cotea since last night, he doesn't appear to have softened in his opinion of me any.

Marclinus swivels. "Well, there's another who can be of use."

When I glance around, he's striding toward Lorenzo. The prince of Rione's dark face tenses, but he gives a stiff bow to his emperor.

As I hurry after Marclinus, Lorenzo's gaze flicks to me and jerks away again. He doesn't look any happier to see me than he does my husband.

It shouldn't matter. I made my choice. I'm lucky even Raul still cares about me.

None of those facts stops a pang from resonating through my heart.

"Prince Lorenzo," Marclinus says in a jauntier tone, "I'd say the hall of entertainments could use some music this afternoon."

My stomach turns. Emperor Tarquin was making a habit

of pushing Lorenzo and his gift to the limit, not even knowing just how much casting the illusion of divinely beautiful melodies over the entire court cost him.

I catch Marclinus's arm before he can go on and focus completely on him with an apologetic smile. "Husband, why don't we call on the court musicians instead? I do find it so much more enthralling to listen to multiple instruments in harmony. Why should we settle for just a vielle or a lyre on its own?"

Marclinus chuckles. "You do have a point there. And we should appreciate our native Darium talents."

He beckons to a page and instructs the woman to gather the musicians who've actually been hired for the job. At the edge of my vision, Lorenzo drifts away without a backward glance.

I don't know whether he's grateful for my intervention or offended by it.

The pang of that uneasiness jostles another idea loose. When my husband sends the page off, I lean closer to him. I might as well start testing what little bits of influence I can wield so far.

"We should discuss that banquet I'd like to hold. And there were a few treats I've heard the nobles mention that I was hoping I might get a chance to try…"

CHAPTER SEVEN

Aurelia

When the last of the banquet's dishes have been laid out on the expansive table in the middle of the dining room, I lift my wine goblet. The nobles swarming the room pause in their chattering.

Over the past few weeks, I've stood before all these high ranking Darium citizens naked, bleeding, vomiting, and every other imaginable humiliation. Somehow the weight of their attention feels even heavier now.

This is my first official court event as their empress. Until they've fully accepted me in that role, every move I make will be scrutinized.

"Good evening to all my friends of the court," I call out with a gracious smile. "Thank you for joining me tonight for what I hope will be a delectable feast. Consider it my thank you for

welcoming me into your world. You'll find all sorts of delicacies to try. I've had the palace chefs give a variety of foods beloved in Accasy their own Darium spin as a demonstration of just how well our two countries can work together. Please, enjoy!"

Applause ripples through the crowd. It's hard to tell how much is politeness rather than enthusiasm. As the nobles turn toward the banquet table, the expressions I catch hold a fair bit of uncertainty and skepticism.

I sampled all of the new creations being offered tonight as the chefs perfected their recipes. If the imperial kitchen staff's work doesn't win over at least the court's tongues, nothing will.

Marclinus teases his fingers up my neck to give one loop of my hair a playful tug. "It certainly smells delicious. I'm going to dive in myself and see what bounty you've created for us, wife."

I follow him over, taking a plate that one of the servers hands me. I purposefully arranged for this banquet to be a buffet, with small portions that the nobles can nibble on as they continue circulating through the room if they wish to stay on their feet.

The setup will allow me to circulate between *them*, making the most of this opportunity to talk with them while they're enjoying my generosity. With a little luck, at least a few of them will view me in a more favorable light by the end of the evening.

Now that I'm empress, the imperial tasters try every dish I'm interested in before I take my portion. I start with the honey-glazed duck and stewed lacquernuts before meandering between the clusters of nobles.

Emperor Tarquin and his son have beaten the expectations of respect into his court. I can't pass anyone's sight without them bobbing their head to me. It's a bit absurd, but it gives me plenty of openings to strike up a conversation.

At the acknowledgment of two pairs of barons and baronissas, I join their small group. "I hope you're finding the meal to your liking."

I doubt they'd admit it if they didn't, but the speed with which they're devouring their first round lends their effusive words some weight.

"It's always exciting to discover new flavors," one of the baronissas gushes.

I beam as if in delight. "I've found the same—and there've been so many new things to discover since I've arrived in Dariu. I know the loss of our former Imperial Majesty has cast a pall over the court. If there's anything I might not have thought of on my own that would ease your troubles or raise your spirits, please don't hesitate to let me know."

Her husband hums. "It is a great loss, but everything has been handled splendidly. I wouldn't mind seeing more Ularian wine served at our dinners, though."

The leadership of his country and the entire empire has changed without warning, and he's most interested in his beverage selection?

Well, perhaps he's afraid to say anything that could come across as more critical.

I offer another smile. "I'm sure I can see to that."

I amble onward from one group to the next. A couple of marchionissas deny that anything in the world could be improved, but a viceroy brings up a graver concern.

He dips his voice low as if he's worried he'll spark a panic. "I appreciate knowing that the empire can count on Accasy's loyalty with you standing by our emperor. I trust Your Imperial Eminences are keeping a close eye on our nearer neighbors."

I can't stop my eyebrows from arching. "Has there been unrest reported in the other territories?" I haven't heard of any, though I suppose it's possible Marclinus wouldn't have brought me into those discussions.

The viceroy clicks his tongue. "The rebellious elements never know what's good for them—always looking to cause trouble. They might see Emperor Tarquin's passing as an opportunity to strike out. But of course our new emperor will stamp out any signs of dissention swiftly and firmly."

Marclinus had better do that, he's actually saying, just wording it so it can't sound like he's telling the imperial family what to do.

From what I've seen and heard, the empire's conquered countries are far too beaten down to spring into major rebellion at a moment's notice, but I can't say I'm surprised the Darium nobles would worry about it. "He absolutely will," I say confidently, with a twist of my gut at the thought of just how brutally my husband is likely to crush even a whiff of discontent abroad.

As I continue my circuit of the room, I encounter a few more anxious murmurs—overheard or spoken to me directly —about the possibility of rebels testing the new emperor's strength. But most of the matters raised are as vapid as the first baron's wine preferences.

At least the more superficial matters are easier to address without feeling I'm encouraging hostility toward the outer territories. I smile and nod, nod and smile, promising that I'll see that the city's most prominent shoe designer stops by the palace soon, that more marigolds will be added to the gardens, and that a new bath oil scent one marchionissa has heard about will be ordered in.

One gray-haired marchion isn't so eager to talk. He bobs his head in acknowledgement and takes in my question with chilly eyes.

"The thing I'd most want to ask for cannot be offered," he says flatly, and returns to the buffet table.

I watch him go, recognition tugging at my mind. His features reminded me of one of my competitors in the trials —maybe Giralda?

Is that her father? Does he blame *me* for the loss of a daughter, simply because I survived and she didn't?

I wouldn't have let anyone die if it'd been up to me rather than Tarquin and Marclinus, but I don't think going over and reminding the marchion of that will warm him to me. It's much easier to resent the interloper than the men who've held such sway over his life.

As I amble on, my path brings me toward Bastien and Lorenzo more than once. The two princes always happen to drift off in another direction before I get close enough that they'd need to acknowledge me. I catch Raul's eye and thank him for the combat lessons he's promised, but saying more feels unwise.

My heart beats a little faster just feeling his dark gaze on me as I move on.

By the time I add more food to my plate and take a moment to sit at one of the tables, I have quite a list of court requests in my head. Whether it'll engender good will toward me for more than a moment or two, it's difficult to tell, but at least it's a starting point.

I accept the compliments of the nobles whose table I've joined and make the same appeal for advice. After they've informed me of how they'd love to see a new statue of Tarquin erected, perhaps one of solid gold, my smile feels even stiffer.

The dining room is full of light and mouth-watering scents, but I can't sense any of the warmth that would have permeated a banquet back in the main Accasian palace. For a few seconds, I'm overwhelmed with longing for the spirited conversations and companiable laughter between my family and colleagues that never felt calculated the way every remark and giggle does here.

My friends would have found these concerns absurd. I can so easily imagine Cataline shaking her head in bewilderment. *Don't they ever think even of the people of their baronies or whatever other territories? The ones they're supposed to watch out for?*

Nica would snort and speak up with her sarcastic lilt. *Don't you know a gold statue of the emperor makes all our lives richer?*

Picturing them with me lifts my spirits while deepening the wave of homesickness. My gaze drifts over the rest of the room—and jars to a halt on my husband.

Marclinus has come up beside Vicerine Bianca. He leans so close his lips brush the shell of her ear, whispering something to her as he trails his fingers down her back. He caresses her as if the gold marriage band gleaming by his sleeve didn't exist.

Of course, he's never cared about her marriage vows either.

It's not a surprising sight—Marclinus has outright groped Bianca in front of me in the past, and she's made no secret of their intimate association—but it's the first time he's overtly approached another woman since our wedding. I hesitate, unsure how I should react.

Even I'm not supposed to criticize our Imperial Majesty. Should I pretend I haven't even noticed?

A flush has darkened Bianca's smooth brown skin. She says something back to Marclinus, turning partly toward him, but she keeps her hands clasped modestly by her waist. Her gaze darts across the room… to me.

Her dark eyes hold mine for the space of a heartbeat. I can't help thinking there's a question in them and in the slight slant of her mouth, as if she's confirming she has my *permission.*

I don't know why she'd think she'd need to seek it. She's enjoyed throwing her closeness with Marclinus in my face plenty of times before. I outright told her I wouldn't interfere with their ongoing relationship after we married.

I meant what I said. The situation might have struck me with a momentary awkwardness, but not a particle of jealousy nips at me.

If he dallies with her, it should spare me having to use a dose of my special potion on him for a third night in a row, with all the playacting that goes into my performances.

I incline my head slightly and return my attention to my plate.

Is that how a proper empress is supposed to act? Is that what Marclinus's mother would have done, in the few years she stood with Tarquin after his crowning before she lost her life to childbirth?

As thorough as my training in royal etiquette has been, it somehow never prepared me for the scenario of how to handle a husband who flaunts his affairs in front of your entire court. Marclinus seems to require an additional set of rules of conduct.

There might be more I could learn from the empress who came before me—the one so beloved by the common people they gave her an honor all her own. Perhaps I can use this banquet to get a little something for myself as well.

When I've cleared my plate, I weave through the room again, watching for any of the older nobles who'd have been in court three decades ago during Tarquin's early years as emperor. Here and there, I stop to mingle.

After a little small talk about the food and the atmosphere, I work in a question in a casual tone. "You know, I've heard so many lovely things about Empress

Fionille, it seems a shame I never had the chance to meet her. I wonder what foods she'd have brought out for a banquet?"

The impact the late empress had on the court is unmistakable. The mention brings a soft smile to every face, and everyone agrees that she was wonderful.

I don't learn much of anything specific, though, even about her taste in cuisine.

"She would have loved this feast," one of the elderly vicerines tells me with a pat of my arm.

"She made every meal feel like a banquet," a grizzled marchion says. "Pleased with whatever we were having."

A faded baronissa taps her lips with a distant expression. "I don't know if what was on her plate mattered much to her. She always looked beautiful, whatever the occasion."

I'm left unsure of whether Marclinus's mother had little mind of her own or if it's been so long that recollections are too hazy for details.

She must have done *something* to earn her people's affections.

I meander through the room for a little longer, making polite chatter, but the plates have become quite picked over. The crowd is thinning. When I've exchanged at least a few comments with everyone who's lingered, I set off for the library.

The rulers of Dariu are enamored with their own grandeur. Surely there are accounts somewhere of the significant events of any emperor's rule.

It can't hurt to do a little research into how a Darium empress has typically behaved beyond the royal standards I'm used to.

Given that Marclinus and Bianca vanished from the dining room some time ago, I don't think I need to worry about my husband wondering where I've wandered off to.

Not that he should have any reason to disapprove of this line of research.

I slip past the library's heavy door and stall in my tracks with its thump behind me.

Bastien is standing by one of the central tables, in almost the same place where we spoke the first time I encountered him in this room what feels like a century ago.

The hardening of his expression is as if no time and nothing else has passed between us since that awkward conversation.

I step forward cautiously, studying his stance, aware of the guards who'll have trailed through the halls behind me— who'll follow me into the library as they judge necessary. Most of the things I'd like to say to the prince of Cotea, I don't dare.

I keep my tone mild, my gaze steady. "Prince Bastien. It's my good fortune that I've run into you here. I was hoping to find records about the life of past empresses—perhaps you know where I might find something like that?"

It's a subtle overture of peace, one he could accept or dismiss.

Or smack it away like a stinging gnat, as the case may be.

Bastien's voice comes out as stiff as his posture. "I'm sure Your Imperial Highness can find it on your own, as you prefer to do things."

He stalks to the door, giving me a wide berth. My lips part, the words to try to call him back rising to them—and at the same moment, two guards arrive.

I nod to them with feigned gratitude and tamp down the ache in my heart as Bastien disappears into the hall.

I shouldn't be shocked by his vehemence, should I? From what Raul said, Bastien spearheaded the plan to arrange our escape.

He tossed aside all the caution I know he's clung to so

fervently in his determination to keep his foster brothers safe. He tossed it aside for my sake.

And I threw his passionate gamble back in his face, however necessary that choice was.

If I'd realized his devotion to me ran *that* deep... I don't know if I could have done anything differently. But the knowledge brings a lump into my throat that I can't swallow away.

It turns out I could have used Bastien's help, if the records I'm looking for even exist. I putter around the library until two hourly bells have pealed beyond the palace walls, but I don't come up with anything closer than historic accounts of imperial military campaigns from more than a hundred years past.

Perhaps I've simply missed the relevant books in this vast collection, or possibly those accounts are housed in the records room I don't have access to.

I make my way back to my chambers. When the door shuts behind me, I'm finally alone.

Standing in the middle of the luxurious bedroom, gold glinting and satin shimmering all around me, my pulse wobbles.

What have I accomplished today other than determining that the people of court are frivolous and xenophobic—both of which I already knew—and giving myself a list of trivial chores? Do the nobles have friendlier feelings toward me now, or will they keep whispering to each other just as much about the wild princess who's become their empress?

I tip my face toward the gleaming ceiling and close my eyes, tapping my fingers down my front in the gesture of the divinities. *Elox, I'm following the path you guided me to. How should I proceed in our quest for peace?*

I hold myself still for several minutes in meditative daze.

No matter how I detach my mind and let my thoughts drift freely, no message I can discern comes to me.

My godlen hasn't totally ignored me, though. When I tuck myself in bed in my nightgown and drift off into sleep, a dream is waiting to meet me.

I'm crouched in a vast green field, the grass tickling against my bare shins. Each of my arms is looped around the wooly body of a lamb.

I'm hugging the animals close, but with a sudden bleat, they break from my embrace. The lambs spring off in opposite directions, hurtling away from me.

I can only catch one of them. I *must* catch one of them. But how can I decide which?

The sense of urgency blares through me, and I jolt awake in the darkness. The shapes of the room swim before my weary eyes.

I revisit the images of the dream in my mind over and over, looking for a clue. What do the two lambs represent? What sort of equal division am I meant to choose between?

I received my message, but I can't say I have any clue how to decipher it.

CHAPTER EIGHT

Lorenzo

As the servers bring around our second course of breakfast, a creamy sweet smell reaches my nose. A sudden pang of loss hits me alongside memories of the terrace outside my family's main palace, the view of the ocean to one side and the sprawl of white-washed city buildings to the other.

Then my plate is set in front of me, and I understand my reaction with a punch of recognition.

Next to the fresh-baked pastries sits a pot of a flecked jelly as white as the walls back home.

Coconut jam. It was almost always on the breakfast table when I was a little kid, but I haven't gotten to taste it in years.

Marclinus lifts his voice from where he's lounging at the head of the table. "I hope you all enjoy the treat we ordered in from Rione. My wife had a craving for coconut."

He shoots one of his cocky grins at Aurelia, who dips her head modestly. "Thank you for indulging me."

The morning sunlight streaming through the windows lights up her walnut-brown hair and gleams in her dark blue eyes. At the small smile that crosses her lips, my heart hitches in my chest.

I realize I'm staring at her and yank my gaze back to my own meal.

She didn't so much as glance my way. She hasn't said a word to me since her wedding ceremony.

But she told me out in the woods weeks ago that she'd never tasted coconut before. After *I* told her that coconut jam was one of the things I missed most about my early childhood in Rione, before Emperor Tarquin claimed me as a hostage.

She asked for this treat for my benefit, not hers.

A lump rises in my throat. If my hand wobbles a little when I dip my spoon into the pot of jam and swirl it on the flaky pastry, I hope no one notices.

She also intervened when Marclinus was going to order me to play for the court a couple of days ago. Has she really pretended to enjoy my music in the past, or was she asking for the court musicians to spare me the strain she knows comes with using my gift?

The emotions that've been roiling inside me for the past few days churn even harder. A swell of affection clashes with the lingering pain of watching her rush into Marclinus's arms and a sharp prickle of uncertainty.

She could have been *with* me rather than him. With all of us, away from here, never worrying about catering to our tyrants' whims again. I called out to her the way only I could, laid out the whole plan to reassure her, promised her the entire blasted world—

And she signed her refusal to me with a jerk of her hand

and careened on into a marriage to a psychopath.

I loved her. I don't know whether I should still think about that emotion in the present tense. I don't know whether the woman I fell for even existed, or if she was as imaginary as the illusions my gift can conjure.

The creamy sweetness floods my mouth with each tiny bite I push between my teeth. Thank all that's holy that some capacity for taste remains in the stump of my tongue and the flesh around it.

I do my best to drift away from my turmoil into recollections of careless days roaming through the city streets or exploring the mountain slopes with my older sister and cousins, but the gloom that's shrouded me since the end of the final trial follows me even into my memories.

I polish off every bit of the pot's contents all the same.

Should I say something to Aurelia? Indicate that I recognize the gift—that I'm grateful for it?

Or would doing that only make me more of an idiot?

It's hard *not* to feel like an idiot when we move to the gardens and I have to watch Aurelia sashay between the flower beds and around the fountains with her hand tucked around Marclinus's elbow. She beams up at him and laughs at his jokes, the perfect picture of a devoted wife.

I don't think her offering at breakfast was intended as an invitation. Maybe it was an apology. A consolation prize.

He got the woman I adore, and I got a pot of jam. Am I supposed to be grateful for that?

Now that we're well into summer, it's a hot day even in the late morning with the sun glaring down from a stark blue sky. I wander through the shadows, watching Aurelia as surreptitiously as I can manage.

I shouldn't pay attention to her at all. I should pretend her existence means nothing to me. But her presence tugs at me as if she's snagged a fishhook right through the chambers of my heart.

She brought a light into my life like nothing I've ever felt before. Now that I've tasted that kind of joy, I can't help craving it, more than I crave even my old home.

This isn't healthy. I can't chase after what might only have been an illusion.

Except it might have been real. I can't shake the gloom or the craving while that possibility lingers in my head.

I'm not sure what signs I'm watching for now. Raul insists that she murdered Tarquin, that she *had* to stay so she could end our foster father's brutal reign—the way we meant to end it ourselves, as hopeless as those plans turned out to be. Could the gentle, compassionate woman I thought I knew really have schemed to end a man's life, no matter how awful he was?

She could be fierce and determined too. Who knows what other dimensions she had to her?

It's only... If she's capable of murder, then I can't say I really knew her regardless of the rest.

Bastien crosses my path, takes one look at my face, and catches my arm to drag me over to one of the lawn games that's just started up.

"I know you're mourning," he says under his breath. "But you've got to try not to look like you've just been gutted. Distract yourself."

Is that what he's doing? It's always seemed easier for the others to harden themselves to our losses and failures than it is for me.

And I have been gutted, in one smooth stroke with the flick of a hand, and over and over every time I miss her secret smiles, the knowing glint in her eyes, the heat of her caress.

The balls we lob at the hoops feel heavier than usual on my hand. The sport strikes me as even more pointless than usual. My frustration seeps into my throws: one and then another flies wide.

After I've knocked one of the hoops—not the one I was supposed to be aiming at—right over, I pull back toward the hedges to leave the game to the other players. Counsel Etta drifts over to join me, her pale forehead furrowed.

"Prince Lorenzo," she says in her dry voice. "You've seemed rather out of sorts lately. Is there anything in particular bothering you?"

A chill runs down my spine. Etta is one of Tarquin's—and now Marclinus's—chief advisors. Which means she's wise enough to potentially put the pieces together if the source of my tangled emotions has been too obvious, and close enough to him to easily share any suspicions she has.

My grandfather's voice echoes up from the past—his stern words while he shook his finger at my six-year-old self while tears streaked down my cheeks. *You're a prince. You feel what you feel, but you can't let everyone see it. No one wants a ruler who bawls in front of them every time he's disappointed.*

Bastien's right. I have to get a better grip on myself.

I thought I'd gotten better at bottling up my negative emotions as I grew into a man, but obviously my control is still wobbly. Aurelia's desertion shattered it like a vase knocked to the floor.

With conscious effort, I turn toward Etta and force a smile onto my face. I've spent the past fifteen years here pretending obedience and passivity. That's what everyone expects from me.

I just don't know how to find my way back to that state of "normal" when I've been thrown so off-balance.

Pulling a scrap of paper and a pencil out of the pouch at my hip, I scrawl a quick message. *Stayed up too late practicing a new instrument. Too tired to be at my best.*

It's a plausible excuse. I have traded music for sleep in the past, although the weariness has never left me quite as off-kilter as I am at the moment.

Etta purses her lips, but she inclines her head as if she accepts my answer. "If anything does trouble you, especially if it would affect others' well-being too, I hope you'll share your concerns."

I nod, my supposed agreement a bald lie that doesn't give me so much as a twinge of guilt. The advisors are the imperial family's creatures—they serve Marclinus's interests, not anyone else's.

I pull myself away from the game completely, figuring I'm less likely to show distress if I stick to admiring bright blossoms and enjoying the whiffs of floral-scented breeze. Naturally, my feet end up leading me straight into Aurelia's vicinity.

She's standing with several of the court nobles near one of the marble fountains. I sit on a bench on the opposite side, where I can't see her or make out her voice over the warble of the water.

I'm simply enjoying the cool spray. Nothing strange about that.

I close my eyes for a few minutes, focusing on the patter of droplets as well as I can. The scrape of footsteps over the gravel that surrounds the fountain snaps me back to alertness.

It's only one of the imperial guards. He stands stiffly by the fountain, watching the empress with a somber expression beneath his curly hair. His hand rests on the hilt of the sword at his hip. The broad scar by the corner of his eye suggests any fight today wouldn't be his first.

His presence is to be expected. No doubt there's at least one other guard monitoring Aurelia from a discreet distance. But something about the tension in his stance niggles at me.

Does he think there's a threat nearby?

While he stands sentinel, I study *him* and the area around us as surreptitiously as I can. What reason has he seen to worry?

Then his mouth moves, a low mutter that's meant only for himself. Any sound to the words is so quiet it's lost to the warble of the fountain.

But I've spent years interpreting hasty gestures and mouthed words from across the room when my foster brothers and I need to communicate stealthily. I've developed a decent skill at reading lips.

And the words I think I saw the man's lips form are ones I might have seen just a few weeks ago, when Aurelia first arrived, from my own foster brothers.

"Pathetic Accasian tramp."

My back stiffens in an instant with a lurch of my gut.

If I caught that right, he isn't tense because of a threat he wants to protect Aurelia from. He doesn't want to protect her —*he's* the threat.

Did I misinterpret? Lip reading is hardly an exact science, and some of the syllables of the words I thought I made out are awfully subtle. He could have been grumbling to himself about something else altogether.

As I watch him longer, though, I become increasingly sure. When he scans the garden, his eyes always narrow slightly as they pass over Aurelia's position beyond the fountain. His hand flexes against his sword hilt as if he'd like to draw the blade and use it right now, even though I haven't seen any cause for violence.

Unless he sees the foreign princess-turned-empress as a malicious entity.

I knew some of the common people had hostile feelings toward her—I saw what happened in the square after the funeral speeches. The current palace guards were all hired before they had any idea they'd be serving an empress from the wild north as well as the current imperial family. It isn't totally unexpected that one or two might have a negative attitude.

Gods above, what if he decides to act on his disdain?

Abruptly, he swivels and strides past my bench toward the other side of the fountain. His mouth is set in a grim line.

Panic overrides most of my good sense. I push myself to my feet as if I have somewhere else to be and fling a concentrated illusion straight at his face with the force of my will.

My scrap of magic smacks over his eyes, making him think he can see nothing but darkness. The guard yelps, stumbles, and whirls around—and the effect has already wisped away.

I peer at him as if startled, my pulse thudding fast. There shouldn't be any need to fear consequences for using my powers. Raul told us he'd heard from Aurelia that her guards can't detect magic, and that's obviously held true, or he'd have deflected my trick before it reached him.

Then I look past him and realize the true reason he was moving this way.

He wasn't going on the attack. He was simply following Aurelia as she meandered over to rejoin her husband.

Both she and Marclinus frown at the guard before their gazes slide to me, standing nearby. My heart stutters again.

I give a twitch of my mouth I hope looks bemused and hustle off between the beds of flowers.

Fuck. What did I even accomplish? I could have exposed my powers and gotten myself into a total catastrophe if any of the emperor's guards with a magic-sensing gift had come closer without me noticing.

I've veered off between the taller hedges when a familiar broad hand falls on my shoulder.

I glance over to see Raul has followed me. He offers a sympathetic smile that's really closer to a grimace.

"Getting a little jumpy, huh?" he says.

I twist my hands in the air. *It was a stupid move. I know.*

He pitches his voice even lower. "You're too messed up about her. You need to believe what I told you, and you'll be able to simmer down."

Not that easy.

He squeezes my shoulder and cocks his head pensively. Maybe I should be worried when that sly gleam comes into his eyes. But when he leans close with a conspiratorial lilt to his voice, I can't pull away.

"You need to talk to her yourself. I think I can distract the imperial prick for long enough tonight to give you an opening."

CHAPTER NINE

Aurelia

When I retire to my chambers at the end of the evening, Jinalle and Eusette are waiting to tend to me. They murmur pleasantries as they help pull off the elaborate dress and the heavy jewelry that adored my neck and hair. Then they carefully unpin the brown strands so they tumble free across my shoulders for the first time since this morning.

"What will you wear for the emperor's confirmation rite tomorrow?" Eusette asks, peering into my wardrobe. "I think the blue gown would look very fine."

Jinalle hums to herself and peeks at me shyly. "Or maybe that lovely green one, to match Estera's colors in her honor?"

The thought of tomorrow's ceremony makes my stomach clench. I'm glad that we're getting on with seeing Marclinus officially confirmed as emperor, which will also solidify my place as his wife. But what can I expect from the civilians who'll be watching us every step of the way?

How many of them still feel the same way as whoever hurled that bloody animal organ at my mourning dress? What else can I do to prove to them that I support their new emperor and the empire?

If there was a potion that could win over the hearts of a country permanently, I'd be making it right now.

I contemplate the two suggested dresses in the wardrobe. The midnight blue silk will emphasize my eyes and set off my tanned skin nicely, but I do like the idea of showing my respects to the godlen we're appealing to. Not that Estera, overseer of learning and wisdom, generally cares all that much about fashion.

It's a light grass-green that reminds me of Elox's peaceful fields. I can honor my own godlen at the same time.

"Let's go with the green." I reach for my nightgown where it's folded on my dressing table. "Thank you for your help. I can take care of my washing up on my own."

My maids curtsy and slip out of my bedroom with no sign of offense. After a few days in their role, they're already used to my independent streak.

The moment the door has shut behind them, I exhale in relief. For a brief time, I have no one to perform for.

A familiar pain fills my chest. It'd be better if I could be myself with company once in a while. To sit here and chat with Rochelle like I used to as she brushed my hair or fixed my gowns so they emphasized all of my figure's best qualities…

I couldn't tell her everything, but I could be so much more open with her than with any of the other ladies of the court. She gave up so much so I could make it to this point.

There's no way left for me to repay her. I can't secret her off to the medic she'd fallen for. I couldn't even see to a proper funeral. Tarquin sent her savaged body to her home province before I was in any position to have a say.

Even having Cici, my maid from Accasy, by my side would be a comfort. But as the idea flits through my head that I could summon her back now that I'm empress, I'm already dismissing it.

I can't drag her into all the dangers I'm facing here. When I still have so little sway over my own fate, it would be pure selfishness.

Until I can establish my standing with both Marclinus and his people, I can't offer any real protection to anyone I care about.

The last thing Rochelle said to me was that I have to win. The trials may be over, but I haven't truly triumphed yet.

I can do that much for her and everyone else who's counting on me.

Right now, though, I don't even know whether my husband intends to call on me tonight.

My thumb rubs over the side of my ring, too lightly to trigger the needle that dips into the hidden cavity. Then I reach for my nightgown and tug it on.

Perhaps if I'm already in bed and at least appear to be asleep when Marclinus comes by, he'll leave me to my rest rather than disturbing me. There'll be no need for the full pretense, no need to share my chambers with him.

It's a small chance, but better than none at all.

I hurry over to the expansive bathing room at the far end of my chambers. On the threshold, I jerk to a halt. My hand shoots to the gilded doorframe to grasp for balance.

Lorenzo stands up from where he was perched on the edge of the empty marble bathtub. The prince's dark gaze holds mine, his stance tense as if braced for my reaction.

My heart restarts at twice its usual pace. All my thoughts

about Marclinus barging in come racing back to me, sending the frantic thudding right up my throat.

I take a step into the room to make it even less likely that the guards stationed outside will hear my voice, as low as I keep it. The door to my apartments is thick, but I don't want to take a single unnecessary risk.

"What are you doing in here? Marclinus could come by any second—even if you hide yourself, his guards will sense your magic—"

Lorenzo stays where he is on the other side of the tub. It yawns like a chasm between us.

His hand jerks through the air to cut me off. *It's okay.*

As anxious as I am, I can't help frowning at him. "It's not. It was risky enough when you all would sneak into my old rooms, but now..."

The prince attempts another gesture that he aborts partway through, perhaps realizing that what he needs to say is too complicated to convey by his more furtive means.

His illusionary voice, the rich baritone I haven't heard since he asked me to run away with him, resonates into my head. *"Raul is distracting Marclinus. He promised I'd have until at least the eleventh bell to speak with you uninterrupted."*

I fold my arms over my chest. "I don't see how he could guarantee that."

Although knowing how the princes look out for each other, I find it hard to believe Raul would have made the promise if he wasn't sure he could follow through.

Lorenzo simply shrugs. We eye each other across the tub, which suddenly feels tiny compared to the vast gulf my refusal opened up between us days ago.

A lump rises in my throat. It's still difficult for me to imagine that I won so much affection and devotion from any of these men that they were willing to throw away their entire future to be with me.

But Lorenzo was. And I turned my back on him. I wouldn't make a different decision even now.

What am I supposed to say to him?

"Was there something specific you wanted to talk about?" I ask tentatively.

It's hard to read the emotions that travel across Lorenzo's deep brown face. His jaw flexes, his gaze flicking down and up again, his stance swaying slightly as if he almost stepped closer but thought better of it.

"Raul says you dealt with Tarquin. That you stayed here in order to do it."

I never admitted to the murder in so many words even to Raul, as accepting as he was of the act. My lungs constrict against the idea of voicing my crime out loud.

How much loyalty can I count on from a man whose heart I broke?

I lift my chin toward Lorenzo. "Does the possibility bother you? He told *me* that you all were planning to do the same for years before I ever showed up."

"Because we were angry and a little scared, and it seemed like the whole continent would be better off without Tarquin, back then. Now it's just been handed over to Marclinus."

The despair in his words wrenches at me. Gazing back into his dark eyes, I see those boys of ten or eleven years old whispering in hallways and secret rooms. Planning their immense sacrifices around the idea of bringing down their tormenter and saving their kingdoms.

Watching that dream crumble to dust just a few years later when the eldest of them snapped and fell in a bloody heap at a stab of a guard's sword.

Despite the tension between us, I want to challenge that despair. Perhaps because I've teetered so close to the edge of it myself.

My voice softens. "And I'm married to him. I'd think I

have a better chance of steering the empire in a more peaceful direction as the emperor's wife than as Tarquin's daughter-in-law."

Lorenzo is silent for a moment, simply staring at me. *"And that's what you intended to be, as quickly as possible, all along."*

The lump in my throat expands until I feel as if I'll choke. I will it down as well as I can. "I never lied to you. I told you I had to marry Marclinus. I told you I was here to do whatever I could to see my country—and yours—have a better future. I just didn't tell you exactly how far I was willing to go."

"But you… You're dedicated to the godlen of healing. You were always trying to stop the violence…"

My mouth twists. "I didn't say I enjoyed what was required of me. But Elox gave his blessing. You aren't very familiar with him if you think I've strayed from his teachings. He's always believed that violence is sometimes necessary to save more lives in the end. I'm the one who could come here. I'm the one who could clear the way. So I did."

Lorenzo's expression twitches. All at once, he strides around the tub. His expression is so intense, my body goes rigid when he reaches for my arm. "Lorenzo, don't—"

He freezes with his hand simply touching my elbow. *"I'm not going to hurt you, Rell. I wouldn't. I just— It's not only up to you. I'm here with you now. I might not be able to do much, but I can hold you and take on a little of that burden. It shouldn't have been all yours to begin with."*

The fond nickname brings a burn of tears to the back of my eyes. I blink hard, my heart still thudding fast, but I'm not sure what there really is to be afraid of now.

Ever so tentatively, I tilt toward Lorenzo. With a raw sound, he gathers me against his chest.

I rest my forehead against his shoulders and breathe in

the warm, tangy scent I've missed. My next words come up in a mumble muffled by his shirt. "I'm sorry."

The prince's embrace tightens. *"I'm* sorry. *I was thinking too much about what would make me happiest and not enough about what matters to you. I should have known you well enough to be sure you had good reasons."*

"I mean, the whole point was for it to not look as if I could have had anything to do with it, so I can't really blame you for having trouble believing I did."

"Raul knew. I should have trusted him and you more."

A soft laugh tumbles out of me. "Well, he hasn't always been right about me, so I think you can be forgiven there too."

Lorenzo draws back a few inches, his fingers brushing over my cheek and his head dipping toward mine. My breath catches with the longing to experience the press of his mouth once more, but a quiver of ice races through my veins at the same time.

I've already indulged in more pleasure than I was owed. I have to think about the security of the men I care about as well as my own.

I set my hand on his chest with a gentle nudge, just enough force to halt him. Lorenzo peers down at me with a question in his eyes that he doesn't need to put into words.

My voice comes out in a whisper. "I want to, but I have to see things through with Marclinus. It's going to take everything I have if I'm going to win him over enough to make a difference. I can't afford to lose focus. And… and I don't want to put you in any danger."

I already lost my head once with Raul. I swore I'd fortify my self-control.

Lorenzo knits his brow. *"I don't want to put* you *at any more risk than you already are. You don't have to worry about me. Whatever you need from me, I'll be happy to give it.*

Happy that I'm finally accomplishing something that might matter."

"I know. It's only—with that—"

I stumble over my words, the ache in my chest squeezing tighter.

But maybe Lorenzo should know this. He's shared his heart the most freely with me from the start.

Knowing my history might make it easier for him to keep his distance when it'll keep him safe.

I can't quite bring myself to pull right out of his embrace. My head droops, my cheek grazing his jaw.

"I thought once that I could have love and everything that comes with it. When I was sixteen, there was a man just a little older than me who joined the palace guard back home. He was often posted outside when I'd go for walks in the grounds, and we spoke a little, and then when he was off duty, he'd join me... I'd meet him secretly at night. After we'd been seeing each other for over a year, we started talking about running away together."

Lorenzo strokes his fingers up and down my back in a soothing caress. He asks his question with a gentle twist of his other hand within my view: *What happened?*

"We got to the point of making detailed plans. I convinced myself that leaving wouldn't be betraying my kingdom—that I'd find other ways of helping Accasy without needing to act as a princess..."

I wince at my past delusion. "He took a trip home to visit his family outside the capital. There was some kind of altercation with Darium soldiers who were passing through —he stepped in when they were harassing a couple of locals —it ended in a fight. One of them stabbed him right through the heart."

Lorenzo hisses a breath through his teeth and pulls me back into an emphatic hug.

It's been long enough, the pain dulled enough, that only a faint prickle touches my eyes with the memories. I just need *this* man to understand. "That's what happened the last time I got selfish and put my desires over the duty that comes with all the privileges I was born into. That's what happened to the man I built those fantasies around. I can't let it happen again."

"It wasn't because of you or any plans you made. Those fucking soldiers—"

"It was their fault too," I agree. "Theirs and Emperor Tarquin's for letting them run wild up north. But I knew what was right, and I ignored it. If I hadn't been dallying with him, he might have gone home at a different time or felt less bold—or perhaps even one of the godlen took offense and somehow nudged events to turn out that way."

Lorenzo lets out a dismissive grunt. *"You're never responsible for anything that happens to me, Rell. I make my own decisions. I'd rather be punished for taking a stand with you than stay safe at a cowardly distance."*

"I don't know what stand there is to take. I had no idea what Marclinus would be like when I came here—I had nothing specific planned beyond getting to this point. He's so... set in his ways. Everyone in court is equally self-serving. The rest of the country doesn't know what to make of me. I'm still figuring out how *I* can get anything important done."

A little of my worry must bleed into my tone. Lorenzo draws back to gaze into my eyes, his own steady and determined. *"I've known Marclinus since he was twelve. He was already much the way he is now. Sometimes he'd ignore me; sometimes he'd prod at me until I couldn't bear it and ran away. But he did seem to care what Tarquin thought. If he could listen to one important person in his life, he could listen to another.*

A little hope blooms inside me at his words. "It might take a long time, if I ever get there."

"You've already done so much so quickly. When you're ready to make another move, we'll be here. Me and Raul—and Bastien will come around eventually. He's just stubborn."

A wry smile tugs at my lips. I suppose all four of us struggle with that particular fault. "I'm sorry," I say again.

"Don't apologize. You need what you need. I can figure out how to take joy in your presence even if it has to be from afar."

Beyond the palace, ten peals of the city bells ring out. Lorenzo cocks his head, an avid glint coming into his eyes. *"It isn't very much compared to your heroics, but do you want to see how I've made the court pay in the small ways I can?"*

Curiosity tugs at my gut. "Absolutely. But we can't walk out the door when—"

"We don't need to. I work from the hidden passages."

The prince ushers me across my bedroom and opens the secret panel that he must have entered through. When I step into the passage after him, the narrow space closes around us. The dim enchanted glow washes over us like twilight.

I try not to think about the passion I shared with Raul here just a few nights ago or how much I'd like to pull Lorenzo to me now.

As the prince of Rione guides me through the passages, his illusionary voice quiets as if he's being more cautious of his power slipping away from him. *"I learned in the first couple years of having my gift that I could cast illusions into people's minds even when they're asleep. Which is a very convenient time, since they'll assume that anything they encountered in that state was only a natural dream. Or nightmare, as the case may be."*

"You disrupt a lot of the nobles' slumber, do you?" I murmur with amusement.

"Only when they deserve it. Unfortunately, a lot of them do

a lot of the time. It's convenient that there are plenty of unnerving folk stories and supernatural tales in the library to offer inspiration."

Ah, so that's why he lurks in the library nearly as often as Bastien does. "Who are we paying a call on now?"

"I think Lord Connus, one of the viceroys' sons, is a fair choice. His rooms aren't far over from yours one flight down, and he was trying to goad Neven this afternoon."

"Sounds reasonable to me."

We ease down a cramped flight of stairs and stop several paces over from it. Lorenzo leans toward the wood-lined wall. I can barely make out his features in the darkened space, but I feel the concentration tensing his body.

After a few minutes, a wavering cry sounds in the room on the other side, loud enough to filter through the wall. It's followed by another, and then a wordless shout as Lord Connus must thrash awake.

Lorenzo lets out a faint chuckle. I grin at him, and he beams back at me as if my approval has doubled the victory.

It might not be much, but it is something. Little by little, we can pick away at them.

Even a mountain crumbles in time.

CHAPTER TEN

Aurelia

The open-topped carriage that's leading our procession to the Temple of Boundless Wisdom puts all other carriages to shame.

The gold-gilded frame stretches half the width of the broad city road, forcing the spectators gathered to watch our passage to squeeze into a dense line along the buildings and crane their necks from the side streets. It's twice as long, with velvet cushioned benches and smaller seats for as many as a dozen passengers to ride in luxury.

A gold statue mounted on the bow depicts two miniature soldiers holding aloft the imperial crest with its credo *CONQUER ALL.* More etchings of vines and flowers, animals and weaponry, gleam all along the sides and back.

By necessity, the carriage moves slowly through the streets, rocking with the plodding steps of the four harnessed horses. A contingent of twenty actual soldiers marches ahead

of us, with several more flanking the sides of the carriage and many more all along the parade of smaller, less spectacular vehicles behind us.

These soldiers wear the ceremonial uniforms I've only ever seen here in Vivencia: black slashed through with dark gray and indigo, like the imperial guard uniforms but a little plainer. How many of our audience have ever seen the menacing garb the Darium army dons when enforcing Dariu's rule abroad or doing battle as they attempt to reclaim their former territory across the Seafell Channel?

The memory of the black helms, jackets, and pants emblazoned with stark white skeleton bones sends a shiver down my back.

I keep my posture relaxed and my smile gracious, pretending nothing about this horde of military figures could disturb me. That some of their colleagues didn't murder the first man I loved and so many other Accasian citizens besides.

There isn't much else for me to do except offer periodic friendly waves, following Marclinus's lead. My husband and I are poised on the highest bench at the fore of the carriage. Three from each of our usual host of guards crouch lower on the carriage floor, in front of us and at our sides.

I can't say whether I feel more defended or suffocated.

The guard near my left foot by the middle of the bow hasn't given me more than a glance, focusing his attention on the crowd along the road ahead of us. My gaze flicks to him periodically, watching for any hint of a threat.

Lorenzo warned me about a guard who made a disparaging remark about me in the garden yesterday. Based on his description—curly light brown hair, a scar near his eye —I believe it was this man.

If he makes any hostile move, I intend to be prepared. The other guards are close at hand, but they won't expect an aggressive act from one of their own.

The prince of Rione himself stands farther back by the walls of the carriage along with his three foster brothers, each demonstrating a talent to awe the spectators. Naturally, Lorenzo has been assigned to tap into his gift, which as far as the rest of the palace knows is only for music. He glides his bow over the strings of his vielle.

The music doesn't sound quite as divine as I'm used to from him, but I can't imagine how much effort it must take to project his illusionary skill over such an immense crowd. He'll have to moderate himself.

Next to him, Bastien is showing off a skill I hadn't known he possessed. He's using a decorative bow to shoot enchanted arrows up into the sky, where they burst into bright streamers and glittering confetti that rain down over the crowd. I suppose his secret gift for manipulating the air made archery an easier study.

After his first few impressive shots, I aimed an awed smile over my shoulder at him. The only response I got was a hardening of his expression.

If Lorenzo related his renewed faith in me to the prince of Cotea, it clearly wasn't enough to sway the other man.

On the other side of the carriage, Raul slashes a ribboned sword through the air in flamboyant arcs, demonstrating the combat prowess I saw in the city's arena a few weeks ago. He's careful never to sweep the blade too close to Neven, who's crumbling the edges of slabs of limestone with his bare hands and handing over the rough sculptures to an attendant striding alongside the carriage so they can be handed to one or another spectator.

Among the nobles of the court, it's only the empire's hostage princes who are being asked to perform. All four of Marclinus's chief advisors have joined us in the head carriage, but they've been allowed to sit in dignified fashion, encircled by the demonstrations.

As we round a corner onto the road that'll take us the rest of the way out of the city, thunder rumbles overhead. The clouds that have smothered the sky since we emerged from the palace have darkened even more.

I hold my smile in place and offer another wave as if the dim daylight and the dampness in the air don't bother me. If the rain that's threatening pelts down on us, is Marclinus going to carry out the confirmation rite drenched to the bone?

The voices of the spectators get louder. Plenty are cheering or hollering encouragement to their new emperor, but the words "bad omen" reach my ears.

I can't stop my head from ticking toward the sound. My searching eyes can't determine who said the phrase.

As I scan the crowd, I spot several civilians flicking their fingers down their front in the gesture of the divinities as they look at me. Their solemn expressions suggest they're appealing to the gods *against* me rather than for me.

A woman near them swivels her hand in front of her in a warding motion we use all the way up in Accasy too. Her gaze burns into me as the carriage rattles past her.

My smile gets stiffer. I notice a man warding himself while he stares at me, and another woman doing the same.

They're not daring to call out in open protest against their new empress from beyond Dariu's borders, but they feel they need protection from my presence. Do they think the weather is another bad sign on top of Tarquin's death?

I summon all the benevolence and serenity I can into my expression and my wave of greeting. I'm not the enemy here. I want to see all of them living happy lives—gods can be sure I care more about all of them than the man beside me does.

How do I convince them of that fact?

The curly-haired guard adjusts his position near my feet.

My pulse skitters for a second before I'm sure he isn't making any unexpected moves.

Surely he wouldn't do me any overt harm in front of all these witnesses anyway?

Another rumble of thunder reverberates from the sky. Lorenzo's lyre music mingles with it. An arrow arcs gracefully toward the clouds and pops with a shower of swirling sparks like a cloud of dancing stars.

And one of the soldiers who's been marching next to the carriage swings around and heaves himself toward me.

I've been so focused on the guard in front of me that my attacker is nothing more than a blur of motion at the edge of my vision. In the space of a blink, he's leapt up and hooked one arm over the side of the carriage.

He swings his other hand straight toward my bare throat with a blade gleaming in his grasp. A ragged shout of purpose bursts from his mouth at the same moment. "Remove the wild woman before she dooms us all!"

I yelp and flinch away, colliding with Marclinus. The guards around us heave to their feet, swords hissing from sheaths, the nearest whipping toward my would-be assassin.

Except the blow isn't needed, because the soldier is already sagging over the side of the carriage. The dagger falls from his limp fingers to thump on the carriage floor. His dangling legs bump against the gold etchings he's sprawled over.

The fletching of a brightly colored arrow protrudes from where the shaft plunged straight between my attacker's ribs.

The carriage grinds to a stop. The guard who was about to stab the attacker in my defense steadies his sword.

We all stare at Bastien, who's just lowering his bow.

He shot the soldier—he reacted faster than even the guards trained for that purpose.

He reacted that quickly to save me, even though he's given every appearance of wishing I was already dead.

My jaw has gone slack. A swell of gratitude and something like relief fills my chest.

I haven't really lost him after all, whatever good it does either of us.

I should thank him, but Marclinus speaks first. Perhaps that's for the better, because he's clearly put together at least some of the same pieces I have.

He waves to the guards. "Get this traitor's corpse out of our sight and find out who vetted the villain. Then get this procession moving again."

As the carriage rocks back into motion, Marclinus's attention veers to my savior. "Prince Bastien. That was quite the shot. I hadn't realized you were so invested in my wife's well-being, but I can hardly complain about the results."

Despite the last part of that remark, his tone is cool enough to send a chill over my skin. Instinct kicks in, making me laugh as if it was all a bit of folly and touch my throat where my attacker meant to sever my life from my body. "Neither can I."

Bastien's knuckles have paled beyond his usual pallor where he's clutching his bow. He dips his head to Marclinus, not even glancing at me.

His voice comes out carefully even. "I actually thought he meant to hurt you, Your Imperial Majesty. I couldn't let any harm come to my most esteemed foster brother."

Yes. Pretend it had nothing to do with me. That's the safest route.

The narrowing of Marclinus's eyes suggests he doesn't fully believe that explanation. "The wretched fellow would have had quite the reach to stick that blade into me."

Bastien's shoulders lift in a twitch of a shrug. "It happened so fast, I didn't have the chance to think the situation through. All I knew was he was lunging in your general direction."

And even more so mine.

"Well," Marclinus says with a hint of a drawl that doesn't ease my nerves for a second, "I appreciate you stepping in on my wife's behalf as well as my own. It isn't as if there's any shame in defending both of us."

Bastien bobs his head. He reaches to the quiver at his back for another enchanted arrow as if he considers the matter resolved. "Naturally, Your Imperial Majesty. I'm glad to have assisted you one way or the other."

He turns away from us to launch the new arrow toward the sky. Glowing streaks in a rainbow of colors haze the bottoms of the darkening clouds.

I touch my throat—unguarded by the charmed fabric of my dress. The guard must have known it was one of the few spots where a blade could harm me.

The ominous hush of our audience seeps through my stunned state. I yank my attention back to the spectators.

They're peering up at us with puzzled expressions. I push a smile onto my lips and give another wave to show I'm perfectly fine.

Nothing to concern themselves with here. Just a momentary attempted murder.

The last thing I want them to see is the dread winding around my gut.

One of the soldiers hired as part of our own imperial entourage thought his world would be better without me in it—so much so that he was willing to give his own life to accomplish it. He couldn't have imagined he'd survive the attempt even if he'd managed to drive his blade home before my guards intervened.

He believed that I'm going to bring doom on them all. Just how many of Dariu's people feel the same way but aren't brash enough to deal with the imagined problem so violently?

At least, not yet.

Marclinus studies Bastien for a few moments longer before offering his own jaunty wave to our audience. The sharp glint in his eyes turns my skin clammier.

I don't know what he makes of Bastien's response. I have no idea what deeper answers he's searching for.

Something about the prince's sudden move bothers him. Something that makes him aim that evaluating look my way next, along with his arrogant grin.

Whether Bastien has truly forgiven me or not hardly matters. If my husband is scrutinizing any association between me and him, I need to put even more distance between myself and all of the princes I care for.

CHAPTER ELEVEN

Aurelia

As our procession passes through the arching gate in the city wall, High Commander Axius moves around the carriage's seats to put himself right behind Marclinus.

His voice is firm and solemn. "I apologize for the inexcusable oversight, Your Imperial Majesty. As soon as the rite is finished, I'll personally interrogate every guard and soldier stationed in and around the palace to root out any additional hostile sentiments."

I notice he's apologizing specifically to my husband, not me, even though I'm the one his soldier attempted to murder.

Marclinus appears to take that approach as a matter of course. "If we have any more incidents like that, I'll be holding you personally responsible, High Commander."

His voice has gone even colder than when he was speaking to Bastien. The burly military man sits back down without change to his grim expression, but I'd imagine he's aware of just how dire a punishment his new emperor might deal out.

Should I find a way to mention Lorenzo's suspicions about my guard? The curly-haired man might have made a disparaging remark before, but he did spring to my defense just as quickly as the others.

What reason do any of the soldiers or the crowd of civilians following along the road to the temple have to respect me? No one but the nobles and a handful of guards saw how hard I fought in the trials to win the title I now hold. I just had a man launch himself at me with full intent to kill, and all *I've* done about it is say a few words in mild gratitude to those who acted on my behalf.

Behind me, Bastien sends another arrow spiraling toward the clouds. I clench my hands against the urge to look back at him, to try to glimpse what's going on behind his impassive face.

Such a difference one fleeting act can make when it's the right one. In a split-second with one loosing of his bowstring, he turned every harsh word he's spoken in the past several days, every glare he's aimed at me, into a lie.

My gaze travels over the growing swarm of spectators as I offer another regal wave. Tension coils around my stomach.

Has Emperor Tarquin's death had the same effect on Dariu's people, only in the opposite direction? Every pretty phrase and smile I've offered could be dismissed as easily as Bastien's vitriol if they associate my presence with the loss of their beloved ruler.

I can't just sit here. I have to act myself—in some way that will overcome the tragedy my ascension has been tied to.

It's not enough to tell them I'll be a devoted leader or present a picture of one. I have to prove it to them.

Even Marclinus has to confirm his legitimacy, after all...

The spark of inspiration makes my pulse hitch. But this isn't the time to play it safe. Some of Dariu's people are already willing to kill me in an attempt to set their country back to rights.

I may have precious little time to convince them that I'm the woman who can right wrongs for them after all.

I glance over at my husband, who's tipping his head to the crowd with a glint of his golden crown. The jutting stone towers of the sprawling temple building have come into view at the top of the rise ahead of us.

"Husband," I say carefully, "all that's required for this ceremony is that you navigate a relatively short maze. Is that correct?"

Marclinus's eyes flick toward me. "That's the gist of it. There are a few dramatics for effect, but easy enough to prepare for. There's certainly no need to worry about my fate."

As I meet his gaze, I force my smile to soften as if with fondness. "Oh, I'm sure it'll be no challenge for you at all. I was only thinking—it's clear there's a little unrest focused on me because of the tragic timing of your father's death and perhaps my coming from outside Dariu... I'd like to demonstrate to your people just how committed I am to serving them as their empress. Would it be an imposition if I went through the confirmation rite as well?"

Marclinus's eyebrows leap up. Behind us, Counsel Severo leans over with a disgruntled sound. "A secondary confirmation would be highly irregular. I don't believe it's ever happened before."

"And it's meant for the imperial line, not the wedded

consorts," Marclinus adds, but his tone sounds more curious than dismissive. "Couldn't you simply hold them a festival or what have you?"

I look down at my hands in feigned modesty. "I suppose I could. But receiving a sign of the godlen's approval should do much more to resolve any doubts in those who'd consider harming me. I'm not sure what else could have the same effect. The empresses who've been of your line and ruled the empire have gone through the rites as well, so I assume women aren't excluded?"

Marclinus's grandmother, the woman who ruled the empire before Tarquin took the throne, must have carried out these ceremonies, along with the handful of empresses who inherited the position before her. First born is all that ever matters, not one's sex.

My husband looks over his shoulder toward Cleric Pierus. "I don't suppose Estera would take offense to passing judgment over both of us, as far as you're aware?"

The religious man opens his mouth and closes it again as he appears to grope for an answer. "We could put that question to Cleric Nellia at her temple. But we wouldn't want to diminish the spectacle of your own rite."

Marclinus snorts. "I hardly think that my wife following in my footsteps will make my own triumph any less. If anything, it would show even more of my wisdom in picking such a dedicated partner."

Counsel Etta's mouth has twisted. "Your Imperial Majesty... She hasn't had all the same preparation as you..."

Marclinus shakes his head at her, his eyes gleaming with increasing enthusiasm. "All the better. It'll be a real confirmation of her faith in the gods—and theirs in her."

He turns back to me with a grin so sharp that my nerves jitter. "You aren't fully informed of the details. It'll be more of a challenge to your wisdom than it is to me. There'd be no shame in rethinking the idea if you have your own doubts."

A note of challenge resonates through his voice, punctuated by a crackle of distant thunder. I keep my smile on my face, but I'm abruptly sure with a sinking of my gut that Marclinus hasn't warmed to the idea only for how it'll benefit my standing with his people.

If there's more to the rite than I know, he could tell me—but he hasn't. Does he see my participation as a test of his own, to ensure I'm not actually the bad omen some of his people are claiming?

Or perhaps he simply wants to confirm my mettle one more time. If I'm overstepping with this request and fail, I can't imagine he'll feel the slightest shred of guilt about replacing me.

I can't back down now. Then I'll lose not only my chance to earn his people's favor but perhaps any respect I've so painstakingly won from my husband as well.

I touch my hand to the bodice of my dress over the godlen sigil branded into my skin. "I'm sure Elox and what wisdom I possess will guide me."

Marclinus rubs his hands together. "I think it's an excellent idea, then."

His advisors' expressions still range from skeptical to outright uncomfortable, but they don't raise any further argument. I avoid looking toward any of the princes along the edges of the carriage, not wanting to see what they make of my decision.

It's meant to be a simple test, merely symbolic. Whatever Marclinus's additional knowledge is, surely the rite can't be *that* difficult without it?

The crowd's clamoring of anticipation intensifies as our procession reaches the crest of the hill. The imperial carriage comes to a stop right outside the main temple doors.

Cleric Nellia is waiting on the front steps, her deep green robe fluttering around her slim frame with the unruly wind. She motions us along a route that's been prepared with a strip of green silk.

As we follow the path around the silken side of the temple, Marclinus murmurs to the cleric in quiet conference. From the flick of her gaze to me, I assume he's mentioning my intent. It looks as if she asks a couple of questions, but her ultimate answer must satisfy my husband. He glances back at me with a subtle nod and a pleased smile.

We come around the temple's last rambling tower and find ourselves at the edge of a vast hollow holding a structure of smooth beige stone.

The polished stone walls we peer down at form an immense square filled with many more identical walls. They bend around each other, intersect, and split apart seemingly at random, like a twisted house of tiny, warped rooms that's missing its roof.

Estera's maze.

At the bottom of the slope before us, a flight of stairs leads up to the top of the nearest wall. Another set of stairs stands at the opposite end of the structure, just before a small marble dais festooned with green ribbons and gold figurines of Estera's favored animals and plants.

Ah. For this maze, we don't walk between the walls. We walk on top of them.

The structure must loom at least ten feet above the floor of the hollow. It's a good thing the walls look wide enough that balance shouldn't be too big a concern.

The soldiers who escorted us have formed a ring around the hollow on a ridge a few feet down the slope. The growing audience gathering around the edges gazes over their heads at the maze.

At another rumble of thunder, Cleric Nellia glances up at the sky. "I suspect we will see some rain."

Marclinus taps his finger against the scar on his lips and peers over his shoulder. "I suppose I could ask my gifted foster brother to send off the clouds…"

That's right. I've never seen Bastien use his gift with air for that purpose before, so I'd almost forgotten the story he's given the rest of court. Everyone else believes he can only summon or disperse rainclouds.

I resist the urge to hug myself against the damp wind. How much strain does it put on the prince of Cotea to propel a heap of heavy clouds away with the wind?

Before I can decide whether it's safe to speak up in favor of sparing the man who just defended my life, my husband shakes his head with a definitive air. "But the weather may very well be the gods' will. An additional challenge for both of us."

He shoots his sharp smirk at me again.

I square my shoulders. "Indeed."

Cleric Nellia doesn't argue with Marclinus's assessment. Without further comment, she escorts him down the slope to the base of the first set of stairs.

There, she swivels to take in the spectators all around the maze. An amplification charm lifts her voice over the murmurs of anticipation. "A ruler can only be as strong as their strategy and insight. His Imperial Majesty will now complete Estera's rite by navigating her blessed maze and then welcome the approval of our godlen of wisdom!"

Applause breaks out through the watching crowd. Marclinus raises his hand to them in acknowledgment and strides up the steps with total confidence.

At the top of the first wall, there's only one direction he can turn. He walks along that first stretch with his head high, his golden crown blending into the slightly paler curls of his hair. I trace his course, preparing to make the same journey myself in a matter of minutes.

He's just made his first turn toward the middle of the maze when I realize the rite is more complicated than I assumed.

With a grating sound that reverberates through the hollow, most of the walls within the outer square slide and rotate. Old paths disappear; new ones open up.

Figures throughout the audience let out awed gasps. How many of them will have gotten to see this spectacle of magic nearly three decades ago when Tarquin carried it out?

How often does the maze change while the rite is going on? How many different configurations are possible?

How do you manage to stay standing if the wall you're on shifts beneath you?

There must be a trick to it—the extra knowledge Marclinus mentioned. He pauses until the walls have settled, steps onto a new route, and waits again when other walls spin around him. After a couple more iterations, it's clear he somehow knows how to always step onto a portion of the maze that'll remain still beneath him, even if that wall jerked or pivoted every other time.

He makes the process look easy. It can't be more than a few minutes before he's stepping onto the final wall and loping down the far steps, his teeth flashing with his grin.

Cleric Nellia has come around the maze to meet him. She ushers him onto the decorated dais and spreads her arms toward the citizens swarmed around us. "Emperor Marclinus has proven his understanding and intellect. Estera welcomes him onto the throne!"

As if to emphasize her words, a streak of lightning slices across the clouds. Its glow flares off Marclinus's crown.

Even knowing what a psychopathic prick he is, my breath catches a little at the spectacle.

The audience roars their own approval. Marclinus lifts his arms to accept it, tipping his face toward the sky. Then he motions for the cleric to pass over her amplification charm.

"Thank you for witnessing my first rite of confirmation, my good people of Dariu!" he calls out. "You're lucky enough to get to observe an additional honor today. My wife, Empress Aurelia, will complete the rite herself to prove how worthy she is to stand by my side."

That's not exactly how I'd have put it, but it isn't the worst possible framing.

The applause that follows my husband's announcement is more hesitant. I wave to the watching civilians and head down the slope as if I'm every bit as sure of my success as Marclinus was.

When I reach the bottom of the first set of stairs, I tap my hand down my front in the gesture of the divinities. *Estera, see me through this trial so I may guide the empire in a wiser direction. Elox, give me a calm mind so I can recognize what needs to be done.*

As I climb the steps, the loudest burst of thunder yet cracks the clouds. Raindrops sprinkle down on my coiled hair and patter against the stone.

I swallow thickly and keep walking.

Wonderful. Now the tiles will be slippery as well.

It won't matter as long as I choose the right path. There has to be a strategy, something that'll become clear to me if I pay enough attention.

I can't let myself think about falling—about how easily my bones could break and my neck snap if I tumbled into the midst of these shifting slabs of stone.

The cool dampness seeping across my scalp and dappling my face shocks my mind into sharper alertness. I step onto the tiled surface on top of the wall and start forward in the same, obligatory direction Marclinus did.

My gaze slides ahead of me—and lingers on images carved into some of the tiles up ahead.

The grooves etched in the stone are shallow enough that I couldn't see them from the edges of the hollow. The first one lies just a few paces away, near the first turn Marclinus took.

It's an owl—Estera's patron bird. Is that a clue to my course?

As I come up on it, the walls swivel around me. Two swing to a stop on either side of the owl tile, both with a similarly styled carving at their ends.

To my left, there's a tree. To my right, what looks like a smoking chimney.

This one point was fixed all along. I know Marclinus veered to the right.

Recognition flares in my head.

There's a fable about Estera in which she gives advice to an old man who later discovers an owl in his chimney. *The truth will come to you if you search for it, but it's often not as easily found as lies.*

You could say owls belong in forests far more than chimneys, but that clearly wasn't the point of this association. Are we meant to think of Estera's deeper messages rather than common understanding?

I step to the right and hold still there. The rain picks up, soaking into my dress.

The wet silk clings to my legs. I can already feel how clumsy I'll be if I make a wrong move and end up on a moving wall.

So I'd better not let that happen.

As they did for Marclinus, the slabs rearrange themselves again. I don't think it's quite the same configuration he was faced with, though. From what I remember, he took his next turn from the middle of this section, but no other passages branch away from that spot now. My next options wait all the way down at the end, five paces away.

There, I can either step onward onto another wall straight ahead or turn to my left.

The tile in front of me shows an image of a feather—no, a quill, for writing. Beyond it lies an image of a scroll. To the left, a pot of ink.

I don't have much time before the walls move again. I stride forward, inhaling deep into my lungs. What association would Estera say matters more?

Having the material to construct a message is more important than what you place it on.

I swerve to the left. The second both of my feet have hit the tile, the wall I just left lurches away.

But the one I moved to remains in place. I choose correctly again.

All right, Aurelia. You've got the hang of this now. Just keep moving toward the end.

As I walk on, I summon all the stories of Estera I can remember from my childhood reading and sermons in the temples back home. I step from a tortoise to a waterlily, from a monocle to a vase, and from a sprig of sage to a lit candle.

The rain pelts down harder, blurring my vision. The tiles are growing slick beneath my leather slippers.

My forward foot comes down on a thin puddle and skids farther without warning.

I stifle a yelp, my whole body swaying within the confines of my now-drenched gown. The muscles in my inner thighs twinge with strain, but I manage to catch my balance, braced as if I'm halfway to doing the splits.

Dragging my legs back together, I peer ahead. The racing of my heart fades.

I'm almost at the end.

I hurry forward more cautiously, coming to a stop at an

image of an iris. Either of the walls branching out beside it could lead me to the final staircase, depending on how the slabs around them move in turn.

To my left, there's a carving of an open book. To my right, a winding snake.

The book seems like the obvious answer. What clearer symbol could there be of Estera's dedication to learning?

Which means it could be too obvious.

What stories are told about her and irises? Are there any specifically about a book as well?

I draw my posture straighter, delving into the well of calm in the center of me.

An image swims up from my memory: a painting that decorated one side of Estera's alcove in a smaller Temple of the All-Giver in Accasy, one near our secondary palace farther north.

A banded asp slithering through a field of irises. A lesson she taught about the danger that can lurk if you focus only on superficial appearances rather than studying deeply enough to get the full picture.

Breath held, I step to the right.

The slabs around me heave and rasp. A wall clicks into place right beside me, leading to the outer wall with the stairs descending from the maze.

I scramble through the rain with as much grace as I'm still capable of. Cleric Nellia grasps my hand to lead me to the dais, where servants have erected a canopy to shield Marclinus from the rain.

As I clamber up to join him beneath it, he brushes my damp hair back from my forehead, his hard-edged face beaming with satisfaction. "There's my empress."

He raises my hand before the audience that's stayed throughout the thundershower. Cleric Nellia declares Estera's approval for all to hear. This time, the surge of cheers is nearly as emphatic as it was for Marclinus.

I smile, water still trickling cold down my back from my drenched hair.

I've made my first real stand, but there are still three more rites to go. And I intend to complete every one of them, no matter what I have to do to convince my husband and his advisors to agree.

CHAPTER TWELVE

Aurelia

Lanterns glow throughout the dusk-draped palace gardens. Some shine a natural fiery amber, while others gleam imperial purple or Esterean green.

The illumination catches on the multi-colored finery of the court nobles, turning the gardens into a rainbow of both flowers and fabric. Music winds around the hedges and fountains as feet prance and skirts swirl.

As we carry on our own dance, Marclinus adjusts his grasp on my fingers and slides his other hand down from my waist to my hip. His gray gaze bores into me with unnerving intensity. I'm not sure I've ever seen his grin quite this manic.

His voice is all jaunty exuberance. "Isn't it a wonderful night for a celebration? I think it's all the better that we had a brief delay."

I paste my smile even more firmly in place, restraining a

cringe when he reaches around to paw at my ass. "It is indeed a lovely atmosphere and a worthy celebration."

My husband has been in a particularly jovial mood since dinner last night after the confirmation rite. His hand never left my thigh throughout the meal, and he ushered me straight back to my bedroom afterward, barely waiting to get through the door before he was on me.

If his drug-induced absence from the regular evening activities was noted by his court, no doubt they saw enough of his lustful enthusiasm not to suspect anything worse than an extended romp in my bed.

The celebration of our—well, mostly his—success with the rite has continued through today. We spent the morning and afternoon parading around the capital's streets and squares with Marclinus soaking up his people's adoration as palace staff distributed food and wine.

While most of the city folk's attention was on their emperor, I received some respectful nods and eager words of greeting myself—more than on my previous ventures into the city. I only noticed a couple of warding gestures, one of which was followed by a neighbor telling the doubter off.

My demonstration has warmed the citizens to me at least a little.

Tonight is dedicated to a celebration in court. Yesterday's humidity has left the palace stuffy, so Marclinus ordered us all out into the darkness of the gardens. The lawns and paths are serving as our ballroom.

This is the third dance he's claimed with me so far, each time equally leering and enraptured. I have the impression he's tracking every flick of my eyes, every twitch of my muscles.

What he's searching for, I'm not entirely sure. But given how often his hands have strayed to my breasts and ass, I suspect I don't have much longer before he drags me off to my chambers again.

Apparently victory riles up all his appetites. If a simple confirmation rite energizes him this much, Great God help me if he ever manages to reclaim the western half of the continent.

In the brief lull between songs, he kisses the back of my hand, followed by my wrist, leaving my skin crawling. Then, to my relief, he releases me. "I'll find you again soon."

I'm not sure if that's a promise or a warning.

One of the elder marchions approaches me, and I take his offered hand. He's old enough to be my grandfather, and the wary glance he aims after my husband suggests he won't take the slightest risk of overstepping politeness.

As we step to the newly rising melody, he smiles benevolently down at me. "I have many years behind me, but this is the first time I've seen our ruler's consort complete the divine rite. You've come from Accasy with interesting ideas."

I keep my stance relaxed, though my chest has tightened up. "I want all the people of the empire to have every confidence in me after their sudden loss."

"An admirable goal. It's reassuring to all of us to see that at least one of the godlen approves of you too, especially when Marclinus has no heir as yet." The marchion peers down at me with a twinkle of amusement in his eyes. "I expect you'll be helping him with that before long."

Better not to mention that at the moment, the thought of carrying anything to do with Marclinus *inside* me provokes a full-body shudder.

I dip my head modestly. "I look forward to helping the imperial line continue with all expected strength."

Sometime possibly years in the future when I can stomach it.

I think I've made a little progress with my husband already. It's hard to tell with his shifting moods, though.

I'm not at all sorry to see the dance end. When I turn around, considering whether I can get away with retreating to the fringes of the party, Raul is standing waiting for me.

The prince offers a deferential bow, but there's a teasing gleam in his pale blue eyes. "Your Imperial Highness, would you do me the honor of a dance?"

I can hardly refuse him without people wondering why.

I accept his hand, and he sets the other on my waist— with much more care than Marclinus offered. He leaves plenty of space between us as if he assumes his presence isn't all that welcome.

Raul might be hotheaded, but he isn't stupid.

As he tugs me deeper into the crowd of dancers, I feel the need to say something anyway, in a low voice no one else will be able to make out over the music and chatter. "Remember that we barely know each other. He's been watching closely."

Raul hums and spins me around with a twist of his hand. The paler scars that crisscross his knuckles gleam in the lanternlight.

A teasing note creeps into his voice too. "I'll be nothing but a gentleman to my empress."

I restrain myself from glowering at him, as much as I long to lean into his embrace. "I mean it. I don't like the mood he's in."

"I've been enduring my imperious foster brother's moods for many years longer than you have. I can navigate them well enough." He caresses my palm with the subtlest stroke of his thumb, sending a flicker of heat down my arm. "I'm supposed to begin your combat lessons soon. He'll have to tolerate me being a *little* close to you."

"That's not why I suggested them."

"Of course not. I appreciate any time I get to spend with

you, however impersonal. Given what that prick of a soldier tried with you yesterday, we should probably fit in your first lesson before you're setting off for the next confirmation rite."

The memory of the lunging soldier chills me. "Yes. We have a few days for that. And I also need to know everything there is to find out about that second rite—Prospira's."

Raul's gaze turns slyer. "I know at least one or two minds that could be put to that task on your behalf."

We lapse into silence, all of my attention narrowing down to the warmth of his skin against mine, the tiny gestures of affection he manages to offer, and preventing my expression from reacting to any of them.

"There," he says as the melody starts to wind down. "All we had was a dance. No catastrophes."

"I'm not sure it was wise to risk it regardless." My gaze flicks to the nobles around us, but thankfully I don't spot any suspicious expressions. "It's a difficult balance to maintain."

"Ah, but I'm meant for that, you know, even if I haven't been the best example of balance so far." Raul grins. "Lavira is the central hub of this half of the continent, after all. My mother used to say that our kingdom is the conductor of one vast dance, coordinating communication and trade back and forth with our neighbors, following each other's cues and pace. I can manage to match yours when it's for such a great reward."

He doesn't press his luck. When the song fades, he gives my fingers the slightest squeeze and steps away with another bow. "Thank you for indulging me, Your Imperial Highness."

I need a little space to cool the secret passions he's stirred up in me. As casually as I can manage, I wander over to one of the tables that's been set up with bottles of wine and goblets.

I let the server pour a fresh glass for me and wait for one of the imperial tasters to sample the glass before taking a sip of my own. The rest of the court frolics before me, but I can't help picturing the wilder lands of the terrain outside the main Accasian palace.

How much would I give to wander away into those vast woods and let their cool, deep serenity wash over me? Even the forested part of the imperial palace grounds is too cultivated to stir quite the same sense of peace.

My roving gaze snags on a head of shaggy auburn hair by the large fountain nearby, highlighted by a nearby lantern. All thoughts of home vanish.

I haven't had a chance to speak to Bastien since he leapt to my defense yesterday. How long might it be before I get a better chance to do so without being overheard?

As if simply taking a stroll, I meander past the table, around a garden bed, and end up standing before the fountain next to the bench Bastien is sitting on. I study the marble statue of Sabrelle striking down a foe, admiring the artistry.

My guards will have followed me, but from their usual discreet distance. No one else has wandered within several paces of this spot. The warble of the water will prevent my voice from carrying.

I watch Bastien from the corner of my eye. He's still gazing straight ahead, away from the fountain, but his shoulders have gone rigid.

All the words I'd like to say clot in my throat. It's a moment before I can pull together a coherent comment.

"I was starting to think you'd enjoy seeing my throat cut. I'm glad that's not the case after all."

Bastien's jaw ticks. His voice comes out low and flat. "Even if I wanted to hate you, it seems I'm not very good at it anymore. What do you want from me now, Aurelia?"

It's a strange relief to hear him say my name so informally

after all the "Your Imperial Highness"-ing I've faced, even if the phrasing of the question stings.

I reach my hand out to let the cool water lick over my fingers. "I was only hoping to thank you properly. I know… the choices I've made might have been difficult to accept, but I'd like you to be able to make peace with them. I've only ever done what I thought was the best for the most people."

"So you've convinced Raul and Lorenzo." He pauses. "Taking on the rite was impressive. It was harder for you than it was for Marclinus, wasn't it? You looked as if you had to think your way through it."

"He went in with more preparation."

"But you mastered it anyway. It seems you really can do just about anything you set your mind to." Bastien adjusts his position on the bench. "I was dancing with you when the recent 'tragedy' happened. How did you pull *that* off, if you really did?"

I don't need to ask what he means by "that." The instant when Tarquin fell, the smoldering fury in Bastien's gaze in the moments before, is seared into my memory.

Of course, out of all the princes, he'd be the one who needs to understand the practicalities before he can fully accept it. I shouldn't have expected anything else.

I resist the urge to rub my ring. "The trinket you once stole was valuable to me for more than its gold and gem. It was carefully crafted as a subtle delivery vessel for… potions. And I'm sure you're aware that a gift can be skewed away from its most essential purpose if you simply focus it in the right way."

Like convincing my gift for concocting cures that I'd need to put a man into a paralytic fit to heal him, after which it was only a matter of increasing the concentration.

A rough chuckle escapes Bastien. "You knew you'd go that far before you ever left Accasy."

It isn't a question. I think he believes me now.

I answer him all the same. "Everything was prepared well in advance."

"You never gave any sign of your full intentions."

"And you know that I can be very determined about what I reveal or don't."

Bastien swipes his hand past his mouth in a jerky motion. "It was stupid of me to forget that. To stake all our lives on a situation I so hugely misjudged—even more than with Pavel— Hope can be a dangerous thing, can't it? But obviously you have your own sense of duty. I suppose seeing us killed would have been an acceptable sacrifice to the greater good."

The anguish in his voice sends a lance of guilt through my heart. I have to hold my gaze on the fountain through sheer force of will. "I didn't think I was putting you in danger. I never would have wanted to. I assumed you'd leave on your own, that no one would have a chance to catch on."

"Oh." Bastien's silence stretches too long for comfort. "It wasn't worth everything we'd be giving up if we left without you. Although maybe that's where I was the most stupid. I thought—"

He falters again, and this time he doesn't go on.

I can't leave him sounding so miserable. "What?"

"You had everything a woman could want between Lorenzo and Raul. You only needed me because I'm the one who calls most of the shots. I let the pretense go to my head —I let my heart override my mind… Stupid."

My throat constricts. He can't really think what he seems to be saying, can he? "Bastien, it wasn't a pretense with you any more than the others. I—"

He pushes to his feet abruptly, cutting me off. "You don't need to keep pretending. It's less painful if you don't."

He strides off in the opposite direction toward a cluster of tall hedges even farther from the rest of the court.

A vise seems to have clamped around my entire torso. To have caused him that much pain already, over an assumption that isn't even true—

I only manage to hold myself back for a couple of heartbeats before I'm swiveling on my feet. They carry me toward the hedges at the most leisurely pace I can restrain them to.

Bastien must hear me approaching. As I veer around the first of the hedges, he spins where he's stopped deeper in the shadows.

His voice drops to a harsh whisper. "What are you—?"

I only have a matter of seconds before my guards will follow closely enough to observe me. I propel myself across the last few steps toward him, grasp the front of his shirt, and kiss him with everything I have in me.

Bastien's breath hitches, and then he's kissing me back as if I'm the air he needs. I give myself over to the heated passion of our collision for one fleeting moment before I yank myself back.

Footsteps rasp beyond the hedge. Bastien's eyes go wide. "You could have gotten yourself murdered."

My fingers clench, the feel of his shirt lingering on them. "Hearing you talk like that makes me feel as if I've already died. I consider myself blessed that you were willing to take the chances you have for me, and I'm going to do everything in my power to make the best of this wretched situation for you as well as me... even if I don't have much power yet."

I don't dare dally among the hedges any longer. I walk past him and weave on between the sculpted shrubs, back toward the dancers.

Coming up on the edge of the lawn, I pause to gather myself. When I wet my lips, they tingle from the kiss.

No one hurls any accusations. I got away with that brief lapse.

I just wish I didn't feel so sick about refocusing my loyalties on the man who least deserves them.

After a couple of minutes, Bastien emerges amid the garden beds. He doesn't look my way, but there's something easier about his stance that melts a little of the ache inside me.

Marclinus saunters over to me with his mouth set in a smirk. I set the glass I've been carrying around with me down on the nearest planter, expecting that he's coming to claim another dance.

Instead, he crooks his finger at me and tilts his head toward the palace. "Come with me, wife. There's a matter I'd like to discuss with you and my foster brothers."

Chapter Thirteen

Bastien

I've never trusted Marclinus farther than I could throw him. As he ushers his wife, my fellow princes, and me through the palace halls, I have even less certainty about his motives than usual.

Did someone catch a glimpse of my kiss with Aurelia after all? If he's taking some kind of vengeance on me, why is he insisting on bringing the others along?

Or has he somehow discovered our plot from nearly a week ago and come up with a sadistic scheme of his own to make us pay for imagining we could escape the empire's chains?

Aurelia glides along next to him, the picture of serene grace. If the image of her frantic expression when she approached me in the darkness wasn't emblazoned in my memory, I might have believed she was totally unconcerned.

The imprint of her mouth is burned into my lips. My

pulse never had a chance to stop racing before Marclinus summoned us over and gave it a very different sort of reason to scatter.

She willingly admitted her treason to me. She gave me the means to prove it if I decided to be more vengeful.

She put her life on the line to show how much I matter to her and kissed me like she couldn't bear to spend another moment apart.

How can I doubt her now? How much was my earlier anger even justified rather than the shame that the risks *I* took that didn't pan out the way I hoped?

No matter what she's said, I can't shake the sense that I've been stupid somewhere. I missed things. I presumed things.

What if this situation is even more tangled than I'd have guessed five minutes ago?

Raul saunters along with a nonchalant front, but I catch a hint of the tension he's suppressing in the flexing of his hands. Lorenzo hasn't been able to restrain a frown.

Neven marches among us with his shoulders braced and his forehead furrowed, as if he's ready to fight but confused about whether he needs to. We're going to have to keep a particular eye on the kid, no matter where this scenario leads.

Marclinus directs us into one of the palace's smaller sitting rooms, which means it's still a little larger than my very respectable bedroom. Several embroidered armchairs wait in a loose ring around a low table.

The emperor takes the most ornate chair on one side of the table and motions for Aurelia to sit next to him. As the rest of us sink into the chairs opposite them, one of the staff arrives with a platter holding six goblets and a large bottle of wine.

Marclinus grins in approval and waves the woman over. "Here we go. Something for everyone."

He sets out the goblets himself with a flourish, one in

front of each of us, and then leans back while the woman pours the wine. A slender man I don't recognize slips into the room and remains near the doorway, just a few paces from the four guards who've also followed us in. He studies us, his face taut.

What in the realms is going on here?

Marclinus dismisses the server with a flippant gesture and picks up his goblet. His tone is as jaunty as ever. "I thought we should have a drink and a chat together—me and all my companions from beyond Dariu's borders. My foster brothers, you haven't offered our Accasian princess a very effusive welcome. If there are any sour feelings about her rising to a station so high above your own, I hope tonight we can find some common ground."

Is that all this private get-together is about?

I pick up my glass, no less wary than before. "I hold no animosity toward our empress. We all want what's best for the empire, don't we?"

I lift the goblet as if in cheers, a gesture Marclinus eagerly matches. The others grasp their own cups to join us.

It seems safest not to watch Aurelia tip her goblet to her lips, not to trace the bob of her sleek throat as she swallows. I can remember all too well how the soft skin there heated against my mouth just days ago, when for a brief moment she was completely mine.

After I've taken a swallow of the tartly sour liquid, I lower my glass. Lorenzo nods as if to say he agrees with my statement.

Raul relaxes into his chair with a faintly amused expression. "If we've failed to be gracious enough in some way, feel free to list out our mistakes so we can fix them."

Neven takes another hesitant sip. "I didn't realize anything was wrong."

Marclinus tsks his tongue at us. "A little jealousy of the

new arrival is totally normal, I'd imagine. But now you have the chance to speak with her openly. Find out whatever you like about my bride."

He sweeps his arm extravagantly with a slosh of his goblet that sends a smattering of wine onto the rug. As far as I can tell, he doesn't even notice.

Aurelia studies him, her expression cautiously puzzled. "None of your foster brothers have troubled me," she says in a mild tone, which is such a brazen lie I'd laugh if I were drunker. "At least, I haven't expected anything from them that they didn't offer. I'm sure they have plenty to keep them busy without thinking all that much about me."

"We'll see the truth of that soon enough." Marclinus flicks his hand in an upward motion. "I hope you're enjoying the wine while we're at it. It's an excellent vintage."

Aurelia smiles in agreement. "Very good." She brings the cup back to her lips.

Marclinus tilts toward the rest of us with a clap of his hands. "Let's get on with it then. I suppose we could start with you all sharing—"

Aurelia suddenly sways to the side, her goblet wobbling in her fingers. My gut lurches.

Her husband turns to consider her, a thin smile playing across his mouth. "Ah. It didn't take long at all."

Aurelia blinks at him. Her arm shakes harder, and she sets her goblet down on the table with a clunk. "What—?"

Her question is cut off with a wheeze. She clutches at her chest.

Then her limbs slacken. Her shoulders shudder and buckle.

Her body crumples right off the chair, her head narrowly missing the edge of the table before it thumps against the rug.

Horror jerks at my gut, but the satisfied glint in

Marclinus's eyes holds me in my seat. This is some kind of sick game he's playing.

Lorenzo, tender heart that he is, has jumped to his feet. He stares at Marclinus, emitting an urgent noise.

Raul cocks his head, but his shoulders have tensed. "It seems your wife could use some assistance," he says in an even tone that only shows a bit of strain.

"Oh, indeed she does." Marclinus flashes a grin at us. "Her goblet had a rather vicious poison in it, I'm afraid. She has perhaps ten minutes before it shuts down all her essential organs."

On the floor, Aurelia sucks a breath through her teeth with a hiss that sounds as furious as it does desperate. Her sleeve rustles across the carpet with a groping of her arm.

My heart hammers at my ribs. What under the god's gaze is this psychopath actually after?

I yank my gaze away from Aurelia's form sprawled by the table and find that our emperor is watching the four of *us*, not his wife.

A rush of cold prickles over my skin.

He's testing us. Evaluating our reactions to her distress.

Why?

As my thoughts whirl, I will my stance to stay loose, my expression merely confused. Does he think we'll reveal approval at the idea of her death... or a deeper concern than he'd expect from mere acquaintances in court?

Every twitch of her limbs and ragged breath brings me back to the night she collapsed in front of us in her bedroom, after *I* poisoned her, if mostly accidentally. Guilt knots my stomach.

What does Marclinus want from us? What's the right response that'll have him save her?

Gods smite him, does he even intend to?

Aurelia's pale hand twists against the rug, the motion

catching my attention. She repeats the brief gesture once more, swift but clear.

It's Lorenzo's sign to say all's well. She's telling us not to intervene. To pretend there's nothing horribly wrong with the entire situation.

She'd know best what her husband is after, wouldn't she?

Neven's voice quavers. "Why are you doing this to her?"

Raul speaks up before Marclinus needs to answer, in a wry but firm tone that I'm sure is controlling a more fraught emotion. "She must have offended the empire or our emperor in some unforgiveable way. In which case, our foster brother is completely justified."

It's the perfect explanation for his lack of action without leaning too far into concern or rancor. I stiffen my spine. "Absolutely. Nothing good comes of violating Darius's laws."

Lorenzo's jaw is still clenched, but after a glance around at us, he sits himself back down. His expression stays grim but not outright frantic.

They're reining in their emotions that well for her. I'm not sure I've ever seen either of them so willfully controlled.

She's been putting on the riskiest performance of her life to overturn the entire empire. The least we can do is hold our tempers to save her.

Marclinus gives a light laugh. "You have so much faith in my judgment. I appreciate that. But no, my lovely wife hasn't done anything wrong at all. I was merely curious about a few things."

He's brought her to the verge of death out of *curiosity*?

If I didn't know one of the things he's most likely curious about is how invested we are in her fate, I'd be springing off this chair to punch him in the face.

What good would that violent act do Aurelia anyway? We're even more helpless than the night I meddled with her stew. At least then, we could have decided to summon a medic.

We can't help her at all while the man who rules over us wants her laid low. He'd simply have his guards haul us away.

All the same, my mind launches into a panicked calculation behind my dispassionate mask. If all of us lashed out with our gifts right now, the guards would focus on protecting their emperor first. Is it possible we could spirit Aurelia away in the chaos?

What would be the point of trying when she's now down to seven or eight minutes of life and we have no idea how to heal her?

This frozen, desperate despair feels all too familiar. It harkens all the way back to the first time I had to stand by while Darium soldiers beat a man to death in the street outside my old palace, when I was all of five years old with my father's hand gripping my shoulder like a warning.

I've never known how to fight back without losing even more.

Aurelia's the only person I've ever met who's strong and smart enough to pull it off. Unless she's lost that gamble after all?

Another chuckle cuts through my anguish. Marclinus beckons the slender man who entered earlier toward Aurelia and leans over to peer down at his wife. "My darling, I'd like to confirm that your gift is working properly. Use it to tell us what substance would work as an antidote to the poison that's afflicting you."

For a few agonizing seconds, there's only the strained rasp of Aurelia's breath. Then she spits out, "Cottermish."

Marclinus's gaze flicks to the other man to confirm. He dips his head before fishing a packet out of his pocket.

As I stare at him, a twinge of recognition hits me. I think he's one of the palace medics.

I've never paid all that much attention to their faces. Without the typical white robe showing his dedication to Elox, I didn't make the connection.

The emperor smiles down at his dying wife. "Very good. It appears your gift is functioning as it should. You may have some of that cottermish now. I was concerned that something might have gone wrong with your blessing from Elox after you failed to come up with a cure for my father."

My teeth set on edge, but I keep silent. Raul does as well, even though in that moment his glare looks potent enough to sear Marclinus's head off.

Neven doesn't have as much self-control—or as much awareness of how much we're hiding.

"That isn't fair," he bursts out. "We all saw Aurelia try to help Emperor Tarquin. He passed so quickly—how would she have had time to make any cure? None of the palace medics could do anything with *their* gifts either."

As the medic crouches by Aurelia's head to feed the contents of the packet into her mouth, Marclinus slides his gaze to our youngest foster brother. The hairs on the back of my neck stand on end.

But the emperor simply shakes his head with a rueful grin. "So young and so naïve. Everything is worth testing when it's a matter so serious."

Neven frowns, but Raul touches his arm, and he heeds that warning. The kid slumps in his chair, folding his arms over his chest.

In a minute, Aurelia is steady enough to get to her feet. She slides into her chair, her face gone sallow but her spirit as unshakable as ever.

She meets Marclinus's gaze without flinching. "I'm glad to have cleared up any doubts about my gift."

"Yes, excellent, excellent." He pushes her poisoned goblet

aside and offers his own. "Have a little undoctored wine and enjoy yourself now. We can all have a pleasant evening."

I force myself to reach for my own glass, even though I feel ready to vomit.

Did we manage to quell his other suspicions? What will he do to Aurelia if more doubts arise?

No matter what the ordinary citizens of Dariu or our country's soldiers think of their new empress, she'll never be safe. Marclinus has just proven that the greatest threat to her survival is the man she has to welcome into her bed.

CHAPTER FOURTEEN

Aurelia

The seat at the head of the main table remains ominously empty all through breakfast. With each passing minute that our new emperor doesn't appear before me, with each bite of my meal that turns into a lump in my mouth, the food tastes more like ash.

With each breath, a faint pinching sensation jabs my lungs, leftover from the poison he fed me last night. Every nerve recoils from the memory of our interlude afterward in my bedroom.

Marclinus made no mention of his test as if pretending it'd never happened, but he appeared to revel in my lingering weakness all the same. He chuckled when he had to help my shaky hands peel off my gown. He met the sickly sway of my body with eager caresses and a broad smirk.

The only benefit of his exulting in the temporary feebleness he'd inflicted was it gave plenty of time for the

potion in my ring to take hold once I pricked him. I didn't have to endure anything more intimate than I've needed to allow before.

My husband must have left not long after waking from its stupor, sometime in the middle of the night. The other side of my bed was empty when I woke.

I took some pleasure in his absence then. Now, I can only wonder what new horrors he might be concocting.

Based on last night's scheme and the way he reacted when Bastien shot my attacker, I have to think he suspects some kind of collusion between his foster brothers and me. He must know perfectly well that what Neven said is true—if none of the palace medics could save Tarquin with their magic, what hope did I have of brewing a cure in the few minutes before his death?

Marclinus's test didn't even prove that I couldn't have, regardless of that fact. Whether my gift works as claimed or not has no bearing on whether I *chose* to use it.

No, the real test wasn't for me. It was for his hostage princes, to see if any of them appeared overly concerned about my well-being. Possibly hoping they might be moved to violence against their emperor in my defense, so he'd have both proof and an immediate excuse to punish them.

They kept their heads well. Neven was the only one who spoke up for me overtly, with a typical teenage outrage against unfairness that his time in the imperial palace hasn't quite dulled yet. I don't think Marclinus will read anything suspicious into that.

I have no idea whether the results of my husband's test will have erased his suspicions, though. The trials he put his prospective brides through are clear enough proof of how much he enjoys making others suffer.

He might very well prod at the princes several times

more just for the "fun" of it. And gods only know how he'll use me again.

I need him to see that my loyalty is unshaken, that I can set aside last night's cruelty and continue on as his devoted wife. Erase any doubts he might still have about *me*.

If he's absolutely sure I couldn't have dallied with any of his foster brothers, his sadistic inclinations will find a new target.

My husband has occasionally lounged around in his bed after a late night rather than joining the court for our morning meal. As soon as I can graciously make my departure, I head back to the imperial apartments.

The sole guard standing by the door to Marclinus's private chambers simply tells me he's not in. Frowning, I wander through the halls contemplating where my husband might have gone instead.

Did his advisors call an early morning meeting? I remember seeing Counsel Etta and High Commander Axius at one of the tables during breakfast, though.

I wouldn't have expected Marclinus to skip a meal for some solitary entertainment. What is he up to?

I come out of the staircase into the second-floor hallway to find Vicerine Bianca mincing by.

She pauses, taking in my expression and the direction I was coming from. "Are you looking for His Imperial Majesty?"

My entire body tenses against the idea of revealing anything at all to this woman. I might not face such an uphill battle winning over the court if she hadn't done her best to sour her fellow nobles' opinions about me—and I'm certainly not forgetting how she joined in the attack in the palace woods that left me with multiple broken bones.

On the other hand, she is rather familiar with my

husband. She hasn't shown any hostility since the trials ended.

It's always more useful to cultivate allies than to encourage enemies.

I offer a thin smile. "I suppose you know where he is."

Bianca bobs into a brief curtsy, as if the formality has only just occurred to her. "He's in his office, Your Imperial Highness. I just spoke with him—he seems rather distracted. Disinterested in company."

Her mouth tightens with those last words. Her dark gaze rests on me for a moment before she goes on. "But perhaps he's only dismissing the sort I would offer. You may have better luck."

Is she admitting that she believes I can offer the man she's so coveted something she can't?

I blink at her, startled enough to have to scramble for an answer, and Bianca dips her head again before continuing on down the hall.

"Thank you for the assistance," I say hastily, and hurry on to the imperial offices.

To my surprise, Marclinus's guards are poised outside the office where I first spoke to him directly—the one he used when he was merely the imperial heir. There's a larger one for the emperor's use.

But then, he hasn't had much time to make the transition. He might have records or books among his things that he wanted to consult.

Even though I'm now his wife, one of his guards knocks for me and announces my arrival rather than letting me speak to Marclinus myself. The initial silence makes my heart sink, but then Marclinus calls back, "Let her in."

Stepping through the office doorway feels like tumbling back through the weeks to that first private conversation, when I came carrying tea on a tray.

As then, Marclinus is sitting at his desk. He glances up from the documents he's been perusing with an unusually pensive expression.

He casts his gaze over me from head to toe and back again, his expression tightening. His voice comes out brisk but not harsh. "To what do I owe the pleasure, wife?"

I clasp my hands in front of me and offer the sweetest smile I have in me. No harm done, no hard feelings. "I missed you in the dining room and wanted to make sure all is well. Has some concern arisen that's urgent enough to keep you from breakfast?"

Marclinus flicks his hand dismissively. "I can eat later. There is…"

He trails off with a more penetrating look at my face. No doubt he's still hesitant to trust me with all the details of the empire's business.

I expect him to wave me off too and continue his work alone. Instead, he leans back in his chair and motions for me to draw up the smaller armchair off to the side of the desk. "Sit down. Considering the threats you've already faced, I suppose you should be properly informed."

I tug the chair over and sink into it, appreciating the invitation but uneasy about the rest of his words. "Informed of what?"

Marclinus turns back to his papers. "It appears fresh unrest is stirring in Lavira. Reports have come in of attacks on a couple of our guard posts in the countryside."

Ah, I can see why that might have distracted him, especially when his own court has been fretting about the conquered countries rebelling. At least it has nothing to do with me or his foster brothers.

I just have to pretend that I don't think the rebels have a legitimate cause.

I tilt my head to show I'm considering the matter. "Do

you have reason to believe the attacks are part of a larger movement? It could simply be locals lashing out without any real organization. Two incidents aren't too much to be coincidence."

My husband grimaces. "The local forces are investigating. But my father had issues with Lavira shortly after he took the throne—I've just been reading through those accounts. It wouldn't be surprising for us to see a resurgence in anti-imperial sentiments at another transition point."

"I'm sure you'll deal with them as effectively as he did." In horrific, brutal fashion that I'd rather not think about. "If it's only a couple of small, isolated instances at the moment, I'd imagine it's better to wait for more information before drawing conclusions."

"That's your dedication to Elox talking." Marclinus's fingers flex around the metal pen he was toying with. "A couple of assaulted guard posts is how the revolt in Velduny began."

No wonder this particular incident has unsettled him. The rebellion in Velduny is what led to the entire western half of the continent throwing off the empire's shackles.

The loss happened a century ago, well before even Tarquin's time, but the imperial family has never stopped trying to regain their former territory. I can't count how many Accasians—and no doubt civilians from the other conquered countries as well—they've thrown into soldier garb and spurred across the Seafell Channel to meet their deaths in vain.

The possibility of losing more territory must gnaw at Marclinus's ego. How awful would it look if he failed to quell an uprising so soon after he took the throne?

Perhaps if the scenario were different, I'd try to guide him toward a course that would result in that exact outcome. But the empire has stamped out plenty of rebellions in the past.

Velduny's revolutionaries had a couple of major advantages: being far distant from Dariu's center of power and taking the local forces totally by surprise.

The imperial forces were over-confident back then, too slow to see just how great the threat was. Marclinus would rather err in the opposite direction now and crush any hint of mutiny as brutally as possible. Lavira shares a border with Dariu and is trapped amid the other countries of the empire —they can be stormed from all sides.

All that will come of this incident is more people dead— the exact people I'd want still living to support the changes I hope to make in the future.

I craft my response carefully. "I see your point. And you certainly have more experience in the area of warfare than I do. Elox's teachings aren't without their own wisdom, though. Any violence you order in response may spark vengeful anger. I would never deny that you must come down with all force when it's necessary, but maintaining peace where it's already established benefits us as well, doesn't it?"

Marclinus scoffs. "I certainly wouldn't offer a friendly hand to the thugs who killed those guards."

I hold up my hands. "And you shouldn't. Proven criminals must be punished to maintain order. I'm talking more about the possibility of a broader revolt in the making."

My husband sets down his pen and turns to fully face me. "And what do you think your godlen would say about that?"

I ignore the derisive note in his voice, keeping my own tone subdued. "I'd imagine… that you should avoid any punishments based on suspicion rather than clear proof. Have your representatives seek out the reasons for the current rancor. See if there are matters of discontent that you can address without any real cost, and perhaps that will snuff out enough ill feeling that there's no need for it to come to a battle at all."

"*Chat* with the traitors."

I shrug. "You don't know yet which citizens are traitors. And it seems to me that you'll gain a lot more time without additional assaults if the people feel they have no reason to rise up. If they're simply biding their time until they're angry enough not to care about the risks, they could strike again at any moment."

Marclinus swipes his hand over his mouth, the gesture tugging at the scar through his upper lip. Was it one of the rebels in Rione, the one conflict he had a direct hand in tackling under Tarquin's watch, who left him with that mark?

"I can see there's some sense to your words," he says slowly. "Father did always say it's useful to get differing perspectives, whether they adjust your course or steady you in it. I appreciate that I have a wife who's able to form a coherent perspective in the first place."

I can't tell whether that's an insult hidden in a compliment, but I'll take it over outright mockery. "I'm dedicated to supporting you however I can. I can't hope to match the guidance your father would have supplied, but what little I can offer is yours."

Marclinus gazes at me for a few moments longer, until my skin starts to creep with memories of last night all over again. But there's nothing leering or cruel about his expression right now, even if I can't read what's going on in his head behind his cool eyes.

Finally, he shakes his head. "Father was only a little older than I am when he needed to take the throne. I'll manage."

I catch the start of a dismissal in the words and jump on the one thing I can think of to prolong the conversation— and my chances of proving my devotion. "I appreciate having a husband who looks out for my safety. Why did you feel I should know about the potential uprising? Have there been any attacks on Dariu's soil?"

"Not as yet. And if the Lavirians are smart, they won't risk it." The smile Marclinus forms is fierce enough to make my pulse skitter. "Better to be aware than not, though. And we will be traveling not far from their border for the third rite in about a month's time."

We're meant to leave for the second in a matter of days. Perhaps, while he seems positively disposed toward me, I should bring up my intentions. They are an act of devotion of their own, after all.

"True enough. And I was hoping I could accompany you fully in the remaining rites as I did in the first."

Marclinus catches my meaning in an instant, with a tick of his eyebrow upward. "You want to complete the other three confirmation rites? The first wasn't enough of a challenge to sate your interest?"

I let my smile turn wry. "I didn't vie for your hand in order to take things easy after I'd won it. The people seemed to respond well to my demonstration. I'd like all of Dariu to know how committed I am to the empire—and that I have the gods' approval."

"Well, I suppose showing the strength of our combined rule will only work to my benefit." He cocks his head. "You'll have to face the challenges fairly, though. The advance knowledge is reserved for those of the line already blessed by the gods."

Is that how he sees the advantage that all but guarantees he makes it through the ceremonies?

"I trust that the gods will see me through," I say, which is true enough. If my wits and their divine support aren't strong enough for me to emerge from these introductory challenges unbroken, then I'm hardly up to the greater task I came here to carry out, am I?

The intensity in my husband's gaze softens just a little. "I certainly haven't met anyone who could match you for faith, Aurelia, though I suspect your other virtues have at least as much of a role in your victories."

That was definitely a compliment in its entirety. I think I've gained some ground here today, even if I can't tell which part of my approach won Marclinus over however much.

I'd better leave him on a victorious note.

I ease to my feet with a respectful dip of my head. "I'll endeavor to continue impressing you."

His chuckle follows me to the door. "I'm sure you will, wild princess of mine."

He can say that all he wants, but I'll never be his.

CHAPTER FIFTEEN

Aurelia

I catch Baronissa Livisse by the cards tables in the hall of entertainments. "I've been able to locate a supplier for that Icarian fabric you were interested in. Madam Clea is looking through the offerings now and should be able to take commissions using it as of tomorrow."

The baronissa claps her hands together in delight and then rests one on the protruding swell of her belly. "It will be nice to have a new gown waiting for me after our little lord or lady arrives. Something to look forward to. Thank you."

She beams at me, and I smile back. I'm making some progress at warming the court up to me... even if so far their good will is mostly based on what they can get out of me.

Gods only know if the grasping nobles will ever value their empress for more than that. Although somehow Marclinus managed to acknowledge this morning that I have

virtues beyond spreading my legs for him, so it doesn't seem utterly impossible.

As I turn, I catch Vicerine Saldette glowering my way for an instant before she wrenches her expression into blankness. I aim a careful smile at her through a jab of unreasonable guilt.

I've learned that her daughter was Leonette—the woman who survived nearly to the end of the trials with me, whom my last desperate act left for dead. The vicerine has been perfectly polite to my face, but I can always sense a bitter edge underneath.

She wishes her daughter were in my place. Why wouldn't she?

Before I have to find something to say to her, a footman stops in front of me and bows. "Your Imperial Highness, I'm to inform you that your first combat lesson will commence in the palace gymnasium at the next bell. His Highness Prince Raul suggests you make sure you're clothed fittingly."

Ah, I knew the lesson had been arranged for this afternoon, but not exactly when. My husband does still like me to know that he controls my life more than I do.

I smile at the footman too, because we only rise to greater heights with the support of those below. "I'll see to that now."

I can only imagine what attire Raul would consider "fitting" for a sparring session—and what clothes he'd prefer to see me in if he had the choice. Most likely none at all for the latter.

Since I obviously can't arrive nude, and the wardrobe I have consists exclusively of gowns of various opulence, I paw through my options for the plainest dress I own. The sky-blue silk still boasts gold embroidery along the neckline and waist, but the short sleeves are billowy enough to allow easy movement. The skirt is at the lightest and airiest of typical

Darium fashion, leaving my legs with plenty of room to maneuver as well.

It'll have to do.

As I step out into the hall, I fold my arms over my chest, abruptly aware of how the purple blotches on my scarred lower arms are now in view. I didn't worry about showing them back home during the warmer months, but the court isn't used to them yet.

Oh, well. It's a reminder that there *is* more to me than they regularly see in the palace common rooms.

I take a few steps before realizing I'm not entirely sure where I'm going. Swiveling around, I spot two of my ever-present guards shadowing me from farther down the hall.

One of this afternoon's number is the curly-haired man Lorenzo described to me, whose name I've gathered is Kassun. My skin itches with even more uneasiness.

I haven't seen any outright hostility from him so far, but since I started watching him more closely, I have noticed that he generally appears more tense than my other protectors, his expressions darker.

Suppressing my doubts, I beckon them over. "As much as I appreciate your usual discretion, I could use more direct help at the moment. Could you show me to the gymnasium?"

Both Kassun and the square-jawed woman who's his companion today bob their heads in agreement. I catch a flicker of a grimace across Kassun's face, sharp enough that it might almost be a sneer.

Hmm. Perhaps this would be an ideal time to address that particular problem as well.

Whatever his issues with me are, he mustn't have revealed any threatening inclinations when High Commander Axius carried out his investigations. I don't think he wants me dead.

He simply doesn't like me very much.

The knowledge combined with his military bearing and the sword at his hip makes my nerves jangle, but I have to remember that he isn't one of the soldiers who's maimed and murdered my people back home. Every member of the Darium military is their own person.

Many of them awful people, but if I don't give this one the benefit of the doubt, how can I expect him to give me the same?

We set off with the guards marching on either side of me rather than trailing behind as usual. As they guide me to a staircase that leads down to the first floor, I glance over at Kassun.

"How long have you served at the palace?"

Under my scrutiny, he draws his posture straighter. "This is my eighth year, Your Imperial Highness."

"You must be quite familiar with the court and the doings of the imperial family, then."

He makes a hesitant noise of agreement, probably uneasy about where I might be going with this line of conversation.

I keep my tone mild. "I hope you would tell me if you feel I'm acting in any way out of place with them, then."

Kassun's head jerks toward me. His voice stiffens. "It would never be appropriate for me to criticize you, Your Imperial Highness."

"Not even if I asked you to?"

"There is nothing to criticize," he insists, a little too late. His fellow guard scowls at him.

I let out a light laugh. "It's important to me that I'm fulfilling my role here as well as I can. I certainly wouldn't be offended."

Now Kassun simply stares at me. "Why wouldn't you be?"

Interesting. I study him in turn. "You think I should be."

"You're the empress—to allow anyone to insult you—"

He snaps his mouth shut, but I think I understand enough. Lorenzo thought he'd called me "pathetic."

"You feel I'm too soft," I suggest gently. "Did you not see me endure Emperor Tarquin's trials to make it to this point?"

A slight flush has reddened the guard's face. "I would never say you're not strong. We just haven't had many who are dedicated to Elox here, other than the medics. It's not... a common attitude."

Ah. He assumes my peaceful nature will interfere with what strength I could bring to bear.

I suppose that's not an unexpected concern when the Darium empire was built through war and maintained through violent dominance. And when this man has no idea just how forcefully I've been willing to assert my own will for the right cause.

The other guard interrupts our conversation with a clearing of her throat and a gesture toward a doorway we've come up on. "The gymnasium."

I smile at her in thanks and give Kassun one last glance. "I trust in time you'll see that my dedication to healing and harmony only prepares me to defend whatever I hold dear."

As usual, the guards hang back by the doorway as I enter the room.

The space is large enough that I'd imagine a couple dozen men and women could train in here at a time without it becoming overcrowded. Most of the floor is covered with thin mats for absorbing impact. Racks of training weapons stand along one wall. Another is hung with targets of various sorts alongside a few wooden dummies. For all the palace staff keep the place clean, they haven't been able to completely erase the sweaty tang from the air.

In the midst of that space, only two figures are waiting for me. I assume Marclinus reserved the room solely for my use during this lesson—and I can't say I mind the lack of spectators.

Raul moves forward with a nod of greeting. "Your Imperial Highness," he says, with just a hint of wryness at the formal title.

Despite his tone, his expression stays grim. His gaze sweeps over me as if searching for injuries. I suspect from the flexing of his shoulders that he's remembering last night's poisoning—and wishing he could thrash my husband for it.

He kept his cool impressively well during Marclinus's test. All of my lovers did, but knowing Raul's temperament, I suspect it was the most struggle for him.

My husband could learn a lot from the foster brothers he disdains.

Raul's next words come out with a more ominous undertone. "Are you well?"

Even the lingering sting in my lungs has faded since breakfast. "Quite." My attention veers to his hands, which have risen in front of him. His knuckles are freshly bandaged. "I hope you are also."

Raul follows my gaze. His mouth twists, but he's as aware of the guards watching from the doorway as I am. "I have no complaints."

He gestures me over to where our other companion is waiting.

Prince Neven stands on the central mat, his stance a little awkward. His muscular but gangly teenage frame reminds me even more of an overgrown puppy than usual when he offers me a sheepish smile. "Raul suggested I could help."

"We're focusing on defending yourself against attackers," Raul explains. "It'll be easier for me to coach you if I can watch how you handle someone else instead of having to be right in there myself. And this one could use some more pointers himself." He gives his younger foster brother a nudge.

"Of course." I suppose it would have seemed odd if he'd brought in Bastien or Lorenzo instead when neither of them are much inclined toward combat.

I meet Neven's gaze. "I appreciate you contributing your time—and looking out for me as best you can."

Not just now, but last night when he argued with Marclinus on my behalf.

The young prince's awkwardness fades. "You're one of us —come from farther away. That's almost like family."

It appears he doesn't hold any continued animosity toward me for rejecting their escape plan either.

"All right, enough chatting." Raul motions me over to the weapons rack. "These are all blunt. Pick one that's a size and weight you feel comfortable with. Once we know what you can handle best, you can see about getting a proper knife or dagger to keep on you."

The thought of carrying around an obvious deadly weapon makes my skin crawl. "Is that really necessary?"

"Obviously we'd hope your guards can intervene before it gets to that point." Raul shoots a pointed look toward the two by the door. "But if an attacker makes it past them, a blade is your best chance at slowing them down or even stopping them. I'm not going to be able to turn your fists or feet into all that effective a weapon in a single session."

Fair enough. I did get a decent amount of training in physical defense relying just on my body back home. The tutor didn't focus on weapons, as a princess wouldn't have expected to have one close at hand.

I don't want to be walking around with an instrument of violence on clear display, though. That'll give the opposite impression from what I want to convey.

I scan the offerings and select the smallest knife, one that could be concealed in a pocket or behind my belt pouch unobtrusively.

Raul's expression turns skeptical, but he simply shakes his head at me in bemusement. "We can work with that. You'll just need to be very accurate in where you strike."

He sets me up on the mat with Neven a few paces away. "He'll come at you from the side, like so." He beckons Neven, and the young prince makes a mock charge, reaching for my neck.

Raul stops him when Neven's hands are near my shoulder and touches my elbow. The warmth of his touch tingles over my skin as he slides his fingers around my arm to guide it. "In this position, you're most likely to do critical damage if you aim the blade here or here. The more you hurt your attacker, the less likely they can hurt you."

"Such a pleasant thought," I mutter.

He chuckles and leans closer as if adjusting my shoulder position more minutely. His voice drops to a murmur so low I doubt the guards can tell he's talking, though his breath washes over my cheek. "Bastien's going to search out information on Prospira's confirmation rite. I talked to an elderly vicerine who was around for Tarquin's ceremony—she didn't remember it well, but said it had something to do with gathering crops."

I keep my own voice equally low. "That doesn't sound too dangerous. What happened to your hands?"

Raul glowers at me as if he could have expected me not to care. "Nothing you need to worry about. It was either this or Marclinus's face."

He injured his knuckles working out his frustrations after last night?

I'd like to ask more, but we can hardly keep talking along these lines without drawing suspicion. Raul raises his voice again. "That's right. Now try making those blows when he's approaching at a more normal speed. You want to practice until the right movement feels natural."

We run through several of those exercises, with me standing or sitting while Neven springs at me from different angles. In each position, Raul has us hold in place while he shows me the best ways to strike to incapacitate an attacker before trying the moves at a faster speed.

I don't think it's ever going to feel comfortable for me to drive a blade into another person's throat or gut or eye. I can at least say that by the time my dress has dampened with perspiration and my muscles are getting achy from the exertion, my instinctive defensive reaction is more likely to be deadly.

Every time my gaze meets Raul's, I have to suppress the impulse to say something beyond the training. To recognize this fierce and fearsome man who's determined to stand by my side as a person rather than just a tool.

One question seems safe enough. "You've clearly been training in combat for a long time. Is that a typical pursuit for Lavirian royalty?"

Raul snorts, taking a step back after our last exercise. "Not at all. But my family could tell my temper ran too hot for me to be all that effective at moderation or negotiation."

I raise my eyebrows. "It seems odd to judge someone's temperament so thoroughly when they're still a child."

"They were right that patience isn't a particular virtue of mine. At least if I could handle myself in a fight, I could defend whatever political treaties or trade negotiations we oversaw." He strikes an overly pompous pose. "I thought of myself as very valiant when I first started."

Neven covers a snicker with his hand. "But you dedicated to Kosmel rather than Sabrelle."

"Ah, by the time I was twelve, I'd figured out that good combat is all about nuance. There's a kind of might in just appearing to *have* power, and in knowing how to wield it in opportune ways rather than mindlessly. Plus I needed a little help in the cleverness department."

He taps the side of his head. His tone is wry again, but his jaw flexes with unstated tension.

I know the other reason he dedicated himself to the godlen of trickery was to gain the gift he thought would help him destroy Emperor Tarquin—and then realized it wouldn't after all.

"It sounds like you were decently clever already," I say gently.

Raul's smile comes back. He pats me on the shoulder with a surreptitious squeeze of affection. "And you haven't done badly as a warrior, Your Imperial Highness. Next time, we'll have you in one of your frillier gowns so you can get used to the movements even if you're more… encumbered."

"Definitely a concern." I rotate the handle of the training knife in my hand, adjusting my grip, and turn toward the doorway. "I'd like to try a bit more of a challenge right now. Kassun, would you join us in here?"

Raul's eyebrows arch, but he doesn't argue with my request.

The guard cautiously treads farther into the room. "Your Imperial Highness?"

I wave the knife at him. "You have more experience and more training than Prince Neven. My last attacker was a military man like yourself. I'd like to see what it might take to fend off a skilled attacker with a sword. Grab a training blade similar to your regular issue weapon. Please don't actually run me through, of course, but don't hold back too much."

Kassun gapes at me. "Empress, I— I'm not sure this is wise—"

"It'd be even less wise for me to go off on our trek to the

Temple of Fruitful Fields underprepared. Please, let me see where my worst limitations are so Prince Raul may help me mend them."

The guard still looks as if he's just swallowed a lemon whole, but he goes to grab one of the blunted swords.

Raul folds his arms over his chest. "If someone comes at you with a blade that much bigger than your own, your best bet is to get out of the way as much as you can. The sword is going to strike you either way, so better that it hits something less vital. If you can deflect it with your knife or even get in a strike of your own, great, but don't focus on that."

I nod, shifting my weight on my feet. "All right. Kassun, you attack, and I'll do my best to dodge."

Kassun approaches tentatively at first, taking a swing and a jab that I easily leap away from. When I duck under another swipe and tap my knife against his belly, his forehead furrows with consternation. "You wouldn't normally get an opening like that."

I grin at him. "Then don't give me one. Make me fight."

Despite his obvious misgivings, he comes at me faster. His sword slices through the air with enough force to ruffle my hair when it veers close.

I dodge and weave, and fend off one blow with a clang against my knife that reverberates down my arm. More sweat trickles down my back.

"Always move to the side as well as backward," Raul calls after me. "Focus on keeping your head and torso out of reach. Don't be afraid to duck right down to the ground if it keeps you safe."

I end up crouching on my knees and flick my blade across Kassun's shin as I scramble away. His next swing nicks my shoulder. I suck in a breath, and the guard freezes.

"Your Imperial Highness, I'm so sorry—I—"

I stand, holding up my hands in appeal. "I'm fine. It

barely hurt. You're only doing as I asked. But while we're here…"

I swipe my arm across my damp forehead and then slash out without warning. My knife stops an inch from Kassun's eye before he's quite got his sword up again.

He jerks backward, his jaw twitching. "You wouldn't have gotten that close if we were still sparring."

"I know." I lower my knife. "But you didn't expect me to try it. I want *you* to know that if my own security—or that of the people I rule over—is under attack, I'll do whatever is required to protect it. The idea of peace doesn't do anyone any good unless you're willing to fight for it."

Raul's laugh rings through the room.

Kassun gapes at me for a moment before a trace of a smile curves his lips too. He bends into a brief bow. "I won't argue with that, Your Imperial Highness."

"Good. Now I think I'd better retire to my chambers for a time before I present myself before the court again."

And perhaps it'll be with one fewer potential enemy to worry about.

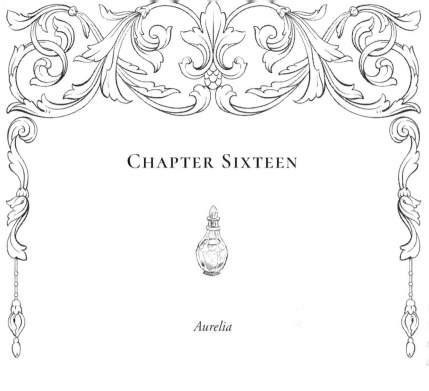

Chapter Sixteen

Aurelia

I slip out of the palace in the pale sunlight just after dawn. Most of the court is still asleep; the only talk I hear is the chirping of the birds.

I make my way swiftly and steadily to the herb garden around the side of the building near the kitchen. We're meant to leave for the Temple of Fruitful Fields tomorrow. I don't know how much access I'll have on the road or at the smaller imperial residence near Ubetta to the various common ingredients I might require for a potion or salve.

It seemed wisest to gather a small stash now in case I should need any of them before we return.

I'm prepared to find one or two of the kitchen staff among the rows of herbs, gathering what they need for the day's planned meals. But when I come around the last row of hedge sculptures, the sight of a woman bending over one of

the small bushes in an elaborate silk gown draws me up short.

Bianca's head twitches toward me at the soft tap of my footsteps on the path. We stare at each other, her smooth brown face seeming to yellow in the wan light.

She straightens up abruptly and pats her sleek upswept hair as if making sure the strands are in order. Her other hand clutches a sprig of thin leaves I can't imagine what she'd do with.

"Your Imperial Highness," she says, her typical haughty voice just slightly roughened. "What a delight to run into you out here."

I tread closer, knitting my brow. "What are you collecting rosemary for?"

The vicerine tucks her acquisition closer to her flowy skirt. "I enjoy the flavor."

Is she planning to simply chew on the stuff? And what's even more odd— "Why didn't you send your maid to collect some, then?"

Bianca lets out a dismissive sniff. "I can do a few things on my own. If even the empress roams the gardens of her own accord, why shouldn't I?"

None of that really answers my question. In fact, her response gives me the distinct impression that she's doing everything in her power to avoid answering directly.

I pause to take in her stance, the cant of her posture, the set of her face. A sharper suspicion prickles up inside me. "You're in pain. What's the matter?"

Rosemary has some mild pain-relieving effects. I wouldn't have expected a court noble to be aware of that, but it's a common enough folk remedy, so there's no reason the vicerine couldn't be.

And the rigidness of her body suggests she's holding

herself very carefully to avoid provoking the problem into worse discomfort.

Bianca shakes her head and gives a crisp laugh that would probably leave most people embarrassed to have questioned her. "I'm perfectly fine. Why don't you see to your own business and let me tend to mine?"

She's being more antagonistic than the last couple of times I've spoken to her, which only convinces me more that she's hiding something. She's trying to get me to leave before I discover what.

If it's a matter of her health, I don't need her to tell me with words.

I focus on my gift and aim my honed attention at her body. What could I concoct that would heal what ails her?

The flurry of images that form behind my eyes make my pulse lurch. She's concealing much more than I would have guessed. No wonder she's barely moved since I came upon her —it must be taking all her self-control not to reveal her injuries.

I could leave her to it, even though the rosemary will merely dull a little pain, nothing more. She once left me for dead, beaten and broken in a hollow in the palace woods.

But every bit of my nature balks at the idea of abandoning a person in need. It isn't as if she's made any move to harm me since the trials were completed.

My voice softens. "You need a lot more than that rosemary will provide if you want to be back to rights soon. You know what my gift is—I have an ointment already prepared that will soothe some of your ills, and I can brew you a tonic that will help with the rest. Unless you'd rather go to the palace medics. They'd be even more able to—"

"No," Bianca interrupts, her face going even more taut. "It's really not necessary. Any of it."

What is she so worried about?

Her gaze flicks beyond me—toward my ever-present guards who'll be hanging back by the hedges. The fact that she came to the garden herself despite her pains, that she wouldn't have visited the medics... Is it something she doesn't want any of the palace staff finding out about?

Nothing my gift showed me indicates any reason for such secrecy. Some part of her flesh is bruised and torn, and an infection is starting to set in.

If someone's attacked her, shouldn't they be brought to justice?

Every bit of her behavior shows that she wants to avoid even acknowledging she's wounded. She obviously isn't willing to admit it in front of company.

I'd rather not bully her into submission, but with difficult patients, it's sometimes the lesser of two evils.

I lift my chin with an imperious air. "I'll gather a couple of ingredients I'll need, and then you'll accompany me back to my chambers so I can tend to you. Either that, or we can keep standing here until more of the staff are moving about to notice your early-morning activities."

It appears I've gambled right that she'd rather as few people as possible see her moving around the palace. With a sigh, her shoulders slump. "You really needn't trouble yourself—"

"I'll be more troubled if I don't do what I can. Consider it an order from your empress."

Bianca holds still while I snatch up a few leaves of one plant and more of another. It's not at all the larger supply I was hoping to collect, but I can return later today.

By the time I'm done, childish laughter bounces from around the side of the building. Some of the palace nursemaids must have brought their early-waking charges out to the gardens for some fresh air. The noble children are so often kept away from court, restricted to their parents' chambers with the staff who care for them, that it's easy to forget they live here too.

The sound of increased activity nearby makes the vicerine tense more. At the beckoning flick of my hand, she follows me toward the palace without further protest.

As soon as she starts walking, her discomfort is obvious. She takes steady steps, but they're slower and stiffer than I've normally seen her move. Her mouth tightens.

I wish I had some magic to convey her up the stairs to the third floor. She climbs at an even more mincing pace, glancing around her as if she's simply taking the time to enjoy the mosaics embedded in the walls, but her knuckles pale where she's gripping the railing. As she takes the last step onto even ground, she can't restrain a wince.

The moment I have her inside my chambers, I motion her toward the sofa at the far side of my bedroom. Bianca sinks onto it with a faint noise of relief and peers around her at the vast space with all its trappings.

"Well, the empress's rooms are nearly as fancy as His Imperial Majesty's. You are looked after well."

"I earned my place," I say mildly, which she knows as well as anyone, and retrieve my tea box and brewing apparatus from my trunk.

Bianca watches with undisguised interest as I pick out a few more ingredients. Right on time for my morning preparations, Eusette's voice carries through the door. "Your Imperial Highness, are you already up? I've brought the water for your morning tea."

I hustle over to the door and take the small pot from my maid, blocking her way in. "Thank you. I'm having a private conversation with a friend, and as you can see, I've dressed myself. Could you come back just before breakfast to give me a hand taming my hair better?"

Eusette's eyes widen with a curious glint, but she bobs her head and departs.

I turn around to find Bianca staring at me more incredulously than before. "Why are you doing this?" she blurts out.

I don't know if it's my calling her a friend or the fact that I'm protecting her secret at all that's bewildered her, but the answer would be the same regardless. "You've been hurt. I can help heal you. We may not exactly be friends, but we aren't enemies anymore, are we?"

She ducks her head with a wince. "No, I wouldn't say we are. But I wouldn't have blamed you for considering me one."

I grope for the right words to encompass all that's happened between us. "I don't think any of us were behaving at our best during the trials."

Bianca sits in silence as I prepare my miniature cauldron over its burner. A weariness comes over her pretty face that unsettles me nearly as much as her difficulty walking.

When she speaks again, her voice is quiet. "You were. No matter what anyone did to you, you played a fair game."

"I can't claim that wasn't strategic in its own way. It's the approach that's always worked best for me."

"Fausta's approach obviously didn't work for her." Bianca rubs a gleam of tears from her eyes. "I won't make excuses for her. She did what she felt she had to do too. It's an honor being part of the court, but it also comes with certain... restrictions. She finally had the opportunity to be something more, something more powerful."

"And you helped her," I say evenly.

"She was like a little sister to me. Of course I wanted to see her elevated as far as she could be. And any threat to her winning would mean her *dying* instead. That was all I was thinking about. It was nothing to do with you personally."

She pauses. "I suppose you were an easier target because

we didn't know you, and a more important one because you'd already won Marclinus's attention once. But in the end, you tried to look out for her too, even though your life was on the line. I never properly thanked you for that."

The way she's laid it out so plainly reminds me of conversations with Nica back home. My friend could sometimes be too blunt for politeness, but she knew how to cut to the heart of the matter when it was important.

Perhaps if Bianca and I had been able to talk this way to begin with, we might have forged something like an actual friendship.

Shrugging off the pang of homesickness, I stir the potion that's now coming to a simmer. "My attempt didn't do much good for her in the end." Lady Fausta still plummeted to a painful but hopefully brief death during the final trial.

"Perhaps not. But the trying matters to the rest of us still here. It matters to me, anyway. I'm sorry for how we hurt you that one night. You didn't deserve that."

She sounds resigned, as if she doesn't expect me to accept the apology, but I think she means it.

I retrieve my ointment for soothing wounds and glance up at her. "I expect you'll forgive me for not wanting to take any midnight walks in the woods with you going forward, but I have no interest in punishing you for the past. I'd rather we move forward with respect and mutual understanding. This needs to go directly on your injuries. Where are you hurt?"

A flicker of panic passes through Bianca's expression. She draws her posture more upright on the sofa, her legs tucking together. "I'd rather see to the application myself, on my own. If you'd allow me the use of your bathing room?"

I would, but her immediate refusal to reveal the location combined with the shifting of her stance sends a jolt of ice through my veins. How many places could she be injured the way my gift suggests without my having noticed her favoring a specific limb or the bulge of a bandage beneath her dress?

My hand tightens around the pot. "Did Marclinus do this? Is he the one who hurt you?"

He's been domineering but never brutally rough when he's taken me to bed—but I've never let him carry out the full act. Who knows what violent intimacies he might be imagining in the grips of the hallucinations?

Bianca's cheeks flare ruddy as she must realize I've caught on despite her attempt at avoiding the subject. "No. I wasn't with him last night. I…"

Her fingers curl into the folds of her skirt. She looks down at her lap and back at me. After a tense moment, she must decide there's no point in making up a story.

"My husband would rather not share my affections," she says tersely. "But of course he would never deny His Imperial Majesty. Mostly he tolerates it, but every now and then he lets out some of his frustration on me. He's never been quite this rough before."

My stomach sinks. How badly must Viceroy Ennius have manhandled her for her to be not just bruised but torn and fighting off an infection?

"That's not right. You *should* see the medics, so there's a record—you could appeal for divorce—"

Bianca cuts me off with a shake of her head. "No! I'm happy with my position. It's not as if I'd be so much better off with anyone else."

I frown at her. "What do you mean? There are plenty of husbands who wouldn't… treat you so forcefully."

"How many of them would ensure my place in court? The kind of life I'd like to live? Tolerating the way they huff and rut is the price women pay for the other benefits of marriage."

My mind leaps back to certain "ruttings" I've savored in recent weeks. "With the right partner, it can be enjoyable."

Bianca snorts as if the idea is absurd. "That's the tale they dangle to soften the blow—and to make us feel like we have to play-act a lot of swooning to appease their egos. What's there to actually enjoy? It's a sweaty, pawing mess. Even with an emperor, as I'd imagine you well know now."

I can't exactly tell her that I've enjoyed myself plenty with men other than my husband—or that I haven't fully experienced what my husband might have to offer. I'm too stuck on the fact that she *has* and yet she's talking like this.

"But you—why do you encourage Marclinus's attentions if you're not getting anything out of it?"

The vicerine peers at me as if I've grown a second nose. "I get plenty—the envy of the other ladies, the gifts and benefits of being favored by the imperial family, the knowledge that a man who could have anyone wanted *me*..."

She falters, and her gaze slides away. "Although, to tell you the truth, I haven't found much satisfaction in that pursuit in recent days. It doesn't feel much like an honor when he has a woman he's so much more devoted to. I'm only a plaything for when he's momentarily bored."

I'd imagine that's what she's always been in Marclinus's eyes. Maybe it didn't feel so much so when he was unmarried, when many available women were vying for his attention and he chose her as one of his favorites regardless.

If she's never seen sex as anything but a chore and a bargaining chip... *is* it simply that she's never been with the right man, or is she simply not inclined to enjoy that sort of physical intimacy at all? One of the dukes in our court in Accasy never dallied with any of the court lords and ladies and adopted the son of a family friend as an heir. He always said he didn't see any appeal in romantic entanglements.

Bianca might have taken a similar position if she hadn't

wanted the advantages her marriage and trysts could offer. And perhaps she was afraid of appearing the odd one out. Or she honestly believes that no woman ever enjoys the carnal act.

Who would have thought that the lady at court who's established herself as having the most seductive wiles doesn't take any pleasure from the most direct result of those seductions?

It isn't my place to poke any further into her personal concerns. My gift judges my concoction done, so I take the cauldron off the flame so it can cool. "I won't invade your privacy. You're welcome to use the bathing room to apply the ointment. Only on external areas. The tonic should help reduce inflammation and speed healing inside, as well as warding off infection. It'll be cool enough when you're done tending to your injuries."

Bianca nods with obvious gratitude and accepts the pot of ointment from me. As she stands up, her gaze turns wary. "Thank you. I— You did say you weren't going to interfere with my relations with His Imperial Majesty—that it was all right—"

Is she afraid I'll be upset after what she's revealed?

"You knew him long before I did," I say. "And I've seen from the start that he's not one to be tied down. Whether you think it worth continuing the association is completely up to you."

She exhales shakily. "All right. Please don't mention this morning's incident to him. I don't want him thinking I might be… damaged."

She hurries away into the bathing room, leaving me wondering how it is that such a vile man has so many of us catering to his every whim above our own.

CHAPTER SEVENTEEN

Aurelia

The music winds through the expansive parlor, so bright and spirited it almost shimmers in the air. Through sheer force of will, I avoid glancing toward the platform where Lorenzo is stroking his fingers over his lyre.

Marclinus hasn't called on the prince of Rione to entertain the court since I suggested that the full company of imperial musicians made for a more appealing sound… until today. I hope the break did Lorenzo some good after all the times Tarquin pushed him to the limits of his gift, but it's coming up on two hours since we retired here after dinner, and my husband keeps motioning for the prince to play on.

I've wandered past the windows and between the scattered armchairs and sofas more times than I can count. I'm sure I've spoken to every noble in the room at least twice

at this point, all smiles and friendly chatter, hearing what else I can do to make them a little happier.

So I'm not lying when I sidle over to Marclinus after he's just left off a conversation with Counsel Severo and one of the viceroys and rest my hand on his forearm. "This room becomes rather dull after a time, doesn't it, husband? Perhaps we could suggest a move to the hall of entertainments."

And perhaps he'd leave off prodding Lorenzo for more music with the change of scenery.

Marclinus clicks his tongue at me chidingly. "Is our court not enough to keep you from boredom? I thought you had more of a creative spirit than that."

His jaunty tone tells me he's teasing, but also that he isn't at all bored himself—and therefore uninterested in changing anything about our evening. But his comment sparks a flicker of inspiration.

I smile at him. "That might be the answer right there. I do love a creative challenge. I wonder how I'd take to the lyre? If Prince Raul can teach me to fight, then surely Prince Lorenzo can offer his empress a quick lesson in his own skills."

Marclinus raises his eyebrows. "Looking to become a musician as well as a medic, wife?"

I shrug, keeping my reactions as casual as possible. "It would do to pass the time. An empress can never have too many talents up her sleeve, can she? Besides, the princes of the other realms need to remember how much respect they owe the both of us."

The smirk that crosses my husband's face tells me I picked the right tactic to get his agreement. "Indeed they do. By all means, requisition his services. Although I don't know how much guidance you'll get out of that tongueless mouth of his."

I restrain a wince at his callous dismissal of Lorenzo's

sacrifice and stride over to the musician's platform with my best imperious airs.

Lorenzo is just sending out the final notes of his most recent song. At the sight of me approaching, he hesitates. His gaze flicks to Marclinus before returning to me.

"Thank you for providing a lovely accompaniment to our evening," I say, as formally as if we've never really spoken before, let alone lain entwined in passion. "I have a mind to see if I can uncover a little musical talent of my own. The lyre seems one of the simpler instruments. Lend me your expertise, and let's see what I can make of it."

He nods in acceptance, with a brief creasing of his brow that I suspect is worry for me, but I hope anyone watching will take as confusion. As he steps down from the platform, I curve my fingers in the subtle gesture to say, *It's fine.*

Lorenzo offers me a mild smile, a deeper affection heating his dark gaze as he offers me the lyre. I attempt to position it in my arms the way I've seen him hold it. He adjusts my grasp, careful to touch only the instrument, not me.

Being this close but having to pretend I feel nothing for him leaves my heart aching. But it's worth it to release him from his constant performing.

Lorenzo reaches past me to strum the strings, demonstrating the ideal pressure and speed. I imitate him a few times until the sound that resonates from the instrument is reasonably appealing. Then he leads me through the notes of a simple melody, adding a few at a time and watching to make sure I can remember the whole composition so far.

The strings dig into my unpracticed fingers. It must take many days of practice to start to build up the callouses that protect Lorenzo's hands.

The thought brings back the memory of those hands

moving over my body with a sudden flush. I will down my reaction and train all my attention on my lesson.

When he's taught me enough that I can play a short but sweet little song, if somewhat haltingly, I cast my gaze around the room as surreptitiously as I can. Is Marclinus distracted enough that he's unlikely to push the prince into resuming his playing?

I can't spot my husband's golden-blond curls anywhere. Has he gone off with one of his lovers? That'll make the rest of the night easier for me.

In any case, he certainly can't give any orders if he's not here.

I offer Lorenzo a polite smile. "Thank you. I'm not sure this is a skill I'll pick up all that easily. I'd imagine you've been practicing for a long time."

He accepts the instrument back from me with another dip of his head in agreement and a broad motion in the direction of Rione, as if to say he started in his early childhood there. I wonder how intensely he focused on that one familiar pastime after he was dragged here as a hostage. His music must have given him comfort—at least until Emperor Tarquin started exploiting it.

Lorenzo makes a stealthier motion of his hand that thanks me emphatically in return. He knows what my real goal must have been.

As much as I long to, I can't tarry here next to him any longer without it looking odd. My husband might not be in the room, but plenty of people happy to gossip are.

I meander through the parlor for several minutes longer, but Marclinus never reappears. Well, if he doesn't feel the need to host this gathering, I hardly see why I shouldn't have some time to myself too, even if I'll have to spend it less thrillingly than I'd imagine he is.

I slip out of the room and head down the hall toward the

nearest staircase. A couple of pages go hustling by from that direction, but I don't pay much attention until the emperor himself emerges at the bottom of the staircase I'm approaching.

"Ah," Marclinus says with a tighter grin than before. "Were you going to turn in for the night? I thought of something we should take care of before we leave for Ubetta tomorrow morning."

I have no idea what he could be talking about, but his measured tone sends an uneasy shiver down my spine. I'm still not sure whether I prefer him buoyantly chaotic or chillingly calculating. Both moods often lead to unpleasantness.

I lift my chin in a show of spirit. "I can certainly help you with whatever that is."

He eyes me for a few heavy thuds of my heart and then motions for me to follow him in the direction I was coming from. "I'll explain once we're all together."

Who is 'we'?

Keeping my expression composed, I trail after him down the hall. He leads me to the audience room where we first met: the long, high-ceilinged space with its two thrones on the dais at the far end.

We haven't held an official palace audience since Tarquin's death. Will I take the seat that was once Marclinus's while he claims his father's, or will some lesser chair be brought in for me as his consort while the other stays vacant waiting for the next heir?

There's no one else in the room at the moment except for one of the pages I saw earlier, who's setting up a small brazier in front of the dais on a stand that brings it to waist height. As he lights a flame inside it, the other page hurries in carrying a wrought-iron rod about the length of my arm.

Marclinus accepts the rod from her and spins it between his fingers. "Very good."

He continues ushering me toward the dais, handing the rod to me when we're halfway there. My fingers close around the cool surface automatically. It's heavy, and one end holds a broader metal disc that might indicate its purpose.

Before I can inspect it, a few more sets of footsteps draw my attention back toward the room's entrance.

Another page is just escorting the three older foster princes inside. Bastien, Raul, and Lorenzo peer at us from across the room.

My stomach sinks. I thought we'd settled whatever Marclinus was concerned about the other night when he poisoned me. What is my blasted husband up to now?

Marclinus beckons the princes over with a sweep of his arm. "Come along, come along. We can get this over with quickly, and then you can go back to whatever you were occupying yourselves with before."

Lorenzo shoots me a quick quizzical glance, but I don't know what's going on any better than he does.

While the pages depart, their work done, my and Marclinus's guards assume their positions along the walls. Marclinus has me stop next to the brazier and stands at its other side. He waits until the princes have almost reached us before motioning them to a halt a few paces away.

Bastien gazes back at the emperor with an impassive expression, not acknowledging me at all. "What's this about, Your Imperial Majesty?"

Marclinus folds his arms over his chest. "It occurred to me with our upcoming treks across the country and the recent unrest beyond Dariu's borders that I should implement a concrete reminder of who you owe your loyalty to ahead of any consideration of your birthplace. You should be as dedicated to the empire as you are to your chosen godlen. So you should wear our brand as well as theirs."

The rod wobbles in my hands. Gods help me, *that's* what it is: a brand. I tip the broader circle toward me and make out the etching of the imperial crest.

CONQUER ALL. He means to conquer his foster brothers down to their very spirit if he can.

And make his wife a party to their humiliation. Marclinus tilts his head toward me. "Your empress will do the honors so that I can focus on ensuring I see no signs of revolt in any of you. Especially our prince of Lavira." His eyes narrow slightly as he considers Raul.

Raul's mouth opens and closes again with a tightening of his jaw. There's no precedent that I know of for this act. Marclinus is acting out of pure tyranny.

But who can say what worse consequences they'd face if they refuse?

I don't know why he's spared Neven in the same fate. Maybe he decided the younger prince didn't pose the same sort of threat—or that the others would be less inclined to accept his request if it included harming the teenager they shadow like protective older brothers.

No, this is about something else. As my husband's gaze lingers on my face, I'm increasingly sure it's mainly about *me.*

He poisoned me to see how they would react. Is he testing me now to see if I'll balk at harming them?

Surely a little protest would make sense given my nonviolent inclinations, regardless of the target?

Marclinus gestures for the princes to sink down. "On your knees. Pull off your shirts so she's got plenty of skin to brand. We'll place it right below your godlen sigils, since I won't claim to be above the gods. Wife, get the brand heating up in the fire. It won't do much while it's cold."

The princes are already dropping to their knees and

tugging off their shirts without further protest. My throat constricts so tightly that for a moment I can't breathe.

I turn toward my husband. "I've never done anything like this to another person before. To inflict that kind of pain —I'm afraid I'll falter and make poor work of it."

Better to focus on how it'll affect me than what I'd rather not do to the only men in this awful place I actually care about.

Marclinus simply shakes his head. "You'll have to steel yourself and get the job done. If you're going to rule over this empire by my side, you need to be able to deal out pain as necessary as well as take it."

Bastien's mouth sets in a tense line. "We're perfectly happy to do what it takes to show our loyalty."

He hasn't looked away from Marclinus, but I know that message is meant for me. He's telling me it's okay, that they understand I have to do this.

All our lives depend on the psychopath giving these commands. And none of these men want to see my own in danger any more than I want to risk theirs.

With a lurch of my stomach, I place the brand end of the rod into the brazier. As the flames lick over the etched disc, my queasiness only grows.

My mind scrambles for any excuse I could use to divert Marclinus, to offer a different course of action he'd find even more satisfying without doing the same permanent damage. No options swim up through my whirling thoughts.

I could simply refuse. Claim I can't bear it and back away.

And then what? He'll probably do the branding anyway. The princes wouldn't be any better off, and I'd have shown my husband that he can't count on me for a difficult task.

Not to mention inflaming any suspicions he still harbors about my interest in his foster brothers.

This is the best way forward, even if it's horrible.

Still, when the metal disc is glowing and I can't put off the task any longer, my gut churns so hard I have to grit my teeth against the urge to vomit. I lift the rod, tensing my muscles to keep my arms as steady as possible, and step toward the princes.

Lorenzo is first in line, Inganne's sigil showing in the middle of his chest, even darker than his deep brown skin. His gaze follows me as I approach with the searing tool.

When I'm close enough that my body will block part of Marclinus's view of his body, the prince of Rione twists one hand in a few small, fleeting movements.

I belong to you.

All at once, I'm choked up for a completely different reason. He's taking this act of possession and making it a bond between us rather than between him and the empire I represent.

As if somehow the agony I'm about to put him through could be a gesture of love.

A renewed swell of affection stokes my courage. Through the racing of my pulse, I clamp my jaw and press the brand forward.

The sizzle of it against Lorenzo's skin makes my nerves jump so badly I almost flinch. Only the thought of how much worse I could hurt him if I lose my grip holds me in place.

Lorenzo gasps, and I jerk the brand back.

The sickly smell of burnt flesh trickles through the air. The brand mark shows as a ruddy near-black shape on Lorenzo's chest.

He rocks into a sitting position, his expression taut. I blink away the tears that prick at my eyes as hastily as I can.

Marclinus speaks with no detectable emotion. "Very

good. I knew you had it in you. Get the brand nice and hot again and then proceed."

It takes all my will and the deepest well of calm inside me to keep my hatred off my face as I carry out his command. Raul waits for me without a hint of concern in his expression, though his pale eyes smolder with everything he can't say.

I can only imagine how much rage he's tamping down, both at the humiliation aimed at them and the agony it's putting me through in turn. Marclinus could never imagine being as strong as these three men have needed to become under his vicious rule.

When I'm poised to go through with the act, Raul gives the same discreet, silent message he must have seen Lorenzo offer. *I belong to you.*

For all the signal might be an attempt to reassure me, the process is no easier with him. Even the toughest of the princes can't hold back a grunt at the hissing impact of the brand.

By the time I'm approaching Bastien, my head feels as if it's detached from my body. I can't let myself sink into my queasiness or horror too deeply, or it'll all spill out of me.

Bastien meets me with his back rigid and the same gesture as his foster brothers. *I belong to you.*

My husband could never be capable of such true devotion either.

Fresh tears well in my eyes. I force myself to press the brand forward.

Bastien's face twitches, what little color his already sallow skin contains draining from it. At his stifled cry, I wrench the brand away.

A tremble runs through my limbs. There. It's done.

Please, let this be the end of it.

Marclinus retrieves the rod from me and douses the

brazier. "Nicely done, wife. You're every bit as strong as I expected. Foster brothers, you may go."

As he turns to set down the brand, I aim a hasty motion of my fingers at the other men. *Meet me in the room below.*

I hope I've conveyed my meaning well enough. I have to do *something* to offset the pain I've unwillingly inflicted on them.

They trudge out of the room, and Marclinus aims one of his sharp smiles at me.

What really provoked this cruelty? Could his suspicions have been renewed by my interrupting Lorenzo's performance?

My listing stomach compresses into an aching knot. How can I protect the men I've fallen for if even the most innocent gesture sets them up to be punished?

CHAPTER EIGHTEEN

Lorenzo

The scorched skin on my chest still stings, more so when I move. I try to recline in the worn armchair, but with every minute that passes without Aurelia's arrival, my hands clench tighter against the padded arms. There's no way I'm actually relaxing.

Raul paces back and forth on the threadbare rug in the sitting room that used to connect the servants' chambers to the hidden passages within the palace walls. It's been several days since we last gathered here, and his feet stir up the thin layer of new dust. It tickles my nose.

He doesn't appear to care if he's agitating his wound. Every muscle on his massive frame bulges with tension. "Are we *sure* this is where she wanted us to meet her? She couldn't have been motioning to the library or the gardens?"

Bastien is poised on the edge of the settee, his lean body braced rigidly as if he thinks he might need to leap up at any

second. "She indicated down and enclosed. That eliminates both. And this is the only place in the palace she *can* meet us without risking being observed. Nothing else would make sense."

"She might not have been thinking straight after all of Marclinus's fucking insanity." Raul sucks a harsh breath through his teeth. "He can't *know* anything, can he? If he was even slightly sure, he'd already have chopped off our heads."

I stay quiet, not knowing what to say. After all the music I enhanced for the court this evening, just the thought of forming my illusionary voice sets off an uncomfortable prickle in my skull.

Bastien swipes his hand over his pale forehead, ruffling his auburn hair and provoking a wince as his shirt must brush the fresh burn. "I can't even tell whether he truly suspects there's some fondness between us and her that we've been hiding or if he simply enjoys tormenting all of us. We've always been easier targets than the rest of the nobles."

Raul looks toward the spot where the imperial crest is now seared into his brown skin. "As soon as I'm out from under this fucking roof, I'm—"

A faint creak on the other side of the paneled doorway brings all our heads jerking up, Raul's voice halting. With a sigh, the panel slides open.

Aurelia steps out, her hair loose and mussed across her shoulders, a glass jar clutched in one hand. Her gaze darts over all of us. Her blue eyes have gone even darker with her urgency.

Her voice quavers. "I'm sorry it took me so long. Marclinus told me to wait for him in my chambers, and then he took until the next bell actually coming, and— It doesn't matter. This salve should help reduce the pain and make the burns heal faster."

I get to my feet with a lurch of my heart at the unstated

implications of her words, her unpinned hair. Marclinus came to her *bed*—she had to cater to his advances again.

Fury and jealousy flare together behind the clenching of my jaw.

Raul's voice comes out in a growl. "If that vicious prick made you—"

Aurelia lifts her hand to stop him. "I dealt with him the same way I always do. It's... tolerable."

Bastien has risen and pushed forward to meet her. Her gaze drops to his shirt. She must be picturing the brand she pressed into his chest, because she flinches. "I'm so sorry."

He grasps her wrist with an emphatic squeeze. "It wasn't your fault. You handled the situation perfectly."

"Marclinus is the only one we're upset with," I add, ignoring the pulse of pain that comes with the illusion and casting it far enough for my foster brothers to hear me too. *"Him and his brutal tests."*

Raul scowled. "He'd better get bored of them soon, or..."

He trails off, because really, how can he go on? What can any of us do right now to stop the new emperor from following every horrific whim that strikes him?

Not even his wife is safe.

Aurelia doesn't look at all reassured by our words. Her gaze slides over all of us, shining with both affection and anguish. "You all held so strong through the whole thing... But you shouldn't have needed to. Gods, I hate him."

She opens the jar with a wobble of her hand and dips her fingers into the pearly blue gel inside. "Let me just— I should have enough. I'll need to brew more when I have the chance, just in case..."

When Bastien raises his shirt at her gesture to reveal the seared flesh, her mouth twists. With delicate movements, she smears the gel over the raw spot.

Bastien stays tensed at first, but his stance softens as the initial soothing effects must sink in. He closes his eyes. "Thank you."

Aurelia gazes up at him and then, just as gingerly as she treated his burn, touches the side of his jaw and bobs up to kiss him.

Bastien makes a rough sound low in his throat and grasps her waist as he kisses her back. The pang of envy that hits me is much more bittersweet than before.

I haven't gotten to kiss the woman I love since before her final trial. But Bastien has struggled the most with accepting how his plan was upended. He always takes on so much responsibility for the rest of us.

If anyone needs the reminder of how much she cares in return, it's him.

Raul's gaze tracks Aurelia as she moves from our foster brother to him. A predatory glint sparks in his cool eyes.

He watches her apply the salve to his own wound, any discomfort he's feeling buried deep. "Is the kiss part of the cure, Shepherdess?"

She gives him a wry look. "I suppose we can count it as that. If only to show I belong to you all too, as much as I can."

The words bring a catch into my breath. No further envy stirs as Aurelia kisses Raul, only a tingle of anticipation.

She comes to me next, gliding across the floor like a figure out of a dream. The salve imparts a comforting coolness into my skin. The sad smile she offers me sends an ache from my throat to my gut.

I touch her cheek. *"I meant it. I'm yours."*

She answers with the kiss I've spent more than a week imagining. Her lips meld with mine, soft and sweet, while her cool, wild scent fills my lungs.

How could I want anything else when I have her?

When she draws back, my hand trails down her face to

tuck the strands of her hair over her shoulder. The gesture reveals a ruddy blotch on the side of her neck.

My fingers jerk away from it.

He marked her. Her wretch of a husband bruised her beautiful skin to stake his claim.

All careful intentions go out the window. I tug her back to me, capturing her mouth for my own, teasing her lower lip with a graze of my teeth before deepening the kiss. As she melts into me, I ease my hand down her side. My palm slides over the tempting swell of her breast—

Aurelia pulls away with a shaky breath. She clasps my hand so the refusal doesn't feel so much like a rejection.

"I want to," she says, the hunger turning her voice raw. "I just don't think—"

She already explained this to me. I squeeze her fingers, a shameful flush rising to my face, and flick my other hand through the air. *I know. I'm sorry—I shouldn't have pushed.*

Aurelia steps farther back, glancing over all of us. She looks wilder and more gorgeous than ever with a flush of her own darkening her cheeks and her hair flowing unkept about her face.

She screws the lid back onto the jar and lowers her gaze to it for a moment before meeting our eyes again. "With the way Marclinus has been acting and the court setting off for Ubetta tomorrow, I think we should be even more cautious. We won't have any secret passages or discreet rooms to sneak off into in the waystations. And he seems to be watching us so closely…"

My innards tighten even more at the idea of putting additional distance between us. The cloud of gloom that consumed me a few days ago settles over me, but I force myself to incline my head in agreement. *"Whatever you think is safest for you."*

Protecting her matters more than bodily pleasures, as much happiness as a single touch from her brings me.

Raul grimaces. "I realize I've taken chances before, but I don't want to put you in danger. You know the threats you're facing better than any of us. You decide whether our combat lessons continue—whether you even want to talk to us—and we'll follow your lead."

"But we'll still be here," Bastien adds, his face drawn. "If you do need us, in whatever way…"

Aurelia's mouth twists. "I want all of you to stay safe too. If I could, I'd have you all sent back to your home countries already—"

No! I interrupt with an overt jerk of my hand. I'm recoiling from the thought too violently to concentrate on my gift.

As Aurelia stares at me, I repeat the same gesture I did in the audience hall. *I belong to you.* Then I add, *We belong here with you. The fight is ours too.*

She blinks hard—against tears she's managed to hold back until now? "I know, but if something happened to you because of me…"

She's still haunted by the death of that guard she fell for years ago. A duller twinge of jealousy passes through me, but it isn't as if he's competition now.

Maybe she needs the confirmation that he's not a harbinger of our doom either.

I gather my composure enough to conjure my illusionary voice, girding myself against the brief ache of effort. *"It wouldn't be because of you. I don't think it was the time before either. Why don't you tell us all exactly what happened, so we can make sure what we have here doesn't end the same way?"*

Aurelia's gaze darts to my foster brothers. Raul's expression has turned grimmer; Bastien's jaw flexes.

"You know the basics," she surmises. "Lorenzo told you what I told him."

I start to make a gesture of apology, but she shakes her head. "It's all right. I assume you share everything you know with each other. There's nothing I'd tell any of you that I wouldn't be comfortable with you all knowing. But do you really want to hear about Gavril?"

The name makes the man more real in my mind. I can picture a younger version of Aurelia casting glances across the room, ducking out into the gardens, blushing as he charms her.

Raul answers for me. "Lore's right. If it'll help set your mind at ease about our involvement, we should hear it."

Her arms come up to hug herself. "I don't know how much there is to say. I never told anyone I was seeing him—I had a lot more freedom in Accasy. My friends suspected I was fond of someone, but I never admitted who. Freedom or not, it isn't really done for a princess to marry a man who's only a guard. It wouldn't have benefitted our kingdom in any way."

"It would have made you happy," Bastien says quietly.

"Maybe. Or maybe the guilt would have eaten me up if we'd actually managed to run away." Aurelia grimaces. "But that isn't what happened. He always wanted to protect people from Dariu, and when he intervened, the empire's soldiers cut him down. From what the townspeople told us, they were getting pushy with a girl—they'd torn her shirt—and they started shoving her brother around when he spoke up. Then Gavril stepped in…"

She inhales slowly and meets my eyes again. "He should have stayed out of it, just like he should have stayed away from me. But he didn't, and they stabbed him to death. You can't claim you won't face the same fate if you follow me too closely down the path I'm on."

Raul lets out a dismissive sound. "Then we won't follow

too close. Your Accasian guard hadn't spent fifteen years dodging the empire's worst. We know when to keep our mouths shut and our tempers cool." His lips quirk into a smile. "Staying peaceful may not come naturally to me, but all I have to do is think of you for inspiration, and it's not so hard."

"And it was his decision to intervene," I add. *"Just like our actions are our own. You didn't ask him to defend his neighbors any more than you've asked us to defend you."*

Bastien eases closer to Aurelia and sets his hand on her arm. "But we want to. I'd rather be stabbed a hundred times than run off like a coward now that we finally have a chance to make a difference. *You* didn't run away when you had the chance. Give us the same choice."

Aurelia manages a shaky laugh. "When you put it that way, it's hard to argue."

Raul gives her hair a teasing tug. "Then don't."

"All right. No more talk about sending you away. But we do still need to keep our distance." She looks toward the panel. "And I should probably be getting back before anyone can suspect I'm gone."

Bastien's posture pulls a little straighter. "First—I hadn't found the chance to tell you—this afternoon, I came across some records about Prospira's confirmation rite. The written accounts are sparse and leaning more toward poetry than facts, but they mention something about watering the plants from the emperor's body… I think it may require the spilling of your blood."

I wince. Hasn't this woman been wounded enough?

Aurelia's expression barely twitches. "That's helpful to know. I have ways I can prepare for that."

She wavers for a moment, her fingers curling toward her palms at her sides. "I'm not sure we should even speak, at least until that rite is over with. I'll have to judge Marclinus's moods. Sometimes he has seemed as if he's starting to trust me. Please remember that I'm doing this for all of our countries. It's just not always easy to see the best way how."

I swallow hard. *"We know you're doing your best, Rell."*

She aims her sad smile at me again. "I'd better go. Marclinus might wake soon."

We all nod. I suspect my foster brothers are restraining themselves from wrapping her in a final embrace as much as I am.

As Aurelia slips away into the passages, a thicker gloom descends over the entire room. Raul glowers at the lantern on the table, as if it's to blame for our circumstances.

It occurs to me that he has more reasons than just our separation from Aurelia to feel discomforted. Murmurs of rebellious behavior in Lavira have been passing through the court, and Marclinus himself referenced it tonight.

We all know how brutally the empire cracks down on any sign of dissent. My memories of watching Tarquin and his son crush the minor uprising in my own home country summon echoes of that past distress.

I didn't go back to Rione while the fighting was happening, but Tarquin toured around the country with me at his side shortly afterward to remind the kingdom of his authority. The images of the savaged bodies hung from pikes all around the main city square rise up like ghouls in the back of my head.

"You must be worried about your people back home too," I venture.

Raul huffs. "If they're going to be idiots about it, there's not much anyone can do for them."

His brow furrows all the same.

Bastien glances toward the wall our empress vanished through. "So far, Marclinus hasn't taken quite as extreme an approach as I'd have expected. Maybe Aurelia really is already moderating his harsher inclinations."

All at once, I'm twice as choked up as before.

Every time Aurelia tries to nudge our new emperor away from his initial plans, she's putting herself at risk of his wrath. But she's taking that risk for all of us, maybe even more so than herself—for Lavira, for me just tonight when she interrupted my playing.

How much more will she be able to accomplish if she can simply survive long enough to see her hopes through?

Resolve sweeps through me, more potent than the melancholy that gripped my chest just minutes ago. *"She can talk about our safety all she wants, but it's only hers that really matters."*

Bastien studies me. "What do you mean, Lore?"

I ball my hands into fists, speaking through the growing ache in my skull. *"We've hidden our full gifts all this time in case we get a chance to use them against the empire... She could overturn everything we hate about the tyrants. If there's a moment when I have to choose between using my power in a way that might expose it and losing her—I don't care what happens to me. Our old plans, all the secrets, my* life—*protecting her means more than any of it. I'd rather die knowing she'll keep fighting for the future we wanted."*

Raul blinks at me as if startled by my vehemence. Then he raises his own fist in the air between us. "I'll second that vow."

Bastien's mouth curves into a crooked smile. "I can't argue with your logic. To Aurelia and the end of the empire's tyranny."

We knock our fists together like we used to, years ago before all our hopes seemed lost.

CHAPTER NINETEEN

Aurelia

Marclinus's travel arrangements appear to echo his ego. I'd have thought the huge carriage we've set off for Ubetta in was more than enough, with its velvet cushions on the benches, silk curtains by the windows should we want privacy, and gold plates with etchings of the imperial symbols all over the sides from base to roof.

Apparently not. Because a second, even larger carriage hisses across the paved road behind us, enclosed except for a locked door at the back and apparently holding every possession the emperor might wish to access while he's away from the primary imperial palace.

He generously accepted one trunk of my own clothing inside, for my use once we reach Ubetta. For the week of the journey, I'm restricted to the two loaded onto the carriage we're riding in.

Clothes are hardly my biggest concern at the moment,

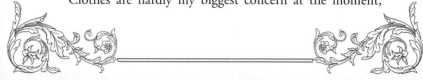

though. I can't help noticing that the color and grain of the polished wooden walls around me and those of the vehicle behind me look like bream cedar. The faint sweetness that seeps through the smell of the varnish makes me queasy.

How many of the Accasians forced into service died just to transport the breamwood logs that created this vehicle down to Dariu? How many were maimed and left destitute on the empire's orders?

It's arduous work and a dangerous journey, which is exactly why no emperor or empress has wanted to send their own citizens up to the wild north to carry it out. Certainly not while they have plenty of conquered subjects they can command instead.

My parents and grandparents and generations of Accasian royals before them have attempted to moderate the breamwood trade as well as they can. We don't have much leverage when too forceful a complaint could be claimed as treason.

An executed ruler does their citizenry no good at all.

There's an Accasian one step from the imperial throne now, though. So many ills I want to heal—I simply have to play my cards right.

I peer out the window at the passing terrain, rolling grassy hills baking beneath the blazing summer sun. My thoughts drift down the line of carriages behind us.

Where in the caravan of court nobles are the foster princes riding? How are they faring since last night's torment?

Those are questions I don't dare ask or even show a hint of while my husband lounges on the bench across from me.

To my relief, Marclinus appears to have simmered down since last night's cruel intensity. He's spent the first few hours of our journey paying more mind to a sheaf of reports and records he's spread out on the cushion next to him than he has to me.

I'm not sure what it'd be safe to say to him, so for now I've kept quiet. We're going to be spending a whole week on the road to the site of the Prospiran confirmation rite. I'll have no shortage of my husband's company.

I can bide my time.

A squadron of cavalry trots at the head of the imperial convoy, with more flanking our carriage. Our personal guards sit on the carriage's outer benches. Kassun is among those riding with us today, and his brief tip of his head to me in respectful acknowledgment heartened me a little.

All the same, memories of the attack during the parade flash back to me at random moments. I mostly keep my composure, letting the flickers of panic wash through me and subside. But when one of the mounted soldiers veers toward my window abruptly, I can't restrain a flinch.

Marclinus's head ticks upward. I brace my hands against the bench to steady myself, and the soldier doesn't even glance my way. She was only dodging a large rock on the field close to the road. After a moment, she eases farther away from our carriage again.

My husband studies me. "Axius vetted the full military host personally. He wouldn't have risen to the top of our military ranks if he didn't know what he's doing—and he's aware I'll have his head if there's another attack."

I offer a sheepish smile. "I know. But being certain of a thing in your head and convincing your bodily instincts of it are rather different matters, aren't they?"

Marclinus's lips curve slightly upward in return. "I suppose you have a point. It does remind me, though—I had something forged for you…"

He digs through the small trunk by our feet and retrieves a slim knife. The sheath gleams with a trim of intricately carved gold, but the grip is covered in smooth leather, and the entire weapon is barely longer than my hand.

Marclinus hands it to me. "I gathered from what I heard of your combat lesson that you prefer a discreet blade. It does seem suitable for a woman who prefers not to fight at all. Still, you should be able to take some comfort that you can defend yourself if need be."

I draw the blade from the sheath and turn the knife experimentally in the air. It's light enough not to strain my wrist but maintains a heft that reassures me it can get the job done. My fingers fit perfectly around the grip.

My husband wasn't even present for my one lesson so far, but he's observed me closely enough to specify a weapon utterly suited to me.

"Thank you," I say, with a mix of gratitude and apprehension. And then, because I doubt I'll get a better opening than this one, "Do you think I need to fear attack from parties within our own court?"

Marclinus cocks his head. "What do you mean?"

I motion vaguely toward the procession of carriages behind us. "You seemed concerned about your foster brothers' loyalties. Have you seen any reason to believe they pose a threat? Should I be particularly on my guard around them?"

My husband's gaze lingers on me a beat longer than is comfortable before he replies. "If I had evidence that they were working against me, I'd have already eliminated the threat. I simply thought it was wise to remind them who holds the power in the empire, even if they're royalty at home."

If he had ulterior motives regarding my reactions, he clearly isn't going to admit as much.

I can't risk my concern for the princes bringing more

harm down on them. What can I say that would sound like a woman considering them a problem rather than allies?

I rub my chin thoughtfully. "I suppose they do seem to keep to themselves rather than mingling much with the rest of the court. That sort of detachment is a little concerning. If they were going to conspire together, they'd have plenty of opportunity."

Marclinus leans back in his seat, his fingers tracing over the hilt the dagger sheathed at his own hip. "You raise a reasonable point, wife. How would a dedicat of Elox propose we address that concern?"

How indeed?

I make a show of pondering, my mind racing through the possibilities. I need something that would deflect suspicion without disturbing my secret lovers more than necessary.

"Perhaps they need to be prodded to integrate more with the rest of the court," I suggest. "Have them spend the rest of the journey to Ubetta apart, riding with different groups of nobles. If they come to see your allies as friends, so much the better. And your allies could inform you if they notice any seditious inclinations."

Marclinus laughs. "I don't know how friendly my nobles will be to *them*, but the gist of your strategy has merit. It's possible my father was too lenient on them, allowing them to shun the rest of us when they took a mind to. Let them shun each other for a little while. I like it."

That isn't how I'd have put it, but his approval settles my nerves. His expression has relaxed, no more hawk-eyed stare.

The sooner he trusts my advice, the sooner I may be able to sway him in the directions I actually want.

On the second morning of the trek, Marclinus glances around as we're heading back to our carriage with a jaunty air. "I fear we'll become boring if we spend too much time just the two of us, wife. Why don't we pick a few companions to share our carriage until lunchtime?"

He doesn't even wait for my response before waving toward Bianca at one of the other carriages. "Vicerine Bianca, I'd enjoy your company for the morning. Ah, and Marchionissa Pontelle, I'm sure you'll offer lively conversation as well."

His gaze slides back to me, his gray eyes glinting. Waiting to see who I'll suggest.

Is he still thinking about the princes—wondering whether I'll take an excuse to spend time with them under the cover of the strategy I put forward yesterday?

I'm not that much of an idiot.

I catch sight of Raul standing by one of the carriages with a few of the other nobles and twitch my hand at my side in a subtle gesture of apology. His gaze passes over me as if he's barely noticed me, but he gives a brief nod a moment later.

Who here can I safely invite who won't make me feel as if I've asked a viper on board? I cast my attention farther and spot a couple of ladies who recently arrived for a stint at court—two baronissas married to each other.

I turn back to Marclinus. "Why not Baronissas Damina and Hivette? I haven't had much chance to get to know them yet."

And given their romantic inclinations, I may be spared watching my husband paw at *four* other ladies in front of me rather than just one or two.

Marclinus shows no sign of disappointment. "An excellent gathering. Let them join us, and we'll be on our way."

As Bianca climbs into the carriage after me, she shoots

me a crooked smile that looks apologetic. I offer one in return that I hope shows I don't resent her presence.

It isn't as if anyone can refuse the emperor, even if she would have wanted to.

"I hope you're well," I say politely, remembering our fraught conversation over my cauldron.

She bobs her head a little more emphatically than is necessary. "Quite, thank you, Your Imperial Highness."

Then Marclinus is clambering after us and tucking his hand over her thigh, and all I can do is watch and chatter as if this is the life I always dreamed of.

On the third day, as we partake of the lunch prepared at one of the waystations along the road, Counsel Etta and Cleric Pierus approach the imperial carriage. Marclinus has opted for boredom after yesterday's socializing, so there's plenty of room when he motions them inside.

Etta brushes her hands together and gets straight to the point, her close-set eyes fixing on me. "Your Imperial Highness, I gather you're intending to participate in Prospira's rite as you did Estera's?"

I sit up straighter and set aside the roll I was eating. "I am."

Are they making preparations now? We still have a few more days before we're even near the temple where the rite takes place.

Pierus purses his lips and looks at Marclinus as if he expects the other man to weigh in. My husband merely waits with a mild expression for them to go on.

The cleric seems to decide it's better to focus directly on me. "You may find this rite more… demanding than Estera's.

I wouldn't want you to put yourself in an uncomfortable situation."

I can't tell whether he's truly worried about my wellbeing or making up an excuse to ensure the sole focus is on his emperor.

"You could explain what's involved, and then I'll be prepared for whatever it'll require from me," I say.

Marclinus tsks at me before his advisors need to say anything. "You know that advance knowledge is reserved solely for those of the imperial line, Aurelia. If you're concerned that you won't be able to face the challenge without it, you'd be better off sitting this one out."

The last thing I want is to appear cowardly or insecure in front of him. "I have all faith that I can earn Prospira's approval as I did Estera's. I was simply hoping to address the worries it appears Cleric Pierus has."

My husband raises his eyebrows at the cleric. "I think she has you there."

Pierus's round face reddens. "I don't mean to diminish Your Imperial Highness's abilities. It is already irregular for the imperial consort to participate—we have to think through every eventuality."

Etta clears her throat. "It's our job to be on guard against any circumstance that might diminish the emperor and his associates in the eyes of the larger public."

I meet her gaze steadily, even though my stomach has twisted. "Then I'll make sure to confront the task with all the strength and courage they'd expect from the imperial family. My goal is to increase the confidence of the public and set their minds at ease. I won't let myself fail."

Marclinus has drawn his dagger. He spins it between his fingers as he sometimes likes to do as he's thinking. "I would never criticize your strength, wife. But if I tell the people to respect you, they will."

Like the soldier who tried to stab me did? Like my own guard muttering insults in the palace gardens?

Etta tries again. "There will be more pressure with such a large audience. It may be harder to maintain your composure."

While I bleed to water a plant, as Bastien determined might be the case? How much more is there to this rite?

It doesn't matter. I've committed to this course, and I have too many people to prove myself to before I'll be more than a pretty doll on the emperor's arm.

"I'm no stranger to crowds. I promise I won't embarrass myself or my husband." I glance at Marclinus. "And I feel respect earned directly is more valuable than that which is demanded."

"Reasonable enough." He points his dagger toward his advisors. "It appears my wife's mind is set. Why shouldn't more people beyond our court get to witness her commitment? I look forward to the demonstration myself."

He aims a grin at me so fierce my skin starts to crawl.

No matter what this trial brings, I cannot fail.

CHAPTER TWENTY

Aurelia

Midway through the fourth day of our journey, clouds swallow the sunlight. By the time we're preparing to set off again after lunch, raindrops drum on the carriage roof.

Marclinus grimaces at the ceiling with an overdramatic shudder. "If I have to listen to that racket the entire afternoon, I'll go mad." He leans toward the window and snaps his fingers at the guards stationed nearby. "Someone get Prince Bastien over here."

My heart sinks. I scramble to think of some way to dissuade my husband from this course, but I can't come up with any reason I believe he'll consider to spare Bastien the strain.

Bastien trudges over through the rain, his damp-darkened hair bringing out the deep green of his eyes.

"You called on me, Your Imperial Majesty?" he says evenly.

He must already be able to guess what this summons is about.

Marclinus gestures for him to get in with us. "Sit and use that gift of yours to clear off this horrible weather. Perhaps you can entertain us with some conversation as well afterward. All these days on the road do get awfully dreary, don't they?"

"Indeed." Bastien bobs his head to me with an impassive expression and clambers inside. Since naturally Marclinus isn't giving up room on his bench if he doesn't have to, I scoot over to make space.

It seems expected enough that I'd watch the prince of Cotea as he works his magic. I've never seen it done, after all.

I school my own expression into one of mild curiosity, tamping down the more avid interest and concern that both clamor inside me. Curling my fingers against the urge to grasp Bastien's hand in support.

While the prince focuses on the storm clouds beyond the window, Marclinus calls over one of the barons to join our ride as well. The carriage sets off with a hiss of the wheels over the wet road.

Marclinus frowns at Bastien, but the prince's face is so tensed with concentration that I don't think he even notices. The drumming on the roof slows. A streak of sunlight beams across the nearby fields.

My eyes widen in spite of myself. I yank them away from Bastien to peer out the window on my side.

The darkest clouds are drifting away across the sky, off behind us where they won't trouble us farther down the road either. Even the fluffier ones above are thinning into little puffs of white.

He's really managing it. He's using his gift to blow an

entire rainstorm away. I can't hear the warble of the wind from all the way down here, but I make out little eddies amid the tufts of cloud.

I knew he was capable of it—he's known for that gift, after all. But no one else realizes what it really takes out of him, how much directed effort it requires to channel his actual gift into this purpose.

When my gaze slides back to Bastien, my pulse stutters. Other than a few reddish blotches, his skin has sallowed like it did after I branded him. His jaw has clenched. When he drags in a breath, an audible wheeze carries from his chest.

My thoughts dart to my tea box and the brew I made to ease his single lung before, but it's stashed away in one of the tightly packed trunks. Marclinus turns to the baron and makes a wry comment about the contents of our lunch as if his superficial request hasn't worn his foster brother ragged.

I swallow thickly and hold my tongue. I don't dare show much concern of my own and provoke my husband's suspicions.

Listening to Marclinus and his friend, I manage to interject a couple of comments of my own as if I'm engaged by their conversation. My attention lingers on the prince at the edge of my vision.

After a spell of sitting silently other than his raspy breaths, Bastien's posture gradually relaxes. The rattle eases from his chest.

It might look equally odd if I ignore him entirely. And I do actually welcome the chance to learn more about the steadfast man I've fallen for.

I wait another few minutes before I judge it won't add too much strain for him to talk. "I understand you asked for your gift with rain mainly to summon it rather than repel it. Droughts are a significant problem in Cotea?"

Marclinus's eyes flick toward us. I keep my smile subdued, as if I'm only looking to make polite conversation.

Bastien tips his head, looking toward the window as if he could see his home country from here through the renewed sunlight. "You wouldn't think so with the Seafell Channel all along our border. But the flatlands in the northeast don't see much rain naturally. I think it worsened with the leaving of the All-Giver. And since the conflict with the western countries, some of the streams and rivers have been diverted into canals to better serve the fortresses closer to the border."

He speaks carefully, not indicating any judgment over those decisions, but I can judge them myself from what he's said. The Darium empire has put a significant strain on his people's resources for their selfish ambitions.

Marclinus clicks his tongue. "Anyone there has the whole rest of the country to move to. It's their own choice to be stubborn."

Bastien looks as if he's bitten back a sharp remark. His next words come out even more measured. "There are farmlands up there it'd be difficult to abandon. But we make do as best we can."

Does Cotea produce some crop that the empire demands as it does Accasy's breamwood? I wouldn't be surprised.

"Your people can take comfort that their ruling family cares enough to take on gifts and the necessary sacrifices on their behalf," I say.

Bastien's mouth ticks with a hint of a smile. "That's kind of you to say, Your Imperial Highness."

I wish I could pour enough of my admiration on him to spark a proper grin, but my husband is still following our discussion with interest. It feels wisest to shift my attention back to Marclinus. "Is drought a concern in any part of Dariu?"

Let him believe I care about nothing more than I do his

own country. Let him only see the most willing and devoted of wives, while my heart aches for the men who are everything he's not.

It's getting late in the afternoon on our fifth day of travel when the convoy comes to a sudden halt.

Marclinus frowns and leans toward the window. Before he needs to holler for an explanation, High Commander Axius appears outside, his graying hair rumpled and his eyes steely.

"Your Imperial Majesty, we've been reached by a messenger from Lavira. I think you should hear the news immediately."

The way he focuses only on Marclinus as if I'm not even in the carriage feels pointed to me. Perhaps Marclinus gets the same impression, because he beckons the high commander inside. "Come in, and we can keep moving while we talk. You can say whatever you need to in front of your empress as well."

Axius has the decency to look mildly chagrinned. "Of course, Your Imperial Majesty." He nods to me as he climbs inside. I slide over so he can sit across from Marclinus for easier conversation.

I can't really complain about the intrusion. I'll take the rigid military man over the guffawing, fawning nobles Marclinus normally invites to ride with us any day. Especially if it means staying abreast of the news from Lavira.

Marclinus gestures out the window, and the convoy lurches back into motion. He fixes his gaze intently on Axius. "What's going on in Lavira now?"

"We've had word directly from Tribune Valerisse," Axius says. "She was the most senior officer stationed nearby, and she's been heading the investigations and military response. The sabotage has escalated. A fire was set at a larger fort near the city of Daviro—it was caught before any soldiers were lost, but it burned through the stables first and destroyed several horses. Two days ago when she wrote the missive, it appears tainted food was brought to another fort near Rodrige. Most of the soldiers fell ill—so severely a few had already passed from the poison at the time of the letter."

A shiver races under my skin. It does sound like a larger rebellion is brewing, one mainly concerned with doing all the damage it can surreptitiously rather than facing the enemy head on. Which I can hardly blame the Lavirians for, but if there are no clear culprits for the empire to punish, it's likely many innocent lives will be ruined in their conquest for revenge.

Marclinus touches on that subject immediately. "Have any of the perpetrators been apprehended?"

The high commander shakes his head. "Not with any certainty. The workers responsible for delivering the most recent batch of food were interrogated, but they claimed to be unaware of the tampering or who might be responsible. They were executed for either collusion or incompetence, either of which did equal harm."

Already, people who might have been perfectly loyal subjects have been killed over this mess. I wince inwardly.

"Someone must have *some* idea who's lashing out at the empire," Marclinus says. "We can hardly execute the entire country just to make sure we eliminate the dissenters."

"Yes, of course. Tribune Valerisse mentioned that she's beginning a broader swath of interrogations and putting pressure on the locals in the vicinity of the incidents to give up information. She promises she won't relent until she's uncovered the traitors." Axius pats the leather satchel at his side. "I'll be sending a message back to her by our swiftest messenger. I wanted to know if you have any additional orders for her."

Marclinus hums. "Give me an hour to think on it, and I'll speak to you again when we stop for dinner."

The high commander dips his head in acceptance. With another wave out the window, Marclinus halts the convoy just long enough for Axius to return to his post overseeing the cavalry.

As soon as the horses press on, my husband shifts his attention to me. "You took all that news in. I suppose you'd say we should ply the possible collaborators with gifts and favors rather than beat them into submission."

The dry edge to his voice tells me exactly what he'd think of such a suggestion, but his tone is light enough that I don't think he's outright disparaging my opinion. He's inviting me to offer something different.

He could have settled into his thoughts and made up his mind on his own, but he *wants* to hear what I'll say.

My spirits leap at the opportunity. I still have to play it cautious and within the bounds of what I think he'll be willing to accept, but that doesn't mean I can't steer his response in a direction that's a little less brutal.

"You poke fun at my peaceful mindset," I reply, equally light. "I certainly don't believe in rewarding criminals or those who may be concealing them. There's quite a range of options between the lax extreme you laid out and having your soldiers torturing hundreds of Lavirians who may honestly hold no resentment toward the empire at all—at least, not before the torture."

Marclinus tucks himself into the corner of the carriage and folds his hands on his chest, as if he's about to take a nap at a picnic. But his cool eyes stay trained on my face. "Why don't you illuminate me on some of the options you see, wife?"

A prickling sensation runs up the back of my neck with the impression that this is yet another test, but it's one I've been angling for.

How can I focus him on strategies that'll hurt as few people as possible—and hopefully calm down the rebels until I can offer the whole country a better future?

I smooth my fingers over my skirt. "As one point, I don't think offering rewards is an absurd idea—if it's to the right people. You want to protect *your* people who are stationed in Lavira. Offering bonuses and other advantages to the local workers who've continued to serve other forts and outposts well would help ensure their continued loyalty and give them more incentive to distance themselves from the uprising."

"I can see the value of that step. But we do still need to turn up the traitors, ideally before they do much more damage."

I rub my mouth while I think it over, and inspiration sparks. But as I turn the tactic over, I'm not sure I'll be able to convince Marclinus of the wisdom in it if it comes straight from me. He might even suspect me of supporting the local monarchy over his own authority out of my sympathy as a fellow conquered royal.

Can I lead him to strike on the idea apparently by himself?

My heart thumps faster, but I will my voice to stay even. "I'd imagine the biggest problem is that when it comes to the Lavirian citizens who are inclined to lash out, they already see anyone from Dariu as an intruder and a threat. Having Darium soldiers hurt them will only convince them that they're right. I wonder what they're hoping to see happen if they *could* drive the imperial forces out of the country?"

Marclinus snorts. "Presumably they imagine rulership will become the sole domain of the Lavirian royal family. As if the past centuries of their line have any true experience with what it takes to keep even a single country in line."

I shake my head as if in derision. "If they think their local rulers would never make decisions they disagree with, they'd be in for a harsh awakening even if they got their wish. So much unearned trust. No one can govern a country through kindness alone."

"Indeed." His gaze goes briefly distant. "They do have quite a bit of trust in their fellow Lavirians of whatever status, if only in contrast to Dariu. There are still plenty of Lavirian soldiers we monitor, but none of *their* bases of operation have been attacked."

He's already thinking along the lines I hoped. I knit my brow. "What are those soldiers doing while their countrymen harm their supposed allies?"

"Not enough, clearly." Marclinus pushes himself off the wall, an eager light coming into his pale face. "But they could be. Would you object to threats and torture if it was Lavirians carrying it out against each other, my pacifist?"

I swallow a smile. "I prefer to avoid violence when possible, but when it's necessary… I'd say the native forces would be more likely to determine who the real dissidents are, wouldn't they? And more likely to convince those in the know to reveal information without having to crack down unduly hard. And why shouldn't the supposed rulers of Lavira take responsibility for rooting out their own traitors?"

Raul's family will also be able to cover up the rebellion if they see the chance—carry out strategic punishments of the worst offenders, convince those less committed to temper their aggressions. Whereas if the Darium forces handle the situation, they'll conduct a full-out slaughter without consideration of the nuances.

"A very good question," Marclinus mutters. "I think my father would have approved of making them take care of their own mess. And if any of the local contingents balk at intervening, then we'll know they're equally traitorous."

"Yet another benefit." May it not come to that.

My husband pauses and studies me even more closely than before. His mouth slants at a wry angle. "You won't harbor sour feelings over us setting Lavira's royals on their own? If you have some objection, I'd rather hear it now than after the thing is done, even if I can't say I'll change my mind."

I hold his gaze steadily. "I think it's a brilliant strategy, quite worthy of an emperor—a balance of cleverness and strength, immediate impact and recognition of long-term consequences. I understand that any revolt must be stamped out. I simply hate the thought of inciting a worse conflict rather than taking the quickest route to peace."

Another grin flashes across Marclinus's face, warmer than I'd have expected. "If we both like it, then it must be brilliant. Patience is worthwhile if it means getting more effective results in the end. And I'll see that your suggestion about rewarding those we've been able to count on is passed on as well."

I tip into a shallow bow, letting a smile cross my own lips at least. "I'm glad you found my thoughts useful, husband. It's a pleasure to strategize alongside you."

The more I can weave my influence into these conversations, the closer I'll be to truly winning the empire.

CHAPTER TWENTY-ONE

Aurelia

The palace on the outskirts of Ubetta doesn't loom nearly as large as the immense marble building in the capital city, but the sprawling two-story structure still takes my breath away. The pale gray walls glow in the late morning sun with a silvery shimmer that highlights the intricate carvings of figures and foliage decorating them.

As I stare at the spectacle from the carriage window, I have to catch my jaw to stop it from going slack.

A knowing smirk crosses Marclinus's lips. "Wait until you see the inside. The imperial chambers are just as impressive as you've gotten used to, and there are a couple of extra benefits here as well."

When the carriage rolls to a stop, we wait for a footman to open it before stepping out. Marclinus offers an exuberant wave to several of the other disembarking nobles before leading me up the front steps himself. A few pages scurry along behind us, clutching the trunks we were riding with.

My husband strides past golden sculptures and delicate mosaics, glittering chandeliers and paintings enchanted to ripple with movement. We continue down the main hallway, up a staircase, and around a couple of corners into the farthest west wing.

There, he motions me past a gilded door into a vast room with fine marlwood furniture, a thick rug that caresses my feet, and broad windows reinforced with wrought-iron bars —detailed with flowers and vines, but clearly intended for security over décor.

As the pages set down my trunks behind us, Marclinus strides to the window closest to the silk-draped bedframe. He unbolts the sturdy lock and pushes the double panes wide.

They rustle the leaves on the low branches of a tree growing just outside. Pale yellow fruit dangle amid those branches.

Marclinus leans out to twist one off. "Apparently a distant empress—my great-great-great-grandmother or some such—loved pears, so she had a few trees planted along the outer wall here." He flips the fruit playfully in his hand and then tosses it to me. "You can have them fresh without leaving your room."

While he grabs another for himself, I take a tentative bite. The pear's flesh is tart and chewy but invigoratingly sweet. "They are good."

Marclinus shoots me another grin. "Don't fill up on too many before lunch. The staff always prepares quite a feast whenever the court is back in residence. Then we'll be off to see our people and earn that blessing from Prospira."

He saunters out of the room, leaving me alone.

I ask one of the pages to bring a pot of boiled water and sprinkle the leaves of my best calming brew into a teacup. As

I sip the steeped liquid, the bittersweet warmth trickles through my nerves like a balm.

After several days of being shut up in a confined space with my husband for nearly every waking hour, simply existing on my own feels like a miracle.

The air in the room is a bit stuffy, but a pleasant breeze drifts through the open window. I open the others partway to encourage more airflow before returning to my trunks to confirm that all my most important possessions are in order.

We're only going to be here for a matter of days, but I may need my full brewing apparatus. And there's one particular concoction, cooled into a solid tablet that I slip into the pouch at my hip, that I'll want before this afternoon's confirmation rite.

My gaze lingers on the offering bowl tucked away in one corner of the trunk. The urge itches at me to lay out some tidbit for whatever daimon might still be roaming through Dariu for whatever luck their good will can bring me.

But I'm trying to keep my husband as happy with me as possible. I already know the Darium nobles look down on the practice of appealing to the spirit creatures that flit through our world.

I have to keep making my own luck.

I'm just closing the trunk lid when something rattles against one of the window frames. As I hesitate, the sound is followed by another brisk tap.

I ease over to the window and peek outside.

Beyond the pear tree branches, a familiar figure stands in the grounds below, dressed in an emerald-green shirt that sets off his dark skin and black hair to impressive effect.

Lorenzo has positioned himself in profile, his face turned to the side as if he's paying no attention to the palace at all, but he's clearly watching for my arrival. When I step closer to

the window to bring myself into view, his fingers twist at his
side in a series of swift gestures.

*We're here if you need us. Lower floor, around the corner.
Bastien two over, me five, Raul nine.*

His hand relaxes, and he ambles off as if to explore the
gardens. An ache forms at the base of my throat.

Even when we're forced to keep our distance, he wants
me to know I can count on them.

In line with the priorities of its neighboring temple, the city
of Ubetta looks like a haven of growth and abundance. As
our procession weaves through the wide streets, we pass
building after building constructed partly out of living
plants: wooden walls merged with blooming trees, roofs of
woven vine still sprouting leaves.

On every corner, a tree bearing one sort of fruit or
another shades the street, although most of their current
yield looks unripe.

At a couple, children clamber through the branches
checking the bounty while their parents examine the lower
boughs. Hope lights in their pinched faces when one of the
kids tosses down a ruddy apple.

From their scruffy clothes and skinny bodies, I'm
guessing they rely on the public trees to supplement their
meals. How do they fare when the growing season is over?

They pause to wave to the imperial carriage, not letting
their hunger distract them from the awe of seeing their ruler
in person. Marclinus grins and waves back.

Does he even notice that their lives must be far from
plentiful?

The closer we get to the Temple of Fruitful Fields, the

more locals swarm the streets. Cheers rise up while those farther back bob on their toes for a better view.

Beyond the city's edge, stark rocky mountains rise in the distance to the east. But the landscape around the temple is all verdant fields true to its name.

Like much of the city, the temple itself stands as part of four towering oaks with windows tucked into the corners of branches, rustling leaves sheltering the roof. The walls built between the grand trees echo Prospira's promise of abundance with carvings of flowers and food, bounding rabbits and milk-heavy cows.

As the cleric of the temple leads Marclinus and I around the living structure, murmurs flow through the air after us. An even larger crowd of locals continues to gather around us to watch the confirmation rite.

Most have drawn close around the ceremonial site behind the temple. Like the setting for the Esterean rite, this one takes place in a wide hollow so those watching have a clear view as they peer down at us.

But Prospira isn't interested in mazes. The godlen of fertility and harvest watches over a swath of dark-leafed plants that blanket the bottom of the hollow, their viny stems winding around each other. I can't make out a speck of the earth beneath them.

I still don't know exactly how the rite is going to work, but as the cleric motions to an ornate altar set up at the far edge of the hollow, I pop my concocted tablet into my mouth. An acrid flavor seeps over my tongue as I chew a few times and swallow.

The ingredients I combined should dampen any pain I experience in the next couple of hours. The effect won't be immediate, but I didn't want to risk ingesting it too early. I have to wait for Marclinus to go first, after all.

The cleric lifts his arms toward the gathered people.

"Many ages ago when the gods walked our lands, Prospira traveled through this region. The people of Ubetta went out of their way to offer her good food and comforts even though many had little to spare. As her thanks to us, she saw this temple founded and blessed us with our most sacred plant. Now our emperor and empress will both follow in her path."

He sweeps his hand to indicate the mass of vegetation beneath us and hands Marclinus a gold-rimmed basket. "Goldglobe requires great care and worship to grow well, but when it produces fruit, every one contains all the nourishment a grown man requires for a week. You will walk through the goldglobe field, nourishing it in turn with the waters of your body as you expect to nourish all Dariu's people during your rule. When you have collected ten of the melons, you will present them in Prospira's honor on her altar above."

That sounds simple enough. I watch to see how the cleric will arrange the blood-letting, but he makes no further move toward Marclinus. Instead, he sets off around the rim of the hollow to meet his emperor at the altar.

Marclinus shrugs off the thin purple robe of embroidered silk he was wearing, which a page darts over to collect. Beneath, he has on one of the typical billowy Darium shirts, but breeches that only drop to his knees. He's left his upper calves bare above tall leather boots of light beige.

An inkling passes through my head of what this might signify. A chill tickles down my spine.

My husband strides down the slope of the hollow with total confidence, which of course he'd have when he's been properly outfitted for this task. He takes only a moment to gaze at the field of goldglobe plants before he marches on into their midst.

Those boots must have been tailored specifically for this test. The highest leaves reach just above the leather rim.

They slice across Marclinus's bare shins, drawing scarlet lines in his milky skin. The color of the boots immediately makes sense as the blood dribbles down the leather surface toward the earth.

He wants everyone to see what he's sacrificing for this rite, the red standing out starkly against the pale material.

Those scratches can't hurt all that much, though. As Marclinus walks on, blood continues to trickle over his boots, but only a few more leaves scrape over his flesh. Most of them simply drag across the leather without doing more than smearing the blood, drawing the blotches larger.

I flex my toes within my typical leather slippers—which aren't specially made and don't even reach my ankle bones. The chill has condensed in my chest.

I can't back down now, not when my participation has already been announced, not in front of all these people whose hearts and minds I need to win. I've bled in Marclinus's trials before.

At least this time, it'll be for a purpose I'm happier to serve.

Marclinus dips down here and there to pluck one of the melons off the plants. The bright yellow globes fill his entire hand with long fingers splayed. More red lines dapple his knuckles and wrists with each acquisition.

His confident smile never leaves his face. He knows how to put on a show—I'll give him that.

He barely veers from his straight course across the vast patch of greenery. When he reaches the opposite side with a heap of ten melons in his basket, he hefts it high with two blood-streaked hands and carries it up the far slope like a trophy. Once he's set it on the altar, he bows to the cleric with a dramatic flourish.

My heart is thudding hard enough to drown out the

words she says accepting his completion of the task. The crowd around the ceremony site cheers.

As the cleric calls out for the empress to join her as well, one of the temple devouts pushes a matching basket into my hands.

Here I go.

Sucking in a deep breath, I tread down the slope toward the goldglobe. The skirt of my dress ripples around my legs.

I did choose well in one element of my attire. I went with Eloxian white to emphasize peace and security—and so that the blood I spill will stand out against it. The crimson will bloom even more brightly on the silk than it did Marclinus's beige leather.

With my first step into the mass of vines, I hold the faint hope in the back of my head that my enchanted clothing will offer some protection. It only takes a couple of paces to realize the full extent of my predicament.

The leaves etch little cuts into my legs from my ankles to just below my knees, tearing the silk of my skirt as they do. The magical protections woven into the fabric must only work against blades of metal, not natural vegetation.

Or maybe no magic at all could fend off this god-blessed plant.

The sharp edges also score the supple leather of my shoes. Marclinus's boots must have been made of tougher stuff. Within another couple of steps, the first prick of a leaf slices right through the sole into my heel.

Pain radiates up my thighs, dulled by the suppressant I ingested but still potent enough to niggle at my nerves. Gods only know how awful I'd feel if I *hadn't* taken my own small precaution.

Scarlet splotches spread across the white fabric around my legs. The silk sticks to the wounds and detaches with every swing of my feet across the ground. A fresh sting emanates with every movement.

I breathe slow and even, casting my gaze across the dark green vegetation in search of those brilliantly yellow globes so aptly named.

Marclinus seemed to find his easily enough. He must have picked all the ripe melons growing close to the middle of the field.

A gleam of yellow catches my eye, and I veer toward it, restraining a wince as more leaves rake across my flesh like tiny claws. Inside, I sink my focus into the serene space I hold tight at my core.

Elox, stay with me. Let me meet this challenge with all my composure. Let me see it through to the end.

The growing ache in my limbs turns my breath ragged. I bend down, set my jaw at the prick of the leaves across my fingers, and yank out one melon.

Another lies close by—a minor boon. I detach that one too and glimpse another farther on.

With more and more blood streaming through my skirt and onto the ground, I follow a weaving path across the patch, following the melons that present themselves. Never letting myself stray too far from the altar waiting for me up ahead.

When I straighten up after retrieving my fifth melon, my head swims with dizziness. I stiffen my posture against the sensation, managing not to sway.

Curse it all. I didn't expect to be offering up *this* much of myself in the rite.

The effects of the tablet might dull the pain, but it won't bolster my strength while I drain myself quite literally of life.

Keep going. As quickly and efficiently as possible. Even if my vision blurs for a second as I scan the clumps of leaves for another glint of yellow.

My hands feel as if they're going numb. The sixth melon slides in my bleeding fingers. A burn sears into my calves, flaring hotter with each swipe of my tattered skirts.

As I reach for the seventh fruit, a sharper wave of dizziness rushes over me. I nearly tip right over face-first into the leaves.

My stomach lurches, and I manage to catch my balance by jamming my hand into the mass of leaves. More jabs pierce my palm.

I wrench myself upward, cradling the basket against the middle of my belly so it doesn't tip me to one side or the other.

One step. Another step. Suppress a shudder at the liquid coursing over my raw skin.

Then a voice slides into my head, soft and faint but clear. *"You can do this, Rell. You're almost there. A medic's waiting for you by the altar. I know you can make it that far."*

It's Lorenzo. He's risking using his illusionary magic not far from Marclinus's guards to help boost my spirits.

"The next melon is just a couple of steps ahead of you. I'll be right here with you the whole time."

My body still feels shaky, but my spirits rise. I push onward with all the vigor I have in me.

The eighth fruit. Two more to go.

"One day when all this is done, I'll take you back to Rione. We'll sit on one of the palace terraces and look out over the turquoise sea in the most refreshing breeze. We'll eat coconut jam and pastries and fish fried so fresh it melts in your mouth."

He's drawing a picture for me, a place where I can escape the worst of the pain. I wrap the image around me as I trudge onward to the ninth melon.

There. I'm almost at the edge of the patch.

I only need one more.

My ragged shoes squish beneath my feet, soaked through with my blood. I pause, and the whole world blurs around me.

Lorenzo's projected voice wavers. A strain creeps into his tone as it fades, but he keeps going. *"All the gods will be on your side, Rell. You can beat Marclinus at his own game. Keep coming back to me."*

Great God only knows how much effort it's taking him to concentrate it solely on me across the distance, ensuring no one else picks up on even a trace of the illusion. How much longer will he be able to speak like that before he wears himself out completely?

He's not letting himself falter. I have to push on too.

I swallow hard, and my sight sharpens just enough for me to notice a yellow sheen right near the edge of the patch. I shuffle toward it with all the strength I can summon.

As I set the tenth melon into the basket, an eager murmuring ripples through the watching crowd. I'd almost forgotten they were there. So much for the pressure of an audience that Etta and Pierus were worried about.

Leaving the biting leaves behind, I slog up the hill. Every footfall jars loose more pain.

But here's the medic in her white robes waiting for me. Here's the Prospiran cleric in his of yellow, welcoming me to the altar with open arms.

As I set the basket down next to Marclinus's, the healer is already grasping my hands. With a pulse of her healing magic, the cuts there seal. She bends down to extend her ability to my legs.

With the flow of soothing energy, my flagging strength revives.

The cleric pours a bucket of water over my basket to wash the fruit clean as well. Beyond her, Marclinus is grinning fiercely, as if he'd find it even more fun to toss me back into the mass of leaves and watch me thrash around in them.

I don't want him to win. Not even in this one rite.

He completed it much more gracefully than I did, but I can show how deeply I understand Prospira's wishes for the world—wishes this callously selfish man would never consider for anyone except himself.

I reach for my basket again. "I'd like to honor our godlen of abundance in one more way."

The cleric blinks at me but nods. "As you wish, Your Imperial Highness."

Marclinus makes a startled sound and opens his mouth as if to interrupt me, but I speak first, loud enough for my voice to ring out over the crowd. "I give this one goldglobe melon to Prospira."

I set one of the melons on the altar. Then, clutching the basket, I step toward the watching civilians beyond the ring of guards protecting our spot by the altar.

"These fruits should nourish those who need it most. You know your neighbors better than I do. Which families in Ubetta are most in need of an extra meal? Who's been struggling to make ends meet? Let them be blessed by Prospira's bounty today."

Awed eyes stared back at me. Urgent conversations break out throughout the mass of figures.

"Volmus and Sirena should have one to share with their children," someone hollers to a chorus of agreement. The spectators nudge the couple toward the guards.

I offer one of the melons, and the woman hugs it to her chest. "Thank you," she says, abruptly teary.

I choke up a little myself before I manage to raise my voice again. "Who else needs a helping hand to live as they should? I have eight more to offer, and I want to see them given where Prospira's help is needed most. Let us all live the happiest and most plentiful lives we can!"

Eager applause reverberates through the crowd alongside more shouted suggestions of the deserving, and I know I've truly confirmed myself as their empress today.

CHAPTER TWENTY-TWO

Raul

Lively music flows through the sunlit fields outside the palace walls. Thousands of Darium citizens from Ubetta and the neighboring towns have flooded the terrain, chattering and laughing, waving streamers of imperial purple and hollering the emperor's praises.

But not only the emperor's. As I've prowled along the edges of the area cordoned off for the court nobles' use, I've heard nearly as many voices calling out blessings and gratitude to Empress Aurelia.

Every time, I have to hold my expression in its careful nonchalance, as much as I'd like to grin. The buoyant enthusiasm for the woman I adore—the devotion she deserves from everyone whose life she touches—has nearly washed away the horrific images of her clambering through that patch of vicious vines two days ago.

Her whole dress was splattered scarlet by the end. It took

all my self-control not to charge in and carry her up the side of the damned hollow rather than watching her swaying steps.

I may be tutoring her in combat, but I'm learning all kinds of lessons from her in the patience my parents fretted I'd never be capable of.

She still managed to give off a perfectly serene air as she handed over most of her collected bounty to the needy families whose neighbors called them forward. She looked like a godlen brought to life—a moving, breathing manifestation of the divinity of peace.

I already knew she was incredible, but watching that demonstration, I could believe she really will conquer the entire empire through the sheer goodness of her heart. Clearly an awful lot of Darium's common folk were equally affected.

Even now, in a new airy dress of dove gray, she's standing at the edge of the imperial area, beaming at a couple who've approached and resting her hand briefly on their young daughter's head as if in benediction. Her guards remain poised on either side, braced to leap in at any sign of threat, but Aurelia shows no sign of concern.

This is the role she's meant to fulfill. Not a lesser princess bullied and tormented at the emperor's whim, but a ruler in her own right, one who leads through respect and honor rather than brutality.

A few months ago, I'd have said that idea was a fanciful dream. Now…

Even though I can't risk ambling close enough to hear her words, even though I may never get to caress her skin or summon her sighs again, more faith is stirring in my chest than I've felt in my entire life before.

In the midst of our reserved area, Marclinus hops up onto the temporary dais and claps his hands. The amplification charm he's donned pitches his jovial voice over the entire festival grounds.

"We've had a wonderful time celebrating with you all these past days! I thank every one of you for your joyful welcome. My court and I must return to the palace for the afternoon to see to the well-being of the empire, but you may continue to partake of all the refreshments and entertainments through nightfall. We look forward to joining you again tomorrow."

Thank the gods. I might appreciate the affection that's being offered to my woman, but the extended celebrations that come with the confirmation rites get tiring after a while. And I'd rather not have to listen to one more civilian gushing about Marclinus's greatness.

We proceed out from under the baking rays of the summer sun into the slightly cooler halls of the palace. Savory smells of the upcoming luncheon feast trickle from the kitchen, but it appears Marclinus isn't ready to dine just yet. He leads the lot of us into this palace's hall of entertainments.

There's a spring to his step that's a little unsettling. He's giving off the kind of manic energy I've become uncomfortably familiar with in my many years as his foster brother—the kind that usually produces some sadistic idea of "fun." I drift to the edge of the large room, giving him a wide berth.

Marclinus veers from one cluster of nobles to another, his mouth stretched in a wide grin. His laughter peals through the room with a harsh edge that sets me even more on guard. He taps his fingers against his sides, his gaze darting this way and that.

Something twitches in his expression, and he draws aside one of the footmen. In a matter of minutes, a few of the staff have pushed the chairs and card tables at one end of the room toward the walls, clearing a wide-open space.

I catch Bastien's gaze where he's lingering by the dart boards. The tensed set of his mouth suggests he's just as apprehensive as I am.

Another servant arrives carrying a bundle of fabric he spreads out on a table beyond my view. Marclinus beckons us all over to the cleared area of the room. He tucks his hand around Aurelia's elbow, tugging her close.

His lips curl with an especially wicked smirk. "My court, I've thought up a special entertainment just for us! Why should the commoners have most of the fun, am I right?"

The nobles let out several whoops and exclamations of agreement, but many of the faces around me look wary too.

"My empress and I have put ourselves through tests of mind and might while the rest of you loaf around," Marclinus goes on in a teasing tone. "And as my wife has rightly pointed out, the other royals in our midst haven't truly made themselves part of this court. If they enjoy setting themselves apart from the rest of us, I think we should make our resident foster princes at least offer a little amusement."

A chill condenses in my gut.

I know what's about to happen wasn't Aurelia's idea. She may have made a comment during our trek that prompted Marclinus to separate the four of us and force us to socialize with only the other nobles, but that would have been with an eye to deflecting suspicion.

She'd never have encouraged any course of action likely to do us real harm. Her expression now is perfectly placid, but her hand mostly hidden in the folds of her skirt has balled.

Marclinus is already waving us forward. "Come on now. Let's see all four of our princes. It'll be a good test of your own mettle for whatever roles you find yourself in with your royal families."

All four of us. As I trudge out into the cleared area, my gaze slides to Neven, who's emerging from the crowd of nobles with a scowl slashed across his face.

He had a hard enough time keeping his cool when it was Aurelia being harmed by Marclinus's machinations. If it's the rest of us...

I need to keep a close eye on him.

Bastien and Lorenzo join us, Bastien grim and Lorenzo's forehead furrowed with worry. Marclinus draws Aurelia off to the side of the open floor, near the table I can now see glints with several weapons: blades of various lengths, a mace, a battle hammer.

The imperial prick motions to the offerings. "You'll each choose your weapon, and then we'll have a thrilling melee. The last one standing will be announced the prince of princes and receive a special meal at our luncheon."

My stomach flips over. I'd rather starve than attack my foster brothers. What fucking madness is Marclinus playing at?

Aurelia glances at her husband. She keeps her tone light and good-humored. "Husband, this challenge hardly seems fair when one of their number is an experienced victor of the arena battles and the others, I assume, have rarely fought."

Marclinus chuckles. "I suppose those three will need to be strategic and try to topple Prince Raul as a joint effort before they battle it out between themselves. Go on now. Pick your weapons."

Aurelia's jaw flexes as if she's held back something else she'd want to say. I flick my hand by my side in a hasty gesture I learned from Lorenzo, the one she's warned us off with more than once. *It's okay.*

She can't intervene more without leaving him wondering

why she cares that much about our well-being. The consequences for her and us will be so much worse if he ever guesses her true feelings.

I stride over to the weapons table. My foster brothers follow more hesitantly.

"You'd better not think you can get one over on me," I declare, as much for our audience's benefit as theirs. "I know exactly how to take each of you down."

With our backs to Marclinus, I risk a longer chain of gestures. *I'll look after you. Fall when I strike.*

I am the only one with much combat skill. Neven has plenty of strength, but he lacks the discipline to be strategic in a fight. Bastien's main skill is with arrows, his awareness of the air currents helping him judge the best shots. At hand to hand, his missing lung will leave him depleted before he can put up much of an attack.

And Lorenzo has always hated even the controlled sparring of our periodic workouts. He'd rather be sitting in a corner strumming some instrument.

So if we're going to put on a performance for Marclinus's enjoyment—and that of however many nobles enjoy seeing us bash and stab at each other—I need to take charge. I can drop them to the floor in a way that looks painful but with injuries more superficial than deadly.

Bastien gives a subtle nod to show he understands. Lorenzo grimaces and replies with a gesture of his own: *Be careful.*

Neven huffs as if insulted by my bluster, but when he glances at me as he picks up the mace, worry has darkened his bright brown eyes.

"We'll see what you can do," he says, waggling the weapon at me. I know he means that he'll follow my lead.

I pick up a short sword with a thick pommel at the end of the grip. As I step back from the table, I give it a few experimental swings that draw a couple of gasps from our spectators.

Marclinus clicks his tongue, sounding giddy with delight. "Let's not have any outright murder take place in front of us, Your Royal Highnesses. I don't want to be making awkward explanations to your parents. Hit hard enough to leave your opponents unconscious or at least incapable of standing up, not dead, or I won't be able to call it a win after all."

Wonderful to know he has some standards of propriety. Does he really think we'd have slaughtered each other for his stupid game if he hadn't mentioned that rule?

Bastien picks up a slim sword that suits his slender frame. Lorenzo grips one of the daggers awkwardly. We eye each other across our misshapen circle in the cleared area of the room.

It's a strange sensation, finding myself needing to take the lead. I'm used to handing that role over to Bastien with all his older brother airs and cool-headed practicality.

They're counting on me to guide them right this time. I need to be worthy of their trust.

My stomach knots, but I swipe my blade through the air. "I'm not going to stand around and wait for you to find your guts."

Then I charge at Neven.

It'll be easiest to knock him down first—and easiest to avoid any questions about how I'm fending off all my attackers if it's the other two I have to keep at bay. I dodge the kid's first tentative swing of the mace, smack him across the ribs with the flat of my sword, and circle him to keep away from Bastien and Lorenzo.

Neven winces at the impact. Guilt jabs through my chest, but the blow can't feel worse than an actual sword shoved through his flesh if I were really invested in this battle.

The watching nobles start hollering out encouragement

and insults, egging us on and wagering on who'll come out victorious. I focus all my attention on the shifting of my muscles and the thump of my heart. I have to ignore them, the emperor, and Aurelia standing rigidly by.

All the training from my first stumbling lessons with the head of the Lavirian royal guard to the brutal lengths the imperial arena master pushed me to rise up from the depths of my mind. The imagined prickle of sand in the back of my throat grounds me.

Neven whips around as if giving the fight his best effort and lashes out at me again. I deflect his mace with a clang of my blade, nicking a small cut across his cheek at the same time.

With a growl, he heaves toward me. I can't tell whether he's purposefully making my intentions easier for me or he's letting his temper get the better of him like I worried he might.

With a sidestep, I kick his legs out from under him. He tumbles forward to sprawl on his hands and knees. As he rolls over, I aim another kick at his belly—checking my force at the last second so it looks as if it'll have landed harder than it actually did.

Neven grunts all the same and flails out with his mace. I leap around him and bring the pommel of my sword slamming down on just the right spot on his forehead.

The kid's arm drops. His eyelids flutter and drift shut as his head lolls with his stupor.

I think I've actually knocked him unconscious. I didn't want to—I just didn't know if he'd actually play along with the way he was fighting back.

A surge of nausea bubbles up to the base of my throat, but I can't give in to my horror. I whirl around, my sword at the ready, in time to deflect blows from both of my other foster brothers.

Bastien offers a feigned sneer to offset the anguish in his gaze. "You think you're so much tougher than the rest of us. We'll give you a challenge, all right. Come on, Lorenzo."

Lorenzo's face is fixed in a distraught expression, but he slices his dagger toward me. They move around me at opposite sides as if trying to throw me off.

Bastien adjusts his grip on his sword, a hint of warning right before he springs at me. Lorenzo launches forward at the same moment.

I duck and spin around, jamming my heel into Lorenzo's knee and smacking my weapon against Bastien's wrist. The sword spins from his grasp; blood streaks across his pale skin where I couldn't help cutting him even using the flat of the blade.

As Bastien scrambles after his sword with his first rasped breath, Lorenzo makes a disgruntled sound and throws himself at me again. It's too easy to shove him backward, aiming a punch at his chest where his ribs will absorb most of the impact.

I dance around him and ram my elbow into his spine. As he stumbles, I whack the back of his head with my pommel.

A thin whimper seeps from his lips as he falls flat on his face.

I didn't hit *him* hard enough to really rattle his brains, but his body goes totally limp. Good man. He understands the real challenge is in the performance we give, not any actual battle.

Bastien is already sprinting at me again despite the wheeze reverberating from his chest. "You asshole!"

"I do what I have to do," I snap at him, channeling my anger at Marclinus into the words.

It only takes one swift swipe of my leg to knock Bastien's feet out from under him. He gasps and lashes out with his sword, drawing a shallow scratch across my side.

With a forced snarl, I wrench his arm aside and smack his head in turn.

Again, I hold back my full strength. Bastien helps by rolling his eyes upward and sagging onto the floor as if I've cracked his skull.

My stomach is roiling now. I straighten up and face Marclinus, willing my foster brothers to keep up their act. Willing the emperor to buy it.

The sight of the prick's smug expression makes me want to slam my sword straight through *his* skull. My fingers flex against the grip, remembering his victorious smirk when I competed in my first arena exhibition—as if the triumph was his rather than mine for letting me join in.

Remembering how much I wanted to carve open his arrogant face and drowning in the urge to do that right now.

I can imagine it so clearly. I can hear the cries of horror from the crowd, the light snuffing out in Marclinus's eyes, the blood gushing down across his slackening features.

I tense my legs against the surge of fury, gritting my teeth.

No. I know an attack wouldn't actually turn out like that.

The guards right behind the emperor would block me with their magic before I drew a single drop of blood. Then it'd be mine spilled all over the polished floor.

I have bigger dreams now that I'm not willing to give up.

So I stand still and rigid while Marclinus begins the round of applause. "Nicely done, Prince Raul. You shall have your prize."

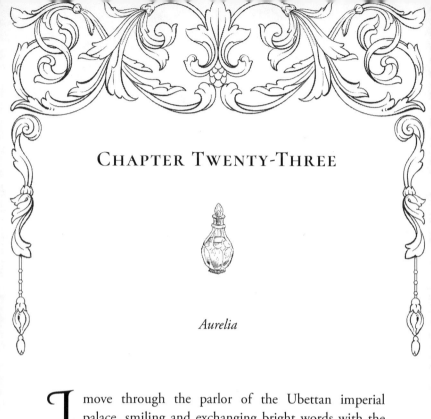

CHAPTER TWENTY-THREE

Aurelia

I move through the parlor of the Ubettan imperial palace, smiling and exchanging bright words with the gathered nobles, but apprehension weighs on every step. The small bit of lunch I forced down sits in my stomach like a lump of lead.

Raul stands by the unlit hearth, accepting patronizing compliments on his "victory" with a grin that looks increasingly feral. It must be taking more strength than he applied to the earlier skirmish to hold himself back from snapping.

As soon as the mockery of a battle was over, medics hustled into the hall of entertainments to help revive the other princes and lead them off to the recuperative room for additional tending. I can't imagine Raul hurt his foster brothers any more than absolutely necessary, but every passing minute without their return sits heavier on my gut.

What got into Marclinus that he thought pitting the princes against each other in front of the court was a good strategy? What was that strategy even supposed to accomplish?

I thought he was aiming to integrate them more among the Darium nobility, diffuse any conflicted loyalties. Did he somehow think that ordering them to fight each other to the point of unconsciousness would make them feel *more* friendly to the court egging them on than to their fellow hostages?

He even brought Neven into this morning's cruel display —making the teenager fight with the men he sees as his older brothers.

I don't know how to explain it, but I can't ask my husband either. Any hint that I disapprove of his choices, especially when it comes to the princes, could be disastrous.

And I've already seen that he can be brutally callous simply on a whim. He just... He'd started to seem almost *reasonable* during some of our recent conversations.

One shift in mood, and he's swung to the opposite extreme again.

I'm ambling toward the spot where he's laughing with several of his noble friends when High Commander Axius steps into the room. He catches Marclinus's eye and makes a quick gesture to indicate he needs the emperor's attention.

My husband has at least enough sense today to decide discussing military matters in front of his entire court would be unwise. He parts ways with his conversational partners with a few jovial remarks and claps on the back before strolling out of the room after the high commander.

My stomach lists uneasily. Has there been more news from Lavira?

An empress has a right to know what's going on throughout her empire, doesn't she?

I amble over to the doorway as if I'm in no particular hurry, not wanting to stir gossip, and slip out into the hall. Marclinus and Axius are already veering around a bend up ahead, talking in lowered voices. Marclinus's guards trail several paces behind.

My husband's snicker carries down the hall, raising the hairs on the back of my neck.

I set off after them. I'm not sure where this palace's meeting rooms or imperial offices are located, but it doesn't appear to matter. Just as I reach the corner, the two men duck into one of the smaller sitting rooms, which I suppose they consider private enough.

Marclinus's guards draw to a halt by the doorway. One glances my way, but he doesn't move to stop my approach. Perhaps he feels I have some right to join the conversation as empress.

I walk slowly but steadily, keeping my ears pricked. When their voices become clear enough for me to make out Axius's words, I slow even more, gazing vaguely into the distance as if pondering some other concern.

"—more than a hundred executed, and twice that in custody," the high commander is saying. "The raids and interrogations will be continuing as we speak."

My pulse hitches, and then stutters harder at Marclinus's answer: "Oh, I think Tribune Valerisse can hit the wretched traitors even harder than that. Everyone in those cities needs to know they can't get away with so much as scowling at the representatives of their empire."

Axius hesitates before going on, his next remark more halting. "The local forces still haven't been able to determine who the actual conspirators are, or—"

Marclinus snorts. "I'm sure we'll wipe them out along with a bunch of the other rats who simply haven't taken the gamble yet. If they aren't betraying us, they're hiding the ones who did. Let them all die."

I can't linger here merely listening any longer. Lifting my chin, I stride into the room.

A step over the threshold, I stop and raise my eyebrows. "So this is where you wandered off to, husband." I slide my gaze to Axius and then back to Marclinus. "What's pulled you away from our gathering? Is there urgent news?"

My husband's tone stays as flippant as when he was ordering the executions of hundreds moments ago. "Only an update from Lavira. Nothing that needs to concern you." He nods to the high commander. "I think you know where to take it from here."

Axius dips his head lower in respect and leaves the room, his mouth set tight. I get the impression he isn't all that pleased with his orders.

I step closer to Marclinus, pushing my mouth into an adoring smile that feels utterly hollow. "What was the news? It sounded as if you were talking about Lavirians dying—has their royal family identified the culprits?"

I'd rather not admit how long I was eavesdropping.

Marclinus lets out a dismissive huff. "As if I'd trust those incompetent fools to crack down on their own people. Our soldiers are getting done what needs doing and teaching the lessons needed."

"Oh," I say carefully. "When we discussed it before, you seemed eager to put responsibility for the sanctions on the local royals."

When did he go back on his seeming agreement? Did he have that conversation with me and immediately turn around and pass on instructions to do the opposite, or did his opinion change sometime during the days afterward?

Marclinus tugs a lock of my hair free from its upswept style, winding it around his finger. It's a seemingly playful gesture, but something has hardened in his cool gray eyes. I feel as if I'm staring into irises of polished limestone.

"I'd imagine it seemed that way to *you*, wife, with all your Eloxian devotion. Did you really think I was going to go along with your soft-hearted nonsense?"

My words catch in my throat. I'm not sure he's ever spoken quite so disparagingly toward me, even when I was only vying for our marriage.

I summon a cautious remark. "Involving the Lavirian royal family and their own soldiers—you came up with that idea."

"I could see that your poor nerves needed soothing, so I presented some bullshit to set your mind at ease. You should be glad I know how an uprising actually needs to be quelled. Give them one inch of compassion and they'll be razing everything they can to the ground. But we'll smash them first." With a feral grin, he smacks his fist against his palm.

So everything he said to me during our conversation last week... The consideration he offered me, his curiosity about my opinions, his pensiveness while he thought the dilemma through... All of that was a lie? The whole time he was mocking me in his head?

When I can't come up with an immediate response, Marclinus clucks his tongue at me as if I'm a child he's chiding. "You really thought I cared what you'd make of the situation. *You*, a minor princess from far off Accasy who's spent barely a month in Dariu?"

I restrain a wince. "I'm always open to learning what I lack. If I'm going to serve the empire as well as I can—"

He snaps his fingers in my face. "That is your mistake. You don't serve the empire. You serve *me*, while I give the empire what it needs. Did you figure performing the confirmation rites proved you were meant for more? All it's done is show what a pathetic figure you are. Going out of your way to hand out the fruits of the rite to commoners, as if you're some kind of almsgiver rather than the wife of the emperor?"

Marclinus's lips curl with a sneer, his gaze cutting into me.

He's not just dismissing my contributions. He's angry.

Because I stole some small part of the attention he felt was his due? Because the people of Ubetta reacted so enthusiastically to my offering?

My fingers itch with a spurt of my own anger. I have a brief vision of snatching the small knife in its sheath behind my belt pouch and plunging its blade straight into his heart.

But I have more strength than this man will ever give me credit for. I will not be baited.

I let my head droop, willing my shoulders not to slump in turn. I refuse to outright abase myself before this man unless I have to. "I simply wanted to remove any doubts about my place by your side."

"It's not their opinion that matters." He waves his hand toward the walls. "They're all imbeciles. And if you want to impress me, you'd do well to behave less like one yourself."

"Yes, husband. My apologies for disappointing you."

"Hmph." He ambles away from me, running his fingers over the top of a nearby armchair, and then spins back around. "Your presence does remind me—I've been thinking we should add to our fleet of ships faster than we have in recent years. I'm going to call for significantly more breamwood from Accasy going forward. They'll be happy to supply to both their emperor and their formerly Accasian empress, I assume?"

The bottom of my stomach drops right out. More wood from the bream cedars—that'll require more local workers doing the dangerous work of felling the trees and conveying them along the precarious route down to Darium. More men and women crushed beneath the trunks and drowning in the rivers, never to return home.

"Of course they will," I say, steadying my voice as much as I can. "You'll get the best results if you ramp up production gradually."

Which might give me time to distract him with some other acquisition?

Marclinus simply laughs. "Why should I wait? I'd like to see twice as much arriving in a matter of months. If they can't keep up, you'll need to deal with them like the empress you're so keen to show you are."

He stalks out of the room without another word.

It takes all my strength to stop my legs from outright crumpling under me. I wobble over to a chair and sink into it, gazing at the room but not really seeing its contents. Every part of me feels numb except the queasy churning of my gut.

Marclinus is punishing me by lashing out at my country —demanding so much more of my people when they're already stretching themselves thin to cater to the empire.

He'll force *me* to impose the demands on them myself if they fail to fulfill his request quickly enough.

All to put me in my place and remind me how little I matter to him.

I bring my hands to my face. I thought I'd started to make a few gains with him. I thought I'd earned some small bit of respect. But it was nothing more than another game.

I came all the way from the wild north to secure a better future for my kingdom, and it turns out I've only encouraged the new emperor to make my people a target. How much more will he bully them if I disappoint him again?

No matter how many times I breathe slow and deep, my nerves keep jangling. My store of inner calm has shattered.

No one in the empire will know real peace while that pompous, sadistic asshole still rules.

The thought floats through my head, expanding until I can't focus on anything else.

It's true, isn't it? How many times does Marclinus have to prove that he'd rather ruin lives than raise them up, torment his people rather than cultivate them, crush my spirit rather than celebrate it, before I fully believe him?

He couldn't rule while his father still lived. I never will while my husband still does.

My throat constricts around my next breath.

I might have brought about Tarquin's death, but I didn't relish the act. Every particle of my nature would rather guide those around me toward kinder decisions through sympathy and understanding rather than violence.

Back when my parents, my sister, and I murmured in secret in the private rooms of the palace, obtained my ring and worked out the best ways of using it, we never discussed disposing of anyone other than the old emperor. We assumed Marclinus would be at least a little open to influence, with his youth and his lack of experience.

How could we have imagined just how awful he'd be? That he'd become a terror worse than Tarquin?

How *could* I get rid of him? I can hardly pass off a sudden death as another bout of illness in a man still in the early years of his prime, especially after his father just passed under similar circumstances in my presence. And even if there was a way to free the empire of his awfulness, his people would hardly accept me as their new ruler in his place.

I'm not even Darium. I've only been empress for a matter of weeks. Nothing except a marriage ceremony and the gold band fitted around my wrist tie me to the imperial family.

Perhaps farther down the line, when I'm mother to his

heirs, when I've fully established myself in their minds...
But, gods help me, the thought of lying with him for real
after the insults he just hurled at me makes every particle of
my body recoil.

My gaze drifts across the room again. Sunlight beams
through the window.

The warm brilliance gleams off the ruddy wallpaper, and
a memory of Bastien's dark green eyes beneath his auburn
hair rises in my mind. The shine on the dark wooden cabinet
brings Lorenzo's image swimming up after it. The glint in the
bluish crystal of a vase in the corner summons Raul's pale
gaze.

The men I actually want are right here.

My heart skips a beat. I hold perfectly still, unsure
whether this is a godlen-driven vision or simply fanciful
thoughts.

The starkest rays of sunshine dwindle. The images fade
with them, but the swell of longing in my chest remains.

Perhaps... Perhaps there is a way.

The jolt of that inspiration sends me to my feet. I waver
there for a moment, the implications of what I'm considering
so huge that I've lost my breath completely.

Do I really dare? Would such a plan be outright madness?

Marclinus's sneering face and vicious words come back to
me, and my hands clench at my sides.

What am I consigning myself and everyone else I care
about to if I *don't* take action?

It's so much, so big... So far beyond what I originally
planned...

Resolve unfurls inside me, grounding me. I head out of
the room and through the halls to my chambers.

My maids have come through and tidied the room, but
it's empty now. I settle cross-legged on the rug and tap my

fingers down my front in the gesture of the divinities. With each inhalation and exhalation, I give myself over to the meditation.

Elox, you've led me well before. Be my shepherd. What if another murder is the only way to peace? What would you have me do now?

The light plays across my closed eyelids, filtering through the pear tree leaves rustling outside the windows. The breeze tickles across my skin.

The field I've seen before in dreams and visions forms behind my eyes. I'm kneeling in the grass, the green blades splattered with crimson.

A lamb stands before me. As I study it, it steps forward and rests its muzzle on my shoulder as if embracing me.

A sputter of a laugh bursts from my lips and breaks the scene.

If that's supposed to be Marclinus, he's never going to come to me like that. He sees everything I do, everything I am as pathetic.

But of course, there is no clear answer. I lean back to lie on the rug, peering up at the ceiling and puzzling the image over.

Was the lamb meant to be the emperor? The field was bloody too, as if battles had been fought there. The animal could simply represent the peace I'm striving for, indicating that it is within reach.

It could represent a child I'll one day hold in my arms.

I know my godlen has never approved of violence unless it was absolutely necessary. Elox might be telling me to be patient—but what if I end up sacrificing both my country and the men who've won my heart because I bided my time?

I sit up again, my jaw setting firmly. I can be patient for a little while, because I'll need to be anyway. My monster of a husband will have at least nine months to prove himself to *me*.

First things first. I need to concoct a potion that'll flush the mirewort from my body.

I open my trunk and take out my brewing equipment.

CHAPTER TWENTY-FOUR

Aurelia

I sway and spin on the dance floor, now in Marclinus's arms and now in one of his noblemen's. This once, it's easy to keep my smile on my face.

The deep well of calm I've often turned to has spread through my chest, cool and soothing, as if I'm soaking in a tranquil pool.

I'm taking back control over my fate. There's more than one way to transform a pawn into a queen.

At the end of a dance with one of the viceroys, I happen as if by chance to be standing a few paces away from Bastien. When he glances my way, I twitch my hand at my side to catch his attention and then form a few hasty gestures without glancing straight at him.

You three meet me in your room. Eleventh bell.

Bastien meanders onward, but not without a twist of his fingers that simply indicates, *Yes.*

From the corner of my eye, I note when he and Lorenzo depart the ballroom, with Raul following two dances later. I glide to the music for a few more songs just so the connection isn't obvious. Then I contrive to put myself in my husband's path once more.

Marclinus appears to have tired of dancing. He's standing off to the side with a cluster of nobles, one hand raising a goblet of wine to his lips and the other resting on Bianca's ass where she's standing next to him.

A tremor runs through the serenity I've cultivated. My ploy will be much more difficult than I expected if my husband has already set his mind on tumbling a different lady tonight.

I slip between the chattering nobles to my husband's other side and tuck my hand around his elbow when he lowers his goblet. "Such a fine night, husband."

Marclinus peers down at me. He hasn't mentioned our fraught conversation from this afternoon. As we've danced, I've caught an avid glint in his eyes as he watches me, as if he's eager to see what lingering effect his words might have had.

Now, he grins and swirls his wine in the cup. "So glad you're enjoying yourself, wife. It's always a good time when we can revel with all of our people—at least, the people who matter."

He flicks his gaze toward his friends. They all titter with the laughter he was seeking.

I tease my fingers up the back of his arm and bob up on my toes to murmur close to his ear, for only him to hear. "I thought I might show you just how well I can serve you tonight? In every way you might enjoy."

Marclinus's grin stretches into a leer, but he tugs Bianca a little closer by her waist. "My empress is looking to deprive the rest of you of my company. That hardly seems fair."

In the midst of the following chuckles, I grope for the right words to achieve my seduction.

I hardly expect Bianca to lend a helping hand. But she pats Marclinus on his chest, gazing up at him through her eyelashes. "We would never want to deny you the pleasures of marital company, Your Imperial Majesty. It will give us much joy to know you're being so... satisfied."

She manages to make it sound as if taking me to bed would impress all of them—and perhaps even stir her own desires for later encounters.

And as many complaints as I may have had about the vicerine's conduct, she does know Marclinus well. His eyes smolder down at her and then dart to me with even more interest.

"It certainly would be poor form for me to neglect my husbandly duties when my wife is clearly in need of a good pleasuring," he says in an amused tone, without any sign of caring that he's now all but spelling out what we're going to do. But then, this is the same man who paraded me naked in front of his entire court. "Especially when I benefit just as much. Revel on in my honor, my friends!"

He hands his goblet to a passing servant and guides me toward the door with his hand on the small of my back. I catch Bianca's eyes for a second, and she offers a minute nod as if to say, "He's yours."

I knew she hadn't been feeling as enthusiastic about their intimacies lately, but I never imagined she'd push him into my arms. I'm not sure whether to take the gesture as an apology for past sabotage or a thank you for the recent help I offered.

Either way, I have my husband almost where I need him.

Before we've even reached my chambers, Marclinus is stroking his fingers around my neck and across my shoulders.

As we step over the threshold, he gives the lacing on the side of the dress an emphatic tug to loosen it.

"I like having you begging for it. Let's see just how well you can serve your husband, hmm?"

I smile back at his smirking face and press my ring before brushing my hand across his wrist. "There's nothing I want more. Please take me, my emperor. I've been burning for you all evening. I can't wait any longer."

The false words taste sour spilling over my tongue, but Marclinus shows no sign of noticing. With a laugh, he yanks at my dress hard enough to rip the fabric.

I restrain a wince and grasp the collar of his shirt in turn. He crushes his mouth against mine, pushing me backward to the bed as he does.

"My wife," he mutters against my mouth. "My simpering Accasian wench. Only mine. You belong to me."

The harsh edge to his claim sends a chill over my skin, but I giggle breathlessly as if I'm entranced.

I peel his shirt off him, and he shoves me right onto the bed. When he reaches for my drawers, my heart hiccups with the thought that he might race straight to the culmination of this act before the drug kicks in.

I nudge him playfully to the side and grab his trousers. "I've hardly had a chance to serve you at all. Your wife should be on her knees before you at least once every night."

A ragged chuckle seeps out of Marclinus. He props himself against the pillows to watch me better, grazing his fingers over my hair as I unfasten his trousers.

I tug them down slowly, forcing myself to kiss his pale thigh as if I'm drawing out the anticipation for his pleasure. To my relief, just as I've tossed off his shoes to remove the trousers completely, his head lolls to the side.

"Mmm, Aurelia," he growls, but his eyes have hazed. His hands grope at the air.

My stance relaxes. I strip off my undergarments as I always do, so he'll have vague memories of taking in my naked body when he wakes. When I trace my fingers down his well-built chest, he groans.

It only takes a few minutes before he reaches his climax on his own. As he sinks into total oblivion, I clean him up as briskly as I can and then go to my trunk.

I don't know exactly how long I'll be gone tonight. It's safest not to leave anything to chance.

The second potion I brewed this afternoon has cooled into a grainy paste. I smear a little on my fingertip and bring it back to my husband.

His lips part easily at my prodding. I run my finger over his tongue.

Based on its scent, the sedative will have a similar aftertaste to alcohol. If any flavor lingers when he wakes, he should assume it's from the wine he was drinking. For good measure, I take the goblet I carried back here after dinner and dribble some on the bed near his face before setting the glass on the side table.

The sedative should ensure he sleeps several hours. Which means I'll have to endure his snoring the entire night after I return rather than hearing him depart in the wee hours of the morning, but I can tolerate that discomfort to gain everything else I hope to.

I pull the least cumbersome of my packed dresses out of my trunk and wriggle into it. Then I ease open one of the windows to peer into the darkness outside.

Only a few lanterns gleam amid the palace grounds. There's no entrance on this side of the building. The guards will be stationed by the doors at the front and back, as well as along the outer walls of the estate.

I clamber onto the window ledge and reach into the pear tree. Gripping one branch, I swing myself out and settle my feet near the trunk. I tie a tasseled rope I liberated from one of the curtains there.

It only takes a few careful maneuvers to work my way far enough down to feel comfortable dropping the last short distance. The tied rope dangles to just a few feet above the grass, well within reach for when I need leverage to scramble back up again.

And neither my personal guards nor Marclinus's have any idea I've left my rooms.

Brushing my hands together, I skirt the side of the palace through the still darkness. Night-dwelling insects chitter, and a dog howls somewhere in the distance, but I can't make out any sounds from inside.

I peek around the corner to ensure there's no one nearby in the gardens and then sneak along the windows at floor level.

The first room I pass is dark. The second, the one Lorenzo indicated is Bastien's, holds a faint glow from a partly shaded lantern.

The two windows that belong to that room are closed. I tap on the pane as loudly as I dare, pause, and then tap again.

At my second beckoning, it only takes a few seconds before Bastien's pale face appears beyond the glass. Eyes widening, he pushes the window open.

Raul pushes over beside him and holds out his tawny arms to help haul me inside. I scramble over the ledge just as Lorenzo hurries over from the room's small sitting area.

Tension thrums through the air. None of us speaks, not even Lorenzo's conjured voice in my head, until Bastien has shut and re-latched the window.

"What's happened?" Raul demands. "If that prick has some new awful scheme—"

I touch his hand, and he cuts himself off, his scowl softening with whatever comfort my touch provides.

As I step farther into the room, away from the window, Bastien jerks the curtains closed without needing to be asked. With all their gazes on me, the proposition I'm about to make feels even more immense than it did in the solitude of my chambers this afternoon.

But I have one more urgent matter to consider first. I peer closely at Bastien and then Lorenzo, searching for any signs of pain. A prod of my gift during dinner didn't reveal any lingering injuries that needed attention, but I need to hear confirmation from their own lips.

"Are you all right? The medics ensured that you're completely healed?"

Bastien nods, with a flicker of a smile toward the prince of Lavira. "Raul didn't hit us all that hard to begin with. We managed to get away with a bit of playacting and some bruises that've been well-soothed."

Lorenzo echoes his foster brother's reassurance with a couple of twists of his fingers. *All's well with us. And you?*

I square my shoulders, girding myself for the possibility that my plans may end before I've done more than speak them. "I'm well enough, but... I'm the one doing the scheming tonight. Marclinus has gone too far. I thought there was a chance that I could nudge him onto a better course, but it seems no matter what I do, he only gets worse."

Bastien's jaw tightens. "Tarquin taught him too well."

Lorenzo's resonant voice fills my head. *"It isn't your fault, Rell. He never listens to anyone."*

Raul has latched on to the first part of my declaration. "What are you up to? You know we'll help you however we can. Especially if it means seeing the imperial asshole get a taste of his own medicine."

My chest constricts. I've all but admitted my murder of Tarquin to these men, but I never discussed it with them beforehand. I'm not entirely sure how they're going to react now.

I wet my lips. "I don't think I'm going to accomplish anything I hoped to as empress while our new emperor is making the decisions. But if I can continue winning the rest of Dariu over as I've started to—if he then met some unfortunate end…"

Bastien's face tenses and Lorenzo simply stares at me, but Raul guffaws in approval. "You are bloodthirsty under all that talk of peace, aren't you, Shepherdess?"

I can't stop myself from glowering at him. "I'd rather not harm anyone at all. But if it's that or watch Marclinus harm who knows how many more people, it's clear which action is more on the side of peace."

Bastien sets his hand on my shoulder with an affectionate squeeze but worry shining in his eyes. "To pull it off—you couldn't use the same trick as with Tarquin. Any kind of illness so soon after his father's might raise suspicions."

Ah. He isn't bothered that I've made the suggestion, only that it might get me into trouble.

I brush his rumpled auburn hair away from his temple, reveling in the brief warmth that blooms between our skin. "I wouldn't go about it any way that I thought could be tied back to me or seem connected to Tarquin's death. And I'll have quite a bit of time to strategize."

"You're waiting until after all the confirmation rites?" Lorenzo suggests. *"That shouldn't take more than another month or two."*

"Well, there's something else I'll need in order to solidify my place as empress, considering that I'm not part of the imperial line—not even distantly, not even Darium myself." I inhale slowly. "I need to be the mother of the next emperor or empress-to-be."

All three of the princes stiffen.

Raul's eyes flash. "You shouldn't have to let that maniac of a husband—to have to carry his spawn inside you—"

I hold up my hand to stop further protests. "I don't like that idea either. Which is why it occurred to me... the child doesn't have to be his. Not as long as everyone else believes it is."

The stunned silence afterward stretches even longer than the first. Lorenzo's lips part and then press shut again. *"You mean..."*

Even after the hours I've spent thinking about this moment, a blush burns my cheeks. "I won't be taking any more mirewort. Based on my cycle, this should be an opportune time... I hadn't thought I'd bring a child into the world this early, but if it's the only way to protect everything I'm working toward, I'd rather it was with someone I actually admire."

Raul shifts his weight on his feet, looking uncharacteristically awkward. "You know I can't provide that service."

I meet Bastien's gaze. "It would have to be you. Your coloring is much closer to Marclinus's than Lorenzo's." I glance at Lorenzo with an apologetic grimace. "Not that I wouldn't want you just as much—but the chances that the baby's appearance would raise questions—"

He dips his head in understanding. *"I never would have thought I'd have the opportunity in the first place."*

Bastien sputters. "Neither would I."

I wrench my attention back to the prince of Cotea, reaching to caress his cheek. "You don't have to agree. It's a huge thing to ask. You'd probably never be able to treat the child as your own—I don't know how much you'd get to interact with him or her, even if I can remove Marclinus from the throne, depending on how careful we still needed to be ..."

Bastien's jaw works, his dark green eyes piercing into mine. He dips his head toward me to claim a kiss, one I offer up without any hesitation at all.

His hands settle on my waist, holding me in front of him. His mouth melds with mine, gentle and then more demanding. A giddy shiver races down my spine at the promise of passion.

Bastien keeps his desires tightly in check most of the time behind his studied reserve. But I've gotten a taste of how easily he can turn his authoritative airs into a dominating presence when the mood is right. He's anything but a passive partner.

When he breaks from the kiss, he stares down at me, his gaze heated but pensive. His voice comes out commanding. "Tell me why you'd want me even if it wasn't for this scheme. Why this means more than simply outmaneuvering Marclinus."

As confident as he sounds, the order hints at his earlier insecurities about my affections. A pang shoots through my chest.

I loop my arms around his neck, stroking the hair that tumbles to the nape, and gaze right back at him. "From the moment I arrived in the imperial court, I could tell you have a mind and a will to be reckoned with. And if sometimes you turned that cleverness against me, you're also canny and kind enough to admit when you're wrong and make amends. I trust you to be both strong and tender when I need it. You've been willing to risk what little security you have to protect me. I know my heart and my life are safe in your hands."

The corner of my mouth ticks upward. "And it certainly doesn't hurt that you're absolutely stunning to look at."

I pause, and the deeper truth I've been resisting since I first started falling for these men rises up my throat.

Why should I deny it any longer? Why shouldn't he hear just how much he means to me?

The sweet, naïve feelings that stirred in me years ago in Gavril's presence are nothing compared to the ache of devotion that burns in me now.

My voice goes raw, but the words come out clearly enough. "I love you. I wish we could be together like this every day instead of just stolen moments."

Bastien makes a rough noise, and then he's pulling me into another kiss, his mouth capturing mine with a searing heat that has me melting into him.

"I love you too," he murmurs against my lips. "You're so much more than just a medic princess—you're… you're a signal star, lighting our way through despair. I don't know if there's anything I wouldn't do if it meant seeing you free."

Bittersweet tears prick at my eyes. I kiss him again with all I have in me, but the emotions whirling inside me niggle at my conscience.

He isn't the only one I need to say those words to.

I draw back from him just enough to look at Raul and Lorenzo, who are watching with uncertain stances. No matter how tangled our circumstances are, a smile I can't hold back stretches across my face, offsetting the tears now streaking down my cheeks.

"I love you," I say to Raul, and then, to Lorenzo, "And I love you. I don't know how I'd have held it together over the past few weeks without all of you. When Marclinus is gone, maybe there'll be a way… But until then, I still want you all to be a part of this act. This will be *our* child, not his."

A cocky grin curves Raul's lips. "Fuck yes, it will be."

He steps in and claims a kiss of his own, even though I'm still in Bastien's embrace. His foster brother doesn't protest other than a light-hearted huff.

When Raul pulls back, Lorenzo is there, grazing his

fingers over the side of my face and into my hair. His kiss is gentle and lingering, but no less giddying.

"You know how much I love you," he says without lifting his mouth from mine. *"There's no one I'd rather see on that throne. I'd set you on it right now if I could."*

A ripple of wind that must be Bastien's gift stirs the skirt of my dress. "Let's give our empress everything she needs, then. We can treat her even better when we have an actual bed."

The prince of Cotea traces the curve of my ass, and I whimper, turning to seek out his mouth again. Raul plants his lips on the side of my neck, while Lorenzo cups my breast through the thin fabric of the gown.

Bastien's next commands come out a little breathless. "This isn't just about ruling the empire or setting things right. This is about the four of us, and we should make our woman feel as good as possible. Get this dress off her and show her how an empress deserves to be treated."

Raul wastes no time obeying, yanking at the fabric and tugging it up over my head.

Lorenzo dapples kisses over the scars on my forearm, continuing that trail all the way up to my collarbone while he teases his fingers along the edge of my chemise. *"You deserve every pleasure and all the devotion in the world, Rell. No matter what Marclinus says or does, never forget that."*

He lifts that last layer of silk that covers my chest and takes the peak of my breast into his mouth. The tingling jolt at the pressure of his lips draws a gasp from my lungs.

Bastien drinks that sound in and plunders my mouth in turn, his tongue drawing mine into a thrilling dance. When Raul strokes his scarred knuckles across my other nipple, I can't hold back a whimper. My hips sway between my lovers.

The prince of Lavira dips his hand into the shadows between our bodies, and suddenly a sensation slides all across my legs and torso as if a dozen hands are caressing me at once. He's used his gift to solidify a swath of darkness so he can trail it across my skin.

Bastien doesn't intend to be outdone. An air current stirs to life, quivering across every inch of my body that isn't already touched. Its delicate touch sets off enough sparks through my nerves to leave me moaning.

A satisfied smile crosses Bastien's lips. He lowers his head to flick his tongue over one nipple my other men have briefly left unattended and nudges me backward. "Onto the bed. I want to see what you'd look like if you really were mine."

Another tingle passes over my skin. I let Raul tug my drawers off me and climb onto the satiny bedspread. In the middle of it, I sprawl out on my back. "I *am* yours."

Bastien lets out a noise like a stifled growl and stalks after me, wrenching off his shirt as he comes. The sight of the brand I burned into his pale skin below his dedication sigil to Jurnus wrenches at me, but he erases that grief without hesitation. Kneeling between my knees, he drops his head between my legs.

At the first swipe of his tongue over my sex, my hips buck upward. He holds them in place, plundering me as if I'm the most delicious meal he's ever had. The wave of pleasure coursing up from my core has me shuddering in an instant.

As I clutch at his hair, my marriage band around my wrist glints in the lanternlight. But it's nothing but a frivolous bangle to Marclinus. Why should it mean anything more to me?

Bastien sucks on my clit, and my body writhes to meet him. My other lovers sink down on either side of me.

Lorenzo catches my mouth with a deeper kiss. Raul fondles my breast before lapping his tongue over it.

A keening sound I can't restrain seeps out of me,

embarrassingly pleading. I tug on Bastien's hair, and he looks up at me. The sly smile that crosses his slick lips almost makes me come on its own.

"What do you need, my signal star?" he asks in a low voice that makes my sex clench with desire.

I grasp his shoulder. "You. Now. Please."

"You never need to beg me."

The contrast with my husband's arrogant words sets off a fresh prickle of tears in my eyes. I jerk at Bastien's trousers to help him out of them, and he braces himself over me. With one tender kiss and another, he removes the traces of grief from the corners of my eyes.

Then he gazes down at me, all heated determination. "We'll make it right. Whatever it takes, however long it takes."

As he sinks into me, he brushes his lips against mine. Gripping the sides of his face, I return the kiss through the feeling of fullness and the bliss that expands from the spot where our bodies have joined.

He fills me completely, withdraws, and plunges forward again, faster this time. My knees rise as if of their own accord to urge him on.

With each thrilling thrust, our mouths collide. Raul and Lorenzo stir even more flames, pressing their lips and trailing their hands over my arms, my neck, my shoulders, my chest.

Bastien's breath has gone ragged, but he shows no sign of flagging despite his sacrificed lung. He ducks his face to nuzzle my cheek between kisses. "You are mine. You're *ours*. And we're yours."

Raul lets out a gruff sound of agreement. "I love seeing you give yourself over to us," he mutters in my ear.

At the same moment, Bastien pushes even farther into me. His cock strokes the most sensitive spot within, and my jaw twitches with the deeper burst of pleasure.

My teeth scrape across his lower lip. With our next kiss, a metallic flavor seeps into my mouth.

I brace my hand against his chest to stop him, peering at his mouth. Blood is welling from a nick on his lip.

Guilt dampens the rush of my desire. "I bit your lip— you're bleeding."

Bastien flicks his tongue across the spot without any sign of concern. A starker determination firms his expression.

"You've bled for us. Why shouldn't we bleed for you?"

"But I don't—"

He cuts off my protest with another kiss, soft but still passionate. "I swear by it—I swear by my blood—we'll end Marclinus together, or I'll die trying."

The second part of that oath sets off a jab of panic, but there's no denying how emphatically he means it.

Raul's gaze darkens. He snatches a pocketknife he was carrying from his trousers and pricks the blade against his thumb. "We'll all bleed for you, as much as it takes."

He lifts his hand to my face, and I part my lips to let him brush a drop of his blood across my tongue to join Bastien's.

"All of us," Lorenzo says, holding out his hand. When Raul passes the knife to him, he repeats the gesture with his own thumb.

Bastien lowers his head again, washing the metallic tang of their vow away with the sweet force of his kiss. He picks up his pace again, driving into me with renewed urgency.

I rock with his thrusts again and again, opening myself as much as I can, welcoming him deeper. The pulses of delight swell and surge until I'm trembling under him.

Lorenzo slips his hand between us and swivels his fingers over my clit. Once, twice, and the headiest wave of pleasure crashes over me.

I cling to Bastien as I shudder harder, every particle of my body singing with my climax.

Bastien groans and pulls me tight against him. His last few bucks send me spiraling higher before he sags against me with his own release.

I hug him tightly, nestling in between my men. Hoping that we've sparked more than pleasure here tonight—that inside me might soon be growing a new life that will lead the way for so many more lives to be saved.

CHAPTER TWENTY-FIVE

Bastien

I flip through the leatherbound tome, careful with the aged paper. The magic the imperial archivists embed in the palace libraries' holdings protects the books from basic wear and tear, but the pages can still rip if handled roughly.

There's supposed to be an account of Emperor Malvius and his wife's joint march into battle toward the end here... Ah, this chapter.

In the thin light that filters this far between the shelves from the library's windows, I skim the text to confirm it has at least a little detail about that past empress and then tuck it back into its spot, leaving it protruding just half an inch farther than its neighbors.

So far, I've given six other books the same treatment. Only a couple have more than a chapter or two regarding one of the empresses—there's a slim volume that's one of the

early ruling empress's journals, and a treatise on the initial attempts to regain the western half of the continent that regularly mentions the empress who ruled during much of them.

I did also find a biography of an emperor a couple of centuries back whose ruling mother died when he was only six, and whose father ruled as emperor until the boy came of age despite only being connected to the imperial family by marriage. Aurelia might find some benefit in the account of that consort who took over the throne.

I step back to contemplate the rows of books, nowhere near as familiar to me as the shelves in the capital imperial palace where I've spent most of my life. The smell of the old leather fills my nose with an invigorating tang.

So much information I haven't had a chance to fully peruse. So many records that could guide us on the path to victory.

I wet my lips in thought, and my tongue flicks over the healing cut on my lip—the little break where Aurelia's teeth caught on my flesh. The prick of lingering pain sends a deeper rush of pleasure through me.

I close my eyes for a second, reveling in the images from last night: her body under mine, her arms around me, her hips welcoming me into her pliant heat.

My cock twitches partway to attention as if it thinks we're going to see that kind of action again so soon.

But the memory I keep returning to, the one that brings a brighter sort of warmth all through my chest, is of her gazing up at me while she told me all the things she most admired about me. Her soft, clear voice as it formed the words, *I love you.*

I know this situation is absurd from any logical standpoint. She *can't* be mine. She's literally married to another man, one who'd sooner gut her than see her in someone else's arms for anything beyond a chaste dance.

Great God help me, I don't care anymore. I don't want any other woman.

If the rest of my existence is spent drifting on the sidelines, working toward the shining future our signal star has spoken of however I can and indulging in whatever secret moments we can steal, I can't imagine being happier. I can't imagine being happy at all leaving Aurelia behind, knowing she's sacrificing so much of her own happiness and freedom for the rest of us while I pursue a life without her.

Lorenzo had the right idea. We made our biggest sacrifices years ago, and we may still be able to use the gifts we received to end Dariu's tyranny. It'll just be by protecting the woman who's proven up to the challenge, ensuring she can carry out all of her plans.

I wish I could toss every lout and would-be assassin away with a blast of manipulated air. I wish I could summon a fearsome wind to hurl her prick of a husband into the Sunblown Sea to drown.

Since I can't risk either act just yet, retrieving the books she asked me to seek out for her is the best way I can offer my support.

The bell to mark the third hour of the afternoon rings through the palace walls. I scan the shelves one last time, but there's nothing more I can add to my work in the last few minutes.

The library door sighs open. I amble out of the aisle as if I was on my way out anyway.

Aurelia halts at the sight of me. She stiffens her voice as if she's a little uncomfortable speaking to me, but her eyes stay warm. "Prince Bastien. I suppose it's a good thing I ran into you. You seem to be a frequent visitor of the palace libraries.

If you're in a more obliging mood today, could you direct me to the shelves where I'd find books on the empire's history?"

I match her tone, clenching my jaw when her guards slip into the room behind her. "Of course, Your Imperial Highness. Right this way."

I spin on my heel and stalk off toward the aisle I just left without waiting for her. It's best if the staff who follow her around think I'm annoyed by her presence.

They can't have any idea that we arranged this meeting ahead of time.

Aurelia follows me with brisk footsteps. I slow once I'm out of view of the guards, and she catches up with me a few paces down the aisle.

For a brief moment, her hand slips around mine. Our fingers twine together. Warmth blooms between our palms.

I lift her hand to press a swift kiss to her knuckles, holding her sparkling blue gaze. Absorbing the brilliance of her smile.

Gods above, I had no idea it was possible to love a woman the way I love her. Like a vast cavern inside me has been filled with an unshakeable glow.

At the creak of footsteps behind her, I reluctantly release her hand. Stepping farther away, I motion to the shelves around us. "This aisle and the one just next to it hold most of the historical accounts. I trust you can find what you need from here."

I march back out just as the guards position themselves like shadows at the end of the aisle.

All the way down the hall outside, my pulse beats at a lighter but faster rhythm. How can I feel so elated when there's so much to fear still ahead of us?

Worry still pinches at my gut, but I have enough hope in me to smooth down its sharpest edges.

Most of the court headed out to the gardens after lunch. I make my way there, willing all of my joy off my face. It wouldn't do for anyone to question what I'm looking pleased about.

With my first steps into the harsh sunlight, the last voice I'd want to hear calls over to me. "Prince Bastien, I wondered where you'd gotten to."

Marclinus's words, cool and even in tone today, bring back a twinge of an ache in the back of my skull. Raul didn't hit me as hard as he'd have needed to in order to truly knock me unconscious, and one of the medics soothed the bruising, but the effects of that fight can't completely vanish in the course of one day.

I turn to face my new emperor, setting my mouth in a careful smile. "Good afternoon, Your Imperial Majesty. There was something I wanted to look up in the library before joining you all out here."

It'd be no good lying about my whereabouts when Aurelia's guards no doubt report her every interaction to him.

He hums to himself, his gray eyes glinting like steel. "After yesterday morning's display, perhaps you should be researching combat techniques. Archery only gets you so far."

I spread my hands as if in supplication. "Unfortunately my sacrifice makes me rather unsuited for the intensities of hand-to-hand combat. But I may seek out more training when we're returned to Vivencia."

From what I understand, we're only going to remain here near Ubetta for another few days, touring the countryside for more festivities and lounging at the palace in between.

"A wise man develops every strength he can," Marclinus says in a tone I can't read, but he turns away a moment later, releasing me from the conversation.

Was he trying to rub my failure in my face—as if any of

his own nobles could have bested Raul in battle either? Or is he already working some new scheme I haven't gotten a clear picture of yet?

With renewed apprehension, I stroll between the flower beds, veering toward the shade of the neatly spaced trees to avoid the full blaze of the summer sun. There's little breeze this afternoon. The floral scent hangs in the air, cloyingly thick.

I pass many chattering nobles, one cluster of which Raul has inserted himself into. His laugh is dark enough that I don't think he's enjoying himself, but since he's the only one of us who's ever socialized much with the Darium nobles, one of his tasks is joining their gossip and listening for any information that might reveal one of Marclinus's weaknesses.

Aurelia's whole plan will fall apart if there's no way she can take the emperor down without being exposed as a murderer.

I meander on toward the garden's largest fountain and hesitate at an unexpected pairing that's come into view by a nearby hedge.

The sun glares off Neven's white-blond hair where he's standing with High Commander Axius. The imperial military advisor makes a few brusque gestures of his hand to emphasize what he's saying, and Neven nods as if to show he's taking it all in.

What would my youngest foster brother be talking to one of Marclinus's closest colleagues about? Did Axius draw him apart from the rest of us for some reason?

Or possibly the kid sought out the high commander for this conversation. I know his ego was smarting after his quick dispatching in yesterday's scuffle.

Does he think the highest military officer in the empire is going to offer combat tips? Raul would happily arrange more sparring sessions.

I walk over to the fountain to enjoy the faint coolness offered by the running water, though there isn't enough breeze to produce a spray. Someday, perhaps I'll be able to summon one without needing to worry about the consequences.

After a few minutes, Axius claps Neven on the shoulder in an unnervingly companionable gesture and strides off. The kid watches him go with a flinty expression, as if he's girding himself for some difficult mission.

I don't like the looks of that at all.

I join him, taking on a casual air in case anyone notices us. "I didn't know you were friendly with the high commander."

Neven's face twitches with a hint of guilt. "I just had a few things I wanted to ask him about."

So he's the one who approached Axius rather than the other way around. I don't know if that's better or worse.

My lips twist into a sympathetic grimace. "You shouldn't take the fight yesterday too hard. Raul has five years of combat experience on you, including all the real arena battles he's fought in. Once you're finished with your core studies in a year or so—"

Neven cuts me off with a shake of his head and a flash of his eyes. "It's not about that. There are bigger things for us to think about than one stupid skirmish that was more like a show, aren't there?"

I pause, studying him. "What do you mean?"

He guffaws with typical teenage defiance. "Things are changing. We have to be prepared. Do you think I don't know that you three are always going off and deciding things without me? I need to be ready too."

A chill washes over me. "Neven, we've never meant to shut you out. If there's anything that's bothering you, we'd rather you came to us—"

He shrugs me off. "It's not that important. You wouldn't understand anyway. I just need to figure some things out for myself."

He strides away without a backward glance.

CHAPTER TWENTY-SIX

Aurelia

"It was *so* impressive watching you fight up close," the baronissa simpers, peering up at Raul through her eyelashes as she strokes her fingers over his brawny arm.

On the other side of the carriage from the pair, I will my jaw not to clench and my smile to stay mild. When Marclinus invited the prince and a couple of other nobles into our carriage for our third day on the road back to Vivencia, I have to think he predicted the ensuing flirtation. It's not as if Raul's reputation in court is any secret.

Is he evaluating my reaction to the other woman's pawing and Raul's cocky grin in return? Raul's interest or lack thereof while in my presence?

Or is the pairing part of some other game I can't guess at yet? He might be punishing the woman's husband, who's sitting next to me, for a transgression I'm not privy to.

Regardless, I have to stay here and respond to my husband's lively chatter as if I've barely noticed what's developing on the opposite bench. Raul has no choice but to lean closer and make his teasing remarks as if he welcomes the attempted seduction as he would have before.

The nobles will wonder at his lack of interest if he leaves off his rakish ways too suddenly. Has he kept up his pastime of bedding married ladies as some kind of revenge against the court at large?

No matter what promises of devotion he's offered me, he probably *should*. Even if the thought of him drawing this woman into his embrace makes me want to toss her right out of the carriage.

Marclinus lifts the bottle of wine he liberated from the kitchen at the last waypoint as if in toast. "We should have another arena exhibition while we're back in the capital. Give the prince of Lavira some proper opponents to show off his skills against!"

He grins with all his teeth, takes a swig from the bottle, and passes it to the baron beside him.

The other man is just lifting the bottle to his lips when the carriage jerks to a stop. As the baron sputters around the sudden slosh of wine into his mouth, one of our soldier escorts appears at the carriage window.

"The bridge is out just up ahead by Norbina, Your Imperial Majesty. The townspeople are already working at repairing it. They think it'll be secure in another few hours."

Marclinus sighs. "What's the next nearest route over the river?"

The soldier grimaces apologetically. "There's a bridge down by Thavess, but it'd take until the end of the day just to backtrack to the crossroads and make it over there."

"Fine then. I suppose we'll wait." My husband rubs his

hands together. "I'll see if I can motivate the workmen to get on with it a little faster."

My stomach sours with dread. I ease out of the carriage after Marclinus, not certain what I could do to moderate his whims but feeling I should be in a position to try.

The contingent of cavalry from the front of our convoy has spread out to reinforce the thinner ranks that ride alongside the carriages. Beyond those who've remained at the front of the procession, people in plain shirts and trousers are milling around the bank of the river. A heap of wood and stone lies nearby.

Dozens more civilians have gathered along the bank and spread out across the field next to the road, peering at our parade of opulence.

Marclinus strides to the front of the convoy, his guards hustling close behind. He lifts his hand to catch the workers' attention. "Thank you for your service, my good people! I'll see that a fine reward is sent your way once I reach the capital. The faster you can get us across this river, the finer it'll be!"

My anxiety fades. Apparently the wine has left my husband relatively good-humored.

I suppose he wouldn't last long as emperor if he terrorized even his own country's people on a daily basis.

Marclinus ambles back along the procession and strikes up a conversation with a couple of marchions from a carriage a couple down from ours. I give our horses a scratch behind their ears and then meander around the vehicle to stretch my legs.

And also to avoid getting back into that enclosed space with my secret lover and his potential new paramour.

A tense muttering passes between some of the soldiers. When I glance toward their protective line along the convoy, the crowd of watching civilians has drawn closer. I think it's expanded as well, with more townspeople venturing over from their homes to gape at the traveling imperial court.

"Give us space!" one of the captains hollers at the nearest onlookers, tugging on his reins so his stallion stamps its feet warningly. "Stay well back from Their Imperial Eminences."

It's Marclinus the spectators are particularly interested to observe, isn't it? Several necks crane as the crowd tries to peer beyond the soldiers to see what he's doing.

A few of them gaze my way, leaning to look around the cavalry. One woman's face brightens when our eyes meet. "There's Empress Aurelia!"

Oh, maybe they're curious about me as well. I lift my hand in a polite wave.

The focus of the crowd appears to shift, more people moving my way as if hoping to catch a glimpse. As they edge closer to the soldiers again, a flurry of murmurs carries with the faint breeze.

The bits and pieces of comments that reach my ears are a mix of eager and urgent.

"...carried out the rite just like he did!"

"Can you imagine..."

"...can't be good, Emperor Tarquin passing on the same night as..."

"...all the way from Accasy..."

"...giving the bounty to the people most in need, so generous of..."

"...when the gods send an omen like that..."

The last remark comes with a hurried warding gesture. I resist the urge to rub my arms self-consciously.

Word about my participation in the confirmation rites has obviously spread, but it hasn't been enough to reassure every Darium citizen, especially those who weren't there to see my efforts.

Losing their emperor the night of my wedding is an association that's difficult to get over.

They're watching me now, evaluating the way I'm standing here. Trying to judge whether to cheer me on or shun me?

At least a few people have decided on the former. "Hurrah for our new empress!" someone hollers from farther back in the growing crowd, punctuated by a couple of nearby whoops of approval.

I wander a little farther along the convoy, not wanting to look as if I'm hiding but not sure what I can do that would sway anyone in my favor right now. It isn't as if I can help them mend the bridge. The soldiers don't look inclined to let me even speak to the civilians face-to-face.

After past incidents, I can't blame them for their vigilance. And Marclinus has already berated me for stepping beyond my supposed place. I can't meddle much without risking his wrath again.

As I stroll along, more voices call out in my praise. I aim a few more waves at the spectators. I nod at the nobles I pass who've stepped out of their carriages, but their answering smiles look a little stiff.

I pause by one of the staff carriages to accept a goblet of juice to take the edge off the heat. Bianca sidles over next to me to claim a drink of her own.

"You're causing quite a stir," she says under her breath.

I glance toward the watching townspeople. "I didn't intend to. It's not surprising they're curious."

"Not just curious. And it isn't only them getting riled up." Bianca tips her head toward the rest of the convoy. "Some of the court has been grumbling this past week about the attention they feel you've been encouraging, as if you're trying to set yourself up as better than those of us from Dariu."

Gods smite me, is there anything I can do—or have done in my general vicinity—that the imperial court won't use as an excuse to criticize the "wild princess" from the north?

I stop myself from rolling my eyes. "I simply want the people of what's now my home country to warm up to me, since I'm *not* originally Darium. It won't help any of us if they think I'm an ominous presence."

The vicerine's lips curve at a wry angle. "I'm sure you've already noticed that most noble folk are mainly concerned with what benefits us directly and immediately—and looking as good as possible while we're enjoying those benefits."

For fuck's sake. Am I now expected to polish the common people's opinion of the entire court as well as myself?

I do need the lords and ladies on my side too. Giving them gifts clearly wasn't enough to win them over. What could possibly mollify them when it comes to a complaint like—

A flash of inspiration passes through my head. I pause, holding back a laugh at the idea that seems absurd.

Perhaps it isn't. Perhaps it's actually genius.

It could calm their complaints, give them all the more reason to appreciate me, and serve the townspeople at the same time.

Bianca arches an eyebrow at me. "You look as if you've had an interesting thought."

"I have. I have indeed."

I stride on toward the farthest of the imperial carriages. Bianca trails behind me out of apparent curiosity.

Two marchions and marchionissas who've been traveling together watch my approach with a vaguely apprehensive air. "What can we do for you, Your Imperial Highness?" one of the marchionissas asks.

I clasp my hands in front of me and put on a tone of

pure earnestness. "I was just thinking of these poor workers striving away and having to wait so many days for compensation. Wouldn't it be lovely if we showed the people of Norbina just how generous all of the imperial court can be?"

Her husband perks up, though his tone is cautious. "What do you mean?"

I motion toward their gilded carriage. "I'm sure you're carrying some coins or trinkets of value you could part with for the rest of the journey. We'll take a collection and have it presented to the workers on behalf of the court nobles. When we return to the capital palace, I'll see that you're repaid twice over."

They can hardly argue with the chance to double the worth of their valuables while appearing ever so benevolent in the process. An excited titter passes between the marchionissas as they clamber into the carriage to decide what to contribute.

"Quite the stratagem," Bianca remarks as I turn to proceed along every noble carriage in the convoy.

I raise my eyebrow right back at her. "I hope you'll join in the generosity too, Vicerine?"

She laughs, more warmly than I think I've ever heard before. "I'd imagine I will, for such a reward."

By the time I've made my way through the entire procession, the nobles from the tail end are already bustling toward the front of the convoy with pouches of silver and plainer bits of jewelry. That's good enough—the townspeople might not be able to easily exchange full court finery for anything they'd actually find useful.

I give an explanation to one of the captains, whose forehead furrows but who swings down from his horse to take up the collection.

As I return to my own carriage, Marclinus saunters over,

his smirk more crooked than before. "I hear you're attempting to empty my imperial treasury for a single bridge, wife."

My pulse stutters, but I make my own smile as sweet and innocent as possible. "The people are working so hard to ensure that our journey is delayed as little as possible—and they should know what a fantastic court you lead, shouldn't they?"

"All due to my own influence, I'm sure," he says.

He doesn't move to intervene, though, simply watching as the final nobles hurry to offer their contributions. When the captain presents the workers with their reward, a volley of awed voices rise up in response. "Thank you, Your Imperial Eminences. Thank you, everyone of the court! It's our honor to serve you."

I think that should be well enough settled, but the swarm of onlookers in the field presses closer to the line of soldiers again. "Empress Aurelia's kindness is spreading," someone says.

"She's setting such an example for the court."

"What a blessing on our country!"

More of the horses shift uneasily on their hooves. "Give the convoy space!" the other captain shouts.

A couple of his underlings glance back at me with the briefest of frowns.

Damn it all. I've lifted up my fellow nobles but caused more trouble for those guarding us.

My heart thumps faster, but perhaps I should consider this moment another opportunity. The townspeople want to see me, to hear from me.

I can give them that and support the men and women in arms at the same time.

I return to the captain who handed over the collected

reward. "Do you have an amplification charm? I'd like to borrow it for a minute."

His expression turns even more puzzled, but he hands over a small rod that contains the enchantment.

I hold it beneath my chin and speak in a clear, firm voice that the charm pitches across the field ahead. "People of Norbina, as your empress, I have a request to make. I understand you're interested to know more about me and this court, but please gather farther back on the field. These fine soldiers have one of the most important duties in the empire, which is keeping your emperor—my wonderful husband—safe. They're committed to that purpose and have never failed us yet. Let us show our respect for their fantastic service."

Several of the nearby soldiers sit up a little straighter at the praise. The crowd's murmurs sound somewhat discontented, but the civilians do pull back a few paces.

I ease toward my carriage. Raul and his baronissa companion have long since climbed out, and the prince is now standing near the wheel by the driver's seat. Perfect.

"Thank you!" I say to the common folk. "Perhaps even a little farther back—because then you can get a better view."

Lowering the charm, I turn to Raul and take on an imperious tone. "Help me up."

He blinks at me, but when I grasp the side of the carriage, a smile of understanding flickers across his face. He grasps my slippered foot and boosts me high enough that I can pull myself onto the ledge above the carriage doors.

Being Raul, he also manages to stroke my ankle with a surreptitious caress before he lets me go.

I scramble the rest of the way onto the roof of the carriage and carefully straighten up. Now standing well above the heads of the cavalry, I can see all across the mass of townspeople and the buildings of their home a little farther down the river.

The faces that gaze up at me still show a mix of delight and apprehension, but even those who don't trust me yet should recognize this gesture of good will. I spread my hands on either side of my airy dress, presenting myself to their observations.

With a huff that might hold an unnerving amount of irritation, Marclinus hefts himself onto the carriage after me. Naturally he doesn't like to get the impression that he might be outdone.

He stands beside me and tucks his arm around my waist, raising his hand in welcome to his people as if this was all his idea from the start. But I don't mind. Having him show that he'll stand by me will only improve my significance in these people's eyes.

I just have to hope that I haven't fallen even further in his.

CHAPTER TWENTY-SEVEN

Aurelia

"What are you reading?"

My husband's cool tone puts me on guard before I even lift my eyes from the book. He's barely spoken to me in the couple of hours we've been on the road this morning, the last short stretch before we reach Vivencia after the delay by Norbina set back our schedule.

Marclinus hasn't criticized my handling of the situation a few days ago beyond the few snarky remarks he made in the moment, but I get the impression he's simply pretending it never happened rather than accepting. For the entire journey, he's alternated between filling our carriage with friends so he doesn't need to speak to me except in random chatter and burying himself in records and private pondering even more deeply than on the journey east.

This might be the first time in our eight days on the road that he's shown any interest in my activities while we're alone. I don't know if the question is a peace offering of sorts or the prelude to a new battle.

I lift the book so he can see the cover with its ornately lettered title. "It's an account of the Grotillian Period of Revolt and the imperial strategies for ending the series of uprisings. I thought it might provide some insight useful to the present unrest, should it continue to escalate."

Actually, I'm mainly interested in the sections that discuss the one empress who ruled during that period and the brief mentions of the wives of the emperors before and after her. I don't think it'll do me much good to mention as much to Marclinus, though.

He raises his eyebrows. "You dug that out of the vast library back home when there'd been nothing more than a couple of outpost attacks?"

He considers the capital palace to be "home" then, does he? It makes sense when it seems he and his father spent more than half of their time there compared to the various other imperial estates.

I dip my head as if abashed. "I actually discovered it in the library at the Ubettan residence, which was a little less intimidating to peruse, after the matter seemed worthy of more concern. I hope it's all right that I borrowed it."

Marclinus studies me for long enough that the back of my neck prickles. Then his lips curve with a trace of a smile. "I can hardly complain about you immersing yourself in our country's history."

He's certainly complained about many things I'd think show equal commitment to my new role, but I'm not going to mention that either. I bob my head and drop my gaze to return to my reading.

Perhaps some hint of my annoyance showed through

despite my efforts, or perhaps Marclinus is simply poking at me to see what he can turn up. He waits several seconds, long enough for me to read through a short paragraph in which the author appears to think the empress's new gown is the worthiest point of focus, and then speaks up again.

"You're angry with me."

My eyes dart up with a jolt of surprise I can't completely suppress. Marclinus gazes back at me, neither his expression nor his tone revealing how *he* feels about that statement.

My stomach lurches with the sense that I'm standing at the verge of a precipice. Another trial my husband has decided to spring on me. The carriage rocks with a pothole, setting me even more off-balance.

The literal jolt at least gives me an excuse to brace one hand against the seat, my fingers sinking into the velvet cushion. "Pardon me? I don't know what you mean."

Marclinus's stare doesn't waver. "You've been excessively quiet since Prospira's rite. You haven't asked me for news of the current uprising or offered your opinions on it, even while you're reading up on a similar subject. It seems obvious you're upset that I changed my mind about how I'd handle Lavira."

I don't know whether to be more irritated that he's prodding me on this subject after he specifically lambasted me for offering my opinion or that he's missed all the other reasons I'd have to resent him.

It doesn't matter, since it wouldn't be wise to admit to the irritation at all.

"You told me that it wasn't my place to suggest possible strategies," I say as evenly as possible. "That I should only worry about serving you personally rather than the empire. I thought you wanted me to stay out of that matter." I glance down at my book. "This is only for my own understanding, so I have a better sense of what you're going through."

Marclinus's jaw works, as if he's grappling with his temper.

What does he want from me? Is he honestly going to lay into me for *not* hassling him about his response to the rebellion after he tore into me the last time I dared to question him?

He inhales slowly. "Did it not occur to you that you might serve me by continuing to share your views so that I can be sure I've left no possibility unconsidered?"

I can't stop a bit of an edge from creeping into my voice. "Not when you called the strategies I favor 'nonsense' and 'bullshit,' no."

My husband blinks. For a second, I could almost believe he doesn't remember the insults he hurled at me.

Perhaps he doesn't. Perhaps it was merely one of many dressing-downs he delivered in the course of that day, no more significant than the breath he just took.

"Ah." He swipes his hand past the scar on his lip. "I see your point. No wonder you've been upset."

My fingers ache from the strain of *not* digging them into the cushion in frustration. "I never said I was upset. I'm trying to ensure you're as happy as possible with my part in this marriage."

Marclinus sighs and leans back on the bench, folding his arms loosely over his chest. "What if what I need from you varies somewhat from day to day?"

"Then I suppose I'll do my best to keep up. But it is difficult to be sure when what you appear to welcome one day turns out to have gravely offended you."

I'm not a fucking mind-reader, you infuriating prick.

Marclinus waves his hand dismissively. "I wasn't offended. Sometimes I may be more extravagant with how I express myself than is strictly accurate. It was a long day with trying news, and I was not in the mood right then to be challenged."

I can't hold back the question that's clawed by my throat. "Are you suggesting that I *shouldn't* take you at your word?"

"I'm suggesting that you need to learn how to determine what I'm really getting at. And not be offended yourself if I'm not perfectly polite."

"I'm doing my best. It would be appreciated if you'd be forgiving when I err, especially at this early stage in our marriage. And if you understand why I might prefer to make those errors on the side of caution rather than risk provoking hostile moods."

With the last words tumbling out, I snap my mouth closed. My heart stutters in a sudden panic.

I haven't been quite that forceful with him before. I managed not to outright criticize him, but the implicit chiding isn't exactly subtle.

My husband's eyes have narrowed. "I wouldn't have thought you'd have made it through all those trials only to be crushed by a few harsh words."

Is that all he thinks he's punished me with over the past few weeks?

I push a demure smile onto my face. "I'm quite all right. As I said, I simply wish to see you content and to serve you as well as I can."

His cool gray gaze lingers on me through several more beats of my heart. I'm afraid to look away.

Something shifts in Marclinus's expression with a twist of his mouth. "I may have been overly extravagant with my demands on Accasy's breamwood trade as well. Obviously doubling production would be over-stretching. I was merely making a point. A ten percent or so expansion should be more than satisfactory."

So he *can* decipher that I have reasons beyond my own comfort to be concerned about his moods. The punishment still stings when I'd hoped to decrease the pressure Dariu is putting on my family's kingdom, but I'll take the small win for what it is. "I'm sure my former people will happily fulfill that request."

Marclinus adjusts his position restlessly as if he's not completely satisfied with my response. "You do need to recognize that I'm the ultimate authority in the empire. The decisions are mine and mine alone to make, regardless of what we've discussed. Any great leader must have the ability to change his or her mind as circumstances call for it."

He already thinks of himself as a "great" leader, does he? I wonder what the Lavirians his soldiers are stringing up would say about that.

"I wouldn't want you to do anything you feel is bad policy," I reply. "When I ask questions, it's so I have the full picture. I much prefer knowing what's going on around me to being kept in the dark, whether I have any say in what's happening or not. And I think I can be a better partner to you the more I'm aware."

"Yes. That's reasonable." Marclinus brushes his unruly golden curls away from his forehead, his gaze sliding away from me. "I've prepared for this position for a long time, but the promotion was rather… sudden. I've gained many vital duties and lost the one person I fully trusted for guidance all in one swoop. It will take a little time before my footing is perfect. I appreciate your patience while I find the right balance."

That almost sounds like an apology—or far closer to one than I've ever gotten from him before, in any case.

It's my turn to blink at him, just for a second before I gather myself. "Patience is one of my greatest virtues. You can thank my dedication to Elox for that."

A thin but definite smile stretches Marclinus's lips. "I

should never discount the wisdom of any of the godlen. And your input has generally been both thoughtful and relevant."

He glances down at his wrist, his fingers grazing the gold band that symbolizes our marriage vows. "We *are* meant to be a partnership. Perhaps what would serve both our interests best is if I ask you for your opinions when I'm sure I can give them due consideration, and you believe that if I do ask you outright, I mean to consider them?"

When his eyes meet mine again with a glimmer of warmth shining in them, a lump rises in my throat.

In this moment, he sounds genuine. But after all the cruelty he's shown in the past, after the many times he's turned on me on a whim, how can I possibly trust him?

Neither I, the men I love, nor the countries we hope to protect will be safe until this man is ashes like his father. Him being slightly nice to me for a minute changes nothing.

But I should take the opportunity to touch on one delicate subject I'm going to have to address sometime.

I offer a soft smile in return. "That sounds like a fair compromise. May I ask *your* opinion on something?"

"What's that?"

"You expressed some misgivings about my participation in the confirmation rites. I had planned on completing the final two as well. If it's your wish that I abstain, so be it, but I worry about the impression that will give our people."

Marclinus nods slowly, his eyes going distant as he thinks through the implications. "It might seem as if you backed down out of fear—or lacked the commitment to see them all through."

At least he's clever enough to put those pieces together.

My smile tightens. "Exactly. I wouldn't want to tarnish the start of your reign with an empress who's seen as not only a bad omen but weak or fickle as well."

"You've certainly made some progress toward turning

that first perception around." He chuckles. "And I'm curious to see what you make of the final two rites. If I seem irritable about it later, simply remind me of this conversation."

And hope that he doesn't claim it was all a lie?

I'm hardly reassured, but I can't ask for more approval than that. Whatever happens in the future, I'll deal with it then.

Right now, in this strange moment, the silence that falls between us in the carriage feels nearly companionable.

Why couldn't he be this man—arrogant and demanding, yes, but also contemplative and open to some small compromise—all of the time? I could tolerate being married to that man for the rest of my life, finding my ways of working alongside him.

As it is, I never know how quickly he'll go back to poisoning me or mocking my moral standards.

He's worn down the vast stores of patience I do possess bit by bit...

My fingers close around the spine of the book. Maybe that's the beginning of a strategy right there.

I don't have to knock him down in one blow. I can prick at him gradually, weaken him in some subtle way that'll only matter in the face of a supposed accident.

All I need to do is determine what sort of accident he might happen to stumble into with the right nudge.

Chapter Twenty-Eight

Aurelia

As I slink through the dim passages within the walls, a twinge runs through my belly, reminding me of the disappointing news I'm bearing. I swallow hard and push myself onward.

As soon as I saw Marclinus leaving this evening's entertainments with one of the court ladies, I signaled to the princes to meet me in our hidden room after a couple of bells. I hadn't been counting on returning to my chambers only to discover a splotch of red in my drawers.

I descend the stairs, rubbing my nose against the tickle of dust, and set my jaw. One lost month isn't much. It'll be a pleasure just getting to spend time with the men I love without the pressure of watching eyes.

I tell myself that, fixing a determined smile on my face as I ease aside the panel to step into the room. But the moment

I see my three lovers' faces brighten in the glow of lanternlight, a burn comes into my eyes.

Raul's expression turns fierce in an instant. "What's wrong, Aurelia?"

I blink hard, willing back the threatening tears. "It's nothing particularly startling. These things take time. I started my monthly bleed."

The two nights of closeness we ended up sharing back in the Ubettan palace weren't enough. I'm not yet with child.

I don't need to spell that out to my men. Lorenzo comes straight to me and slips his arm around my waist, drawing me against his well-built frame. Bastien steps near enough to cup my cheek and offer a kiss.

"We have time," he says. "And we'll get plenty more chances."

Raul makes a gruff sound and claims my mouth the moment Bastien eases back. He stays at my side, stroking his fingers over my hair while Lorenzo dips his head close enough to rest his cheek against my temple. "I can't see why the godlen wouldn't bless *you* of all people with a child quickly. Who would be a kinder, more patient mother than our Shepherdess? And you have a much bigger worthy cause on top of that!"

I make a face. "I don't know how many of the godlen consider murdering the emperor a 'worthy cause.'"

Bastien lifts his chin. "They don't get to decide our lives. If they have a problem with getting rid of Marclinus, they should have guided *him* to be a better human being."

Their emphatic support brings a trace of my smile back despite the melancholy lingering around my heart. "I was just hoping we could already be on our way. We're not even really started yet."

Lorenzo tightens his embrace. *"You have all your skills,*

and all of ours as well, as much as you need them. Nothing ever holds you back for long."

His comment about my skills sends inspiration tingling through my head. I've never put my gift to this particular purpose before, but— "I could brew a fertility potion. I should have thought of that to begin with! It isn't exactly *healing*, but it's close enough…"

I drift away from the men as I reach to my gift, focusing on the purpose of encouraging a new life to take hold in my womb. Images of the necessary ingredients and the ways to prepare them flit behind my eyes.

One draws me up short. "Oh. It never occurred to me to keep a supply of socha." Probably because up until now, I've been much more focused on preventing pregnancy than encouraging it.

The princes have watched my pacing. Raul cocks his head. "Will it be hard to get your hands on some?"

"Not exactly… It's a sort of moss that grows only on the trunks of evergreen trees. Pale green with a star-like shape to the leaves and tiny orange flowers. I've seen it in the woods here on the imperial grounds at least once."

Bastien nods. "I know the kind you mean. I've definitely come across it."

"I don't think it has much medical use *other* than encouraging fertility, though." I suck my lower lip under my teeth as I think over the implications. "And it's not the sort of plant I might be gathering simply for decoration. I'm not sure I want my guards wondering what I'm up to and mentioning it to Marclinus. When I do get pregnant, it should seem like the natural course of things, not something I went out of my way to ensure."

I don't want there to be any chance at all of someone tying my future child to a plot to murder the emperor shortly thereafter.

Bastien catches my hand with a brief squeeze. "You don't even need to worry about that. I can go find some right now and bring it back to you without any guards being the wiser. It's not as if I have a host of them following *me* around."

Of course. I have to keep reminding myself that I'm not mired in this awful situation on my own.

I grip his hand tightly in return before letting it go. "Thank you. You don't have to gather it right away—it won't matter for several more days at least—"

"Better to get it done now while I definitely have the chance to bring it to you unnoticed." He lowers his head for another swift kiss and heads into the hidden passage.

As I watch the panel shut behind him, another uneasy thought rises up. "We're going to be leaving for Rexoran to carry out Creaden's confirmation rite soon. Another week on the road each way and who knows how long at that imperial residence without being able to reach each other through secret hallways."

"We have other ways of getting around the guards' notice," Lorenzo reminds me. *"We've seen for sure that yours can't detect magic. As long as Marclinus isn't nearby, I can use my gift to conceal you."*

I touch his cheek, warmed by the affection shining in his dark eyes even if I doubt his suggestion will be carried out so easily. "Whisking me away right under their noses will be quite a feat."

He smiles. *"You've only seen a few glimpses of what I'm capable of."* He glances toward Raul. *"I think our empress could use cheering up. Why don't I give her a trip to more familiar ground?"*

I knit my brow. "What do you mean?"

Lorenzo brushes a kiss to my temple. *"I've been doing a little different reading from usual. There are a few accounts from delegates and other travelers who ventured up to the wild north.*

One of them even included little paintings in her journal. I just won't be able to concentrate enough to create my voice while I'm also doing this…"

The room around me shimmers. The dull walls and pieces of worn, mismatched furniture fade away.

Suddenly I'm seeing bronze fixtures beaming from walls of dark wooden paneling topped by leaf-patterned wall paper. The floor has transformed into a matching polished wood. A vast hearth crackles with a cheery fire, and a thick-beamed ceiling arches high above our heads.

I lose my breath. Everywhere I look, I pick up on more familiar details: the treetop imagery etched in the mantle over the fireplace, the sturdy style of the side table holding a carafe of some beverage.

Even the air tastes almost right. A hint of pine and woodsmoke winds through its coolness.

It's not exact. But if I woke up in this place instead of having it created around me out of much drabber surroundings, I'm not sure how quickly I'd realize it's an illusion.

I spin around, absorbing every facet of the conjured space with a soaring sensation inside me. "This is incredible. It looks just like a common room in one of the noble houses back in Accasy." My gaze darts back to Lorenzo. "You captured it so well."

One corner of his lips curves upward again. I can only imagine how much effort it's taking to produce such a solid and detailed illusion. No wonder he can only speak with his hands while he's doing it.

His fingers curl between us. *All for you.*

With a tick of his head, music winds through the room —the usual sprightly melody of the imperial court dance, not an Accasian song, but he wouldn't have been able to learn an entire musical style from a few sparse records.

Lorenzo holds out his hand to me with a questioning gesture. *May I have this dance?*

All I can do is let out a giddy laugh and twine my fingers with his.

None of this is real. Not the music or the achingly familiar imagery of home or the impression that we're free to dance together without any fear of consequences.

But this temporary, illusionary escape is the best gift I can imagine getting right now, reality being what it is.

We glide around the room, Lorenzo resting one hand on the small of my back. He draws me close against his toned chest and nuzzles my hair at a lull in his conjured music. When his mouth grazes my skin, I tip back my face to welcome a fuller kiss.

Raul clears his throat, watching the two of us from the side of the room with an amused expression. "I think you've gotten to show off enough. Our empress deserves a chance to dance with all of us away from prying eyes."

As Lorenzo releases me with a friendly grin, I arch my eyebrows at the prince of Lavira. "It often seems your eyes— and gift—are doing much of the prying."

"Hmm." He leans in, tucking me flush against his massive frame in a way we'd never dare in front of the court. "I'll never venture farther than you want me, Shepherdess. I just intend to keep ensuring you want me everywhere."

His suggestive tone sends an eager shiver over my skin, even though I hadn't planned on letting tonight's encounter get very intimate.

As we step with the music, Raul teases his fingers all the way down my spine to my ass and up again. "What else would we do if you brought us home with you? Other than taking plenty of tumbles in your wild northern bed, of course."

I let out a soft snort, though I'm sure he isn't wrong.

My thoughts drift beyond the imagery Lorenzo has crafted. "I'd show you the big wild woods we're fond of—much more breathtaking than the tame imperial forest. Hold a festival in the capital so we could dance among the city folk rather than ringed off by guards. We've some gifted musicians of our own." I aim a smile at Lorenzo over Raul's shoulder. "And you'd have to sample treats from all my favorite bakeries and cafes in town…"

"Hmm. I think we'll have to make that dream real someday too."

I tip my head against the massive man's shoulder, tamping down a pang of homesickness. "I'd like that. And I'd like to see all of your homes too."

Raul chuckles. "I can just picture you politely sparring with my parents and sisters. The fiercest of diplomats, all of you. But of course I'd have to whisk you off to have you all to myself for a little while. There's this secluded cove along the lakeshore where we could tuck ourselves away…"

He dips his head to nibble a path down the side of my neck, and a gasp slips out of me. I'm starting to think maybe the mess of stripping down in my current state would be worth it when Lorenzo reclaims me.

The prince of Rione's eyes shine as I rest my hands on his chest. His thumb strokes a gentle line over my ribs.

I beam back at him. "I already know a little of what you'd like to share of your home. The picture you painted with words during the rite of Prospira was beautiful."

Lorenzo lifts one hand so he can sign his answer. *More beautiful with you there.*

Even after everything that's already passed between us, a blush warms my cheeks.

I dance with him through another song and then sway back to Raul, letting everything but the illusion fade away. Then the panel in the wall slides open.

With a startled laugh, Bastien passes into the illusion, gaping at the imagery conjured around him. He aims a crooked smile at Lorenzo. "I didn't know you were planning a party."

Not planned, his foster brother answers. A sheen of sweat has formed on his forehead, but he adds, *I can hold it so you can dance too.*

"I'm not going to refuse that offer."

Bastien turns to me as Raul releases me without complaint—though with a provocative caress of my thigh. The prince of Cotea presents me with a small cloth carry-bag. "I thought you'd want something discreet to keep it in. I hope I brought enough."

I tug the bag open to check the lumps of socha moss inside and grab Bastien in a hug. "It's plenty. Thank you so much."

He embraces me tightly in return. "It's to all our benefit too. Now how about that dance?"

I haven't twirled around the room with Bastien since our last dance when Emperor Tarquin collapsed. Perhaps he's remembering that too, because as he sets his hand on my waist, his expression turns briefly solemn. "It should always have been like this. It should always *be* like this. One way or another, we'll make it happen."

I grasp his shoulder, wishing I never had to let go. "I won't stop trying until we get there."

After our second dance, the traces of strain in Lorenzo's face have deepened—his jaw flexing, a crease forming in his brow. It's a complex illusion to maintain for so long.

I step back from all of the men, my joy bittersweet. "Let's end this wonderful evening here. I shouldn't stay away from my room for too long."

The trappings of an Accasian parlor fall away, leaving the

abandoned servants' room that looks even drabber now. A sigh slips from Lorenzo's lips.

I grasp his hand to emphasize how much I loved his offering. "It was lovely. I had no idea... No one really knows how much you're capable of, do they? Have you even told your family about your real gift?"

He shakes his head and answers with his hands. *Safer if secret. They'd still think I'm broken.*

I bristle instinctively. "You're not *broken*."

They see it that way. Can't talk long even with gift. Tires me out.

"That shouldn't matter. You can express yourself in all kinds of ways."

Lorenzo shrugs and cups my face with one hand while he swivels the other. *I don't care. This is my family now.*

He indicates the other two men and me. A lump rises in my throat. "It's an honor to be part of it."

When I step toward the panel, Raul joins me. "We'll see you back to your apartment like the gentlemen we supposedly are."

Bastien and Lorenzo follow without complaint. As we weave through the shadowy passages, we drop our voices to mere murmurs.

"I did get a chance to do some research into the Creaden rite," Bastien tells me. "Unfortunately, the information I found is about as vague as with the Prospiran one. It sounds as if you'd be leading citizens in some way—that might be metaphorical —and as if it relies a lot on your sight. There were multiple references to 'seeing the right path' and 'discerning the route.'"

I consider those details. "I can probably concoct some kind of 'cure' that'll sharpen my eyes temporarily. Let me know if you come across any other descriptions."

"Of course."

"And we'll keep doing what we can to encourage support for you as empress," Lorenzo says, his illusionary voice a little rough after the energy he's already expended.

I shoot him a nervous look. "Be careful not to be too overt."

His smile turns sly. *"My gift makes subtle nudges much easier."*

"I can pull off a trick or two myself," Raul puts in. "What I've mainly been trying to figure out is how we're going to topple that prick when we're ready."

That is the big question that's haunted me too. I worry at my lip. "How did the four of you expect to do it back when you were making your own plans?"

Bastien answers for his foster brother. "Come at him with all our gifts in quick succession—an illusion to startle, a shadow solidified so he'd trip, a gust of wind pushing him in an unfortunate direction... Something like that. But it wouldn't work. He has protection from any kind of direct magic as well as from blades and other weaponry. And we need it to look like an accident. How—"

He cuts his hushed voice off completely at a much louder remark that reverberates through the wall up ahead, just beyond the panel leading to my room.

It's Marclinus's spirited tone. "Here you go. I've brought you some company while I enjoy my wife's!"

He must be talking to my guards—referring to his own staying outside with them while he comes in.

My heart lurches. "I have to get back into my room."

Raul is already lunging ahead down the passage. As he presses the spot to open the hidden panel, I dash after him.

There's no time for good-bye kisses or even a loving glance. I spring out onto the rug next to the bed, the panel whirs into place behind me—and my bedroom door swings open.

Marclinus saunters in with a jaunty stride. I smooth the skirt of my dress and smile through the racing of my pulse.

Am I flushed from that last short dash? Gods help me, where would we be now if I'd returned even half a minute later?

This is the first time my husband has called on me after he's seemed to take up with other women for the night. I'll have to be even more cautious about my clandestine meetings in the future.

"Husband," I say, managing to smooth my nerves out of my voice. "What a wonderful surprise."

Marclinus cocks his head. "What are you up to, just standing around here?"

His tone sounds teasing, not suspicious. I think I'm all right... for now.

I meander over to my trunks and toss the bag with the socha into one. "Oh, just sorting through some of my things before I turned in for the night."

My husband ambles up behind me and slides his arm around my waist. "No turning in for a little while yet, wife. I'm in need of your attentions."

Of course he is. I force a sweet smile and flick my finger over my ring. "Anything to serve my emperor."

CHAPTER TWENTY-NINE

Aurelia

Excited voices reverberate through the vast arena before the exhibition has even begun. I adjust my position on my cushion next to my husband's as surreptitiously as I can, reining in my trepidation.

I didn't enjoy the first arena show I had to watch. At least back then I had a friend by my side. A friend who understood that using violence as entertainment goes against every principle I have.

A friend who died because of the brutality of the man I have to sit beside now. May Rochelle's soul be at peace with her godlen.

As with that previous exhibition, Marclinus is full of energy, guffawing with the nobles seated around us and offering extravagant sweeps of his arm to the audience of commoners who're packing into the dingier stands. I echo

those gestures of greeting with more modest waves of my own.

"Ah, this is going to be a good one. A fitting gift to our people before we take our leave again." Marclinus elbows me, just hard enough that I have to suppress a wince. "Are you looking forward to it, wife?"

I smile and add one more lie to the pile I've told since I arrived in Dariu. "Very much so."

My gaze veers along our luxurious section of the stands and snags on two figures standing up against the outer wall. Viceroy Ennius has his wife cornered by the railing, one arm penning her in while he grips her wrist with his other hand. Bianca's typical flirty smile looks tense, the dip of her eyelids more anxious than coy.

I get the impression she'd rather leap over the railing into the masses below than continue the conversation, if she thought the spectacle wouldn't be too embarrassing.

What is he badgering her about? From the way his hand flexes, his knuckles paling, I have to think he's holding her tight enough to hurt.

Marclinus doesn't appear to have noticed his long-time lover's discomfort—or perhaps he has and simply isn't inclined to intervene when he'll get no benefit out of the effort.

I balk for a second, my gut twisting with the memory of all the cutting words the vicerine has thrown at me in the past, the pain she dealt out. But she, at least, has proven she's capable of being different from that. She nudged Marclinus toward me when I needed him. She warned me of the court's discontent.

I have to reward what little shreds of loyalty I can get.

And I still don't like seeing any person in pain.

I push to my feet with a swish of my skirts. The chattering nobles around the higher imperial bench scoot back to make room for their empress. A few gazes follow me as I glide across our terrace, but most of my companions go right back to their gossip.

Bianca notices me coming before her husband does. At the twitch of her expression, Ennius leaves off the harsh words he was muttering at her and glances over his shoulder.

Seeing me, he loosens his grasp on Bianca's arm and turns to face me so he's no longer caging her against the wall. "Your Imperial Highness. What can we do for you?"

I aim my smile at Bianca. "I've been curious to know more about those hair ointments you mentioned the other day, Vicerine. I thought now might be a good time to get your insight, while we're waiting for the fighters to finish preparing."

Bianca dips her head, and the viceroy releases her arm completely. Ruddy marks stand out against her smooth brown skin.

My teeth grit behind my smile, holding back the sharp words I'd like to direct at him. Motioning for Bianca to join me, I tread back along the benches to my seat.

The nearby nobles have already scooted over to make room for my new companion. I have no idea what they make of my calling on the woman who's claimed my husband so overtly in the past. Perhaps they assume I'm being friendly on his orders.

As Bianca settles into the seat a couple of inches below my own, she speaks in an undertone only I can hear. "You didn't need to do that. I'm used to handling him."

"It didn't look as if handling him was a very pleasant experience at the moment." I pause and glance over at her. "You've helped me more than once in the past few weeks. I don't mind returning the favor."

"Well… thank you." Her lips slant into a crooked grin. "You know, it's occurred to me that earning the friendship of the empress may be more valuable than having the interest of the emperor. Your wild northern ways certainly add something to the court that we didn't have before."

I have no doubt that if her neck was on the line, all thoughts of "friendship" would fly out the window. But I'll accept the overture, however calculated it might be. "I'm glad you've come to see things that way. I wish my presence hadn't come at such expense."

Her jaw tightens, presumably with the thought of her own lost friend. "Yes. You'd save us all if you could, wouldn't you?"

Before I can decide what to make of that ambiguous remark, louder cheers roar from all around the stands. Today's warriors are striding out from the ground-level doorways at the edges of the arena.

Raul is among them. I'm not surprised, but my heart squeezes for the moment I let my gaze linger on his brawny frame. His mouth is set in a cocky grin, and he whirls his blade in a showy circle, all confidence.

Then a gleam of white-blond hair catches my eyes as it emerges from a far doorway, and my gut plummets.

Prince Neven is striding out onto the sand-strewn earth, his expression rigid and a mace clenched in one hand.

I turn to Marclinus with an arch of one eyebrow, suppressing my queasiness. "You decided to bring an untried teenage prince into the mix?"

I keep my tone dry, as if I find the matter bemusing rather than horrifying.

Marclinus smirks. "He begged for the chance. Why not two princes rather than one? The audience loves it. He'll have easier opponents for his first time. The last thing I need is a second revolt on my hands, hmm?"

He doesn't sound as if he's taking the possibility of the prince's death all that seriously.

As he stands up to welcome the crowd and encourage their enthusiasm, my attention slides back to Raul. His stance has stiffened as he stares across the arena toward his younger foster brother.

Neven didn't mention his intentions to the other princes, clearly. What is the kid thinking?

Maybe it's a momentary impulse driven by the need to prove himself, and after he's conquered the arena once, that'll be enough for him.

Assuming that my husband has judged Neven's abilities correctly and he *will* conquer whatever's thrown at him here today.

As with the earlier exhibition, this one starts with the warriors facing off against each other in pairs. After the first few blows, I'm as relieved as I can be to see that Neven has been pitted against a man of similar size whose movements look a bit clumsy.

Out of all the skirmishes, Neven manages to heave his opponent to the ground first. When he looms over the other man, shoving him harder into the ground with a booted foot on the chest, Marclinus leaps up.

"Let's have a proper ending!" he hollers into his amplification charm, which carries his voice through the whole arena. "Claim yourself some bloody triumph, Prince of Goric!"

Neven has watched enough of these exhibitions to know what his emperor means. He hesitates for a split-second and then drives his sword straight into his opponent's neck.

Bile rises in my throat. Is that the first time the teenaged prince has killed a human being? As part of an imperial spectacle, with a horde of Darium citizens whooping and stomping their feet in approval?

I can't even begin to conceive what that would do to a person, let alone one little more than a boy.

Raul finishes his own opponent off without need for encouragement, though I notice he makes it quick and clean rather than some of the more brutal executions carried out by the other warriors. I sink into my seat, knowing the second part of the exhibition should be less fraught. The animals are dangerous, but far more predictable than a fellow human being.

As with the person-to-person matches, the beast released near Neven is a smallish leopard that doesn't look as if it'll prove much of a challenge. With powerful efficiency, Raul faces off against a hulking tusked boar.

I have a suspicion he wants to finish this particular performance even faster than usual so he can go give the younger prince a piece of his mind.

When all the animals have fallen and four of the warriors are left standing, my stomach's churning starts to settle. The spectacle is awful, but it's over. Now all that's left is—

Marclinus's jaunty voice breaks through my thoughts. "Hold there, Prince Raul. You're going to be the star of our show this afternoon."

My gaze jerks up. Raul is just coming to a halt where he was heading toward one of the doorways like his fellow warriors. He stares up at Marclinus warily, his massive frame tensing all over again.

Whatever my husband is up to, the prince wasn't prepared for it.

I will my expression to stay carefully blank. Any concern I reveal might incite Marclinus further.

He does glance down at me briefly before going on. "Some of my foster brother's countrymen have disgraced themselves before the empire, throwing the good we've done for them in our faces. I'm sure the prince of Lavira would be more than happy to demonstrate how valiantly he'll fight for *us* when called on."

Raul gives his emperor a salute that might contain a trace of the crude gesture I'd imagine he'd rather be making.

"Let's see how he fares with all your attention on him, my people," Marclinus finishes, and lounges back in his seat.

I swallow past the constricting of my throat. "I see you've decided to shake the exhibition up even more."

Marclinus rubs his hands together. "Sabrelle blessed me with a most excellent idea in a dream last night. I follow my godlen as she guides. She inspired some of the best of your trials too, you know."

The trials that killed one or two noblewomen at a go. A clammy sensation spreads through my chest.

One of the barred openings to the animal chambers rasps open, and an enormous bear charges into the arena.

I can see at once that something's wrong with the animal. It hurtles straight at Raul with a ragged bellow, showing not the slightest self-preservation instinct or hunting strategy. Wild, murderous rage emanates from its every pounding stride.

It's barreling toward the prince like a man so desperate there's nothing in his mind but doing all the damage he can. Like the most dangerous sort of foe.

Marclinus must have had someone rile up the bear's temper to such fearsome heights with magic or a drug or perhaps a combination of both. Spittle froths along the beast's gums as it lets out another vicious roar.

Raul dodges to the side, whirls and stabs, ducks and leaps. I can't imagine he's ever faced an animal like this.

Within a matter of seconds, one of the bear's paws wallops the prince of Lavira across the back. Its claws scrape bloody lines through his tunic.

He stumbles and manages to strike the animal in the shoulder, but it hurls itself onward without heeding the injury and knocks Raul right off his feet.

As the prince manages to roll away from the bear's jaws, its gnashing teeth rake through his upper arm. Spilling more blood across the sand, Raul scrambles to his feet.

He slashes at the beast's throat, but it's already hurling itself at him so forcefully he can't complete the motion. They crash back into the earth.

I clench my jaw against a cry. My pulse booms inside my skull. The thing is going to kill him. Smash him to bits and tear him apart.

Why would Marclinus want this?

A snarl and a crack of breaking bone reverberate through the hush of the audience. The bear slams its paw into Raul's head—

And Marclinus is on his feet again, beckoning to someone down below.

All at once, several imperial guards spring from the entryways. They swarm the bear before it has the chance to recognize its many new opponents, driving their blades home. As the beast slumps, they wrench it off Raul's crumpled form.

I tuck my hands into the folds of my skirt so no one can see how tightly they're balled.

Two of the soldiers haul the prince upright. He staggers, blood dribbling across the hard ground beneath him, but he's alive. My frantic pulse only slows a little.

A maniacal grin has curved my husband's lips. His voice rings through the arena. "Let us always remember that our subservient nations are too weak to stand on their own. It's only through the strength of the empire that they've survived and thrived. Dariu conquers all!"

He starts to clap, setting off a thunder of applause throughout the stands. The nobles around us leap up to celebrate their emperor's point even more emphatically, so I heave myself to my feet too, even though I'd mostly like to heave my lunch up my throat onto Marclinus's polished boots.

He nearly had Raul killed to make a point about his conquered countries and the rebellion.

Why wouldn't he? He poisoned me, murdered a dozen ladies of his court. What's a little more bloodshed to my wretched husband?

Numb to the bone, I clap and watch the soldiers lead Raul off the arena floor to where a medic is waiting. The other guards drag the carcass of the enraged bear away, its blood smearing the earth with a dark red trail.

Such a majestic beast was turned into a tool for Marclinus's sadistic amusement. If even Raul with all his might and prowess couldn't fell the creature alone, *no one* could have, Darium or otherwise...

My breath catches in my chest.

An animal isn't a weapon or an enchantment that our magical wards or guards are prepared for. But as my husband has just demonstrated, an animal can be shaped into a means of destruction against even a very powerful foe.

Perhaps Sabrelle has blessed *me* with her idea as well.

As the nobles around us collect themselves for our departure, I turn to Marclinus and push my lips into an ingratiating smile. "What a particularly thrilling exhibition, husband. Where are the wild beasts kept when they're being trained for the arena?"

Chapter Thirty

Raul

As soon as I've finished gulping down my lunch, I take the opportunity to wander away from the carriage our blasted emperor assigned me to today. The company has hardly been "inspiring," as he suggested with that manic glint in his eyes.

If I'm going to get through the rest of the day on the road to Rexoran without stabbing one of my noble companions, I need to make a little progress toward that later date when I never have to put up with this shit again.

I pretend I'm simply stretching my legs and shaking off the stiffness of the last three days of travel. I do actually need the effort—when I roll my shoulders, the muscles on my back twinge where the bear tore its jaws through me. The ache in my thigh where its claws gouged my flesh hasn't totally faded either.

Every pang sets my teeth a little more on edge with a

burn of humiliation under my skin. Marclinus decided not just to have me perform but to use me as a demonstration of his empire's might, the fucking prick. I'd like to demonstrate *my* might by shoving his crown down his throat.

Of course, his guards would intervene before I could so much as lay a finger on him. So I'll have to continue taking a page out of Aurelia's book and find my more subtle means of undermining him.

This waystation is along a particularly colorful stretch of terrain, bright green leaves of bushy trees standing out against the low pinkish-yellow cliffs that jut up here and there farther off. After the fuss at the bridge during our last journey, the soldiers have ordered all of the people from the nearby town to stick to their own streets, other than the handful of workers who are assisting with the meal preparation and clean up.

Halfway along our convoy, many of the soldiers are hanging around outside the main waystation building—a long, low structure of the same pinkish-yellow stone. The sigil of Jurnus marks the lintel, with mosaics of soaring gulls and diving whales decorating patches of the walls.

The godlen of travel isn't the only one honored at this spot. Not far from the waystation's entrance, a fountain dedicated to Sabrelle burbles with water from a small spring. A sculpture of the godlen poses amid the current, brandishing a shield and sword.

Perfect. I can make excellent use of that.

I amble toward the fountain, but before I've made it past more than a couple of carriages, the exact asshole I'm least enthusiastic to see strolls into my path.

Marclinus grins at me with a sly cock of his head that sets me twice as on guard. The two barons who were trotting at his heels fall silent in eager curiosity.

"Ah, prince of Lavira," the emperor says in a blasé tone.

"You must be getting impatient to find yourself close to home again."

The city of Rexoran isn't too far off from the border between Dariu and Lavira, but it's still a fair trek from there to our capital where anyone I know resides. I doubt Marclinus is going to give me leave to take a week-long detour.

I dip my head in a little bow that only I know is mocking. "It's nice to see familiar terrain, but I'm more interested in finding out what Creaden's challenge entails."

Marclinus chuckles. "You can be sure I'll conquer it. And while I'm up there, perhaps I'll settle the empire's latest conquering of your people once and for all. Maybe I should send you across the border to teach the rebels a lesson with your swordplay—just as long as you don't run into any bears."

Both of the marchions break into chuckles of their own. I smile thinly, my hand aching with the urge to ram the dagger I'm carrying into their guts, right where it would mean slow, agonizing pain before death.

In the back of my head, I send up a prayer to my own chosen godlen. *Kosmel, let me stay as stealthy and discreet as you can be. Let me hide my anger so well they never see it.*

The thought of all the power I hold that's unknown to them steadies me. My hand relaxes at my side.

I very considerately refrain from stabbing anyone.

Our merciless emperor isn't being anywhere near that considerate with Lavira's citizens. I've tried not to picture the slaughter he's ordered back home to punish my people for the brewing rebellion.

How many of those he's had tortured and murdered were totally innocent? How many simply justified in their anger against the empire?

There's nothing I can do to stop the carnage. If anything,

he'll take any rebelliousness I show as an excuse to come down on them even harder. But I'm not powerless, as my appeal to my godlen just reminded me.

I'll simply hit him in ways he never expects, as I intend to right now.

I nod to Marclinus again and move to step around his little entourage. "I serve my empire as I'm able."

As I veer around the nearer man, I cast a thread of my awareness into the shadows woven through his clothing. My lips tug into a wider smirk. "That's quite the stash of hazebloom you have on you, Baron. I hope you don't find our emperor's company so dull as to need all that enhancement."

I leave the baron sputtering and Marclinus turning on him with an arch of his eyebrows. If the vapid fool does need to smoke a little of that elating drug from time to time to put up with imperial obnoxiousness, I can't actually blame him.

Meandering on toward the cluster of soldiers around the fountain, I notice a figure approaching from the opposite direction. Lorenzo catches my gaze for just a second with a brief flick of his fingers by his side. *Talking to the kitchen.*

He means he's going to use his gift to nudge the locals in an ideal direction. He'll send out an illusionary murmur or two speaking Aurelia's praises to get the bunch in there chattering along the same line.

Excellent. While he's building loyalty to our empress with the common folk, I'll steer our military men and women farther along the right path.

I circle the fountain, giving the soldiers gathered in front of it a wide berth, and sink down on the rim at the far side as if resting my legs. When I dip my fingers into the warm water, I can grasp hold of the shadow that drapes across its rippling surface.

Grasp hold and meld its shape to my will.

The soldiers are nattering about some new stallion added to the cavalry's stables and who'll get to claim it. I wait until one of them motions toward the fountain's statue. "Maybe better we leave it up to our godlen of battle, huh?"

As several of the glances flick toward the representation of Sabrelle, I push my will through the shadow.

I can't see it directly, but the picture I'm creating forms in my mind's eye: a faint silhouette of a feminine figure in a crown cast across the statue behind the shield, as similar to Aurelia's looks as I can make such a vague depiction.

I only let it linger for a moment before I release the shadows to fall back into their usual patches.

One of the soldiers has grunted; another inhales with a hitch. "That was—did you see that?"

"What?" asks one of the women who I suppose hadn't been looking.

Another soldier speaks up in an awed tone. "I think it was a sign from Sabrelle. For a second it looked as if her statue was embracing the empress—shielding her."

I hold back my satisfied smile and keep sitting there as if I haven't even noticed their conversation. The reverent murmurs continue for several more exchanges, discussing how much strength Aurelia has shown in the rites so far.

"We'll have to see how she fares in Sabrelle's rite at the end," one concludes, but it's clear they've taken the supposed vision of support to heart. Gods willing, gossip about the incident will spread through their ranks.

Every bit of good will we can generate for our empress gets us a little closer to our goals. With luck, Lorenzo has stirred up more enthusiasm on his end as well.

One of the captains calls to the cluster of soldiers to prepare to move out. As they scatter to their positions and their steeds, I push to my feet.

When I come around the fountain, my feet jar to a stop.

Neven is walking briskly toward me—heading for his own carriage, presumably.

The kid hesitates at the sight of me, his tan face flushing slightly beneath his white-blond hair. I've been trying to have a conversation with the prince of Goric since his stupid performance in the exhibition a few days ago, but he's been dodging me and surrounding himself with other nobles at every turn.

He's not getting away with avoiding me this time.

I stride over and grasp his arm to tug him back around the fountain, where we'll have a tiny bit of privacy. Neven's jaw sets, but he follows me without struggling.

As soon as we're out of view of most of the convoy, I let go, mainly so I can toss my hand in the air in a gesture of frustration.

I manage to keep my voice low, but it comes out in a growl. "What the fuck were you thinking, joining the exhibition? You could have gotten yourself killed. Do you really want to do that to your parents?"

The kid's chin juts out even more defiantly. "I didn't, though, did I?"

"You couldn't have known that. You can never totally predict what'll happen in the arena." I drop my voice even lower. "Look what that prick did to me."

His expression twitches, the only sign that the raging bear's attack frightened him. "He made sure you survived. He needs us."

"Not that much, as you well know." I don't have to remind him what happened to his brother.

Neven squares his shoulders and aims an even more defiant glare at me. "You've been fighting in the arena for years. If you can take the chance, why shouldn't I?"

"I trained by sparring with the soldiers and practice

animals for years before that. You've only done the basics. And I was older than you for my first exhibition."

"I'm more ambitious, then."

I narrow my eyes at him, but his refusal to listen to reason unnerves me at least as much as it angers me. "What's going on, Neven? You're throwing yourself into the arena, chatting up high commanders, shutting the rest of us out… If you've got a problem, we're the ones you should be coming to."

"Why?" Neven demands. "Working together hasn't gotten us anywhere in all this time. And now we can hardly talk anyway. The three of you like to make your own plans. I've got to do something for myself."

I knit my brow. "We don't bring you in on every single thing because we're trying to keep you safe. We all have our own concerns that we don't involve everyone with. You can have yours. I just want to know why it's *this*."

Why is he playing into the empire's hands? Getting chummy with the higher powers and showing off in front of them?

Neven's hand darts down his front in a hasty gesture of the divinities. "You believe in stealth, and Bastien wants to talk everything through, and Lorenzo just plays his music. I'm supposed to be the might. I have… I have a duty to find out where my strength can take me."

Something about his phrasing and his appeal to the gods niggles at me. I glance at the statue I just manipulated to my ends and back at my younger foster brother, an uneasy inkling rising up in my mind.

"You think this is what Sabrelle wants."

He's dedicated to the warrior godlen, sacrificed most of the teeth in his face to her for his gift, getting the painful steel replacements. I've never seen him cater to her inclinations quite this much, though.

Neven crosses his arms over his chest. "I know it's what she wants. She showed me that I need to step up. I don't need *you* looking out for me when my godlen is pointing me in the right direction."

Before I can say anything else, a sharp bellow calls any lingering nobles to return to their carriages. Neven spins on his heel and hurries off without another word.

I head to my own vehicle, my stomach sinking. I don't know what Sabrelle conveyed to the kid by sign or dream or whatever other means, but I can already tell I don't like it at all.

How in the realms are any of us going to convince him to listen to us over a god?

CHAPTER THIRTY-ONE

Aurelia

The first thing Marclinus does after he's escorted me to my chambers is throw wide the double doors at the far end of the bedroom. "*This* is the most laudable quality of our Rexoran palace. Take a look, wife!"

I venture over beside him, willing away my travel weariness, and peer out beyond the doors.

The bright mid-day sun streams over a walled garden right inside the palace itself. The building stretches in a looming stone rectangle around the inner grounds. Graceful trees shade marble benches, a burbling fountain, and cobblestone pathways between plump shrubs and flowerbeds, all of which give off a mix of heady perfumes.

I take a deep breath of the warm, floral air. For once, I don't have to lie to my husband. "It's lovely."

Marclinus grins and motions exuberantly to a wall only one story high that cuts through the inner grounds. "The

section on this side is reserved for imperial use—you and I alone. The only doors that open into it are from the imperial apartments. The part on the other side of that wall for the rest of our court is larger but I'd say not half as stunning."

He draws back with a yank of the doors as if to indicate that the view isn't for me just now and swipes his hands together. "All right. If you're insisting on doing this, get yourself presentable for Creaden's rite. You can hardly put yourself before my people all travel-rumpled."

My smile tightens. I dip my head in acknowledgment, and he lopes out of the room with a holler to one of the footmen bringing along our trunks.

He sounds as if he's lost any enthusiasm in my participating in the rite again. Is there something about the long days of travel that provokes his temper and turns him more sour toward me?

I'd like to think it's possible he'll soften once the rites are over and we can settle in at one residence or another for months at a time, but we were perfectly settled at the capital palace when he poisoned me.

We're meant to carry out the rite in just a few hours. I calm my own mind as well as I can, barely listening to my maids' fawning chatter as I soak in a bath and then let them primp and prepare me.

I've chosen another white gown for the task ahead, even though I don't know what it entails. Reminding the people of my desire for peace and healing has seemed to work well in the past.

When my hair is completely pinned up in its delicate swoops around my head and my face has been powdered, I dismiss my maids with the excuse that I'd like to meditate before the rite. I do spend several minutes on that, shoring up my well of inner serenity, but then I go to my trunk of supplies.

I concocted an ointment for the sharpening of one's vision before we left the capital. The effects should last for the rest of the day.

Carefully, I dab a little of the cool gel into my eyes and blink to spread it across their surface. A faint stinging sensation spreads through them, but no tears form.

Using the same test I did when I was perfecting the mixture, I set a book open on my vanity and step back to see if I can read it from a distance. With my normal vision, I need to be no more than five paces away to make out the print.

With my concoction, I can manage eight. A significant improvement.

Let's hope that Bastien's information will serve me well and that seeing clearly in a literal sense will help me through the rite ahead.

The city bells announce the hour. A knock sounds on my door. "We'll escort you to the temple now, Your Imperial Highness."

Kassun is among my personal guard this afternoon. As we walk through the gleaming marble halls to the waiting carriage, he steps slightly closer, his voice pitched low. "Are you sure you'll be all right, Your Imperial Highness?"

He speaks carefully, but I can hear the genuine concern in his tone. My throat constricts.

He was shadowing me when I argued with Marclinus at the residence near Ubetta—he no doubt overheard the disparaging remarks my husband aimed at me over my participation in the rites. And it isn't as if I had an easy time with either of the previous confirmations to begin with.

As much as it warms me that the guard cares for my well-being now, I hate that he thinks he needs to worry. That he's afraid I might be making the wrong decision, one I'll be too weak to see through.

That's exactly why I have to continue demonstrating how much strength I can bring to bear, isn't it?

I keep my own voice gracious. "I trust that the gods see my faith and will support me through whatever may be required of me."

Kassun doesn't speak again. Even asking the first question was an unusual imposition from the figures who are supposed to fade into the background when they're unneeded.

Marclinus is already waiting in the carriage. He simply nods at me before leaning toward one of the gilded windows.

As we lead the procession around the palace, through the city, and beyond it to the Temple of Stalwart Crowns, he raises his hand high to the people gathered along the roads and beams at the praise they holler. I offer my own more subdued waves and smiles, my sharpened eyes picking up every detail.

Some smile wider at the sight of me. Others' mouths tense as if in suspicion or uncertainty. I catch a few furtive gestures of warding.

I still have many more folk to win over here.

It's impossible to know if word of my exact deeds has spread this far from the locations of the other rites. I'm sure travelers and news-bearing messengers have reported that the new empress carried out the rites after Marclinus, but those stories might not have been conveyed with much detail.

They certainly all know that I married their current emperor on the same day the previous one died.

Some of my attention veers to the elaborate buildings behind our spectators. Creaden oversees the art of construction as well as leadership, and his influence shows throughout the city.

Balconies emerge from second and third floors in feats of balance so delicate they look as if they're floating. Rooftops arch and curve in ways that must channel rain to useful purposes.

The colors and materials are more varied than I've seen anywhere else in Dariu, from the reddish-brown of fired clay to shining gray stone to creamy yellow blocks I believe are made from a sand-based mixture. I get the impression the city's builders like to stretch their abilities and welcome a challenge.

Beyond the last of the city buildings, the largest temple of Creaden in the country comes into view. Its structure is a patchwork of materials and a spectacle of architecture merged into one. Swaths of clay blocks merge with others of stone, sand, wood, and colored glass. Turrets veer off at seemingly impossible angles. One staircase winds along the outer wall rather than remaining inside.

Yet as chaotic as it should feel, it gives a sense of cohesion, as if all those parts were placed in exactly the right way to have the most impressive effect. As if no building not made of so many disparate parts brought together could ever function so well.

I suppose it represents Creaden's attitudes about ruling as well as his constructive skills. There's been ample proof of the validity of both.

Supposedly, this structure has stood for hundreds of years on its sturdy foundation. It's said that the first emperor prayed here for the means to build Dariu's authority before he led his victorious campaign to claim a large piece of Lavira for his new empire.

Beyond the temple, a structure made of a darker material than any part of the temple stretches up toward the sky, perhaps twice the temple's height. The glossy black surface gleams with spots of sunlight but mostly absorbs the beams into its depths.

What in the realms is that? Some sort of monument?

It appears to be part of the rite. Our procession veers around the temple toward the black obelisk.

Marclinus and I emerge from our carriage at the edge of a ring of soldiers. They stand about twenty feet back from the sloping stone tower on all sides. A throng of civilians crowd close behind them, staring up at the dark structure.

There's no need for a hollow to allow easy viewing of this rite. I assume we'll be clambering up that tower where everyone on the ground can see us.

I swallow past the dryness of my mouth and glance at my husband. Marclinus has changed into a fresh suit of the typical imperial purple and dark gray, gold embroidery gleaming along the jacket's trim. Nothing about his attire looks different from usual, but then, his clothing didn't offer any clues about the first rite either.

I won't know exactly what awaits me until he launches himself into the ceremony with all his exclusive foreknowledge and preparation.

The temple's cleric moves to greet us, her steel-gray hair pulled tightly back from her square-jawed face. Her violet robes ripple around her robust frame as she gives Marclinus a small bow.

Her amplification charm projects her voice across our audience. "Your Imperial Majesty, it is an honor to host your third confirmation rite. Creaden wishes to witness how you will guide our people and our empire to greater heights."

She holds up a harness of leather straps and a small purple banner imprinted with the imperial crest. "Choosing your handholds wisely, you will lead one of your people all the way to the top of this tower, where you will claim it for the empire with this banner. Both you and your subject must complete the climb without significant injury."

But insignificant injuries are all right?

I study the tower, picking out the even darker splotches

of handholds here and there, before returning my attention to Marclinus as the cleric fastens the harness around his chest.

She beckons forward a young man who's a few inches shorter than Marclinus and likely a good fifty pounds lighter, given his slender body. He must have been chosen as a volunteer ahead of time, selected on the assumption that he wouldn't put too much strain on the emperor.

The harness connects him to Marclinus's back with just a few feet between them. Every step Marclinus makes, the other man will need to follow quickly behind to ensure he's not dragged—or pulling his emperor off-balance.

The man stands tall, proud to be part of this spectacle. Marclinus aims a grin over his shoulder. When he sets off for the tower, brandishing his banner in one hand, his civilian partner falls into step behind him.

Applause and whoops of encouragement peal out from the spectators. When Marclinus reaches the obelisk, he makes a show of kicking one of the lower footholds. The dark rock crumbles away at the impact.

Marclinus shakes his head dramatically and reaches for a higher hold that stays solid.

So that's the challenge—leading another person through the climb where some of the holds won't, well, hold.

It wouldn't be too painful to stumble back to the bottom while you're still close to the base, but if you lost your grip even halfway up? That'd make for quite the fall.

From close to the very top, it might be fatal.

As Marclinus clambers upward, his volunteer citizen scrambles after him, grasping every foothold the moment Marclinus has departed it, sticking as close at the emperor's heels as he can. He has to—the straps are nearly pulled taut.

One slip from either of them could bring them both tumbling to the ground.

Marclinus's personal guards draw close around the base of the obelisk. He has four with him today, two keeping an eye on their master while the others scan the crowd for any sign of hostile intent.

They're far enough away from me that Lorenzo must judge it safe to project his illusionary voice. It slides into my head with its reassuring resonance.

"You just focus on getting up that tower, Rell. I'll be reminding the crowd how fantastic you are."

He's been using his powers here the way he promised he would too, then: sending out illusionary voices as if fellow citizens are speaking up with my praises, to encourage the rest of them to do the same.

But none of it matters if I don't prove I deserve their praise.

As Marclinus climbs higher, the crowd falls into a hush of anticipation. He keeps reaching steadily upward without any sign of hesitation or flagging. Not a single hold breaks in his grasp.

As if he knows exactly what path to take. Which no doubt he does.

Is there something about the holds that distinguishes the solid ones from the fragile, or was he simply given a pattern to memorize?

I've tried to keep track, but it's increasingly difficult the higher up he gets.

At the top of the obelisk, Marclinus lifts the banner and brandishes it triumphantly to a renewed wave of cheers. He fits its handle into a spot at the top of the structure.

One of the temple's devouts has climbed a set of narrow steps cut into the opposite side of the obelisk. He shows Marclinus and his companion how to ease around to that side, and they descend to even more applause. As the cleric gives Marclinus her official blessing, he lifts both hands high in the air, soaking up his people's adoration.

For a few seconds, I'm afraid he's obstructed my intentions after all and I'll be left standing here aimlessly. But the cleric returns to my side of the obelisk, carrying a second banner. The devout trots behind her with the harness he's peeled off my husband.

The cleric smiles at me coolly and pitches her voice across the crowd. "Our empress would also like to earn Creaden's approval and show her worth as a ruler. Who here will accept her leadership and take the climb with her guidance?"

My heightened gaze sweeps over the crowd beyond the ring of guards. I catch a flicker of a hand moving down a chest in the gesture of the divinities, and another making a warding gesture. Foreheads furrow and mouths twist.

A thick baritone calls out from somewhere behind me. "I trust our empress!"

The middle-aged man who emerges from the throng stands nearly half a foot taller than me and a fair bit wider as well. Watching him approach, I can't help wondering if Marclinus had someone prod him to volunteer so I'd face the additional challenge of leading someone who could drag me down the tower that much easier.

It doesn't matter. He's here; he's offering his faith in me. I have to offer him the same in return.

My guards look him over and evaluate him as harmless. The devout fixes the harness over my dress. I restrain a cringe at the tightening of the leather straps around my torso.

It feels like a cage, however flexible.

When the cleric hands me the banner, my fingers curl tight around the handle. I slide it beneath the straps that cross my chest so both of my hands will be completely free and aim a reassuring smile at my companion on this journey. "Just follow my lead. We'll make it to the top."

Despite the jittering of my nerves, I put the same confidence into my strides walking to the obelisk. Even up close, the handholds blend into the smooth darkness of the stone. I peer at those at knee and waist height for anything that might distinguish the correct ones, but the semi-circles look essentially identical to me.

All right. I'll just have to rely on my memory of what I saw from Marclinus's climb.

Girding myself, I reach for a handhold at shoulder level. Then I lift my foot onto one of the lower protrusions.

My companion shuffles closer behind me. He peers up at the steep slope of the obelisk. "It looks even taller from here."

His voice quavers slightly. Have I been tied to a man who's afraid of heights on top of everything else?

"Don't look too far up," I tell him in the same assured tone as before. "Focus on where I put my feet so you can grasp on to the same holds and then put your own feet along that path."

He swallows audibly but nods. As I stretch my arms higher and clamber upward, he follows right behind me. His nervous huffs of breath ruffle the hem of my dress.

I picture Marclinus's ascent, pausing and then reaching for the holds I remember him using. It serves me well for the first ten or so feet of the climb.

Then I reach for a protrusion that I think is the right one. My first tug suggests it's firm enough, but the second I put pressure on it to haul myself upward, the rock fractures between my fingers.

My fingernails skid against the stone with a thin squeal. I clutch my other handhold tight, pressing myself against the slope to keep my balance. My pulse lurches, but I remain in place.

Murmurs break out through the watching crowd. I can't imagine they're saying *good* things about my close call.

I can't let the mistake faze me. Gritting my teeth, I reach for another nearby hold.

I've clambered up another several holds when my memory starts to get shaky. I didn't see exactly where Marclinus was grasping from here on.

Breathing as evenly as I can, I pull on one hold, judge it solid, and then another. As long as I'm cautious about it, I should be able to avoid any major—

The protrusion I just stepped on snaps beneath the ball of my foot. I lurch sideways, my leg swinging wild. With a hitch of breath and a yank of my arms, I center my balance on my other foot.

Sweat trickles down my back despite the afternoon's refreshing breeze. Below me, my harnessed companion lets out a sound like a stifled groan.

"Just a minor slip," I tell him and myself. "We're doing well."

But now I know that some of the holds can handle being grasped onto but not the full weight of my body pressing down on them. How can I be completely sure of my footing?

The lapses must be starting to rattle my companion. He heaves himself up the glossy surface after me as closely as before, but his breath has gotten a little raspy.

His concentration has been shaken too. I'm just reaching for another hold when he steps up after me—and jerks downward with a yelp.

The harness snaps, wrenching me down after him. The banner wobbles where it's tucked against my chest.

I skid down the smooth surface, fumbling to snatch at another protrusion. One of the straps twists my arm, sending a stinging pain through my shoulder. Another smacks against my ribs roughly enough to bruise. I clamp my lips against a cry of my own.

Just as my fingers close around a hold, my companion

manages to catch himself and flings his hand up to steady me by the waist. My toes jar to a halt against one of the tiny ledges.

"Sorry, sorry," the man mumbles. "I put my foot on the wrong spot. I'm so sorry."

My shoulder throbs, but it's not my most immediate concern. I'm never making it even halfway up this tower if the man I'm supposed to be guiding continues stumbling.

I dig into my well of calm and put all the soothing vibes I can summon into my voice. "It's all right. Everyone blunders a little when they're getting used to something new. Now you have a better idea of what to do. You've been with me so far. I know we can make it."

"I don't want to let you down, Your Imperial Highness."

"You won't," I promise. "Only think about following me. About the next two holds for your hands and putting your feet where your hands were. That'll take us to the top. We won't lose our way. We can do this together. Are you with me?"

He exhales roughly, but when he speaks again, there's renewed conviction in his voice. "Yes. It's that simple. I can do that."

It's that simple as long as I can pick the right holds to begin with and don't let *him* down.

More worried muttering is drifting up from the spectators below. Every second we linger in our mistakes, the worse we look.

I stare at the handholds around me, the ones that have proven stable and the ones that might not be, searching for any clue that might direct me. My enhanced sight still can't pick out anything significant. The sheer slope above us looks nearly flat in its blackness.

Closing my eyes for a second, I extend my thoughts toward my godlen. *Elox, guide me as I would guide the empire's people. Show me what I need to see to find the right path.*

When I open my eyes, my gaze veers upward just as the sunlight glances off the obelisk at a slightly different angle.

My attention snags on tiny black lines that creep out from the base of the holds just above me. In a blink, the light fades off them again, but now that I know exactly where to look, I peer even closer.

I can still make out the minute crevices, ever so faintly. Without the ointment, I doubt I'd be able to pick up on the slivers of slightly darker shadow at all.

Most of the holds nearby have a spidery crack or two somewhere close to the middle of their base. A couple only have a few thin lines near the edges.

A swell of certainty rises up inside me. The holds with only outer cracks are the sturdy ones. I have to rely on the pieces of rock that are solid at their core.

I have to show I can recognize a strong foundation.

I stretch my arm up for the closest one, ignoring the deepening ache in my shoulder as well as I can. I think the joint might be sprained, but my discomfort can't matter right now.

All I can do is climb.

"I see the way," I tell my companion as I clamber onward. "I know how to tell which ones are too weak now. We'll be all strength from here on."

With each length we climb without another hold crumbling, my companion's movements below me become more confident in turn. I pause only long enough to squint at the next set of protrusions before curling my fingers around them.

We continue up and up and up. The murmurs below fade with the distance, but they're brightening in tone. The breeze picks up, ruffling through my hair.

My companion's breath stutters.

"We're almost there," I call down to him encouragingly, and he keeps following without faltering.

I reach up once more—and the top of the obelisk is there. A choked laugh hitches from my throat. I reach to tug the banner out of my harness and halt.

No. It's not good enough to simply lead my companion up here, especially after our early mistakes.

I need to demonstrate more than just the basics of being a ruler.

Peering at the area around the peak of the structure, I discern a shallow ridge that curves toward the steps on the far side. I ease onto it, flashing a smile toward my companion. "Come the rest of the way up. I want you to put the banner in with me. We did make the climb together, after all. You should share the glory."

His eyes widen with shock, but his face lights up at the same time. He hauls himself across the last few holds.

I extend my hand toward him, gripping the banner. He clutches the handle alongside me. In one movement, we slip it into the hole at the peak next to Marclinus's banner.

A roar of excitement reverberates from below. My companion lets out a joyful chuckle, his eyes outright sparkling now.

He'll never forget how well his empress led him.

The devout is beckoning us over to the stairs. As I slide over to join him, my gaze tumbles down the tower—and lands on Marclinus standing by the altar, staring up at us.

Staring at me with his mouth twitching into the briefest of grimaces, as if he doesn't like what he's seen at all.

CHAPTER THIRTY-TWO

Aurelia

T he potion slides down my throat with its cloying herbal tang. A small shudder passes through me, but I swallow all of the dose down.

As I rinse out the vial in my bathing room, I glance at myself in the mirror that stands next to the sink. I can't see any sign of the fertility potion's effects in my form, but then, I wouldn't expect any external changes.

I had no way of testing this concoction ahead of time like I did with the vision-sharpening ointment. I can only hope that it works as I envisioned with my gift.

It's been a week since my monthly bleed finished. I've seen the signs in my body that one of the medics back home taught me indicate when chances are best for conceiving.

If I'm going to give this vital part of my plan another try, I need to start now.

My heart thumps faster within the vise of tension that

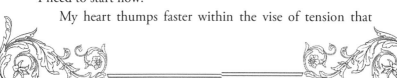

grips my chest. I loosen a couple of strands of my hair to drift temptingly down the sides of my face and adjust the neckline of my dress so my cleavage shows more prominently. I might not have Bianca's voluptuous bosom, but I can make the most of the curves I do possess.

Rochelle would have known how to adjust the gown to show off my figure even more impressively.

The thought of my lost friend hits me with a sharp pang. If she'd been here—if I'd had her to talk to—

No, I wouldn't even have had that comfort. I'd have sent her back to her hometown to marry the man she loved the moment I could.

But then at least I'd have the comfort of knowing I'd saved one person I cared about. I'm not sure yet if I can save even myself, let alone anyone else.

I square my shoulders. I'll go forward and stage the scene I need to with my husband. I'll claim the throne he sits on when the time is right.

I'll do it for Rochelle and all the other people who've deserved so much more than their emperors have allowed them.

Now it's simply a matter of finding him.

Marclinus joined the court in one of this palace's parlors after dinner, but he didn't linger there long. One of the pages slipped in and said something to him that drew him away.

The evening after the rite, he congratulated me on completing it with a smile I'd almost believe was genuine. But since then he's been in one of his more serious, subdued moods, saying very little to me at all even during the public celebrations. I haven't been able to tell if he's frustrated with me or merely distracted by other matters.

We are close to the border with Lavira here—it's only half a day's ride away. I've seen Marclinus conferring with

High Commander Axius more than once. There's probably been more news about the stirring rebellion.

Which isn't likely to put him in an amorous state. I'll just have to work my charms that much better.

Checking the imperial offices seems like my best starting point. I hurry through the halls and come around the bend past the emperor's private chambers.

A couple of his guards are stationed outside a doorway farther down. Here he is already.

As I glide closer, one of the guards draws himself more stiffly upright as if preparing to put me off. If Marclinus asked not to be disturbed from his work, that order may very well apply to me too.

I'm just riffling through possible excuses that might gain me access when the office door swings open.

An unfamiliar woman strides out. Her clothes and bearing immediately assure me that I was right about the matter that drew Marclinus away.

The woman's forcefully athletic movements and the keen dark eyes that sweep over the hallway remind me of my family's hunting hounds. Her long nose and lean frame only add to the impression. She's wearing the dark gray and black jacket and trousers of a higher Darium military official, the imperial crest stitched in gold on the collar that's fastened tightly around her neck.

She swivels on her heel toward me with a swish of her chestnut-brown hair along that collar. It's pulled back from her coppery face in a sterner style than I see from the court noblewomen, woven into three braids on the top and sides that combine into one at the back of her head. I suppose that would fit better under a soldier's helm.

"It appears you have more personal matters to attend to, Your Imperial Majesty," she calls back into the room she just left, with an edge to her voice I can't imagine any of the nobles daring. Does she object to me existing in the palace halls?

My husband appears at the doorway a moment later, his expression tense and his gray eyes stormy. At the sight of me, I'm relieved to see his face relaxes, if only slightly.

His gaze flicks to the military woman. "You haven't yet had the honor of meeting my wife. Tribune, I'm sure you'll offer Her Imperial Highness Empress Aurelia all due respect. Aurelia, this is Tribune Valerisse, one of our most loyal and formidable officers."

Tribune Valerisse—she's the one Axius mentioned who's been overseeing the quelling of the Lavirian uprising.

She bobs her head to me in a quick jerk. "A pleasure, Your Imperial Highness. I must return to my duties."

She isn't much of one for words, is she? Or perhaps she recognizes that saying very little sends a clear enough message all on its own.

At Marclinus's gesture of dismissal, she marches off at a pace just shy of a lope. Watching her, I suspect strolling and ambling are not in her repertoire.

My husband turns back to his office, but he motions for me to follow him.

As the door shuts behind us, he rakes his hand through his golden curls, frowning at the papers scattered on his desk with a vague air. Then he summons a smile. "What do you need, wife?"

His tone isn't as curt as the tribune's, but it's not exactly welcoming either. Even though questions about the news Valerisse brought gnaw at me, I can't jeopardize my goal by indulging my curiosity.

I step closer and rest my hand on Marclinus's chest. He's only wearing one of the silky dress shirts often hidden beneath embroidered vests and jackets, which serves my purposes just fine.

If I can feel the warmth of his skin seeping through the soft fabric, then he can feel mine as well.

I gaze up at him through my eyelashes the way I've seen his noblewomen paramours do often enough. "You've been working very hard these last two days, husband. Isn't this supposed to be a time of celebration?"

Marclinus peers down at me, a hint of a crease forming between his eyebrows before he smooths it away. Almost as if he's puzzled by my overture.

Or skeptical? It isn't as if I often initiate our intimate encounters.

If he realizes I have an ulterior motive—

He eases back half a step, catching my hand in his and holding it loosely. "Are you regretting that I haven't been livelier in the past couple of days? Has my presence not been entertaining enough?"

I blink at him, honestly startled. Gods, no. I could see some members of his court missing his more manic attitudes, but does he really think *I'd* feel that way?

Not that I like being around him all that much either way, but even-tempered he's at least less likely to create some new form of sadistic chaos.

I curl my fingers gently around his. "Quite the opposite. I enjoy seeing you so focused, dedicated to the well-being of our people. But as a dedicate of Elox, I do also know that one can't work hard without any repose and still be at one's best."

Marclinus's next remark comes out drier. "So you came to ensure I wasn't wearing myself to the bone?"

I let the corners of my mouth lift into a smile that's slightly wry to match his tone. "You're serving the empire, and I'm meant to serve you. If encouraging you to take a break is the best contribution I can make to ensuring you rule with all the might you have in you, then I'm more than happy to do my part."

To my surprise, he still hesitates, even though he must understand what I'm offering. "I may not be very good company tonight."

He's never appeared that concerned about my enthusiasm before. What's gotten into him?

I reach up to tease my other hand along his angular jaw. It's a shame such a striking face was wasted on such an awful man. "Let me be good company to you, then. I can take care of you so you'll be ready to approach whatever problems face us fresh in the morning."

Finally, a glint of real heat lights in Marclinus's eyes. He lowers our twined hands by our sides and eases in to run his fingers into my hair. With a dip of his head, he claims a kiss.

My husband has never kissed me quite like this before. There's something oddly tentative about the press of his lips in the moment before I kiss him back, as if he's waiting to see how he'll be received rather than assuming the outcome.

When I loop my arm around the back of his neck, his mouth slides against mine, searing hotter. An unexpected tingle shoots right down the center of me to the warming spot between my legs.

It takes all my will not to overtly cringe in revulsion at the thought of any part of my body responding eagerly to the man who's tormented both me and the men I actually love.

The fertility potion. It must have an aphrodisiac effect as well, one that's clouding my perceptions of Marclinus to make his overtures feel more appealing. I hadn't intended that effect, but it would be fitting to ensure the most necessary act for success takes place.

Marclinus grasps me by the waist, tugging me closer against him. The bulge within his trousers grazes my belly, provoking a shiver that's more uncomfortable.

I can't let this scene play out here in his office, where I

can hardly explain away how he suddenly fell asleep at his desk.

I let my mouth linger against his just a few seconds longer and then pull back a couple of inches. My voice comes out purposefully breathy. "Will you escort me to my chambers, husband?"

Marclinus grins. "Nothing would make me happier."

As he leads me out of the office and down the hall, an ache of longing spreads out from my core.

The potion is certainly doing its job. I only wish it'd taken a little longer to kick in.

I wait until my bedroom door has closed between us and our guards before I twitch my thumb against the side of my ring. When Marclinus pulls me into another kiss, I prick the miniscule blade against the side of his arm. I've flicked it away again before he even comes up for air.

He undoes my slim belt and reaches to loosen the lacing at the back of my dress, but I said I'd be looking after *him*. And it's much easier to set the pace when I'm taking the lead.

I tug the hem of his shirt from his trousers and yank it upward. Marclinus obliges me by helping to peel it off.

As I tease my fingers over his sculpted chest, I smile up at him with all the promises his hallucinations will fulfill rather than me. A pang of need is growing between my thighs, but I ignore it.

I'll give in to my inflamed desires tonight, but the gods can all smite me before I get that close with *this* man.

The potion's aphrodisiac qualities must be skewing my perceptions as well. The answering stroke of Marclinus's hands down my sides and up to cup my breasts feels bizarrely gentle. The branding of his lips against my mouth, my jaw, and my neck are exploring rather than conquering. When he guides me backward to the bed, it feels more like a dance than a demand.

Even if he is being more tender with me tonight, that could never erase all the nights when he's treated me like a doll for his amusement—or any of the horrors he's carried out during our days together.

He finally finishes loosening my dress in the midst of another kiss. As the silk pools around my feet, his gaze trails over me in its wake.

His fingers skim over my scarred forearms and trace the gold marriage band at my wrist in a way I'd call reverent if that made any sense.

Marclinus catches my gaze. "You are lovely, aren't you? Every part of you."

What am I supposed to say to that?

I step around him and nudge him onto the bed. "I have quite the view to appreciate as well, husband."

His more leisurely foreplay has served me well. He's barely settled back onto the pillows before the gleam of anticipation in his eyes hazes over.

I lean over him, stripping off my chemise. His gaze drifts across my body with a vague fumbling of his hands against the covers.

"There you go," I murmur. "Just like that."

When I tug his trousers and drawers off him together, sliding across his erection, he groans. His head tips back into the pillows. His hips rock with the imagined sensations flooding his head.

Just this once, a prickle of guilt pinches me right behind my sternum. The damned potion is messing with my head too much.

I wait until I can clean up after him and then drape an extra blanket across him so he won't get cold. A dab of my additional sedative ensures he'll sleep through most of the night.

Anticipation thrums through my body. The heat between

my legs pulses deeper with every brush of my thighs against each other, but it's too early to leave just yet. I signaled to the princes to meet me at the bell for midnight, when most if not all of the court will have retired to their own beds.

Biting my lip, I wriggle back into my dress, retie the laces, and pick up my book of history to try to distract myself.

By the time those twelve rings reverberate through the palace walls, I could moan with relief. I push open the garden doors and step out into the darkness.

CHAPTER THIRTY-THREE

Aurelia

The air has cooled with the coming of night, more than it normally did back in the capital farther south. I'd find the breeze that licks across my skin and through my dress more refreshing if it didn't put the heated ache between my thighs into sharper contrast.

Arousal pools in my drawers with the friction of my steps. I try to focus only on the stone wall ahead of me, looming in the darkness.

My feet whisper across the tiled path that leads between the trees and shrubs. The warble of the fountain should drown out the sound to anyone not right next to me.

I shouldn't need to worry about anyone at all wandering these grounds or peering from the windows that overlook the garden. The only people currently in residence in the imperial apartments are myself and my unconscious husband.

The inner barrier that separates our private gardens from the more public courtyard stands lower than the pale walls of the palace around me but well over my head. As I approach it, my pace slows. I strain my ears.

One or another noble might have drifted away from the court revelries to steal a private moment in the gardens. As soon as I'm on the other side of that narrow wall, I'm not guaranteed of my privacy.

And then there's the matter of getting to the other side in the first place.

I left the logistics to my princes and their gifts. When I'm just a few steps from the wall, I ease into one of the thickest patches of shadow and wait.

Raul must be able to sense my arrival. It's only a moment before Lorenzo's illusionary voice resonates inside my head.

"All's clear on this side, Rell. We're the only ones in the gardens, and I'll be conjuring an illusion so it'll look as if there's no one here at all if anyone glances out. Bastien can carry you over. Knock if you're ready, then stand still and straight."

My heart thumps faster. I rap my knuckles against the stone surface, just loud enough that I'm sure the sound will reach the other side.

I've just drawn my posture taller when a forceful wind whirls around me. It whips through my loosened hair and catches under my armpits. As it tugs my feet off the ground, a strong gust pushes at the soles of my feet.

My breath hitches with a gasp. The moving air solidifies around me as if it's the supplest of cushions. It lifts me right up over the wall in its invisible embrace, so swiftly and smoothly the sensation isn't remotely frightening, only exhilarating.

In the dimness on the other side, the three princes gaze up at me: Raul grinning with a pale glint of his teeth, Lorenzo's face set with determination, and Bastien following my descent with so much intensity in his dark eyes that my pulse wobbles giddily.

The prince of Cotea lowers his hand to direct the currents of air he's shaped with his gift. I glide down with them as if I'm some sort of godlen entering the realm of mortals from on high.

The moment my feet touch the ground, the solidified air wisps away from me, teasing across my limbs as it does. The heat between my legs flares.

I didn't need a reminder of how much worthier of my trust Bastien is than the unpredictably cruel man I married, but this one act couldn't have served as a better one.

I propel myself forward and yank the prince into a kiss.

With a rough sound, Bastien kisses me back, tugging me tight against him. My arms twine around his lean frame, one hand delving into his rumpled hair as if I could pull our mouths even closer together. For those first fleeting seconds, all I want is to drown in him and welcome him just as deeply into me.

Could we couple right here in the gardens—on a bench or up against a tree or down on the earth?

The thought sends a thrill through my veins. To let go of all the control and caution we've needed over the past several weeks and give ourselves completely over to passion…

I recover enough sense to ease back and glance around. My roving gaze picks out every sheltered alcove and sturdy trunk that could support such wildness.

But it also catches on Raul's massive form where he's watching us with just as much passion blazing in his bright eyes. On Lorenzo, his mouth curved in a dreamy smile even as his posture stays tensed with the concentration needed to work his gift.

A different sort of desire clangs through me more loudly

than the call of my body. I want all three of my men with me. It's been too long since I felt any of their touches.

I can't resist claiming another kiss from Bastien where we're still entwined. Then I ask, a little breathlessly, "Where can we go that Lorenzo can relax too? We should all be able to enjoy this night."

Bastien beams at me without the slightest hint of jealousy that his foster brother's happiness matters to me just as much. "Whatever our signal star wishes, she should have. I think his chambers are the closest to the doorway." He glances toward the other man. "Can you keep us out of sight the whole way to your rooms?"

Lorenzo nods, his features tightening a little more. He flicks his hand through a few signs. *And back here when Aurelia has to go.*

In careful silence, we find the nearest path and hustle along it to one of the doorways into the palace. Bastien keeps his fingers tucked around mine, his thumb stroking over the back of my hand, sending fresh tingles up my arm with every tiny caress.

Raul steps closer to rest his own hand on the small of my back. The protective gesture stirs even more heat beneath my skin.

The burn of desire builds and builds until Lorenzo is opening the door to his chambers. The second it shuts in our wake, I pull Bastien back to me, crushing my mouth against his.

Raul chuckles and teases his fingers down over my hip. "So eager tonight, Shepherdess. Your needs have been neglected for too long."

My cheeks flush. I can't stop my body from swaying with his touch, seeking out all the contact it can get.

"I— The fertility potion I brewed. I think it's... fanned

certain flames." A little growl escapes me. "You have no idea how hard it's been to *wait*."

Raul laughs again, low and full of promise. "You don't have to wait any longer, Lamb." He tugs my chin up so he can capture my mouth for himself.

I do feel more lamb than shepherdess right now, wanting nothing more than to be ravaged. I grope at Bastien's shirt and then Raul's.

Before I can turn to soak up Lorenzo's attentions too, he brushes a kiss to the back of my neck. His deft fingers work over the lacing I hastily tied down my back. *"We'll make sure you're every bit as satisfied as you could imagine. You have all of us, always."*

As the gown's bodice loosens, I spin to meld my mouth to his. A rush of Bastien's conjured wind ripples beneath my dress.

His even voice takes on the commanding air that often emerges when our meetings turn intimate. "Our empress needs us immediately, and I think she should have all of us at once. Did you bring the oil we talked about, Raul?"

I feel Raul's wicked smirk against my shoulder as he tugs aside the fabric of my gown. "I couldn't forget that."

"Let's bring her to the bed, then."

More wind licks beneath my gown and tugs it right off me when Lorenzo eases back. His dark brown eyes gleam with amusement as he strokes his thumb along my jaw. *"He can be awfully bossy, can't he?"*

A giggle tumbles out of me. "I can't say I mind."

As the prince of Rione guides me to the bed, more air swirls around my body. The eddies flick across my skin like the most teasing of touches. My drawers flutter with a current that strokes right across my sex.

I gasp at the pulse of pleasure, and Raul clicks his tongue

at Bastien. "You're just torturing her like that. Our woman needs a firmer hand."

He delves his fingers beneath my drawers to cup my folds. I outright groan, rocking into his hand.

He curls two fingers right inside me and then brings them, slick, to his mouth. Watching him lap up my juices sends a shiver right down the center of me.

I can't forget why I'm here, why I took the potion in the first place. Bastien has already made it to the bed. I grasp at the fastening on his trousers, and he strips out of them and his drawers at my urging.

His cock ruts toward me, rigidly erect. I wrap my fingers around it to pump it up and down, and Bastien's hips jerk. A bead of liquid forms at the tip.

He sprawls on the covers on his back and beckons me to him. His tone has gone rough but no less demanding. "Come ride me, Star."

There's nothing I want to do more. My sex throbs as I squirm out of my drawers and scramble after him with a heady sense of desperation. Raul and Lorenzo follow me.

As I brace myself over their foster brother, Lorenzo sets a steadying hand on my side and brushes kisses along my shoulder blade. Raul twines his fingers in my hair. "Do you think you can take us all at the same time, Empress?"

I sink down over Bastien, taking his rigid length into me with a very undignified whine and a panted breath. Bastien answers for me. "Of course she can. She needs everything we can give her. Make sure she's ready."

His voice breaks as he fills me to the hilt. He catches my neck and tugs me down for another scorching kiss.

But when I arch my hips against him, Bastien grips my thigh to hold me still. "Not yet. Not until we're all together."

Raul lets out a dark hum and traces the cleft of my ass. "I think you'd better be the one to take her here, Lore. I won't make her try to fit me on her first go. But I can prepare her so it's nothing but bliss."

I stay tipped farther forward, my head bowed next to Bastien's, as Raul spreads a slippery oil across my back entrance and then inside with a dip of his fingers. The unfamiliar pressure makes me gasp, but the hunger inside me intensifies.

"Such a good little lamb for us," Raul murmurs. "Is this how much you want to be filled? I can do even better."

His fingers retreat, but only to graze across my entrance again. A second later, I understand why.

A smoother pressure solidifies inside me. Raul eases it in and out, expanding the substance in his grasp slightly with each iteration.

He's grasped the shadow from right inside me and is bending it to his will to pleasure me.

"There you go, Shepherdess. Look how nicely you stretch for me."

The growing pressure and the slick friction flood my whole body with heat. A strange mewling sound seeps from my lips.

Bastien catches it with a kiss and slips his hand between us to massage my clit. I barely hold myself back from grinding against him.

As Raul keeps pumping his shadowy plaything into my ass, Lorenzo kicks off his trousers. He strokes his hand along his cock, watching the scene before him as avidly as a starving man before a banquet table.

"You're gorgeous, Aurelia. And you're ours, as we're yours. Even if no one else knows it. Even if Marclinus acts like you're his. We belong to each other first."

The devotion in his words brings a swell of affection into my chest, as overwhelming as the pleasure that's quivering through my nerves. I find my words amid the maelstrom of sensation. "Yes, we do."

Bastien has been watching my face. A pleased smile creeps across his lips. "I think she's ready to be fully possessed. Get over here, brother."

Raul lets out a rumble of agreement. He releases his sculpted shadow and moves to the side to make room for the other man. "Slow and steady to start is the way to go."

The prince of Lavira has done his job well. Lorenzo slides into my oil-coated entrance one inch at a time, filling me with a tingling pressure that's only got the slightest edge of a burn. A burn that makes the bliss of it that much sweeter.

His breath stutters, and he dips down to press a few kisses along my spine. *"You feel so good, Rell. It's an honor to be this close to you."*

The ache of need has flared from my core again. I'm dying to rock between these two men, but it's not quite enough.

I glance around to seek out Raul's gaze. My tongue darts out to lick my lips in a gesture that feels shockingly provocative a moment after I've done it. "I was promised all three of you."

His grin returns, so heated it could melt me. "What our woman wants, she shall receive."

He strips off the rest of his clothes in a matter of seconds and kneels near my head.

I ease up and down both of the cocks inside me at the same time, reveling in the rush of combined pleasure. Lorenzo traces his fingers along my side encouragingly, and Bastien swivels his thumb over the tip of my breast to add to the giddy sensations. "Go on and take Raul too."

I turn my head and flick my tongue over the head of Raul's cock. He groans, pumping it at the base where his flesh only holds the faintest of curves after his sacrifice.

"Never met a woman who could come close to you. You'll be my shepherdess as long as I live."

I reward him for his loyalty by sliding my lips right around his erection.

His salty, musky flavor floods my mouth. A shudder of pure delight wracks my body.

I'm really doing this. I'm fucking all three of these glorious men in tandem.

My tenuous hold on my urges snaps. I buck between my princes, seeking out every pang of bliss they can send through my body. Soaking up the strokes of their hands, the thrust of their shafts, and the worshipful words murmured between increasingly fragmented breaths.

It feels so right, it's hard to believe I can't remain here always. That I have to pretend to belong someplace else for gods know how much longer.

I'm so primed for the act that it doesn't take much time. As I sway between my men, their thrusts turn jerkier and faster.

My pleasure roars through my veins like a tidal wave. I buck and whimper, chasing it up, up, up—

My climax crashes over me, sparking through every inch of my body. A sharper cry breaks from my throat.

Bastien lets out a strangled grunt and comes with me in a hot gush. Moments later, Lorenzo pants against my back and quivers with his own release.

I suck down Raul as hard as I can, determined to draw him over the edge with the rest of us. His grip on my hair tightens as he bucks against my mouth. "Lamb, I'm going to—"

I don't need the warning. I swivel my tongue around his shaft, and it erupts with a musky spurt I swallow without hesitation.

"Fuck," Bastien mutters, as if he can't quite believe the act he orchestrated.

A joyful laugh spills out of me. I duck down to kiss him hard, and he receives my mouth heedless of the taste of my other lover that must linger there.

Lorenzo withdraws and tugs me over into his embrace as if staking a claim. I sag into the bed between the three men with a sigh that's nothing but contented. The desperate burn of desire inside me is finally quelled.

I'm sated enough that I start to drift to sleep nestled in their warmth. Bastien trails his fingers over my hair, but he's never been one to totally forego caution. "How soon do you need to return?"

There's a reluctant note in his voice. He doesn't want me to leave any more than I want to go. But every minute I delay is a greater risk that my disappearance will be discovered.

Grimacing, I push myself upright. "I suppose I should go now. But we'll meet up at least once more. We should give this month every possible chance to get the timing right."

Lorenzo steals another kiss. *"You know we'll be here for you however you need us."*

Raul grins. "And this kind of 'help' is hardly a chore."

We scramble into our clothes, Lorenzo lacing my dress in a few swift motions. He stands near the door, his deep brown face settling into its mask of concentration.

At his nod to confirm he's constructed the illusion to hide us, we slip through the halls and back across the garden. By the wall, I soar over on a final waft of Bastien's directed wind.

In the smaller private garden on the other side, I simply stand for a minute among the sculpted trees to gather myself. After several steadying breaths, I set off toward the path.

I've nearly reached it when a rustle draws me up short.

My head jerks toward the sound—in the other direction, off near the wall of the palace opposite my apartment.

Is someone else out here?

My pulse lurches. Keeping myself still and silent, I strain my eyes to see through the moonlight.

There's a soft rasp as if of footsteps over stone, but they're heading away from me. As I crane my neck, I think I catch a glimpse of short pale hair between the far-off foliage.

Who could be strolling the imperial-side gardens? One of the guards, thinking Marclinus and I must be too occupied to notice?

What will he think if he sees me sneaking around in the night?

My heart is outright hammering at my ribs now. I stay where I am until the click of a door closing reaches my ears. Then I dart along the path to my chambers as swiftly as I can.

I ease my door open to the sight of my husband still sprawled across my bedcovers. I don't think he's moved more than a tilt of his head toward the pillow.

When I sink onto the bed next to him, a faint snore warbles from his lips. My racing pulse slows.

Whoever was wandering the gardens didn't appear to see *me*, which is the most important part.

The next time I seek out my princes, I'll have to be that much more careful.

CHAPTER THIRTY-FOUR

Aurelia

Purple streamers fly all around the city square in the middle of Rexoran. Jubilant laughter rolls through the air alongside the spirited fiddle tune a nearby musician is playing. Feet patter with dancing steps, and the smells of roasted pork skewers and fresh-baked cinnamon twists lace the breeze.

I stand in the middle of the festivities, but I feel set apart from them all the same. Marclinus's court has taken over the center of the square around its grand fountain dedicated to the very first emperor who pushed beyond Dariu's borders and began expanding their holdings. His statue stands over us with raised sword and fist while similarly armed living soldiers create a barrier all around us to hold back the common folk.

I can't help thinking that the ongoing celebration of Marclinus's ascension looks more thrilling on the other side

of our ring of guards. The city's people are frolicking and downing mugs of frothy ale while we stroll more sedately around the fountain, sipping from goblets of wine.

The court must maintain its appearance of elegant propriety, of course.

Some of the palace servants have at least gotten us our own supply of the local pastries. I nibble on a cinnamon twist my taster already sampled for me, the spicy-sweet flavor flooding my mouth.

Bianca sidles up to me, the goblet in her hand still nearly full. She peers out beyond the guards at the mass of reveling civilians. "They do adore His Imperial Majesty, don't they?"

"Yes," I have to agree. It hasn't escaped my notice that not a single cheer has been raised specifically in my name. I've been mentioned a few times alongside Emperor Marclinus or as the joint "Their Imperial Eminences" but never alone.

That's to be expected. I've only just started making my mark. I'll have many more months ahead of me even if my latest attempt at establishing myself in the imperial family is successful.

The thought is somehow both reassuring and depressing. I push my smile a little higher and aim for a note that's friendly but not overly warm. "I hope you're enjoying yourself."

"Oh, decently enough." Bianca's gaze slides over the crowd again before settling on me. "I suppose you had royal festivals and celebrations of your own back in Accasy?"

A couple of months ago, she'd have delivered that question in a disparaging or disdainful tone, ready to mock whatever I answered. Now, it comes with a curious lilt.

She really is attempting to make good on her realization of how useful I could be as a friend.

Well, as long as I don't forget that she's mainly cozying up to me for her own benefit, I can't see any harm in indulging her overtures. I know some of her secrets. It makes the ground between us feel more even than with the many other nobles who could be scheming just as much but with whom I'm less familiar.

I nod. "The usual godlen festivals, naturally, and a few local holidays. We have less need to worry about security, though, so I'd have mingled more back—"

I'm about to say "back home," but I catch myself just in time. Dariu is home now, to anyone around here who'd be listening to me.

"—back there," I replace it with. "There'd be guards keeping watch, but not outright shielding us."

Bianca raises her eyebrows. "The wild north is a rather peaceful place, then."

The corner of my mouth twitches upward at her ironic phrasing. "For the most part. With fewer people, and all of them sharing similar concerns, there isn't often much to fight about."

Accasians have a long history of comradery and generosity. Those values helped the people of times long past survive our precarious terrain and harsh winters in our isolation from the rest of the continent.

In more recent centuries, we've also stuck together and celebrated the ties between us because no fellow citizen could pose as much of a threat as the conquerors who barge into our streets.

"I do appreciate the company I have here," I add, to be polite.

Bianca hums to herself. "We can create quite a bit of merriment just within our court. It's been a long time since I really went out among the common folk. I used to as a child, when I was at my family's estate…"

She hesitates as if she's afraid she's said too much, but the hint of uncertainty softens me. I touch her elbow to nudge her toward the ring of guards. "We can at least get a better look at what we're currently missing."

A conspiratorial smile curves the vicerine's lips. We stroll together through the gathering of nobles.

Amid the swarm, my gaze catches on Raul's cocoa-brown hair in its usual short ponytail and then Lorenzo's, darker and closer cropped, nearer by. The prince of Rione dips his head respectfully, his face impassive but a gleam I know is affection in his rich brown eyes.

I nod briefly in return and force my attention to slide on over him as if he's of no consequence to me.

As we amble on, Bianca sidles even closer to me. She drops her voice to the barest whisper. "There isn't something going on between you and the princely musician, is there?"

A chill sweeps through my veins. I glance toward her, fighting to keep my expression mild. "Pardon me?"

Somehow my reaction seems to encourage her. The vicerine's smile widens. "Oh, why shouldn't you accept other attentions if you find them pleasing enough? He'll be a major figure in his own country someday, after all. You're smart enough to take the proper precautions."

I manage not to sputter my answer, but it's a near thing. "I don't know what you're talking about."

Bianca arches her eyebrows, apparently not to be dissuaded. Perhaps she's spent so much energy conducting her own intimate connections that she can pick up on the most subtle clues—or perhaps she simply wants it to be true so she holds one of my secrets as I do hers.

"You needn't worry," she murmurs. "You've been more than tolerant of my own trysts. If you should need any help arranging a private interlude or—"

Gods, no. I come to a halt and frown at her with all the imperial foreboding I can summon. "I truly don't know what you mean, so I need no help. It certainly wouldn't to do tarnish my or the prince of Rione's reputations with such speculations."

Bianca pauses, studying me. My heart thumps on, spreading the chill deeper into my gut.

Her smile turns smaller but softer. "My apologies, Your Imperial Highness. I made assumptions and overstepped. I hope you'll forgive me."

I can't tell whether she actually believes me or she's just trying to keep my good will. But what else can I do except hope she won't mention her impressions to anyone else?

I smile back benevolently and force my gritted teeth to open. "I appreciate your apology. Let us move on to more pleasant subjects."

Despite that suggestion, we lapse into silence as we stroll on. My gaze travels over to where Marclinus is standing with High Commander Axius, Counsel Etta, and a few of the marchions.

They look more like they're holding a business meeting than celebrating. Has there been additional news from Lavira?

Is that why Neven is hanging around on the outskirts of their group like a puppy watching for scraps dropped from a table? My husband had better not be drawing the young prince into some larger scheme, no matter how much new eagerness he's shown for battle.

I don't see any sign of anyone talking directly to the prince of Goric, so I return my focus to the goal I claimed to be pursuing. Bianca and I glide right along the line of guards, watching the city folk on the other side dance and drink.

There's some small hope their spectacle of revelry will distract the vicerine from her imaginings.

Several of the nearby citizens turn our way at the sight of me. Murmurs drift through the chatter of the crowd.

"The empress!"

"Isn't she pretty?"

"She went up just like he did."

"That's the kind of partner he needs."

"Did you see how well she climbed?"

Just as my spirits start to lift, a flatter voice cuts through the others, pitched loud enough that I think the man is hoping I'll overhear. "That was all pretending. They'll have given her an easier challenge so she could put on a little show for us."

The remark rankles my pride. If he had any idea—it's his wretched emperor who's had the pampering in these challenges. They didn't see the bruises gouged into my shoulder from the wrenching of the harness; they didn't feel the wind tugging me toward a fatal fall as I neared the top.

I can't say any of that, though. I can only walk on as if I didn't hear, pretending I also don't hear the guffaws and whispers that sound like hushed agreement with the criticism.

How much do I need to do before they consider me a worthy empress?

Bianca rests her hand on my forearm. "Don't pay them any mind. Most of them are louts anyway."

As if I don't know that a great deal of her fellow nobles— maybe even she herself—still have similar doubts about me. As if I don't have just as much to fear from this woman who's trying to be my friend.

I wet my lips, searching for the right thing to say, and my gaze catches on a face just beyond the guards.

For just a second, the woman's skin seems to shimmer. I haven't called on my godlen, but I feel Elox's soothing presence in the effect. It emphasizes her one reddened eye, the lid turned pinkish too.

My gift itches at me automatically—to concentrate on her and see what could heal her ailment.

I hesitate, considering the matter.

Yes. It would be a different kind of show, but no one could doubt I'm performing it through my own talents.

I step closer to the guards, raising my hand to catch the woman's attention. "My good lady, could I have a word?"

Her expression stutters with surprise, but she turns toward me. A man who might be her husband sets his hand on her shoulder as she dips into an awkward bow. "I'm at your service, Your Imperial Highness."

I offer a smile to reassure both her and the guards between us whose shoulders I'm peering over. "I was hoping I might be at yours. I don't know how far word has spread about my gift—I'm dedicated to Elox, with his blessing to create remedies for all sorts of afflictions. It looks as if your eye has been troubling you."

The woman's hand darts to her ruddy eye as if to hide it, her head drooping. "I've seen the herbalist—nothing he gave me worked. We're saving up to hire a medic."

She speaks almost apologetically, as if she's afraid she's offended me with her appearance.

I keep my smile in place and speak as soothingly as I can. "I might be able to give you some relief sooner. Would you let me work my gift for you? The magic won't affect you at all—I can only tell you what should heal the malady."

The man's eyes widen. "We wouldn't ask Your Imperial Highness to—"

I hold up my hand to stop him. "I'm asking you. It would make me happy to lift whatever suffering I can."

As we've talked, many of the civilians around the couple have paused in their celebration to watch. Some of the other nobles drift closer on my side of the ring as well.

I'd better make this a *good* show.

The woman hesitates for a moment longer and then

offers me a shy smile. "If you can see a way to fix it... I'd love to have it gone."

Inhaling slowly, I focus on the redness of her eye, the hints of inflammation that reveal her malady. What would remove those symptoms and set her features back to rights?

The tickle of images that flow through my head reveal why the herbalist's typical remedies wouldn't have worked. From what I can tell, it's a combination of problems—a minor injury and some kind of illness that the treatments have only partly held at bay. Without addressing both in combination, the condition has lingered.

"All right," I say. "You'll need some garlic, brackberries, and willow bark, a little bit of everslip, and some brindle ash sap. Do you think you'd be able to find all that?"

The man's expression turns pensive before brightening as he nods. "We'll manage it."

"Good. The preparation is important too. Let me explain it as well as I can."

I lay out what needs to be mashed and boiled and mixed, how long the resulting tincture should be left to rest, and how to apply it afterward. Toward the end of my instructions, my confidence wavers.

"I've never used my gift purely by instruction before. I sometimes see more subtle steps as I'm brewing—if I'd known and I could have prepared the concoction ahead of time for you—"

"It's all right, Your Imperial Highness." The woman's voice is so warm with gratitude it's impossible for me to disbelieve her. "Just helping us this much—if it works even a little—thank you so much."

Murmurs are passing through the crowd, but they sound more eager than the earlier muttering after that man dismissed my confirmation rite.

Another woman pushes through the crowd toward me,

raising her hand for attention while the other rests on a child's head. "Empress! Can your gift work on sickenings you can't see? My boy's ear has been aching inside for a week now."

One of the nearby guards clears his throat. "Her Imperial Highness can't be expected to tend to every little—"

"No," I interrupt, with a swell of elation. "It's really all right. I'm glad I can help however I can."

This is what I'm meant to be doing here. This is what I came for. I may be healing the empire on only the smallest scale at the moment, but it's a start.

After the boy with the earache, there's a man who's been suffering from breathing pains and an elderly woman who's developed a scaly rash on her hands. All of them haven't had the money to pay for a medic's healing gift, and I suspect the old woman hasn't even scrouged up enough for an herbalist's cure, the balm my gift brings to mind is so simple.

As the number of revelers who've turned into spectators grows, Marclinus saunters over behind me. I don't acknowledge him other than a flash of a smile, but I'm starkly aware of his presence just a step behind, watching the proceedings over my shoulder.

He doesn't try to stop me, but he doesn't offer any words of encouragement either.

Perhaps my husband is simply hoping that people will associate some of my generosity with him.

The next petitioner for my gift approaches the ring of guards with a wary glance at the emperor before focusing on me. The woman looks no more than a few years older than my twenty-one, her loose stringy hair indicating she's unmarried. There's a sallowness to her skin that niggles at me before she even speaks.

She places a thin hand on her belly, which bulges slightly on one side beneath her thin dress. "I've been feeling sick for almost a month now. Can't be a baby because I had my bleed. Hard to keep food down. Hard to work. If there's any way to make it better…"

She trails off, sounding a little hopeless.

I ease closer so it's easier to focus on her rather than the guards and the watching figures all around us. "Let me see what I can tell you."

I gaze at her, calling on my gift.

For the first time this day, my mind remains blank. It's as if there's a dark hollow where the answers should have arrived.

My chest constricts. I've had that result occasionally before, but it's never welcome.

Tamping down my own queasiness, I adjust my thoughts, directing them more toward comfort and secondary concerns rather than healing the main problem. Several images flit past my eyes, none of them contradicting what I already knew.

It takes a moment before I can speak. "I'm afraid I can't see any concoction that could be brewed that would heal what ails you. It's beyond my gift. A medic might still be able to—"

The woman's face has outright blanched. "I can't afford a medic."

I swallow thickly. "I'm sure we could help with that, considering your need. And I can suggest a few things that might soothe your queasiness and some of the other symptoms."

Tears streak down her cheeks before I've even finished speaking. "It's that bad. I knew something was really wrong. They kept telling me I was making a fuss, but I knew. I *knew*."

An angry voice bellows from somewhere behind her. "The empress helped all those others. Why can't she do anything for Vinette who really needs it?"

At the chorus of frustration that echoes him, my pulse stutters. Is all the good I've managed to accomplish going to be undone because of the limits of my talent?

I reach between the guards to touch the woman's shoulder, trying to offer as much reassurance as I can, to let her know that her fears and her pain matter to me even if I can't cure them. The soldier to the left grunts in objection and starts to nudge me backward.

And a gaunt figure lunges past the sick woman to snatch at my arm. "You don't really care at all about any of us, you bitch from—"

His fingers claw at my wrist, the nails digging in for one painful instant. Then a small shape whips past my ear.

My attacker's fingers loosen before the guards have even shoved him away. He stumbles back into the crowd, eyes rolling up as if to stare at the knife embedded in his forehead.

As the gaunt man slumps to the ground in the midst of the startled hush, Marclinus pushes forward. He eases me to the side, glancing at my wrist and then at the staring crowd while he spins another slim knife between his fingers.

He once threw knifes like that at me and nearly a dozen noblewomen to test our mettle. Today he used the same skill to protect me. I never even had the chance to reach for the blade at my own hip.

His voice rings out cool but ominous. "No one harms my wife. Your empress has offered all the help she can. Don't shame our empire by punishing her for her good will."

A shiver travels down my back.

The spectators are already slinking away, leaving the dead man for the guards to collect. The music in the square has faltered; no one speaks above a whisper.

Marclinus defended me, but at what cost? What do all

these people think of me now that a man's been killed over grabbing at me in a fit of anguish?

Just as they might have associated my husband with my efforts at healing, now I'm tainted by his violent inclinations.

I gather myself and step farther away from the ring of guards. Marclinus turns toward me with a casual air as if he isn't remotely affected by the fact that he just murdered a man.

Would I really expect him to be, after all I've seen of him?

"I think that's enough of that sort of excitement," he says with a crooked grin. "Do you need more entertainment than my court has been providing to keep you occupied, wife? Is there something else you need?"

Gazing up at him with my stomach churning, a different stream of images fills my head: all the things I might need to remove him from my life entirely.

"Actually, there is one thing I was hoping I might add to my possessions, if we can find one in town. I'd like to adopt a kitten."

CHAPTER THIRTY-FIVE

Aurelia

I keep accepting dances long after I notice one of my princes and then another duck out of the ballroom. There's no point in dragging Marclinus off to bed in the early hours of the night when I'll just have to wait next to his unconscious form before I can see the men I actually want to embrace.

And the more distance I can put between my departure and theirs, the better, in case Bianca is still speculating about my possible interest in Lorenzo.

I have to take this opportunity. It's only been a couple of nights since our last interlude, but we head back to the capital tomorrow. I can't imagine how we'd find an opportunity to meet up at any of the waystations along the road southeast.

Marclinus turns me in his arms with one of his small

sharp smirks. It's hard to tell if he's looking forward to returning to his most consistent home or worried about being so far from the empire's most urgent conflict again. Tribune Valerisse hasn't returned since the day I met her, but I've noticed at least a few hasty messengers arriving on horseback.

Perhaps it's a little of both, the happier emotions and the more fraught tempering each other in turn. He's had plenty of smiles and chuckles for all the ladies he's danced with and the noblemen he's talked to in between, but not the unnervingly frenetic energy that comes over him sometimes.

This may be the first ball I've attended with him where he hasn't groped my breasts or my ass once. His caresses have been limited to my waist, my shoulder, and the occasional squeeze of my hand.

I'd be relieved not to have our intimate connection on full display, except I'm not sure if it means he's simply not in the mood tonight. Maybe I should have found a way to slip a little of the fertility potion into his wine to ensure he'd be eager for a tumble.

If this month's attempts are successful, it probably doesn't matter if the date of conception doesn't line up perfectly with a night Marclinus thinks he bedded me. I'd rather not leave even the slightest chance for doubt, though.

So much depends on everyone's certainty that the child I'll bear is his.

With a shift in the music, we part ways to entertain other dancing partners. But as soon as I step back from the baron who claims my attention for one song, I find myself facing my husband again.

He offers his hand with a brilliant grin that only emphasizes how ridiculously, unfairly stunning his face is. "My turn again."

I step into his arms without hesitation. Beyond the

palace walls, the bell for the eleventh hour rings. Impatience gnaws at me.

I don't think I can wait any longer. Half of the court nobles have already drifted off to their bedrooms by now. It'll hardly seem hasty.

As I decide on my approach, Marclinus adjusts his grip on my fingers and strokes his thumb up and down my side. "It's been gratifying getting to spend so much time with you this past week, wife. I hope you've had no reason for complaint."

Is he fishing for criticism? I don't even know what he means when I don't think we've been together here more than we have anywhere. We spent a week trapped in a carriage with each other before we arrived.

My only new complaint would be that he hasn't seen fit to let me in on the current situation in Lavira since our last conversation about politics and advising. I'm hardly going to mention that when I promised to leave my involvement at his discretion.

I smile back at him as winningly as I can. "None at all. As much as I enjoy the capital, Rexoran is a lovely place as well."

Conveniently, he's given me all the opening I need. As he spins me around with a swell of the melody, I tuck myself closer against him and let my expression turn coy. "I'd very much like to spend a little more time with you before we leave, just the two of us. Would you like to continue our dance in my chambers?"

Marclinus hums and stops our current dance to lean in to kiss me. The feel of his lips leaves me cold, but I can't help noticing that he's taking the same gentler approach he did a couple of nights ago rather than shoving his tongue down my throat.

Now that he's put me in my place, is this new, less

aggressive version of passion supposed to make up for all his other violence?

I don't need to say anything else. At the end of the song, Marclinus twines his fingers with mine and leads me out of the ballroom. I match his smooth strides through the hallways, glad that I held off on imbibing the fertility potion tonight.

I'd rather not have to deal with any unwelcome desire inside me when I'm with a man who's done so little to earn it.

As we push past my bedroom door, the little ball of black-and-brown-striped fur I adopted yesterday bounds over to meet us with a mew of greeting. I bend down to give the tabby kitten a quick scratch along her jaw.

Marclinus considers the animal with bemusement. "You didn't have enough company already?"

"A pet is a different sort of company." I lift my arms to loop them around his neck, letting my ring graze the skin at the nape. I want my drug taking hold of his mind as quickly as possible tonight. "But not the sort of company I'm looking for when my husband is here with me."

His grin comes back. He walks me over to the bed, tugging up the skirt of my dress as he does, massaging my bare thigh beneath it. "I'll see that my wife is left wanting for nothing, then."

He busies himself with more kisses, working from my mouth down my neck to my chest. Before he's even bared my breasts, his eyes glaze over with the hallucinatory haze.

We've gone through these motions so often that I barely need to think about it now. Put on a bit of a show to direct his delusions, clean him up afterward, and tuck him into bed, tonight with a dose of sedative.

When I walk across the room to my trunks, the kitten

trundles along beside me. I sink down on the floor and let her hop onto my lap.

"You'll help me with him too," I tell her in a hushed voice. "We'll see what we can brew together."

If I'm going to be inciting some wild animal against him, I'll need a test subject for my potions. I can hardly go experimenting on anyone else's pets without raising questions.

We'll start small. I don't want to hurt this sweet creature.

I let her snuggle in my lap for several minutes, contemplating different names I could give her, and then scoop her up to set her on the rumpled blanket she's claimed as her bed.

The fertility potion goes down easier the second time, in part because I'm taking a smaller dose. I didn't like how much it affected my self-control last time.

If I need to make another batch next month, I'll have to focus my gift away from the aphrodisiac implications of my purpose.

At the bell for the twelfth hour, I give the kitten one last pat, cast a glance toward Marclinus to confirm he's slumbering as deeply as I expected, and head out into the garden.

I pad along the path through the cooling air, even more cautious than last time. Every sound that reaches my ears makes my heartbeat stutter. But I catch no sign that anyone beyond a few birds has ventured into the private inner garden.

I ease close to the dividing wall, knowing Raul won't want to extend his shadowy powers very far into the imperial area. I warned the princes that the guards might wander the gardens away from their employer sometimes.

No reassuring voice carries into my head, but a

purposeful gust of breeze whisks around my torso. That's my cue to prepare for the larger force.

I brace myself with a giddy hitch of my pulse. The air rushes up beneath me like it did the other night, propelling me up above the wall as if I'm flying.

I glide down on the other side even more gracefully than before. Bastien lowers his arms with my descent and then steps forward to wrap those arms around me.

He's standing in the small clearing by the wall alone. As I hug him back, an anxious pang resonates through my nerves. "Is everything all right?"

"Yes," he says hastily. "As much as it ever is. Lorenzo and Raul are fine."

He pauses, drawing back a few inches. In the dimness, a blush darkens his pale cheeks. "You've stolen moments with both of them when it was just the two of you. You and I have never really had that. Maybe it's selfish of me, but I wanted this time to be just us. They're keeping watch farther off in the garden, making sure no one stumbles on this spot."

A different sort of pang echoes through my chest at the uncertainty in his tone. Some part of him is still afraid he isn't enough for me. That what we share isn't just as treasured as the love I've found with his foster brothers.

I cup his cheek, beaming up at him. "I don't think it's selfish at all. I only wish I could have all the time in the world to spend with each of you, on our own and all together, without having to worry."

Bastien dips his head closer to mine again, his breath grazing the side of my face with its heat. "If we can see through everything we mean to, then someday... I used to imagine after the empire fell, I'd travel around the continent in honor of my godlen, spreading the truth about the horrors Dariu dealt out and sharing stories from the countries who've been under their thumb for so long. To be that free..."

When he trails off, I tip my face to nuzzle his jaw. "You used to? Not anymore?"

I hear his swallow. "After Pavel died and we couldn't see any way to topple the empire ourselves, it seemed like an impossible dream. I thought the best I could hope for was to get the rest of us through our fostering in one piece. But now, with you—you've brought the dream back to life. It's far off, but I can *hope* again, like I haven't in so long. Except that if it happens, I want you by my side. My signal star."

A lump of emotion fills my throat. I pull Bastien back into a tighter embrace, a prickle of tears forming behind my closed eyelids.

I can't quite smooth the roughness from my lowered voice. "When I found out I was coming to Dariu, I assumed the best *I* could hope for out of my life was the satisfaction of knowing I'd served my people as well as I could. And maybe for my marriage to have a few pleasant moments along with everything I had to tolerate."

Bastien's arms tense around me. "Not much chance of that with Marclinus."

"No. But even though the actual marriage has been so much worse than I expected… I'm still happier than I ever dared to imagine. Because I have you. My heart is yours."

Bastien inhales shakily, and then he's kissing me like the world depends on the melding of his lips. As I kiss him back, heat kindles between my legs with the now-familiar ache of need. The potion is still doing its work, lesser dose or no.

As much as I want to revel in this moment, we shouldn't dally longer than we need to. I'd like all of us to come out of our time under imperial rule alive.

I kiss Bastien again, unable to stop my hips from rocking against his before forcing myself to pull back. "Should we go to your room?"

His smile glints in the darkness. "You looked as if you

liked the idea of staying here in the gardens before. My wild empress out in the wild? Between illusions and shadows, Lorenzo and Raul can make sure no one sees or hears us even if someone ventures out."

A thrill crackles through my veins at the thought of being taken by this man out here in the open. I don't answer other than to yank his mouth back to mine.

Through our deepening kisses, Bastien walks me backward and nudges me up against the cool stone of the wall. When I press against him again, he catches my leg and hefts me upward so his groin is flush against my sex.

At the feel of his taut erection through our clothes, I can't hold back a whimper. Bastien drinks it down, swaying against me with measured strokes that stoke the flames of my desire higher that much faster.

My breath fragments between our kisses. As I clutch at his hair, Bastien groans.

He nips the crook of my jaw and yanks at the lacing on my dress to loosen the bodice. "I don't know how long I can wait before I'm inside you."

A giggle tumbles over my lips. "Why wait? I *need* you."

With a choked sound, Bastien lowers my feet back to the ground. His commanding tone comes out, dark and firm. "Turn around and lean over. Brace your hands on the wall."

I follow his instructions, a heady shiver coursing under my skin. The hard stone rasps against my palms.

Bastien tugs my skirt up to my waist in a heap of silky fabric. As one hand trails along my side, the other teases over the hem of my drawers just below my ass.

"Someday I'll take you here too." He dips his hand lower to graze his fingertips over the already damp fabric between my thighs. "But tonight, this is all mine. Isn't that right, Aurelia?"

He increases the pressure to set off a shock of pleasure. I

gasp. There's something so thrilling about giving myself over to his domineering side, letting him call the shots instead of having to stay in control.

I lean back toward him. "I'm all yours. Take me however you like."

Bastien works his fingers over my clit and the opening beneath, stoking the flames of need even higher. Before long, my drawers are absolutely drenched.

When he retracts his hand, letting the waves of bliss subside, I moan in protest.

"I'm not leaving you wanting for long." He yanks my drawers down to my ankles so I can step out of them. "Spread your legs wider for me, Star."

With a tremor of anticipation, I oblige. The cool night air washes over my heated sex in shocking contrast.

There's a rustle as Bastien frees himself from his trousers. The head of his cock rubs against my folds.

I bite my lip against another moan. "Please."

Bastien's voice has gone ragged. "I'm going to give you everything you need."

He plunges into me in one swift stroke that leaves us both groaning. I push higher on the balls of my feet, offering the best angle I can.

Bastien bows over me, one hand grasping my hip, the other sliding over my ribs beneath my loosened dress. He steadies me as he plows into my sex again and again, each thrust of his cock filling me deeper.

All I can do is pant and sway with the impact and the surges of delight sweeping through my body.

Somehow, Bastien still has the capacity to speak, though it's in a raw murmur. "You know why I love this position, Empress?"

He slams into me with even more force, and all I can answer with is a desperate mewling.

Bastien groans in return and leans even closer to my bent frame. The hand on my hip slides around to finger my clit. "When I fuck you like this, I can hit so much deeper. And at the same time, it's so easy to play with you. Here." He swivels his finger over that tender spot just above where we're joined, provoking a hotter spike of pleasure. "And here."

His other hand glides farther up to tease over my breast beneath my clothes. The flick of his thumb over my nipple makes me jerk against him.

I don't know what woman he discovered this delightful technique with, but I can't be anything but grateful that he's ready to offer it up to me. With every drive of his cock, his hands pulse against my clit and fondle my breast.

My whole body is on fire with sensation. I cry out, grinding back into him as if I can drive him even deeper.

He pinches my clit, and the whirl of pleasure explodes through me in a blaze of ecstasy.

My fingernails scrape against the stones of the wall. My limbs quiver with the giddy rush.

Through it all, Bastien keeps pounding into me. His touch on my clit lightens until I've caught my breath, and then he swivels a fingertip over it in just the right way.

I'm wrung out, but another surge of pleasure is already building. I whimper and press into him as well as I can, chasing the second release he's promising.

As my sex starts to clench around Bastien again, he makes a strangled noise and jerks backward. I don't have time to protest before he's spun me around and pinned my back against the wall, his cock driving home again as our chests align.

Heedless of the rasp that's crept into his breath, his mouth collides with mine. He bucks into me even faster, and another flood of bliss sweeps through my nerves.

I cling to him, giving myself over to my climax. As I

careen over the edge, Bastien pants a curse onto my hair and tumbles with me.

He nestles his head next to mine, our breaths shuddering as we drift into the afterglow together. Just for that moment, I really am only his.

If only I didn't have to walk away yet again.

CHAPTER THIRTY-SIX

Aurelia

As we step out of the carriage to the flash of newly lit-lanterns, Marclinus smacks my ass and squeezes the cheek through my gown.

"What a pleasure it'll be to have some of this meat after dinner!" he declares, vigorously enough that his buoyant voice carries along the length of our convoy. Then he bounds off to grab one of the disembarking marchions from another carriage, with whom apparently he has some urgent matter to bring up.

A blush burns my face, but I keep my mild smile in place as if I'm unbothered. My jaw is starting to ache from clenching back so many winces and retorts.

Over the past two days since we started traveling back to the capital, my husband has been in particularly unruly form. Loud conversations, louder laughter, plenty of wine, and regular pawing at me and whatever other ladies he

picks to join us in our carriage, which he swaps out regularly.

Last night he went off with a couple of baronissas at our waystation, but it sounds like I won't be spared his company tonight.

Is it something about being on the road, a restlessness because of the confinement of the carriage? I don't remember him being quite this thoroughly horrible on our previous journeys.

Perhaps he'll have calmed down tomorrow.

As I clutch that kernel of hope deep inside, Neven ducks out of the carriage behind me. The teenaged prince was one of our companions for this latest leg of the journey, although Marclinus barely spoke to him other than to make a variety of insulting jokes about his home country.

He glances after the emperor with a brief grimace and then looks at me.

"Isn't it wonderful seeing His Imperial Majesty so lively?" I say, with a little more wryness than I might have allowed myself if anyone else was in easy hearing distance.

If the young prince's temper has been riled up as I've seen happen in the past, I'll do what I can to defuse it.

Neven's expression turns more pensive than angry, though. He opens his mouth, hesitates with a flick of his gaze over the departing nobles who are moving toward the waystation's open doors, and appears to gird himself.

His low voice suggests he'd rather no one overhears his remarks either. "I wanted to ask you something about your gift."

Interesting. I nod for him to go on. "Of course. What did you want to know?"

"Well, I…" He pauses again with an awkward dip of his head. "Do you think it's possible to brew a 'cure' for being attracted to someone?"

I can't stop my eyebrows from jumping up before I give the question due thought. If my fertility potion could stir up increased desire, presumably there are other combinations of ingredients that could suppress lustful sensations. "I'd imagine so. Are you looking for that sort of cure? Has something gone sour with your musician?"

I keep the question light and gentle, not sure how much Neven will want to open up to me. I offered myself in a big sister sort of position when we first made our peace, but a lot has happened since then. We've talked very little just the two of us.

He knows I was aware of his interest in one of the court musicians, enough that he only looks a little abashed and not startled by the suggestion. "Not exactly. He actually suggested maybe we could spend some time together when the court returns to Vivencia. I just—I haven't been able to stop thinking about it—I've been *dreaming* about it—"

He stops abruptly with a flush darkening his tan cheeks. "There's so much else going on, so much that's more important. It feels wrong to be distracted by trysts that aren't even happening right now instead of… anything that would be more useful."

An edge of frustration has crept through his words. What's prompted this new attitude?

Neven has been spending a lot of time around the military advisor lately.

I take an even more cautious tone. "Is that something the high commander has suggested to you—that you need to be focused on more serious matters?"

"No. No. I thought maybe I'd get a better idea of what I need from him, but I'm still not sure…"

The young prince trails off, looking lost. A pang shoots through my heart.

I don't have any conception of what it's like to be in his

position: torn away from my family for a decade, forced to live under the authority of a brutal tyrant, aware that my brother died in the same position before I arrived. Gods only know what turmoil he has to work through.

I turn to face him more fully. "I realize we haven't known each other for very long, but I hope you'll believe that I'd like to see you happy and thriving here at court, as much as that's possible. If anything's bothering you, you can tell me as much as you're comfortable talking about. *I'll* help, however I can."

Neven's jaw works, his bright brown eyes going stormy. Finally, he says, "You won't mention it to my foster brothers? Any of them?"

I don't want to lie to him. "If I think I need to so I can stop something awful from happening, I can't keep that promise. But if it's nothing that dire, your secret is safe with me."

He heaves a breath. "Do you ever get visions from your godlen—from Elox?"

Several memories flit through my mind. "Yes, occasionally. Sometimes when I ask for guidance, and more rarely when it seems he believes I need it regardless of whether I've solicited him."

"Then maybe… I've been having other dreams too. I think they're from Sabrelle." Neven presses his hand to the middle of his chest over his godlen brand. "It feels like she's impatient with me. She's urging me to take action, or at least to be prepared to, but I can't tell what I'm supposed to actually be acting *on*. It's all muddled. I just know she doesn't think I've been doing enough."

Oh, the poor kid. Sometimes the divine missives I receive can be a little unnerving, even though they're messages of peace and healing more than anything else. I can't imagine what it's like having the godlen of war and conquest spurring you onward.

Her message has been forceful enough to make a prince think he needs to medicate away his teenage desires to serve her properly.

I consider all the visions and dreams Elox has offered me —so often welcome, but not always—and the teachings of the clerics I grew up with. "You know, the gods have an awful lot of us to watch over. They can't often pay all that much attention to any one person. And they all have different domains that they prioritize. They aren't always *right* about what's best for us, and what they'd believe is best isn't always what we'd agree with."

Neven frowns. "But I dedicated myself to her. She gave me a gift."

I give his shoulder a light pat. "That simply means you generally embrace her principles. It's not a promise to obey every directive. The gods *can't* meddle with our lives directly —they can only suggest. The All-Giver created us to have free will. It's by divine right that we get to make our own choices in the end. All they can reasonably expect of us is that we take their guidance into account."

The prince considers my words, his pensive expression remaining in place. "I don't know what choices would be right for me. Everything feels so chaotic right now."

"I know. But I don't know what you could be doing right now to change that anyway, so I think you have some time to figure out where you stand." I offer a reassuring smile. "And if you decide that you *really* want that potion, I'll see what I can do about concocting it for you."

"All right. Thank you." He aims a flash of a smile at me in return that brightens my spirits a bit and heads over to the waystation building, where most of the nobles are entering beneath Jurnus's etched sigil in anticipation of our dinner.

I'm about to follow Neven when Raul steps into view, his face tight. His gaze flicks to the carriage and back to me. "My foster brother has seemed a little… out of sorts. Has he been bothering you, Your Imperial Highness?"

He obviously means for anyone overhearing to take his phrasing to mean Neven, but the twitch of his fingers at his side indicates *Marclinus*. He's taking the opportunity to check if I'm all right after my husband's shift in behavior.

I'm not sure what the prince of Lavira could do about it if I admitted how much Marclinus *has* been bothering me, but his concern warms me all the same. There's a small pleasure in being able to talk to him at all outside of secret meetings, if only for a moment.

I offer a crooked smile. "I'm sure he'll sort himself out. I'm not overly put upon."

To emphasize that point, I swivel my fingers in the gesture for, *It's fine.*

I catch sight of Lorenzo beyond Raul, turned away from me but with his hand curled by his side. It twists in a subtle motion. *We're here.*

I'd take a lot more comfort from their surreptitious display if my husband wasn't loping back toward us at this very moment.

"Wife!" Marclinus flings his arm around my shoulders and yanks me toward the waystation. "Let's get on with that dinner. I'm sure our princely companions have better things to do than badger you."

He casts his gaze toward both Raul and Lorenzo with a slight narrowing of his eyes that sets my nerves on edge.

I force a giggle. "I'm sorry, husband. Prince Neven asked for a little advice based on my gift, and Prince Raul was simply ensuring he hadn't been imposing. I am quite hungry. Let us eat."

CHAPTER THIRTY-SEVEN

Aurelia

With a reasonable man, my explanation about Neven would be the end of any trouble. With a reasonable man, there wouldn't be any trouble at all over one of his foster brothers asking me a brief question.

But no one needs to tell me that Marclinus is far from reasonable.

We sit together in the waystation's dining hall, quite a bit more cramped than the palace dining rooms and with humbler furnishings but still cushioned with velvet and lit with crystal fixtures that mimic splashing water. Jurnus is one of the godlen of the sea as well as overseer of all travelers, after all.

Marclinus grins, guffaws, and hollers to the fellow nobles

as if he's in high spirits. But every lift of his voice and jerk of his knife across his plate makes me tense up.

There's a frenzied energy beneath his buoyant mood, something darker and more vicious that I can only hope won't seep through the cheerful façade.

He speaks to me only a little, asking me thoughts on each dish. They're all pleasant enough, up to imperial standards.

Then, when the servers have cleared dessert dishes, he stands abruptly without giving the nobles any motion of dismissal.

Grasping my elbow, he tugs me to my feet with him. He leans close, grazing his lips and then his teeth along the edge of my jaw.

I will myself to relax into his embrace. I knew where this night was heading, after all.

Except I didn't really. Because after he mashes his mouth against mine, he grips my waist and heaves me up to sit me on the edge of the table with a thump.

The nobles around us—at the same table and those throughout the room—all glance over if they weren't watching already. Even the few local courtesans who've been circulating the room, seeing if any members of the court want to partake of their services, pause to watch.

Marclinus smirks down at me with an unnervingly chilly glint in his gray eyes. He pitches his voice to carry through the room. "I don't think I've had quite enough dessert yet. I'm going to indulge in my second helping right here."

As the meaning of his announcement sparks a jolt of horror in me, he slams his lips down on mine in a kiss that feels more like a punch. He grasps the folds of my skirt and jerks at the silk. In a few violent yanks, he's dragged the fabric up over my ass, pooling it on the table and baring my drawers to anyone at the right angle to see.

My gut lurches. Most of the nobles around me have witnessed me outright naked before, but Marclinus didn't do more than paw at me a little during that trial.

Does he actually mean to fuck me in front of his entire court as if I'm another dinner course?

Gods help me, I won't be able to stop him. I can't drug him into delusions in front of all these witnesses.

My pulse skitters with the first swell of panic. I clutch the front of Marclinus's shirt, kissing him back with whatever shreds of feigned enthusiasm I can summon, my mind scrambling for a way out.

The men I love are watching this too. Is he trying to provoke them, still testing just how invested they are in me? Is this a punishment to me for some transgression I can't guess at?

Are they all going to be able to keep their cool while he ravages me here on the table in front of them?

Marclinus leaves off plundering my mouth to flick his gaze toward the noblemen nearest us with narrowed eyes. Perhaps he suspects some marchion or viceroy of having designs on me. This could be a test for his entire court.

He lowers his mouth to suck on the side of my neck hard enough to bruise. His hands fumble with my gown's lacing at the same time. His hasty fingers rake across my back.

Great God help me, I can't conceal a flinch.

My husband nips the sensitive skin he's just mauled and lifts his head to peer down at me with a smile that's just shy of a sneer. "Do you have some objection to demonstrating our love in front of our friends, wife?"

If he calls this love, I'd shudder to think what he'd consider hate.

I dip my head in what I hope looks like modesty. "I'm sorry. You know how eagerly I welcome your attentions. But there are certain intimacies I thought we'd keep just between us. It feels more special that way."

At the edge of my vision, I can see Bianca watching us with widened eyes. My gut clenches with the thought that she might provide an alternate explanation—a figure that might have diverted my interest.

Thank all that's holy, her mouth remains tightly shut.

I know my excuse was flimsy, but something shifts in Marclinus's expression. If anything, his grin gets sharper. "My poor modest empress. We'll need to cure you of that bashfulness. But I suppose I could allow you to ease into this sort of fun so it'll be all the more enjoyable later."

He glances around the room, his eyes as hard and glittering as the crystal fixtures overhead. "Why don't we start with just an audience of those who are almost family? Come along, my foster brothers. You can be honored as our first spectators."

He sweeps me off the table into his arms without missing a beat. I spot Bastien by the end of the table, frozen in a rigid stance. When Marclinus jerks his head toward the doorway, the prince of Cotea shoves to his feet.

My husband strides out the doorway with only a brusque, "You too. All of you." My stomach sinks farther at the glimpse of white-blond hair as another figure springs up.

He's dragging even Neven into this horrible spectacle.

Marclinus carries me down the hall. I tuck my head against his chest as if out of shyness, but mostly it's an attempt to steady myself.

Nausea bubbles at the base of my throat. Where is he going to conduct this "fun"?

I don't dare say a word to try to guide him. It seems more likely he'll do the opposite of what I suggest than listen.

The princes tramp along behind us, silent other than the creak of the floor beneath their feet.

Imagining what they must be thinking floods me with a sickly heat, shame and fear mixed together in a noxious stew.

I don't know whether it'll be easier or harder for them to control their instinctive protectiveness when we're away from the rest of the court. They still can't attack Marclinus without the worst of consequences. His guards and mine are trailing farther behind our entourage.

When Marclinus pushes through another doorway, my glance around brings the first whisper of relief.

He's taken us into his own bedroom in the waystation. A couple of his trunks sit at the foot of the four-poster bed.

The guards will wait outside the door like they always do. We have no witnesses except the princes he's forced to observe.

Marclinus glances over his shoulder. "Enjoy the show, *brothers*." The sneer in his voice makes a mockery of the last word.

He all but tosses me onto the bed. I flick my thumb across my ring as I reach for him and brush my fingers against the side of his neck.

As Marclinus clambers over me, he hauls my dress right off. The princes remain four motionless figures by the wall at the edge of my vision, but even there, I can see Raul's hands ball into fists, Bastien's shoulders stiffen.

They don't know exactly how I've handled my husband in the past. They don't know for sure that I'm already handling him now. If they leap to my defense...

I flick my fingers by Marclinus's side in a couple of hasty gestures. *I'm okay. Wait.*

I don't dare look at my lovers. I try not to even think of them as more shame curdles in my gut.

Marclinus paws his hand down my side. "You are mine," he says, just shy of a snarl. "Everyone should know it.

Everyone should see it. You don't get to say when or how I take you."

The lies scrape across my tongue like dull blades. "I'm yours. I'll keep doing my best to serve you however you need."

"That's right." He wrenches off my chemise and bites the tip of my breast harshly enough that I gasp in pain.

Either he takes the sound as pleasure instead, or he was going for pain in the first place. He mouths my other breast just as roughly and shoves his hand between my legs over my drawers.

I suppress a wince and grope at his shirt in the hopes of covering my reaction. Marclinus gives a harsh laugh and tosses the shirt aside.

As he lunges at me again, Raul stirs as if on the verge of springing forward despite my cautioning. I wrench my hand in another urgent gesture to stand back.

And mercy of all mercy, Marclinus's fervor slows. He gazes down at me, the familiar drugged stupor coming over his face.

My breath spills out of me in a rush of relief, but I don't love that the princes will have to see even this part of our typical interludes.

It won't do for them to come into his view or for him to see me talking to them. I don't know how those factors would merge with the hallucinations I need to provoke.

Smiling up at my husband, I repeat the sign for *Wait* as emphatically as I can.

Then I roll Marclinus over so I'm poised above him. Yank down his trousers just far enough that he won't make a mess of them. Linger in his view while his mind conjures lascivious images of our encounter all the way through to his spurt of his release.

If I thought my cheeks burned before, they're scalding now.

As Marclinus's eyelids start to fall, I speak up softly in the hopes of directing the end of his hallucination. "Now that they're gone, I can have you all to myself."

Let him imagine that he's dismissed the princes and decided to doze with me.

I wait until his eyes drift completely shut before hastily wiping him off with my chemise. As I yank my dress back over my head to cover myself, footsteps creak across the floor behind me.

"He's out now?" Bastien murmurs.

I don't know how well the waystation's walls will muffle our voices. I scoot to the edge of the bed and keep my own at a whisper. "Yes. For a couple of hours. I'm sorry you all had to see that."

Raul doesn't waste another second in striding right over to me, his teeth bared. "It isn't your fault. That spiteful asshole…"

He cuts himself off with a strangled growl, fighting to keep his own voice quiet, and slides his arms around me more carefully than I suspect he'd like to. I know it's a miracle he managed to keep his cool as well as he did.

Because he wanted to protect me more than he wanted vengeance. Because he trusted me when I told him I could handle it best alone.

Lorenzo pushes in to offer his own embrace, pressing a tender kiss to my temple as if it can erase all the brutal affection my husband just inflicted on me. He won't dare to conjure his illusionary voice while Marclinus's guards are monitoring the room, but his message is clear enough.

Neven has hung back, the color drained from his face. When I meet his eyes, he drops his gaze. "I… Is that what you always have to do?"

I don't know what he thought, but I suppose none of his foster brothers mentioned that I was knocking the emperor out on a regular basis. Even they couldn't have been prepared for what an encounter like this would look like.

I lift my shoulders in a slight shrug. "It works. It's better than the alternative. He isn't normally quite so... aggressive beforehand."

The young prince's jaw works, and he raises his head again. "He shouldn't— Treating you like that— It isn't *right*."

I have to stop myself from laughing. Of course it isn't. Why should that surprise him after everything else he's seen?

But he is only seventeen years old. Young enough to have a little faith left in humanity.

My own faith feels as if it's drained away even more in the past hour. A wave of despair washes over me.

This is why the moments of gentleness Marclinus showed me in Rexoran couldn't matter. This is why I can't let the fleeting moments of guilt or sympathy shake me from my cause.

No matter how much my husband appears to soften, he always swerves straight back into awfulness before too long. We can never be even wary companions.

He'll always be my enemy. And I'm stuck with him until I can fight my way out of this tangled trap.

"It is what it is," I say, tugging my unlaced dress tighter around me. "I suppose you'd better stay a little longer until the guards won't think it's odd that he'd have drifted off." Time passes faster in the drug's hallucinations than in reality.

Neven's hands clench, but he sits down on the floor by the wall. Lorenzo eases over to perch on the bed next to me and grips my hand.

Raul takes the spot by my other side, and Bastien hunkers down by my feet to lean his head against my knee, tucking his arm around my calf. My breath evens out in the joint embrace, but my heart thuds on.

How much more will I have to survive before I can reclaim my life as my own?

Neven's head slumps, distracting me from my own misery. The comments he made about wanting to do something, to make a difference, come back to me.

He's felt shut out from his foster brothers' plans. Maybe they've protected him more than is truly safe.

I speak up again, equally quiet. "Neven's seen a lot now. I'm not sure it does us any good to keep secrets from him."

As the prince of Goric shifts straighter, Raul glances from me to him with a grimace. But he takes my suggestion to heart.

"We're working on making the situation better," he says in a firm undertone. "Stay away from Marclinus when you can—nothing to provoke him. Lorenzo and I have been nudging as many people as we can in Aurelia's favor."

Bastien nods. "I've been looking into the confirmation rites so she can be as prepared as possible." He meets my eyes. "It's no surprise, but I've been able to determine that the Sabrellian confirmation rite will definitely involve some kind of physical combat. Raul should give you more lessons. I'll see if I can find any more details."

Neven's face brightens. "I'll help with the lessons again. Any way that'll be useful."

Raul chuckles softly. "I'm sure we can find something for you to do. And believe me, when everything's in place…" He tips his head toward my unconscious husband and jerks a finger across his throat.

Neven's lips part in shock, but then the corners lift with a trace of a smile.

Lorenzo squeezes my hand as if to confirm he's here with

me just as much. He lifts his other hand in the air to form a few gestures. *Not like this forever.*

An ache swells inside my chest, but it's bittersweet rather than fully painful now.

I'm not alone. We've made our own kind of family, stronger than the bonds of blood or marriage.

I will get through this as I have so much else, with these men who match my determination around me.

Chapter Thirty-Eight

Aurelia

The hawk plummets out of the sky toward me, its talons poised. All I can see is its golden wings and the expanse of the blazingly blue sky around it.

Every instinct clamors for me to yank up my arms to shield myself, to brace to shove the creature away. But even as my stance tenses, a flood of cool calm washes over me.

No. I need to welcome whatever will come. I need to show I'll accept and embrace the threat, and nothing can truly harm me.

I lift my arms but hold them open wide. The hawk slams into me, raking its talons across my cheek and shoulder.

Pain lances through my flesh, but I remain steady in my pose.

The hawk thrashes this way and that, jabbing me with its beak. Slicing into me with its talons. Battering me with its wings.

I take in every sting and ache and stroke my fingers across its smacking feathers. Hum a soothing tune. Wait for it to see I'm not its opponent.

All at once, the bird spasms. A white form pushes through the golden feathers into my embrace.

The dove shoves the remains of the hawk's body away and nestles against my chest. A glowing light emanates from it, coursing over me and sealing all my wounds.

I made it through, and this is my reward.

I tuck my arms gently around the feathered form and—

My eyes pop open to stare at the dawn-lit ceiling of my waystation bedroom.

The dream falls away. A shudder runs through me at the memory of the hawk's vicious talons.

I touch my face with the irrational need to confirm my flesh is still whole.

My stomach balls into a knot. Elox couldn't have sent a more blatant symbolic vision. The hawk is a symbol of the imperial family—what could he mean it to represent but my brutal husband?

My godlen is calling for peace. For me to keep enduring every insult and attack Marclinus aims at me, with the promise that if I simply keep offering tenderness and compassion in return, that sadistic man will somehow transform into a loving partner.

Is that some kind of divine joke?

As I sit up in the bed, I can't help thinking of my conversation with Neven yesterday evening, before the worst of Marclinus's recent offenses. I told the young prince that none of us have to follow whatever guidance the gods offer us.

That maxim has never felt truer than right now.

I can't stop my jaw from clenching. I've disagreed with

Elox in the past, but I've never felt so outright angry with him.

How fucking *dare* he imply that I haven't tried hard enough? Was I supposed to let Marclinus spread me out on the table in front of the entire court last night and take his "dessert"?

Just how much does the godlen of peace think I should let myself be broken before I'm allowed to defend myself? How much does he imagine I'm going to accomplish for his purpose if I've been smashed into pieces before I get the chance?

No. I did what Elox called for. I committed murder even though it turned my stomach. It was good enough for the godlen of peace that I took down one imperial figure to clear the way for the realms to heal.

I'm simply following the tactics *he* taught me.

A maid arrives with hot water for my usual morning tea, and I clamber out of the bed. My kitten, now named Sprite, weaves between my ankles with a mew of greeting.

I manage a smile and bend down to ruffle her fur. But as I walk to the wash basin, a twinge runs through my lower belly.

I pause with a chill tickling over my skin. Was that the start of a cramp?

Is my monthly bleed already on the verge of returning? I wouldn't have expected it so soon.

I see no trace of red in my drawers when I relieve myself, but as I prepare for the day, a gloom settles over me alongside my frustration with my godlen.

If I'm still no closer to producing an heir, then that's another month I'll *have* to pretend to appreciate Marclinus's callous whims. Another month when I can't do anything except hold as firm as I can while he batters my foundations.

The dark edges of my inner storm cloud nibble at my

mood through a breakfast of Marclinus's jovial conversation, which he continues with the three noblemen he invites to share our carriage. I smile and nod like the wife he wants, longing for the book tucked into my travel case, knowing he'd chide me for unfriendliness if I turned to it.

As we approach the smaller waystation where we'll be taking lunch, a flurry of activity outside the low building draws my gaze.

I lean closer to the window, peering at the folk in simple clothing who are dashing to and fro by the side wall. A couple of the imperial soldiers have ridden ahead and appear to be directing them.

Word must have traveled along the convoy, because the guard riding nearest my window pulls his horse toward the carriage. His mouth is set in a tight line. "You'd better not bother yourself with anything out here, Your Imperial Highness. There was a bit of a mess. The workers are cleaning it up."

My brow knits. "What kind of a mess? What's—"

Then the carriage moves close enough that I can make out the words someone must have painted hastily on the wall, burgundy streaking across the pale blue surface. The letters have faded with the scrubbing of many sponges, but they're still visible in the stark sunlight.

GO HOME TO ACCASY.

My throat closes up. I don't know what else the message might say lower down where the letters are hidden by the workers' bodies, but I can't imagine it gets any warmer.

There's no doubt who it's meant for.

At least one person in the nearest town resents my presence enough that they thought it worth smearing their dislike across an imperial building.

Marclinus slides over and cranes his neck to take in the sight. He clicks his tongue and turns to the cavalryman. "If your colleagues find the perpetrator, see that they're properly punished."

He glances at me with a hint of a smirk. "I'm sure the people will come around as they see how well you serve me."

"These things take time," I say graciously, but I have to make a conscious effort not to clench my hands in my frustration.

I don't want whatever good will I build with Dariu's people to be based only on what I do for their emperor. If that's all I have, then the moment the emperor is gone, they'll see no use in me.

They need to know how well I can serve *them*.

Will everything I've done with the confirmation rites and the other overtures I've attempted satisfy the common folk once word has time to spread? Providing an heir won't even matter if I haven't earned enough loyalty for them to let me steer the empire until he or she is grown.

Marclinus yanks the curtain across the window as if putting an end to any discussion of the incident. The carriage rattles on along the road until we stop right in front of the waystation building.

When I step out to stretch my legs, my personal guards draw closer to me, making their presence known more than I'm used to. I bite back a grimace.

They must be worried about what other hostilities I could face here.

Farther down the convoy, the sun glances off Lorenzo's thick black hair as he ambles toward the still-bustling workers. I suppose he's going to put his gift to use again trying to sway a few more citizens in my favor.

The gloom that settled over me this morning thickens, as if I'm draped in a sweltering fog. The furtive conversation I had with my princes last night and the whispered plans we confirmed feel so paltry now in the light of day.

If I'm going to ignore my godlen's guidance and carve out my own path, I need to fight for it.

But what else can I do that won't harm any of the people I'm fighting for?

While I stew over that problem, the kitchen workers start bringing out our platters of lunch. Marclinus has been strutting along the convoy calling on other friends, but he climbs back into the carriage with me to eat.

I've barely taken a bite of my ham-and-egg tart when knuckles rap against the carriage door. High Commander Axius's grim face shows at the window.

He focuses his attention only on Marclinus. "Your Imperial Majesty, a messenger has reached us from Lavira. I'd like to update you on current developments as soon as you're ready to hear them."

Marclinus's gaze flits briefly to me. I expect him to make some patronizing remark and go off with the high commander to have their discussion where I can't listen in. Instead, his lips curl with another smirk.

He motions for Axius to join us. "You might as well tell me the news right now. I'm sure my wife can find some way to occupy her mind while we talk business."

Ah. He's going to rub it in my face that I'm not supposed to contribute to the discussion. Perhaps this is even another test—confirming that I will hold my tongue, no matter what the news is.

I do want to know what's been happening in Lavira even if I can't weigh in with my own opinions. At least I'll be prepared if my husband ever does let me into his confidence again.

The high commander doesn't look entirely pleased with the situation, but he lowers himself onto the bench next to me so he can face Marclinus, giving me as much space as the carriage allows. While his emperor gulps down bits of tart and sliced fruit with splashes of wine, he gives his report.

"There's been one new incident, an attack of hostile magic destroying a couple of Darium ships that've been carrying goods across Lake Union. Thanks to our soldiers' alertness, one of the perpetrators has been apprehended. Tribune Valerisse is overseeing his questioning personally and is hopeful he'll provide information that allows us to root out the main instigators of the uprising."

Marclinus hums around another sip of wine. "It sounds as though the traitors have been faltering in general. We've put plenty of fear into them."

He casts his gaze toward me once more with a cool glint in his eyes, as if to rub in the fact that his preferred strategy of unchecked violence appears to have been successful.

Maybe his approach did work. Maybe the rebellion will be quelled sooner because of his tactics. That doesn't mean all the innocents who died along the way deserved their fate.

But as he goes on to recommend some methods of torture that make my stomach shudder, I find myself studying my husband from the corner of my eye.

His arrogant assurance and his flippant approach to enforcing his rule have rankled me. I haven't really considered the ways in which they're effective.

His family has held this half of the continent in hand for centuries. They're hardly inept. And they know what their own people want to see to keep loyalties at home strong.

I've resented that Marclinus refused my advice, but I've never asked for *his*.

Despite my queasiness, my conviction grows. I have him right now. Why shouldn't I use him?

Even if in the end, it'll be to bring about his own doom.

Marclinus says something about making an example of the ringleaders and then pauses to swallow the last morsel of his tart. "Well, that should set things back to rights well enough. Where's your lunch, man? I can't have my military advisor starving himself."

Before Axius can answer, Marclinus is waving out the window for another meal to be brought over. The high commander shifts on the bench as if he'd rather be elsewhere, but he stays put to accept the tray.

All the better. He might as well put his mind to this task as well.

I clasp my hands on my lap. "Husband, I've been thinking about another matter. Considering recent incidents, including what we saw here at the waystation…"

Marclinus cocks his head. "What about it? Spit out whatever's on your mind, wife."

I draw my posture a little straighter. "I don't think the efforts I've been making so far have been enough. No one in Dariu should be able to doubt that you've chosen the right partner to serve you. I need to make a larger, more overt demonstration of my loyalties, something that will prove to our people just how devoted I am to them and this empire. You know them better than anyone. I'd love to hear what you'd suggest."

A gleam lights in Marclinus's eyes. "Would you now? Let me think on it. I'm sure we could come up with something delightfully impressive."

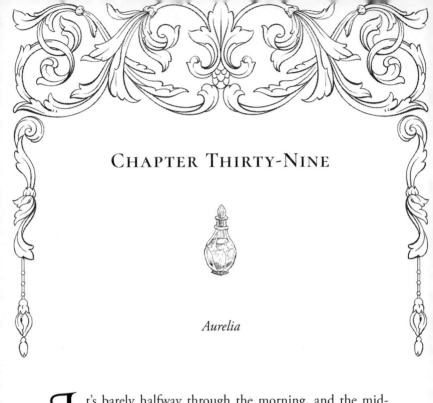

CHAPTER THIRTY-NINE

Aurelia

It's barely halfway through the morning, and the midsummer heat is already sweltering.

The court moved from the hall of entertainments to the gardens an hour ago, but the sluggish breeze hasn't lifted anyone's spirits. The nobles are clustered in patches of shade, accepting glasses of tangy juice from the servants who haven't stopped circulating since we arrived.

It seems the southern weather is determined to suffocate me.

Even Marclinus, who was in exuberant spirits earlier this morning, appears to have deflated slightly. He's taken a prime spot on a bench by the largest of the garden's fountains, where the spray offers a little relief, but his recent laughter has sounded a little weary. He keeps swiping at the sweat on his brow.

I study him surreptitiously from the blanket where I've

settled with Bianca and a few of the other noblewomen, a glimmer of hope lighting in my head. I think I could convince him to come with me into the thicker shade of the palace woods for a private walk—or at least, as private as any of our activities are with our guards lurking nearby.

Yesterday was our first full day back in the capital, and he had a pensive spell that left him locked in his office most of the day. Who knows what moods I can expect in the weeks to come?

I need to take my chances when I can get them.

I drain the last of my juice and hand off the glass to a servant before getting to my feet. "I think I'll get my book from my chambers. It is pleasant to read outside."

My meandering route toward the doors takes me past the nearest of my princes. Raul is sprawled out on a blanket chatting with a couple of ladies, with a lazy grin I can tell doesn't show any real interest.

I don't look at him as I walk by, but I twist my fingers at my side in a silent message. *Come to my room.*

I continue on into the palace, pretending not to be sharply aware of the two guards following behind me, and make my way to my apartment. The moment the door is shut, separating me from their watching eyes, I let out my breath in a rush.

Their constant monitoring is even more suffocating than the weather.

My kitten bounds over to greet me and butts her head against my shin. I scoop her up and cuddle her to my chest as I move across the room. "I hope you haven't been too bored, Sprite. I'll see what I can find for you to play with when I'm not around."

She squirms eagerly in my arms, rolling onto her back and batting at my chin with a paw. I can't help laughing, with a twinge that's both affection and guilt.

Am I really going to start feeding her potions to test their effects? It feels a lot less like a brilliant plan when I've got the subject snuggling up to me on my pillow every night.

I'll just have to be ever so careful about the contents and the dosage. And not start anything until I'm sure of my strategy.

Which today's gambit should help with.

Tucking Sprite under one arm, I retrieve the book that provided my excuse to go inside and also an item of silk I squeezed behind the bed's headboard where the cleaning staff wouldn't notice it. I've just set the kitten down in the bed when the panel in the wall slides open.

Raul props himself against the edge of the hidden entrance and aims a much more ardent grin than he offered the court ladies at me. "What can I do for you, Empress?"

I have to smile back. "I don't think you're going to find this request all that much fun. But it'll give us important information. I'm going to convince Marclinus to stroll into the woods with me. I'd like you to 'accidentally' let one of the hunting hounds loose when we're nearby."

Raul's eyebrows leap up. "Part of your brilliant strategy? You don't expect the thing to attack him, do you?"

I shake my head. "Of course not. I just want to know how quickly his guards will respond to an animal running toward him." I hold up the silk garment. "You'll need to bring these and give the hound a good sniff so it knows who it's supposed to be tracking."

His eyebrows manage to arch even higher. "Are those…?"

"A pair of Marclinus's drawers that he 'misplaced.' I figured they'd hold his scent better than a sock. Don't think about it, just tuck them away."

Raul snorts but accepts the garment with a rueful expression. "The things I do for you, Shepherdess." A sly gleam comes into his eyes. "How are you going to repay me for my trouble?"

I roll my eyes, but I can't resist grasping the front of his shirt and tugging him into a kiss. Raul kisses me back as only he knows how, the heated press of his lips coaxing mine apart so our tongues can tangle together. By the time he draws back, I'm breathless.

"How's that for a start?" I manage to ask.

His grin returns, its cockiness offset by the tender caress of his hand over my cheek. "You never fail to satisfy me. Make sure you take the path that veers closer to the kennels so I'll be able to hear when you're close."

I nod. "I'll wait a little before I suggest the walk to him, so you'll have plenty of time to get everything ready."

Raul claims one more kiss before disappearing into the hidden passage. I wait a few moments to will the flush out of my face before heading out into the hall.

Back in the garden, I make a show of reading a chapter of my book on one of the benches, though if anyone asked, I wouldn't have been able to tell them more than the vaguest idea of what the pages contained. When Marclinus has just drained another goblet of juice, I set down the book and glide over to him.

I hold out my arm to offer my elbow. "Husband, I was thinking it might be refreshing to take a stroll through the woods. Perhaps we'll find a cooler breeze there. At least it'll be even more out of the sun."

The emperor pushes to his feet. "Not a bad idea." He hooks his fingers around my elbow and casts his gaze across the nearby nobles. My plan wouldn't be ruined by company, but I'm a little relieved when he adds, "Let's enjoy the benefits just the two of us, hmm? There should be some reward for all our work."

I make my smile demure. "I'm always pleased to savor your company."

As we amble between the garden beds and sculpted hedges toward the denser vegetation of the woods, I keep my ears pricked for the footsteps behind us. When I glance at my husband, I'm scanning the path behind us from the corner of my eye.

Three of his guards and the two of mine have followed, keeping a distance of perhaps twenty paces. They don't feel the need to stick too closely to our sides when we're within the security of the imperial residence's walls.

That fact might work in my favor too. Although how I'd ever get a truly fearsome beast from where they're held for the arena exhibitions into these grounds, I have no idea.

Marclinus dips his hand into the tumbling water of the last fountain we pass before we reach the woods and slaps the moisture onto his neck, dampening the lowest curls of his hair. "Perhaps we should have one of those large pools for swimming put into the garden. It could be quite enjoyable for much of the year. As long as the ladies don't mind being seen in less than their full plumage."

He flicks his gaze toward me under heavy eyelids as if gauging my reaction.

I cock my head, considering the proposition. "I'd imagine there are ornate bathing garments available that would suit everyone's fancy. This heat is enough to make the idea quite appealing. Does it get very cool here even in the winter? Do you ever have snow?"

"Occasionally, but it's rare. Not like you must see up north. I can't imagine you'll miss the stuff, though. Freezing cold and clogging up all the roads?" He grimaces with a tick of the scar on his lip.

"It can be a lot of fun," I say lightly as we meander on down the path between the trees. I ease toward the branch to the right that will take us closer to the kennels, and Marclinus joins me without complaint. "But yes, it also causes a lot of problems for things like travel. In those months, most Accasians get around by sleigh, which works well enough."

"Perhaps we'll ride in one of those sometime." Marclinus adjusts his grip on my arm and flashes a smirk at me. "Once I'm fully confirmed, we'll need to make a tour of the continent. Make sure everyone's clear on who they're bowing to now."

I doubt we'll want to visit my home country in the winter. The snow clogs the passes between the mountains that separate Accasy from the rest of the continent more than anywhere else. We could end up stuck there for months.

As much as my heart aches to see my family and friends again, I suspect enduring Marclinus's attentions in front of them would be even more wrenching than facing them among the relative strangers of his court.

Before I can think of how to express my thoughts in a way he won't take offense to, my husband changes subjects. "I'm glad to say that your former people have risen to the challenge I gave them quite impressively. We're already seeing increased supply of breamwood logs making it to Lavira and Goric and continuing on the way here."

I swallow my rancor at the reminder of his increased demands. "I'm sure every Accasian is working hard to ensure you're happy, Husband."

"All the more so because they know one of their own stands by my side!"

Marclinus's laugh cuts through me like a cleaver. Do my own people believe that I wanted them to push themselves even harder, sacrifice that much more?

By the time I return to Accasy, they may be cursing me just as much as many Darium citizens have.

A brisker set of footsteps behind us brings both of our heads around. High Commander Axius is marching toward us at a hurried pace.

I'd stop to see what he wants, but Marclinus simply slows a little, as if he wouldn't want his military advisor thinking his presence is important enough to fully intrude on the emperor's pastimes. I think I catch a tick of frustration at the corner of Axius's mouth that he quickly stifles.

He waits until he's caught up with us, falling into step beside Marclinus, before he speaks. "Everything is settled regarding the confirmation rite and the Lavirian prisoners, Your Imperial Majesty."

Marclinus perks up with a wider grin. "Excellent. And it's good that my wife can hear this too."

My nerves jangle with alarm. I glance from one man to the other. "What does Lavira have to do with the confirmation rites? Has the uprising spread into Dariu?"

My husband waves me off as if I've asked a silly question. "They wouldn't dare. No, a perfect idea for showing off your devotion to the empire occurred to me. It should particularly quell any lingering concerns brought about by your *other* dedications—to your godlen and to your former home. What are the details you've worked out, High Commander?"

Axius clasps his hands behind his back. "Cleric Turentan at the Temple of Triumphant Valor approved of the adapting of the rite. He says it's fitting for the spirit of the challenge, and his meditations with Sabrelle were quite favorable. Tribune Valerisse has already arranged to send some half a dozen of the main band of conspirators they apprehended to Vivencia so we can have our pick and use the rest in a more general statement. They should arrive within the week, and we'll hold the rite immediately after."

With every bit of news, my blood runs colder. "The imperial soldiers in Lavira caught the core group of insurgents? I still don't understand how that factors into Sabrelle's rite."

Marclinus pats me on the shoulder. "It was only a matter of time. Now they can serve our own purpose. What better show of might and supremacy—and of loyalty to the empire above all else—than to battle and slay the citizens who've acted out of the most *dis*loyalty to our cause?"

I stiffen so abruptly I have to catch myself from tripping over my feet. "We're going to fight against these people—*kill* them ourselves?"

"Think of it as their much-deserved execution," Axius says flatly. "Sabrelle's confirmation rite is always held in the arena with some sort of combat. This is simply a variation on the theme."

I was anticipating a fight—I could have guessed at that even if Bastien hadn't mentioned it—but I hadn't expected it to be quite like this. To slaughter people who were fighting against the same injustices I want to set right… To do it in front of an audience of thousands…

Marclinus chuckles. "Brilliant, isn't it? You inspired me with your impassioned talk about proving ourselves to the empire."

My stomach lurches. *I* inspired him?

I asked for a bigger way to win over his people, and he came up with *this*?

Why did I ever think anything good could come from turning to him?

In the midst of my inner turmoil, a large dun-brown shape races out of the trees onto the path.

The hound hurtles over the packed earth. It springs toward Marclinus with an eager baying, delighted to have found its requested target—

And an invisible force crackles past me through the air, slamming into the animal when it's still several feet distant from its master. The dog freezes in mid-bound, only one paw brushing the ground. A yelp of surprise bursts out of it.

Marclinus looks over his shoulder at his guards, who are hustling over to us with expressions of consternation.

"It's only one of the hounds," he says with a snort. "Must have gotten loose from the kennel and thought I'd be up to play."

The guard who cast the magic that caught the animal releases it with a jerk of her hand. The hound drops to the ground with a grunt and stands there with its tail tucked between its legs.

The guard frowns at Marclinus. "If something's running at you, we're going to stop it first and determine the size of the threat after."

And they identified the possible threat that quickly, even though a charging hound can't be a typical danger the emperor would run into.

My lips tighten around my smile. My heart thumps dully on, every beat heavier and hollower than the last.

How could I possibly hope that even a magically raging beast would get its claws into Marclinus when his guards are that alert for a basic stroll in the woods? The hound didn't even get close enough to sneeze on him.

It won't matter if I manage to weaken his own reflexes with some subtle potion. I can hardly get away with poisoning his entire guard staff.

My sense of my tentative plans disintegrates. The hollow sensation spreads down through my chest.

As I wet my lips against the dryness of my mouth, Marclinus tugs me onward as if nothing all that eventful has happened.

In his mind, I suppose it hasn't.

He reaches down to scratch the dog on the head and then takes in my expression. Something must show that I'd rather didn't, because he takes on an arch tone that's a little too self-satisfied.

"Of course, if you find you haven't the stomach for it after all, there's no requirement that you participate in the final rite."

Yes. Sabrelle's confirmation rite. The horrible scenario *I* set in motion in my impatience to win Dariu's devotion with a show of my own.

Thanks to me, the people of Vivencia will get a vivid demonstration of why they *shouldn't* trust the conquered countries beyond Dariu's borders and confirmation that slaughtering anyone who disagrees with the empire's practices is fully justified.

Most likely, they'll also get a demonstration of exactly where their empress is weak after all. Because just picturing driving a blade into a civilian who fought so passionately for freedom makes all my innards wobble.

I don't know if I can do it. Any kind of fight is hardly my forte. Being up against an attacker I sympathize with so much...

Will I be able to summon the conviction to overpower my opponent? How can I put my all into this rite the way I needed to with the three before when it goes against every principle that's given me strength?

And if I fail, I'll either die by the rebel's hand or look like a disgrace before all the people I most need to win over.

I want to vomit.

I can't, though. All I can do is hang on to my smile for dear life and careen on along the path I've carved for myself, as awful as it may be. "Of course I'll participate. It's exactly what I asked for."

Gods smite me, I wish I'd never asked at all.

CHAPTER FORTY

Lorenzo

Aurelia moves through the parlor all smiles and bright words. She joins a game of darts at Vicerine Bianca's cajoling and laughs as her unpracticed throws miss the mark. When a couple of the baronissas claim the empress to show off their new shoes, she exclaims over them as if she's never seen anything lovelier.

It's an incredible performance. Even a couple of months ago, when I thought I'd already gotten to know her well, I don't think I'd have caught the signs that something's wrong.

But for most of the past two months, I've had no choice but to watch her from afar as surreptitiously as I can. With every passing week, the subtle patterns to her movements, her intonation, even the angle of her smile have worked their way into my understanding.

Here and there, her shoulders slump just slightly, only for an instant. The light that dances in her eyes shines a little too

glassily. My honed ears catch the faintest brittle edge to her laughter.

She's struggling, like I don't think I've seen since she was in the midst of Emperor Tarquin's trials. Something has shaken the nearly impenetrable determination I've watched carry her through so much torture.

Raul mentioned that Aurelia asked for his help with a minor scheme involving the hounds this morning. I haven't heard any talk among the nobles about an incident.

I'm not sure what she'd have been hoping for, but at least it doesn't appear to have had any horrifying effects.

Who knows what Marclinus might have said or done to her away from our watchful eyes, though? I knew he could be cruel, but I've never seen him jerk around any member of the court the way he has his wife.

By a small mercy, he hasn't seemed all that interested in her since dinner. He's prowled around the room with a few of the nobles he's chummiest with and made occasional wry remarks with a vaguely distracted air.

I drift closer to the emperor, my ears pricked. It's safer to pay attention to him than to Aurelia, and he might say something that paints a clearer picture of what I've missed.

He's just getting up from a cards table, clapping one of the viceroys on the shoulder. "Good game. Maybe next time you'll lose less catastrophically. But it'll have to wait at least a day, because I'm ready to turn in for the night."

Is he? As I track him from the edge of my vision, he says his good nights to a few other nobles and then heads out the door without a word to Aurelia.

A glimmer of possibility flutters up in my chest. If he's gone to bed without calling on her, presumably she'll be safe from his overtures for the rest of the night.

We can find out what's gone wrong and come up with whatever plans we need to set it right again.

Aurelia lingers in the parlor for several minutes longer. I'm not surprised to see that as soon as it's not obvious she's leaving because she knows her husband isn't around to monitor her, she bows out of another game of darts and ambles toward the door.

I position myself where I can carefully catch her gaze and ask a silent question with my hand. *Going to Marclinus?*

She responds as briefly as she's able. *No, my room.*

Perfect.

I seek out my foster brothers across the room, spotting Raul's dark ponytail first. As I ease toward him, a trace of hesitation passes through my limbs.

I haven't had Aurelia to myself in weeks. I was the first of us she turned to, the first she trusted. Maybe it'd be best if I approach her on my own before making a full meeting of it.

If my motivations for wanting a private interlude aren't entirely unselfish, I don't think Bastien or Raul would blame me for it.

The tenth bell can't be far off. When Raul glances over at me, I signal to him. *Aurelia's room, eleventh bell, all of us.*

He tips his head in a hint of a nod. I can count on him to pass the message on to Bastien.

I wait a few more minutes before wandering out into the hall myself. My route takes me in the opposite direction from where Aurelia—and her escort of guards—will have gone… at least at first.

Instead of heading into my chambers, I slip into the abandoned bedroom that we use as an access point to the palace's hidden passages. It doesn't take long to stride through the stuffy wooden corridors in the walls and up a cramped flight of stairs to the section outside the empress's apartment.

I lean close to the panel, listening as hard as I can for any sign that she has company. After a moment, a meow reaches my ears, followed by a soft laugh. A smile touches my lips.

In an abundance of caution, I propel my illusionary voice toward her with my gift, keeping it focused entirely on her. *"Is it safe for me to come in?"*

There's a rustle of fabric as Aurelia stands. Rather than answering with words, she opens the panel for me.

Her unbound hair tumbles down over her tanned shoulders like it always did when I first met her, but her deep blue eyes are shadowed with the worries she couldn't show in public.

Seeing her beautiful face right there in front of me, I can't hold myself back. I step out of the passage and pull her into my embrace.

Aurelia hugs me back, ducking her head against my shoulder. A tremor runs through her breath.

I press the spot on the wall to slide the panel back into place and guide her over to the bed. She sprawls out on the covers next to me, cuddling so close my heart swells with joy.

It should be like this every night.

"The others will be coming later," I say, keeping my illusionary voice at a murmur even though no one could overhear it anyway. *"I wanted to see you by myself first. What's bothering you?"*

Aurelia doesn't ask how I know, just presses her face deeper into the crook of my neck. "Everything's a mess. I don't know how I'm going to do… anything." She lets out a short laugh that's too raw to reassure me. "Toppling a five-hundred-year-old empire is fucking hard—who would have thought?"

My arms tighten around her. *"You're trying to do something incredible. Of course it'll take time to figure it all out. I know you're strong enough to."*

"But what if I'm not? What if I've reached so far and now I'm going to stumble and fall in a way that ruins everything?"

I brush my fingers over her hair and pull back just far enough to see her expression. *"What happened?"*

Her mouth tenses. "I'll explain when you're all here. But I don't see how there's any getting out of it."

"We'll find a way. We always have so far."

Aurelia makes a noncommittal sound that wrenches at me even more, but then she nudges me onto my back. "I don't want to talk about it now. I don't want to think about it. I don't want to feel anything but you."

She nestles onto my taller frame, letting me support her completely.

The feel of her weight on me sets off all sorts of other sensations it's hard to rein in, especially with the wild, sweet scent of her filling my lungs at the same time. I brush my lips against her forehead and stroke my hand down her back.

"I'm here. Whatever you need."

A sigh slips out of her. "I wonder what it would have been like if none of us had been sent here. If we'd met under different circumstances, like regular royals rather than hostages."

The corner of my mouth curves upward. *"I'd have had no reason to distrust you, so I'd obviously have fallen for you that much faster. And then Bastien and I would have had to fight it out with Raul for your hand, and that would have gone badly for me."*

"Hmm. Maybe I wouldn't have wanted whoever was best in a fight. Maybe I wouldn't have been willing to choose even then."

She scoots a little higher on me, the friction sending a pulse of need through my groin, and angles her head for a kiss. There's nothing in the world I can do except kiss her back.

The press of her lips is all sweetness and heat, but there's something unnervingly tender in the way her mouth lingers against mine. As if she's drawing out the moment, afraid that it might be the last time we do this.

As if she's saying goodbye.

My heart skips a beat, but Aurelia eases herself a little higher so she can meld her mouth to mine more deeply. Her legs splay to either side of my thighs. The gasp she emits when her sex presses against my straining erection through our clothes only makes me harder.

Even with the rush of lust, I can't shake the impression I got. Willing down my hunger, I cup her cheek and peer up at her. *"Are you sure—"*

She frames my face with her forearms. "I need you."

Those three words undo me. Then she's kissing me harder and I don't know how to do anything but answer the plea she's making.

I trail one hand down her side to caress her ass, and she rocks against me with torturous pressure. When she tears her lips from mine next, her voice is so ragged it nearly undoes me. "Lorenzo, can we— Do we have time—?"

Before the others get here? The bells have only barely rung ten. But I don't know if I could refuse her even if I expected my foster brothers five minutes from now.

"Take whatever you need, Rell," I say, and groan as she rubs herself even more emphatically against me. It manages to occur to me through the growing haze of desire that I should probably clarify something else. *"I've been taking mirewort, so you don't need to worry about those potential consequences."*

For a second, her stance over me tenses. "It'd have been fine anyway—it should be too late for anything to happen this time around."

I reach up to caress her jaw. *"Maybe it already has."*

Her smile looks sad, but then she dives in to kiss me

again. I tangle my fingers in her hair, wanting to give her everything I can.

Through our ravenous kisses, she hitches up the skirt of her gown around her waist and fumbles with the fastening on my trousers. I help her loosen them and take the moment to stroke her through the dampened silk of her drawers.

Aurelia's breath quavers against my mouth, and then she's tugging my cock free from my own underclothes with a glorious pump of her fingers around the straining length. Before the pleasure of her touch has finished sweeping through me, she's yanked her drawers to the side so she can guide me up into her.

The feel of her hot, slick channel closing around my cock brings another groan to my lips. I kiss her again and again, fondling her breast through her gown, massaging her ass, bucking up to meet the rocking of her thighs.

Aurelia whimpers. The needy sound somehow spurs my desire even farther. I lock our mouths together, thrusting up to meet her.

"I love you. So fucking much. No matter what happens, no matter where you have to go or what you have to do, you'll always have me."

The swaying of Aurelia's body becomes more frantic, her kisses wilder. "Love you too," she mumbles in the fleeting breaks for breath. "Always. Everything."

What voice she has left breaks into a moan she tries to stifle against my jaw. I buck into her harder, faster, and then she's shuddering over me, gasping and clamping around my cock with a bolt of bliss.

I clamp my teeth against the groan of my own release. As I spill myself into her, our swaying slows to a halt.

Aurelia lowers her head next to mine, her lips brushing my shoulder. I hug her close like I did when we were only cuddling, but suddenly the gesture feels hollow.

What have I really offered her with this act? How does fucking her fix any of her problems?

I've told her I love her again and again, promised to be here for her, but what have I actually *done*? What *can* I do?

It hasn't been enough. She wouldn't be faltering under the weight of all her troubles if I'd managed to give her what she actually needs.

The familiar gloom that's so often haunted my mind settles over me, dampening the afterglow of pleasure. I hide it as well as I can, but an ache forms at the base of my throat.

When Aurelia rolls off me after a few minutes, I set my clothes in order and grab a cloth from her bathing room to clean her up. She thanks me with the tenderest of kisses, and damn if I'm not half-hard again by the end of it.

But the uncomfortable sense that I've failed dogs me even as she smooths out her dress.

It doesn't help that a melancholy cast has returned to her face as well. She drifts over to the window and eases back the curtain, gazing out at the darkened grounds and the glittering lights of the city beyond the palace walls.

"There are so many people *right there*, but it feels so hard to reach them. Nothing I do really matters until most of them are happy to see me on the throne."

I slide to the edge of the bed, not daring to join her when someone might spot me from outside. *"If the three of us could realize how wonderful you are even with all our reservations, they will too."*

"Not if Marclinus has his way."

Before I can decide how to answer that remark, the temple bells throughout the city start to peal for the eleventh hour. I motion for Aurelia to close the curtain. *"We should have company in a minute or two."*

I go to open the hidden panel so my foster brothers don't have to wonder whether it's safe to reveal themselves. As it whispers to the side, I make out the scrape of footsteps farther down the passages.

Maybe one of them will know how to tackle Aurelia's concerns better than I do, though even that thought makes my throat constrict more.

Raul emerges first, giving us a crooked smile that's just shy of a grimace. I understand why when Bastien steps out… with Neven right at his heels.

Aurelia blinks at the lot of them. "You *all* came."

Raul jabs his thumb over his shoulder toward Neven, his tone wry. "The kid figured out we were up to something and insisted. After the other night, I thought it was better having him here than leaving him to go make friendly with the imperial army. He knows plenty already."

Neven glowers at him. "I wasn't trying to be friends with the high commander. I thought I might find out something useful from him, especially since the bunch of you hardly tell me anything."

He steps past Raul and dips his head to Aurelia, giving her due respect as empress. "I told you before that I felt like I need to figure out a real purpose. After the things you said, and thinking about everything that's been happening in court, and praying to Sabrelle—it seems like the most important way I can contribute is helping you like my foster brothers are. Protecting you when I can, since you sometimes need it."

A gentle smile touches Aurelia's lips. "I don't want you to put yourself in danger, but I appreciate your support."

Raul folds his arms over his chest. "As if we haven't been offering enough protection—as much as anyone can around that fucking prick Marclinus?"

Bastien presses his knuckles to the other man's arm. "At least Neven's got the right idea. We've gone too long without giving him a real chance."

He shifts his attention to the youngest of us. "You know you can't breathe a *word* of anything we discuss here—or the fact that we meet with Aurelia at all—to anyone."

Neven draws his substantial height up taller. "Of course. I'm not an idiot. I didn't tell anyone about the waystation, did I?"

He aims a shy smile at Aurelia. "We have someone who actually cares about people outside of Dariu in the imperial family now. Obviously we should do whatever we can to keep you there and see that your influence grows."

So now even the teenager among us is taking stands bigger than mine. Was I just wasting Aurelia's time by having them come later and keeping her to myself for the past hour?

"I can't argue with that," Raul mutters, giving Neven a playful cuff to the head, and turns to Aurelia. "How did your experiment with the hound go?"

The sag of her shoulders tells me immediately that's part of the problem.

She sinks down on top of one of her trunks. "It didn't go anywhere. I don't think we can use that tactic—working with animals."

Her new kitten trundles over to her with a mew as if it thinks she's dismissing it. With a tight smile, she scoops it onto her lap and starts rubbing its back to enthusiastic purrs.

"His guards noticed the hound coming and used magic to block it before it got all that close to him," she goes on. "And it was running at him quickly. I can't see how anything would be able to reach him while they're around, and they always are."

Bastien walks over to set his hand on her shoulder. "Now we know that. We have lots of time to think of other strategies."

"I know. That's just the only one I had any hope for so far." Aurelia sucks in a breath. "But I don't even know if I'll have the chance to make other plans. I—I asked Marclinus for ideas for proving myself to the rest of Dariu. They all love *him* for whatever reason, so I hoped he might give me something useful. But instead…"

Her mouth twists. When she lifts her gaze, she's looking at Raul.

His forehead furrows. "What is it?"

Her free hand balls where it's resting on the trunk beside her. "The army is sending several of the main Lavirian rebels to the capital. Marclinus and I are each supposed to fight and kill one as part of the Sabrellian confirmation rite."

Raul's gaze darkens, but he steps closer too. "It isn't your fault. It wasn't *your* idea. And they'll all be executed anyway."

"But it wouldn't have been me doing it. I wouldn't have ended up making a display of crushing the other countries of the empire as part of my rise to the throne. If I even manage to." Aurelia's head droops. "I don't know if I can just push through like I have the trials before. I can hardly stand the thought of doing it. If I falter, for all I know, Marclinus will let me die. Not that surviving the failure would be much better."

Panic skitters through my veins. *"Of course it's better. As long as you're with us, you still have a chance to win some other way."*

"I'll have looked pathetic in front of thousands of citizens, so many soldiers, the court… and my godlen. What if this is my punishment for going against Elox's urging in the first place? He wanted me to peacefully accept the lot I've been given, and I refused, and now…"

"It isn't hopeless," Raul insists. "I'll train you as much as I can. Every night, all night, if we have to. This is his sick idea, not yours."

"That's not how it'll look. Or how it'll feel." She swipes her hand past her eyes. "It seems as if every time I make a move, I set something in motion that's even more awful than what I was trying to address."

Bastien gives her shoulder a gentle squeeze. "In a situation this complicated, setting things right is never going to be a straightforward path."

"I'm just not sure—even if I survive this—what if I never get on the right path at all? What if the sum of everything I do for the empire makes everyone's lives *worse* instead of better?"

Her voice has gone rough by those last few words. The ache in my throat spreads down to my chest. *"Rell…"*

Raul breaks in before I can go on. "There's absolutely no way that's possible. You *have* made things better already. You've gotten the three"—he pauses with a flick of his gaze toward Neven—"the four of us back on track. You've healed people. You've helped people."

Aurelia grimaces. "But how many have I hurt on the other side of that balance?"

He lets out an incredulous sound. "I don't see how you should take responsibility for that prick's choices, no matter what you said to him, no matter what role he makes you play. And anyway, what if you have to get right down in the awfulness before you can find the ways to cure it? Like… Like the empire is a bathtub full of muck, and you've got to wallow deep down in it before you can reach the drain and release it."

Bastien shoots our foster brother a bemused look. "That's the best comparison you could come up with?"

Raul huffs. "So I'm not a poet. Have you got a better metaphor, oh brilliant one?"

Our older foster brother appears to consider the matter. He lifts his hand to trail his fingers over Aurelia's hair. "If someone had a broken leg or a dislocated shoulder—you wouldn't be able to simply bandage it and expect it to get well. The injury would only fester. You have to deal out more pain setting the bone or the joint right before it can really begin to heal, don't you?"

"Okay, that's a better one," Raul grumbles. "I still like mine, though."

Aurelia gives a choked laugh. "I understand what you're both getting at. You could be right. I wish I knew for sure. I had a set path in mind, and it's completely fogged over. I'm stumbling all over the place. And there's so much at stake."

Hearing the doubt in her voice and seeing it etched all over her face sends a discordant twang through my heart.

This is the strongest woman I've ever met. In the past few months, she's fought through ten times more shit than the rest of us have.

So maybe it's our turn to be the strong ones for a little while. To take on as much of the burden as we can.

Because we can. *I* can.

The weight of the gloom still drags at me, but I shove it aside with a clenching of my jaw. I can't wallow in my own doubt and grief when she needs me.

It doesn't matter what I've been able to accomplish in the past. I can push harder, and harder still, just like Aurelia has over and over.

If a princess dedicated to peace can be a fighter, so can a prince who's never offered much other than music.

We'll get her out of this awful task or shift things so she can stomach it. We'll make sure the people of Dariu see just how incredible an empress she is.

My gaze slides to the curtain covering the window she peered out of earlier. Her words come back to me—all the civilians out there she needs on her side.

The idea that hits me makes my pulse wobble. But that doesn't mean it's bad. As it takes hold, my enthusiasm blooms alongside it.

"We'll come up with a plan," I say abruptly, letting my illusionary voice reach all of my foster brothers as well as Aurelia. *"This time it isn't on you to figure out how to fix the problem. We'll get you on the right track."*

Aurelia blinks at me. "I don't think there's any changing Marclinus's mind. You shouldn't stick your necks out. I'm the one who took this responsibility on."

"And we've decided to shoulder it alongside you, so it's time we did our part. You've set so much in motion already—we can build on that. Keep thinking about it, but you don't have to do anything at all. Give us a chance to come through for you."

I glance at my foster brothers. Raul is staring at me, which I suppose isn't surprising, considering I'm not sure I've ever spoken up quite that forcefully before. Then he grins. "And we damn well will."

A soft smile crosses Bastien's face. He leans over to kiss Aurelia's temple. "I'll trust Lorenzo's inspiration ahead of anyone else's."

Even Neven is watching me, waiting for me to go on.

Their reaction solidifies my resolve. I jerk my head toward the hidden passages. *"We can get started right now. No time to waste."* I clasp Aurelia's hand briefly. *"There are things only you can do—and there are things we can do that you can't. Let us fight for you."*

The worry hasn't left her eyes, but her answering smile looks brighter than before. "All right. Just don't do anything too risky. If I can get through this battle, I still want you with me when it's over."

We push into the passage and slip through the palace toward the vacant bedroom.

As we hurry along, Neven speaks in a low voice. "I'm going to be part of whatever you're doing too."

"I assumed you would be," I reassure him.

"What exactly *are* we doing, Lore?" Raul asks, still sounding amused by the fact that I've taken charge.

It'll be easier to explain—and to convince them—when we're already in place. *"Follow me. And keep quiet."*

Once we've left the passages behind, I lead them out the doors to the gardens. As soon as we step into the cover of the orchard, I cast a larger illusion around us, giving the impression to any patrolling guard who glances over that there's no one among the trees.

Thankfully, my foster brothers heed my request for quiet. They walk alongside me in silence. It's easier to hold the illusion when it's only visual rather than needing to alter the impressions of sound as well.

I bring us to a halt when we reach the wall around the imperial grounds. Staring up at the immense stone surface, my stomach drops.

It's at least half again as high as the wall that separated the inner gardens in the Rexoran palace. Have I been overly ambitious?

Raul is watching me with one eyebrow cocked while Bastien and Neven wait more patiently. I drag in a breath.

I shouldn't assume what they're capable of when I never thought I'd be suggesting an idea like this to begin with.

There's no one else around. I let my concealing illusion fade for long enough to explain myself.

"We've been supporting Aurelia's cause in bits and pieces where we can. I think we need to start making a bigger effort. We can't go through the gate without the guards catching us, but they can't monitor for magic all along the walls. So we go over, and then we head into the city and do everything we can to convince people of our empress's greatness."

Raul lets out a sputter of a laugh. "Gods above, when did Lore take over as the bold one?"

"When he took over as the idea man too, apparently."

Bastien gives me a crooked grin that turns more hesitant when he considers the wall. "I don't know... Lifting all four of us that high without any falls will be hard."

Raul is already swiping his hands together. "Not a problem. I'll get us up and you can just cushion us on the way down. That's the easier direction, right?"

"I suppose, but—"

Raul reaches into other shadows along the wall, and Bastien's mouth snaps shut. The three of us gape in awe as the swath of darkness quivers and hardens into an immense, lumpy shape that looks almost like—

"Stairs!" Neven says with a trace of a gasp. "That's incredible, Raul."

None of us have been able to test our powers to their full potential before. Raul smirks, but his eyes have widened with a little awe of his own.

He keeps his hand braced against the step at waist height. "I need to be touching it to hold the shape. You three go up first, and then I'll follow. Less risk of me dropping you."

I summon the illusion of the untampered wall again. Neven starts up the steps first without hesitation. Bastien follows him, no doubt flexing his gift with the air, ready to catch any of us if we take a tumble.

I start up next, running my fingers over the wall beside me as I climb. The hazy darkness beneath my feet stays perfectly solid, as if I'm walking on smoked glass.

When we reach the top, I find myself gaping again. We're standing on a span of stone only a couple of feet wide, a little higher than the nearby treetops. Beyond the parklands beside the palace and stately buildings of the nearby noble homes lies the sprawl of Vivencia proper.

The people Aurelia's fate depends on.

Raul steps onto the top of the wall next to us and releases his grip on the shadows. When Bastien glances at us, we nod.

The air whirls in front of us with a whoosh of sound. I focus on my own gift, still projecting the appearance of a bare wall to anyone who glances this way.

Bastien motions to us, and we step onto the cushion of air.

It's more pliant than Raul's shadowy stairs, my feet sinking a few inches into the blustering surface. But it stays stable, carrying us down to the ground on the other side.

As we hurry over to the road and begin the hike into the city, I glance around at the others. *I'll project voices speaking support for Aurelia and pointing out her accomplishments, as I have before. Raul, you can shape the shadows into "omens." Maybe we should swing by a couple of temples where that tactic will be most effective."*

Bastien nods. "I can make omens of my own, harassing anyone who speaks against Aurelia. And Neven…"

We all pause to study the youngest of us. Neven makes a face at us in return. "As long as Lorenzo can hide me with his illusions, I can shake things up a little when we need it. I'll be able to reach higher and push harder than any of you."

Quite literally, from what I know about the gift he sacrificed more than half of his teeth for. I'm not sure how his skills might come into play effectively, but it certainly can't hurt to have the option of calling on him.

Bastien gives Neven his most authoritative look. "Stay cautious. Check with us before doing anything, all right? We've been working on this problem for a while."

"Yeah, of course," the kid mutters, but his gaze sweeps warily over our surroundings as we continue.

I don't bother hiding us more than the darkness already does while we walk into town. As we reach the narrower streets with their tan and dun buildings packed closer together, I extend my illusionary power again to tweak our facial features and turn our clothes drabber to fit the regular civilians around us.

It's actually less difficult than convincing the entire court that I'm playing the most breathtaking music they've ever heard, and I can keep that up for a couple of hours. I don't think we should push my limits too far, but we do need to return and get some sleep if we're going to be of any use to Aurelia tomorrow.

Bastien points out a temple of Estera, its tall spires poking above the nearby rooftops. We find lanterns still smoldering on either side of the entrance and a few petitioners to the godlen of wisdom praying inside.

As the cleric passes through the room with a book tucked under her arm, Raul dips his hand into a shadow that courses all the way along the wall. The shapes in an alcove shift into an image of a crowned woman spreading her arms as if offering herself to those watching.

The cleric halts in her tracks with a sharp inhalation. Raul releases the shadow, and the image flickers away.

The woman hustles over and starts murmuring to one of her devouts, no doubt spreading the word of the "sign" she witnessed.

The temple is too quiet for me to conjure voices in supposed conversation for a more overt message in Aurelia's favor. We retreat and find a bustling pub a couple of streets over.

The tang of alcohol tickles in my nose, and a puff of hazebloom smoke blurs my vision on the way in, but the packed tables offer plenty of opportunity. As Raul obscures our forms with his shadows, I aim an illusionary voice to carry into one of the densest knots of customers with a gossipy lilt.

"Isn't it good to see the emperor and empress back at home?

Did you hear that Her Imperial Highness carried a man twice her size up a tower to complete Creden's rite?"

I ease closer to make out the eager and surprised responses before adding another remark in a different cadence from a different direction. *"She cares enough about us to show her dedication—and the gods must think she's worthy too!"*

A few people glance around briefly, but then they continue chattering like the others, just assuming it's all part of the regular bar conversation. It wouldn't occur to them that someone would be adding to the din with magic. They hear what sounds like a fellow patron speaking and don't analyze the fact any further.

That's how illusion works best, really. You give people something they wouldn't be surprised to see or hear anyway, and it takes no effort at all to—

I freeze in place with a skip of my heart.

Bastien catches my expression. "What's wrong?"

"Nothing," I say, my heart starting back up at a pace that's almost giddy. *"It might be very right. I think I know how we can spare our empress from that last awful rite."*

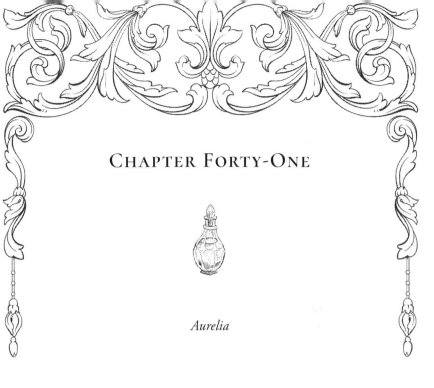

CHAPTER FORTY-ONE

Aurelia

As I lunge and sidestep, another wave of fatigue rolls over me. My sword-arm wavers, and Raul smacks the blade aside.

His frown looks more worried than annoyed. "You need to keep your weapon steady. Your opponent isn't going to care about politeness—he'll be hitting you as hard as he can. Trying to do as much damage as possible before the inevitable."

While I'm doing my best to prevent the inevitable outcome of the rebel's death.

This scenario might play out easier if we could convince the prisoner ahead of time that I'm not aiming to kill him, that we're going to see him safely out of the emperor's hands. But there are too many things that could go wrong.

We don't know which of the rebels being transported to

the capital I'll be set against in the arena. We can't be sure the secret won't slip out, accidentally or out of skepticism.

And the battle for the rite needs to look real, or someone will suspect foul play.

Which means I need to be a good enough fighter to look as if I've killed a man without actually killing him.

I bite my lip and adjust my grip on the hilt of the short sword Raul lent me. "It's taking time to get used to the weight."

"You need to get used to it fast. The prisoners are supposed to be here any day now. There's no way you're winning an arena battle with that tiny blade you like."

I glance down at my dress—will I be given any armor for the rite? I don't even know that much—and the slim belt that holds the small knife Marclinus gifted to me.

My opponent will probably have a proper sword, maybe one significantly larger than even the subdued version I'm training with. I need to get close enough to him to land a few blows and not find myself fatally stabbed in the process.

It's not that late in the night, only a little past the tenth bell, but the exhaustion that's dogged me all day seems to seep right down to my bones, dragging at my limbs and turning my next breath ragged. "I'm sorry. I'm doing my best."

Raul's face falls. He tosses his own sword into the mess that scatters his bedroom desk and tucks his arms around me, his voice softening. "I know. I don't mean to harp on you. I just— Gods help me, it's going to be the worst torture watching you walk into that battle."

I tip my head against his broad chest, soaking in the musky smell of him, wishing I could stay here in his embrace instead of going back to our illicit training session.

This is the third night I've slipped away from my chambers through the secret passages to the vacant room just a few doors down from Raul's. He waits for me there, confirms the hall is empty, and ushers me over to his rooms where we can slash and lunge at each other without worrying about disturbing the draped furniture in some way the cleaning staff might notice.

We also arranged a couple of official training sessions during the day with Neven assisting, but we've only been able to focus on general techniques then. The guards are watching too closely for us to practice the key elements of our scheme.

A spark of hope kindled in my chest when the princes first explained their plan to me. It burns on even now, when all I feel like doing is falling into bed and sleeping for a year or two.

But with each passing day, my energy has faltered. The fatigue weighs on me like the sword does on my arm.

I want to believe we can pull this complicated deception off. I want to believe it'll be enough to prove myself as empress to both my husband and his people.

I want to believe I'm not going to die out there on the arena's sandy earth.

Some part of me must not fully believe any of those things, though, because I still can't seem to completely shake the hopelessness that gripped me when Marclinus announced the details of the rite.

What if he's beaten my spirit down so many times that something inside me has broken for good?

I push away those thoughts and ease back from Raul, bobbing up to give him a quick kiss before I retreat completely. "Then we'd better make sure I'm as ready as I can be for that battle. Let's go again. If I'm just defending myself, that's fairly straightforward. The most important parts are making it look like I've attacked effectively."

Raul nods. "We can focus on those moves. Slashing the forehead shouldn't be too hard. I don't think you have the power to split right into a skull even if you intended to. A shallow gash there will bleed plenty, which'll blind your opponent and make any other wound you deal look gorier."

I lift the sword and swipe the tip carefully through the air just an inch shy of Raul's forehead. We've practiced that move many times already. It isn't the part that makes my gut clench up.

"Then I have to stab him somewhere in the torso, where it'll look to the spectators as if I *could* have killed him, but without actually doing any fatal damage."

"You should get an opening once your potion kicks in, if it works the way you expect," Raul reminds me. "Stab off to the side rather than center, and to the chest rather than the gut. Chances are the blade will glance off a rib, but that won't be obvious at a glance, and no one's going to check very closely when he's lying in a bloody heap."

Chances are I'll only hit a rib. That means there's still a chance I'll accidentally pierce deeper.

And attempting it at all depends on me getting into the right position without my opponent stabbing *me* first.

I inhale and exhale slowly, attempting to dispel both my nerves and another wave of fatigue.

I can do this. It's the *only* way I can do this.

I have to get it right, or I'll be dead one way or another.

Squaring my shoulders, I lift my chin. "Let's run through those moves again, and then we'll go back to general sparring."

By the time the next bell rings, my limbs feel like lead and my eyelids are drooping. I rub them and force a smile onto my face, but Raul touches my cheek. "We've done enough for tonight. It doesn't help you to run yourself ragged."

A raw laugh hitches out of me. "I can afford to be tired when I'm finished with this rite and still alive to enjoy the rest. I'd rather not neglect my efforts when getting to that point is far from a guarantee."

Raul lets out a choked growl and pulls me in closer. He tucks his head next to mine. "You're going to get through this sick ceremony, Shepherdess, just like you did all the psychotic trials Tarquin and Marclinus came up with. *We're* going to get you through, together. And then you're going to claim the entire blasted empire and clean up its horrors."

My smile turns into something more like a grimace. "It's gotten harder to imagine that day."

"You've made a shitload more progress than anyone else ever has."

Raul pauses and then slips his arm around my waist to lead me over to the wall across from his bed. A couple of long tapestries hang from close to the ceiling down nearly to the floor, depicting scenes of Kosmel carrying out two of the tricks the sly godlen is most famous for.

Raul holds out his other hand, flexing his fingers so the mottling of pale scars on the knuckles shift across the knobs of bone. His jaw tightens. "You've always wanted to know why my hands keep getting messed up."

Is he finally going to tell me? I tip my head against his shoulder. "You're allowed to hold on to a few secrets if you must."

He chuckles roughly and reaches to grasp the side of the first tapestry. "It's not all that thrilling a story."

Pulling the woven fabric to the side, he reveals a span of the crimson wall—which is broken with cracks and missing shards of plaster across nearly two feet of its surface.

As I stare at the battered plaster, Raul tucks his arm more firmly around me. "It started as a stupid way to blow off steam when I didn't want to risk anyone seeing me. Punching the wall until my hands bled… Then the cracks started forming, and it meant more. Someday when I've moved out of here, the next person who stays in this room will find that spot and know this palace isn't impervious."

My own throat chokes up. "And you said you weren't a poet."

Raul snorts and nuzzles my temple. "Only for you, Lamb. We're going to beat this place. We'll break down everything that's wrong about it one piece at a time until it's all rubble."

He pauses and turns fully toward me, dropping the tapestry back into place. A deeper intensity than usual flares in his pale blue eyes.

"I still haven't said it. I keep meaning to, and then…"

I frown at him. "What?"

A crooked smile crosses his lips. "I didn't think I'd ever say this to anyone. I had some strange idea that the moment had to be perfect. But it being *said* matters more. I love you. I think I started loving you the first time you told us to fuck off, and the feeling hasn't let go since. I'm never going to offer Bastien's smarts or Lorenzo's dreaminess, but no one will fight for you as fiercely as I will."

Raul touches the thumb he sliced open when all three of the princes made their vow to me. "You're in my blood. Every beat of my heart belongs to you. I'll spill it all if it keeps you safe."

Tears well in my eyes. I'm already nervous enough about my princes' secondary part in our scheme without him talking like that.

I pull him close, pushing up on my toes to claim a kiss. His mouth melds with mine with all the passionate furor the prince of Lavira can offer.

"I love you too," I murmur afterward, feeling the need to say it now even though I have before. "And you're exactly who I need as you are. But let's keep you safe too, please."

Raul's answering snort sounds a little ragged. "I make no promises, but I'll do my best. For you."

I ache at the fervor in his words, but my eyelids are drooping again. I sway in Raul's arms.

He clicks his tongue at me. "Right now we need to get you back to your room so you can sleep. We'll train more tomorrow. Let me make sure the hall is clear."

In the abandoned room, he kisses me once more before seeing me off. I carry the heat of his mouth with me into my trek.

As I walk farther through the passages toward my bedroom, I start to feel as if I'm trudging through mud. But when I reach my bedroom, I don't crawl into bed the way I'm longing to.

I need to perfect the potion that's going to lace my blade when I enter the arena.

It's a variation on the sedative that's kept Marclinus knocked out for hours, but that concoction always turns out vividly green. I can't have anyone wondering what I've smeared on my sword.

My gift has trouble accepting color as a key factor in any kind of cure, so my first several attempts have only resulted in a paler shade rather than the transparency I'm seeking.

Sprite ventures over to watch me pull out my brewing equipment. When I light the flame under the miniature cauldron, she puffs up her fur and backs up a few steps.

I waggle my finger at her. "That's where you should stay." Then I inhale slowly and focus my gift.

I'm halfway through the brewing when I add one last pinch of powder to the cauldron, and the acrid smell that rises up flips my stomach over. Bile rises in my throat.

Clamping my lips tight, I scramble up and dash for the bathing room. The remains of my dinner lurch up my throat just as I bow over the toilet.

I cough and sputter a few times before sitting back on my heels in a tired daze.

What was *that* about? I've concocted brews with the same powdered mineral dozens of times, including just this morning, and it's never had such a discomforting effect on—

My stance stiffens with a jolt of possibility. I count back through the days in my head.

The renewed churning in my gut shifts into fraught anticipation rather than nausea. Wetting my lips, I push to my feet and return to my brewing materials.

From the bottom of my ingredients box, I retrieve the packet our head medic back home gave me before I left. *Because it's good to know early so you can take every necessary care.*

I fish out one of the dried leaves within and study the yellow hue. As my heart thumps faster, I carry it to the toilet, where this time I sit down to relieve myself.

I dip the leaf briefly in the stream and then simply stay there, leaning back against the wall and closing my eyes so I'm not tempted to look. I count a full minute in my head.

Then I hold up the leaf.

The damp material now gleams unmistakably orange in the lantern light that seeps from my bedroom.

A laugh tumbles from my lips, propelled by a surge of joyful relief.

I haven't been exhausted because of despair or melancholy. I'm tired because my body's been hard at work on its own part in my plans.

My other hand comes to rest on my belly. But as I keep staring at the evidence of my condition, a tendril of uneasiness unfurls through my nerves.

I'm pregnant. I'm carrying the key to claiming the empire within my womb.

And that means that in the coming rite of blades and blood, I have yet another life to defend.

CHAPTER FORTY-TWO

Aurelia

Crouched down by the small prickly shrubs at the edge of the kitchen herb gardens, I pluck one pale yellow blossom and another. I attempted a brew with a few of these earlier this morning, but they were younger flowers, still the brighter yellow they show when the petals first unfurl. Some prodding of my gift has led me to believe that the older blooms will result in a more discreet formula.

My guards stand off to the side several paces away. It's awfully difficult to collect potion ingredients in private with them tailing me, but they've had plenty of time to get used to my odd habits like tea-making.

There's no way they could realize that the flower I'm harvesting now is for a traitorous scheme rather than my morning herbal blend.

As I tuck the flowers into the pouch at my hip and straighten up, my heart thumps at a rapid, dissonant rhythm. I'm still not happy with the sedative I've been trying to craft. How many more chances will I get at brewing it before I have to make do with a version that could expose my plans?

It isn't just my life on the line now but the men I love's as well. They'll be the ones carrying out the last part of the plan —the longest part of the plan, with the most chances of getting caught…

My stomach turns with a fresh wave of nausea. I push the anxiety aside as well as I can.

As I turn to return to the palace, I spot Marclinus striding toward me with High Commander Axius and more than his usual coterie of guards in tow. My pulse hitches to an even faster pace.

My husband comes to a stop by the garden and eyes me up and down. His tone comes out cool. "Wife, what are you doing scrouging around in the dirt?"

Raul's words about needing to dive down deep in the muck of the empire rise up from my memory. I suppress a slightly hysterical bubble of laughter and simply smile instead.

"I thought to brew myself a new flavor of tea that will put me in particularly bold spirits when it's time for our next rite."

"I never would have thought you lacked for boldness," Marclinus says with a hint of amusement. "I'll remind you as I have before that we do have servants for certain tasks."

I shrug as casually as I'm capable of. "My gift shows me exactly what I need, but it isn't always easy to convey the exact specifications in words. One wrong ingredient can result in unpleasant effects."

"I suppose that's to be expected when one brings in an

empress who might as well be a medic." He cocks his head. "I assume this tea isn't an urgent matter?"

The potion I actually need to brew is, but I can't tell him that.

I resist the urge to set my hand on my stomach. I've only known about the new life growing inside me since last night, but a new protective instinct has already formed that's focused on my belly.

That new life isn't going to get a chance to come into being if I'm not alive to support it. I have to protect myself before any other consideration.

And I'm not sure yet whether revealing my condition will skew Marclinus's unpredictable moods in my favor or not. I want to time the announcement perfectly.

Now, with my fingers sap-stained and several soldiers looking on, definitely doesn't feel like the right moment, even if claiming a pregnancy-related weakness might get me out of this conversation.

I dip my head in acknowledgment. "Not at all. Is there another matter we need to attend to?"

A sharp smile curves my husband's lips. "I've just gotten word that the Lavirian traitors have reached the city. They're being held in the prison near the arena. I'm off to have a look at them now. Would you like to join me?"

That explains the presence of all these soldiers.

My gut lurches with the urge to balk. The last thing I want to do is gaze into the faces of the beaten figures who tried to fight back against the empire's oppression and failed, one of whom I'm supposed to murder for my own glory.

But an empress who's actually dedicated to her empire and eager to face the rite she volunteered for wouldn't shy from the opportunity.

I gird myself. "Of course. Thank you for coming to find me."

We amble out to the front of the palace where the gleaming imperial carriage is waiting, along with a couple of other vehicles in the much more subdued indigo, gray, and black of the imperial guard. Marclinus doesn't appear to be in any hurry, and I can't hasten his pace without raising questions.

My heart thuds on. If the prisoners have arrived, that means we'll face the rite tomorrow, doesn't it? I can't shut myself away for the entire afternoon and evening attempting different brews.

I'm only going to get a few more attempts at concocting the potion both my life and that of my rebel opponent will depend on.

Axius and another soldier whose uniform suggests he's a ranking officer climb into our carriage with us, our personal guards taking their spots on the outer seats. The high commander sits stern and silent, but I can sense his disapproval with a prickling sensation over my skin.

He still doesn't believe I have any place carrying out these rites. Gods only know how he'd react if he found out I mean to battle a Lavirian rebel while carrying a child supposedly the emperor's heir.

How much does his attitude affect the rest of the soldiers? I know I've gained some ground with them, but it must be hard to ignore the sway of their highest superior's opinions.

At least he's reasonably quiet about his qualms while his underlings are nearby.

Marclinus doesn't appear bothered by his advisor's reserve. He leans back on the cushioned bench with a dispassionate air and glances over at me. "Among the six of the miscreants who helped orchestrate the uprising, there's one woman. It seems fitting that she'll be your challenge in the rite."

It's hard to say whether that should be a relief. A woman can fight just as viciously as a man, especially when she has no other choice. Our godlen of war is female, after all.

At least I shouldn't have to worry about facing an opponent more than a foot taller or vastly outweighing me.

"Fitting indeed," I agree. "I'm curious to see all of them. Have there been no further incidents in Lavira since their arrest?"

He grins. "No reports so far. I hear there was quite a display with the other ringleaders by the royal palace in the capital, while the Lavirian queen and king spoke out against the assaults."

Axius nods. "I don't expect we'll see any further trouble. Our officers will be monitoring the situation closely for some time all the same."

All those defiant spirits have been crushed into submission. How much more pain will my husband inflict on his conquered people before I can crush *him*?

For a second, the enormity of everything I need to accomplish before I can heal the empire presses down on me in a suffocating cloud. I inhale slowly, willing my nerves to settle.

One step at a time. That's the only way I'll see my whole purpose through.

When the carriage stops, we emerge into a ring of guards. They surround Marclinus and me all the way into the dim stone building.

The sour smells of sweat and human waste clog my nose. Marclinus strides on as if unfazed, with occasional flicks of his gaze toward me. He's watching to see how I'm handling the unpleasantness.

I keep my head high and my breaths shallow. Axius leads us down a couple of hallways to a row of cells with barred doors, three on either side.

Wan light seeps through the single window set high in the wall, too narrow for even the skinniest human being to squeeze through. It illuminates six figures with dirt-stained skin and rumpled peasant clothing.

They peer over at our arrival. Most are sitting hunched against one or another wall. One man comes right to the bars, baring his teeth in a threatening sneer.

Another only glances our way briefly in the midst of pacing the short length of his cell. The scrape of his footsteps carries through the space like the underlying rhythm to a horrific song.

Marclinus saunters farther down the hall and points out one of the prisoners. "Here's yours, wife."

The woman glares at him and then me through the lank strands of her mousy brown hair that she's let fall over her face. The arms wrapped around her knees are slim but sinewy with compact muscle. She won't be able to overpower me easily, but she won't be an easy opponent either.

Dark shadows hollow out her eyes, and her lips are cracked, but studying her, I'm not sure she's any older than I am.

She wanted to bring her country a better future just like I do, and this is the thanks she got.

Her voice comes out in a rough croak. "And here's the emperor's whore. Gape all you want, backstabbing cunt."

One of the soldiers bangs on the bars by her face. "Shut your traitorous mouth."

She falls silent, but the prisoners' eyes all around the hall have narrowed.

They don't see a fellow freedom-fighter, of course. They think that I'm here for the same reason as Marclinus: to gloat over the empire's triumph and their failure. They assume I turned my back on my country as much as all of theirs to support these horrors.

And I'm going to have to prove them right in the eyes of all the Darium spectators. I'm going to have to face these glares in the middle of the vast arena, drawing blood and no doubt having my own spilled in a desperate struggle.

My gut twists. I drag my gaze away to focus on my husband instead. "I assume the rite will be carried out tomorrow as planned? I should decide on my weapon so I have a chance to get familiar with it."

Marclinus waves off my request. "The cleric who oversees the rite picks our instruments of battle with Sabrelle's guidance. You don't need to worry your head about that at all."

My skin turns even clammier than I can blame on the atmosphere of the prison.

I do need to worry. I'm going to have to coat the blade with my potion surreptitiously in the moments before my battle rather than getting an opportunity to doctor it ahead of time.

We head back through the halls away from the cells. In the prison's broad front room, Axius draws our squad of soldiers to a halt.

Perhaps a little of my uneasiness has shown on my face despite my best efforts, or perhaps the high commander is merely expressing doubts he feels he can't keep quiet any longer. Either way, he clears his throat.

"Your Imperial Majesty, perhaps seeing the full reality of what awaits her, Her Imperial Highness might reconsider her intention to go through with the rite. It is quite a bit more intense than those before. You're trained for battle—her preferred weapon is that tiny knife. I'd hate to see our empress injured, however fair we make the match."

Marclinus turns to face me. My gaze darts from his penetrating eyes to the soldiers around us. Most of them have tensed, their mouths tight or slanted with traces of their own uncertainty.

All *they* see is a pampered princess in a pretty dress who thinks she's going to spar with a hardened criminal. They probably can't imagine me rising to the challenge of tomorrow's battle.

When I return my attention to my husband, he arches an eyebrow. "It isn't too late to back out. If you feel this is a step too far for you, there's no shame in sitting on the sidelines as the imperial consorts generally do."

A tremor runs through my nerves. In that moment, the idea of taking him up on his offer comes with the sweetest of relief.

I could sit on my cushioned bench and not have to slash or stab, not have to grapple with an enemy whose cause I actually believe in. Not have to worry that the princes I love will meet their own dire fates when they stick out their necks to help me.

I don't even know if the strategy I've devised with my princes will appease Sabrelle. Will she consider it an honor that I've shirked my supposed duty, even if I've made the appearance of fulfilling her rite? How will the godlen react if she *doesn't*?

Will she punish me… or the men who suggested the idea?

I could probably back out without losing respect I've gained with Marclinus through my past efforts—however much respect I've actually gained rather than ire. I'd simply have to reveal my pregnancy and use it as an excuse, and no one could blame me for not putting myself and the coming imperial heir in any danger.

All those thoughts flood my head, dizzying me. But a deeper ache holds me steady.

Our people would understand my shrinking from the challenge now. How will it affect their view of me in the future?

I'll be setting myself up as simply a receptacle for the children I'm meant to bear Marclinus, with no real might or courage of my own. Why would anyone accept a mere vessel as a ruler when their "real" leader is gone?

When I ran through fire to claim the man in front of me as my husband, I was leaving the men I'd actually fallen for behind. That hasn't stopped them from standing with me again, even if it's from the shadows.

I'm not alone in this challenge. I have people I can rely on who are as committed as I am to seeing this plan through. I can't let my fears for their safety hold me back.

I *need* to believe in their strength and in my own if I'm going to think beyond my next move to put myself in the best possible position to accomplish my bigger dreams.

Lifting my chin, I offer an assured smile. "I appreciate your and the high commander's concern for my well-being, but I'm quite certain of my choice. All the people of Dariu deserve to know that I'll fight for the good of the empire in every way I can, even if it means putting myself at risk. If that wasn't the case, I wouldn't be worthy of serving them or you."

The gleam in Marclinus's eyes tells me I've pleased him. Today, at least, he likes me fierce in my devotion.

Just as important are the brief smiles that flash across the faces of several of our guards. They might not believe I'll handle myself all that impressively in the arena tomorrow, but my mettle has won me a little admiration.

"Then it's settled." My husband rests his hand on my shoulder to guide us the rest of the way to the waiting carriages. "Tomorrow morning, you can show our citizens just how much of a fighter you are."

As I clamber into my seat, my stomach lurches. Tomorrow *morning*.

I know I've made the right decision, but the danger in it hasn't vanished.

In less than a day, I need to be perfectly ready, or nothing I've won up until now will matter at all.

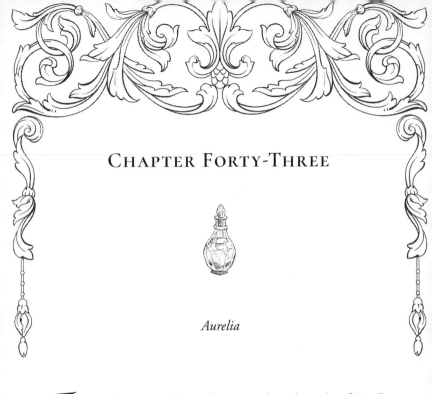

CHAPTER FORTY-THREE

Aurelia

I jab the point of my short sword at the side of Raul's chest one more time. He grins in approval and reaches to touch my cheek. "You've got this. Just stay alive for long enough to cut her one time, and the drug will take over and do most of the work for you."

I exhale in a rush. "As long as I can get the potion onto the blade in the first place."

The smooth metal feels ominously cool beneath the glide of my fingers. After stealing every spare moment I could once I returned from the prison, I adjusted my sedative until it has only the faintest yellow sheen. With luck, anyone who notices the hint of hue will take it for a gleam of sunlight.

Transferring it onto my weapon is going to be its own challenge. I don't know what I'll be wearing for the rite or at what point the cleric will present my weapon. I may have to apply my concoction with thousands of spectators watching.

The memory of how small a human being looks in that vast space when watching from the sidelines doesn't provide much comfort.

"If anyone can do it, it's you." Raul cocks his head at the peal of bells. "Lore and Bas should be here in a moment. Are you looking for a little excitement to cap off the evening?"

He teases his fingers down the side of my neck, and I give him a light swat to the chest. "I only wanted to talk to all of you—briefly, because I really should get as much sleep as I can before tomorrow's fight. Making sure I survive the rite is more important than having a tumble."

"Of course it is." Raul leans in, but the kiss he offers me is an unexpectedly chaste peck to my forehead, as if he's proving he doesn't have to play into his rakish reputation. "I'm honored that you trusted me as a teacher." His grin widens. "And I'm also looking forward to all the ways we can celebrate your victory without worries about the fight hanging over us."

At a knock on the door, he saunters over to let his foster brothers in. I step to the side and put my sword down on his desk, letting my hand linger there to support my balance.

Exhaustion is already winding through my limbs. It's more tolerable now that I know the happy reason for my additional fatigue, but it adds to my own worries at the same time.

I've put together a mildly stimulating tea blend to help keep me alert tomorrow, but the most potent herbs for that purpose are best avoided in my current state. At least I have more slivers of ruddy root to chew on against nausea.

I should probably have headed back to my bed already, but I wanted to see all of my lovers once more. Whether Raul is so confident in my abilities it hasn't occurred to him or he's simply not mentioning it, this could be the last time I speak to them.

There's only one way tomorrow's rite can go well and so many ways it can turn into a catastrophe.

The other two men I love slip into the room. Lorenzo strides straight to me and wraps his arms around me in a soothing embrace.

As I tip my head against Lorenzo's shoulder, Bastien comes to a stop a couple of paces away. The prince of Cotea hesitates there for a moment before propelling himself the last short distance and tucking his own arm around me.

I pull back just enough to give each of them a tender kiss and then gather myself for the discussion ahead. "Do you have every aspect of your plan worked out? Is there any way I can help after the fight is over?"

Lorenzo shakes his head. *"You just need to keep playing the part of victor. We'll take care of everything during the festivities afterward."*

Bastien's expression has turned even more solemn at the reminder of the immense responsibility they're facing tomorrow. "You said the sedative should keep her in a deep unconscious state for several hours, didn't you?"

"I believe so. It's adapting the one I've given Marclinus a few times now, and he's always slept through the whole night afterward. But with different body types and not being able to dose very accurately…"

It's possible I won't just sedate this woman but outright poison her to the death I was attempting to prevent. But making the attempt feels so much more right than giving in to the empire's brutality without at least trying.

Raul joins our cluster and squeezes my shoulder. "We'll get her out of there as quickly as possible. Lorenzo will make sure no one notices us messing with the bodies. We've got a source for a corpse we can toss in her place. Then we stay concealed and haul her out of the city."

I swallow thickly. "Are you sure no one will notice that the corpse isn't her?"

"We'll bash up the face enough that no one would expect to recognize her. It isn't as if anyone will have paid that much attention to her exact looks."

Bastien nods. "It's a big city, which means plenty of deaths every week through ordinary causes. It shouldn't be hard to find a body that's decently close."

"And after you get her out of the city?" I ask.

Lorenzo twines his fingers with mine. *"We'll leave her in a secluded spot well away from the roads, with some food and a note telling her to head home to Lavira."*

Raul lets out a dark chuckle. "She'd better have enough sense to listen to it. But even if she's reckless enough to make trouble here on her own, she'll have no idea how she got out of the city or who helped her. She can dig her own grave if she wants, but she can't dig ours."

I don't think I can ask for more of a guarantee than that.

I ease away from the men to pace across the bedroom, searching my mind for any question I haven't asked, any concern I should raise before we tumble into this possibly mad scheme. Nothing comes to me except a twinge of queasiness that isn't all nerves.

My pulse thrums faster. I look over at my three princes, the men who've followed me so far into mutiny and are on the verge of following me farther still.

I hadn't decided if I was going to tell them this last part —if it would cause them that much more heartache tomorrow if I fail. But perhaps what matters more is how the knowledge will serve them if I succeed and the rest of the burden falls on their shoulders.

They'll have that much more inspiration to guide them, that much more reason to ensure they make it back to me.

I grope for the best way to make the announcement, but most of my words have fled me.

The princes are watching me, Lorenzo knitting his brow. *"Are you all right, Rell?"*

There's nothing for it except to simply spit it out. Why should it be a grand proclamation? People get pregnant every day.

As ordinary as my state might be, a smile touches my lips with the anxious but giddying fact of it.

"It worked," I say softly. "The next part of our bigger plans. There's an imperial heir on the way."

The men freeze for a moment before understanding dawns on all their faces. I can't stop myself from focusing on Bastien.

All four of us conspired to bring this child into being, but it's his the most literally out of the three.

His eyes have widened. He steps forward as if transfixed, touching my cheek and my shoulder and then lowering his hands to my belly, which won't hold the curve that reveals the new life inside me for some weeks yet.

When he meets my eyes again, the smile that stretches across his face sends a pang straight through my heart. I answer it, so much bittersweet emotion swelling inside me that I lose my words completely.

I'm going to bring a child into this world. I couldn't have asked for a more devoted father.

But Bastien may never get to act as a parent to our son or daughter. We can never reveal the truth of this baby's origins. Everything we've worked toward depends on the empire believing the child is my husband's.

His voice comes out choked. "You're still—tomorrow—"

A lump rises in my own throat. "I have to. There's no point having this child if I'm not in a position to protect them in every possible way."

Bastien bows his head, seeking out my lips for the sweetest of kisses. With a rasp of feet across the rug, Raul and Lorenzo join us, encircling me in a ring of warmth.

We're on our way. We have so much to fight for.

By all that's holy, let us see this perilous plan through.

Raul's voice has roughened as well. "You *really* need your rest so you can stay safe tomorrow, Shepherdess. I should get you back to your room."

I cling to them for a few more beats of my heart, soaking in their love. Bastien steals one last kiss, as does Lorenzo, soft and lingering. Then I follow Raul to the door.

Once I've traveled through the hidden passages back to my apartment, I find I'm not quite ready to turn in for the night after all. A restlessness winds through my limbs. The stutter of my pulse stirs up flickers of images from my dreams: the lambs, the hawk.

At least one godlen has reached out to me. I can do the same in return, for whatever good it might do our cause.

I open my door with my head held high. "I'm visiting the palace temple."

As usual, the two guards stationed outside make no comment. I glide through the halls to the temple that's attached to the side of the palace as swiftly as I can without looking frantic.

A few lanterns still glow under the temple's immense domed roof. I glance around at the alcoves dedicated to each of the lesser gods who watch over us and go to kneel on the white cushion in front of Elox's statue.

Tapping my fingers to mind, heart, and gut in the gesture of the divinities, I bow my head. With each even breath, I direct my inner voice toward the godlen of peace and healing.

I know I haven't followed the exact path you laid before me. Please stay with me through tomorrow's struggle. By saving this woman's life, I'm choosing peace. I'm living the principles you've taught, honoring my faith in you.

No answer comes. My throat tightens, but I cast out another message. *I may not be choosing peace when it comes to my husband, but you've seen how little he's offered me. He has several months before I'm in a position to act on my intentions. If he can change for the better in that time, I can change my mind too. If he hasn't, I hope you'll recognize that he's one more obstacle in our way to the kinder future we both want.*

I wait on the cushion for a few minutes longer, lapsing into a light meditation. Nothing I can call even a vague vision passes before my eyes.

Please, let Elox at least be considering my point rather than dismissing me.

When I get to my feet, my attention veers to the statue of the godlen whose interests I'm meant to cater to directly tomorrow morning.

Sabrelle stands stern and mighty, one foot resting on the body of a slain stag. Her marble-carved armor has been polished to such a sheen I could almost believe it's the palest of metals. She stares out from beneath her tufted helm as if daring anyone to challenge her.

I sink onto her scarlet pillow, offering up the three-fingered tap to her as well. *Sabrelle, our principles are often at odds, but I believe I'm still serving yours with my strategy tomorrow. You appreciate clever military tactics as well as brute strength. I'm waging my own sort of war, and to win it I need both might and wits. Please don't take the combination as an insult but as the most powerful approach to combat I can offer.*

The godlen of war doesn't deign to bless me with a vision or any other sort of response either. Finally, I push to my feet.

I've said my piece. I've done everything I can. Tomorrow,

I'll decide my own fate—and perhaps that of the entire empire.

CHAPTER FORTY-FOUR

Aurelia

I don't know if it's the pregnancy or my general level of apprehension, but every sensation in the arena has heightened. The tang of old blood lingers beneath the crisper scent of the dry earthen ground. The warbled voices clamor from the crowd that's packed into the stands all around the imperial box. A wisp of hot breeze touches my face, more a taunt than a comfort. The sun blazes overhead like a rod straight from the forge.

The cleric of the Temple of Triumphant Valor, the Sabrellian temple built next to this stadium of battle, lays out a strip of red silk across the temporary altar set up in the steps below us. The staircase is temporary too, made of steeply layered wooden boards to allow Marclinus and then me to descend into the arena directly from our honored seats.

Cleric Turentan climbs up the rest of the stairs, carrying two gleaming bundles. When he hands the first to Marclinus,

my husband unfurls it into a plated mail vest with chain link across the shoulders and falling to thigh-length.

As Marclinus sheds his jacket to pull on the ceremonial battle armor over his violet tunic and black slacks, the cleric turns to me. The slant of his mouth suggests he's at least as uncertain about my participation as High Commander Axius is.

"Do you still intend to complete the rite, Your Imperial Highness?" he says in a low voice only Marclinus and I will hear.

I dip my head in acknowledgment. "I mean to honor Sabrelle and earn her approval before our people. I'm prepared for whatever lies ahead."

I hope. I adjust the bit of ruddy root I've been periodically sinking my molars into against my cheek, letting it settle another twinge of nausea.

"You may as well don your garb now, then." Turentan hands me the vest and motions to my slim belt. "You should remove all accessories, including that knife. I'll return with Sabrelle's chosen weapons."

I glance down at myself with a twist of my gut. I expected this request, but it's still unnerving to be faced with the reality.

I simply have to stay calm and subtle, and no one will realize I've done anything unusual.

My belt unclasps easily enough. I set it at the edge of my cushioned seat with the pouch's flap facing upward. The plate mail slides over my rose-pink dress—what seemed like a fitting merging of Sabrelle's red and Elox's white—with a hiss of the chain links.

The vest weighs on my shoulders and chest, but not as heavily as I feared. I flex my arms experimentally and find the short sleeves don't encumber them any more than the puff of my gown's.

The purple scars splattered across my forearms stand out starkly in the intense sunlight. They're proof of how much I'm willing to risk and sacrifice for my goals.

I reach for my pouch as if I'm checking that it's securely fastened. As I fiddle with the flap, I dip my hand past it just for a second.

My fingers press against the scrap of fabric I soaked with the gel-like potion I brewed, squeezing out all of the substance I can. When I straighten up, I tuck the slick digits against the folds of my skirt to keep their wet gleam out of view.

Cleric Turentan presents Marclinus with his weapon first: a broadsword with a gold-gilded hilt that looks made for an emperor. Does the Temple of Triumphant Valor keep a large collection of fancy swords, or was his choice a foregone conclusion?

To my relief, the weapon the cleric offers me is significantly smaller though hardly *small*. The narrow blade with its slight curve stretches the length of my forearm.

I grasp the sword's leatherbound grip in my good hand, tilting the blade to the light and then drawing it closer to me as if I merely want to feel the blade. My fingers slide across the sharp edge as swiftly as I can manage without slicing my own flesh open.

The steel shines with an extra, faintly yellow glint, but when I glance up, the cleric has already focused on Marclinus again. No one appears to have noticed my furtive gesture.

As far as I can tell, at least. My pulse keeps thudding at a hurried rhythm. I wipe the remainders of the sedative gel on my dress beneath the fall of the chainmail where no one will be able to see it until after the battle. At that point, any lingering mark can be blamed on sweat, dirt, or blood.

Now all I have to do is slice a woman's forehead open and

convincingly pretend to stab her to death, all while she does her best to carve me open instead. Simple enough.

Ha.

Cleric Turentan leads Marclinus down to the altar. An amplification charm projects the cleric's emphatic voice all through the vast arena. "His Imperial Majesty will demonstrate his might and military prowess before our godlen of battle and the hunt." He turns to Marclinus. "May you do Sabrelle proud."

My husband brandishes his sword in a sort of salute, handling it with an ease that reminds me of the second trial he subjected me and his other potential brides to. The way he swings the weapon in his grasp, you'd think it was as light as one of those throwing knives.

He marches down the steps without a trace of concern, exuding confidence. The sun beams off his golden hair in a ring that might as well be a crown of light.

I did hear that he took to the battlefield himself when putting down the rebellion in Rione several years ago, when he was all of nineteen. This may be one confirmation rite where he needs no additional help at all.

As far as I can tell, he's gotten the exact same equipment as I have, if a larger sword that I couldn't have wielded well regardless. And when he stops on the span of red fabric stretched across the middle of the arena and his opponent emerges, it's clear he hasn't received any favoritism in that department either.

The Lavirian rebel escorted out by a host of four soldiers is the one I noticed pacing in his cell yesterday morning. He matches Marclinus's substantial height and may have twenty or thirty pounds on my husband's well-built frame besides, his shoulders and chest even burlier.

He walks forward with a stormy expression that shows no sign that he means to throw this fight. When the soldiers draw him to a stop across from his emperor, he gnashes his teeth and spits on the fabric.

Boos echo down from the stands, along with hollers about "foul traitors" and "stinking rebels."

A cool grin has curved Marclinus's lips. He flicks his free hand through the gesture of the divinities and motions to the soldiers to release their prisoner.

One tosses a mace on the sheet in front of the man, which I presume is his assigned weapon. Another unlocks the shackles that bind the rebel's wrists. They give him a shove toward the weapon and back up a few paces.

I suppose they'll intervene if it looks as if their emperor's life is in danger—even if that failure means he can't rightfully claim his title as emperor anymore.

Marclinus doesn't need their protection. He holds his sword casually as his opponent picks up the mace, but the second the other man lunges at him, he springs into motion.

I don't want to think anything positive about the callously sadistic man I married. All the same, I can't deny that he's impressive to watch on the battlefield.

Marclinus doesn't have quite Raul's imposing strength, but he makes up for it with deftness. He feints and dodges, always moving, always slicing his sword this way and that to find his attacker's openings.

It only takes a matter of seconds before he's drawn first blood in a deep cut across the rebel's upper arm. The man snarls and hurls himself at Marclinus even more aggressively, but brute force is clearly not going to win the day.

Marclinus sidesteps him and knees him in the ribs. As the man starts to spin around, Marclinus bashes him in the back of the skull with the pommel of his sword.

The rebel staggers and lurches to his knees. In one swift stroke, Marclinus plunges his blade straight through his torso, piercing the man's heart.

He wipes the blade on the man's tunic and backs away from the growing puddle of blood beneath the limp corpse. Watching the scene, bile rises in my throat that the ruddy root isn't enough to contain.

At least I can take a little comfort in the fact that my husband showed enough mercy to end the man's life quickly rather than toying with him.

Though that's probably only because he wanted his completion of the rite to be as clear and clean as possible, not because he wouldn't have enjoyed it.

Marclinus raises his sword in the air to a roar of applause and eager voices that reverberates through the arena. Cleric Turentan strides over to lead him back to the altar and proclaim his worthiness in Sabrelle's eyes.

My mouth goes dry. Now it's my turn.

I stand straight and steady, feeling the gazes of the nobles on the imperial seats fix on me. My princes sit among the figures of the court, but I don't dare look their way. Seeing even a hint of fear in their eyes might unravel me.

Marclinus returns to his seat and tips his head to me. I force a smile and walk partway down the steps to where the cleric is beckoning me to the altar.

Turentan clasps my free hand and holds it in the air. "Our empress will also carry out the rite to earn Sabrelle's favor! If our godlen offers her blessing, one more of the treacherous traitors from Lavira will fall to Her Imperial Highness's blade."

A round of cheers that's not quite as thunderous as that for Marclinus rolls through the stands. The soldiers are already leading my opponent out to the now rumpled red sheet that marks our battleground. The other rebel's corpse has been carted away.

I recognize the woman from my prison visit, but after just a few seconds of observing her approach, my heart sinks.

Her steps sway oddly, as if she's slogging through ankle-deep water rather than air. Her head bobs to one side and then the other. Her gaze drifts across the arena grounds without appearing to focus on anything.

Oh no.

If I actually wanted to end this woman's life, I'd be grateful. Either Marclinus or the temple staff have arranged for my opponent to be drugged so she won't put up much of a fight.

I'd imagine the effect isn't so strong that she won't attack me when I'm right in front of her, but the clumsiness will make it easy to cut her down.

Except cutting her down isn't what I want to do. I meant to *save* her life.

Whatever drug they've given her when combined with the sedative on my sword will almost certainly overwhelm her body. Just the swipe of my blade across her forehead could kill her without my landing another blow.

A chill spreads over my skin. Cleric Turentan is finishing the rest of a speech I've lost track of. Any moment now, he's going to direct me the rest of the way down the stairs and onward to this battle I can't conquer.

What more can I do? I've lost before I had the chance to even try.

That thought sends a surge of defiance through my veins. My fingers tighten around the sword's grip.

I didn't come all this way, go through all the trials and struggles I have, just to give in to the full brutality of the empire now.

I know who holds the real authority even in this rite. I spin toward my husband while gesturing at the woman with my sword. "I need a different challenger. Fighting that one would be an insult to Sabrelle."

The cleric gapes at me. A few seats over from Marclinus, I see High Commander Axius frown.

My pulse hitches faster, but I focus all my attention on my husband.

Marclinus cocks his head. "How so, wife? You approved of her yesterday."

I don't even have to accuse anyone of willfully rigging the odds in my favor. There's an alternate explanation. "I'm very familiar with the signs of illness. She's out of sorts, weak and sick. Look at the way she moves. It would hardly be a fair fight. There were four other prisoners. Let me fight one of them, one who'll be able to fight back properly."

One who'll have a much better chance of harming me. But better that I take the risk than take the life of one of these people on purpose.

It'll be better that than betraying everything I stand for, whether I can voice those qualms to anyone around me or not.

Marclinus studies me through several thuds of my heart. I can't tell what's going on behind his chilly gray eyes.

Axius clears his throat, his frown deepening. Does he suspect I have ulterior motives?

Before the high commander can speak, another voice, sultry but resonant, lifts from the swarm of nobles. "Let her have a real battle! We should get to see just how mighty Her Imperial Highness can be. The wild princess obviously isn't afraid to show her worth."

My attention snaps to Bianca, who's looking at Marclinus rather than me, her lips set in a coy smile. She's giving him even more excuse to accept my request, framing it in selfish terms that won't sound too odd to anyone listening.

Perhaps she really does think it'll be more entertaining to watch me stand off against a fiercer foe.

Bianca's nerve appears to have emboldened others among

the court. Vicerine Saldette speaks up too, in a more brittle tone. "Yes, she's never shied from the struggle before. Why should she be forced to take it easy this time?"

My breath snags in my throat. From her taut expression, I suspect she's hoping I'll meet the same fate that her daughter did in the trials months ago, but her animosity might work in my favor for now.

Marclinus lifts his eyebrows at the two noblewomen. Then he meets my gaze with a satisfied smirk. "You deserve every opportunity to prove yourself. Guards, fetch one of the other prisoners—and make sure they're in good health."

As Bianca turns away, her gaze catches mine just for an instant, with a flicker of a softer smile. An ache forms in my throat.

She doesn't know exactly why it matters to me, but she understood that it did. She spoke up for me.

As far as I know, she's never revealed her suspicious about my possible dalliances to Marclinus either. Is it possible… I can actually trust this woman?

That's a question for later. Because thanks in part to her, I now have to face an even more perilous battle than I expected.

CHAPTER FORTY-FIVE

Aurelia

Cleric Turentan pitches his voice toward the stands again. "Her Imperial Highness fears that her opponent is unwell and would not make for a fair fight worthy of Sabrelle's approval! We will bring out another of the Lavirian traitors for her to prove her mettle against."

Murmurs pass through the audience along with scattered applause. As the soldiers lead the drugged woman away, Cleric Turentan guides me down the steps and across the long stretch of sand-strewn earth to the swath of scarlet fabric.

He turns to me, and his weathered face tightens. I can't tell whether he's disapproving of my choice or simply concerned for how I'll fare.

He bobs his head. "May you do my godlen honor."

Then he walks back to the staircase, and I'm left alone with a mob of thousands staring down at me.

The arena feels even more immense now that I'm standing in the middle of it. The stone walls loom far off and yet still unnervingly high. I'm no mightier than a pebble thrown into the middle of the ocean.

Is this how we mortals always appear to the gods who watch over us?

I flex my fingers around the grip of the sword, getting more familiar with its weight. The sun glares from the east, so I step around the fighting ground until it's burning into my back instead of my eyes.

My fine leather slippers, meant for strolling around the palace rather than combat, slide on the silky cloth. Marclinus wore boots.

After a moment's debate, I slip the slippers off and kick them over onto the packed dirt behind me. My bare feet will give me better traction.

I suspect I'm going to need every advantage I can get.

The dry heat seeps down my throat and into my lungs. By the time the soldiers reappear by the doorway they've been using, my mouth is utterly parched.

The four of them are shoving along one of the male prisoners. Before they've even gotten close, I can tell he's at least a few inches taller than me and plenty bulkier.

His dark eyes sear into me with fury from his pale, dirt-smudged face.

My pulse thumps faster, but I hold myself still and unyielding. Those eyes are alert; his steps are steady. This prisoner hasn't been drugged for my benefit.

I can let one of the rebels who fought for their country's freedom go free himself. As long as I survive the battle with him.

Will the soldiers intervene if he gets the upper hand, like they would have for Marclinus? I don't know what orders they've been given.

Perhaps my husband would rather see me fall than return to his side beaten before the godlen he himself is dedicated to. For all I know, every citizen and soldier in my audience would approve of that decision.

As the escort reaches the edge of the fabric, I brush my fingers down my front in recognition of the gods and brace myself.

As with Marclinus's opponent, one of the soldiers tosses a mace onto the cloth as the rebel's weapon. They release him from his bonds and retreat a short distance, but their solemn expressions don't give me much hope of their protection.

I asked for this battle. I promised I'd serve the principle of peace rather than violence, cleverness rather than stark brutality.

But gods help me, I wish there didn't need to be so much violence to reach even a shred of that peace.

The man snatches up the mace and then studies me. A ragged but mocking laugh tumbles from his lips. Apparently he's sized me up as an easy target.

He strides across the red fabric toward me, raising his mace.

With his first swing and my swipe at him as I dodge to the side, I realize the full extent of my trouble. This rebel's head is those few inches higher than the woman's would have been; his reach is longer.

He isn't going to offer me the kind of openings Raul would have when I simply needed to practice my positioning. The sword I trained with was longer than this one besides.

How in the realms am I going to manage to slash my opponent's forehead without getting so close I let him bash my entire skull open?

I'm a little faster than him, at least. He might not be drugged, but he'll be stiff and weakened from his time imprisoned. Adrenaline can only overcome those effects so far.

Which means I can duck and scramble away from his powerful blows, but only just. Not swiftly enough to leap in and carve open his flesh.

I could try to cut his arms, which are the parts of his body most within reach, but I'm not sure how much force I'd need to use to sever the rough fabric of his long-sleeved tunic. I'd risk wiping off most of the potion on his clothing rather than getting it into his bloodstream.

Maybe if I could nick one of his bare hands…

I attempt a few jabs, but my opponent is hardly *slow*. He whips the mace around, feinting and then blocking. The metal base slams against my sword with so much force the impact wobbles into my bones.

Gritting my teeth, I push myself to the side. The red cloth of our battleground is bunching beneath our feet. Sweat trickles down my neck and beneath the back of my gown.

Shouts of encouragement ring out from our audience, some as simple as, "Empress! Empress!" and others demanding that I "kill the traitor!" or similar sentiments.

How patient will they remain if I continue to struggle?

The rebel hurls himself at me so abruptly I don't quite dodge in time. His mace clangs against the plate mail on my side, hard enough to send a jabbing pain through my chest.

I think he might have cracked a rib.

I inhale sharply and keep pacing around him, clutching my sword. If I can turn the same tactic against him…

I lunge forward with a swing of my blade upward, but the element of surprise isn't enough. My opponent lurches backward and then lashes out with his weapon.

My sword merely whips through the air several inches

shy of his face. The spikes at the end of his mace scrape across my arm just above my elbow.

A cry breaks from my throat. Stinging pain radiates from the gouge in my flesh alongside the patter of blood onto the matching fabric beneath me.

The sword suddenly feels twice as heavy in my grasp, but I can't relieve the strain. With another harsh laugh, the rebel charges at me, pressing his advantage.

I barely scramble away from his brutal swings. One catches me on the thigh just below the fall of the chainmail. The mace's spikes tear through both my skirt and my skin.

I stumble, my leg wobbling under me. The wound throbs with the pulsing of spilled blood.

For a second, my head swims with dizziness. I propel myself farther away, trying not to stagger, my pulse kicking up to a frantic pace.

Before much longer, I'll be too weak to have any chance at all. The soldiers don't seem inclined to step in—and if they have to, then I haven't really won at all.

Most of the spectators have fallen into an uneasy hush. They're watching now to see if their empress is about to be murdered.

I wasn't trained for combat. I'm not as large or as strong as the man I'm up against, and now I'm injured on top of that. How the fuck am I supposed to succeed?

This is why they drugged the woman. They didn't think I could conquer any of the rebels while they were clear-headed, even if all I was trying to accomplish was killing my opponent by whatever means possible.

They assumed I was too weak, just as the man striding toward me does. Disgust is written all over his face.

He spits on the fabric like his fellow rebel did and glares at me. "Looks like I get to take down one part of this blasted empire."

He might not be wrong. I can't even imagine how the princes must feel watching this scene.

Picturing their horror while the rebel trudges grimly toward me, I jolt back to another time when it was two of my now-lovers confronting me. When Raul and Bastien stood in the abandoned bedroom, accusing me of manipulating Lorenzo to some horrible end and of toying with all their affections...

I knew then that I couldn't defend myself with might. I had to play the lamb. Be the soft, simpering princess so many expected.

What if I can turn the tables the same way today?

The possibility steadies me despite the continuing blare of pain and the blood seeping through my gown. I limp back a few more steps, facing my opponent. I let my shoulders hunch and my sword lower.

"I'm sorry," I say, keeping my voice soft so no one in the distant stands will hear it. "It shouldn't have been like this. You shouldn't have been treated this way."

The rebel slows with a sputter of an exhalation. "What shit are you talking? You and your fucking empire brought me here."

I hold his gaze, willing all the sympathy I can summon into my eyes. It isn't hard, because I do feel awful for him. I feel awful for what I'm doing to him, even if it's better than murder.

"Whatever people you hurt or crimes you committed, you were trying to help someone, weren't you? You must have been thinking of your family and your friends, wanting them to have better lives."

The rebel stares at me. His lips pull back in a snarl. "You don't know anything about any of it."

I offer him a tentative smile. "I know that no one fights this hard without believing it's the right thing to do. You cared so much about so many people. There's something admirable about that."

His jaw falls slack before he snaps it shut again. He shakes his head. "You're not making any sense. Shut up!"

The aggression in his stance has faltered with his confusion. He closes his eyes for a second, perhaps to collect himself, and that's all the opening I need.

I spring forward with all the strength and speed I have left and slice my sword tip across his forehead.

As I heave myself backward at the rebel's furious groan, blood gushes down over his face just as Raul promised it would. He rams his mace into my shoulder, one of the spikes digging through the chainmail sleeve, but it can't cut through my elation.

I back up, parrying my opponent's wild blows as well as I can. I only need to dodge a little when he can barely see where he's striking, but I want to look as if I'm still engaged in the fight.

The audience has woken up again with a wave of cheers. A booming of stomping feet reverberates through the arena.

The eager voices wash over me, flipping my stomach. They're baying for more of this man's blood.

And I have to look as if I'm giving it to them.

I note the first moment he starts to stagger. His body sways to the side not much differently from how his drugged associate looked.

I have to move now, before his declined state becomes obvious to anyone else.

With my jaw clenched against the wounds searing at my limbs, I heave myself to the side. Then I ram into him, scraping my blade along his upper torso.

The cutting edge rips through his tunic and pierces his flesh. I feel it jar against his ribs with a flicker of relief.

The sedative and my assault knock the rebel off his feet.

He topples backward and slumps on the ground. His head lolls from side to side as if he's trying and failing to clear his head.

I stand over him, restraining a wince, and slam my sword into his side one more time.

A small grunt huffs out of him at the shallow wound. After a moment, his face drifts to one side so his cheek rests against the earth. His body stills.

If I checked his neck and waited long enough, I should still pick up a faint, sporadic heartbeat. But I'm hoping the soldiers who cart his body away won't bother searching for a pulse when he looks so very dead.

Exhaustion rolls over me along with the din of the crowd's excitement. Part of me wants to collapse too, but I know I have to squeeze every bit of significance I can out of this moment.

Through a sharper flare of pain, I raise my sword into the air above my head in a pose of triumph. The cheers fade with an air of anticipation.

I raise my voice as loud as I can, hoping at least the lowest tiers of the stands will hear me. "For every one of our gods and the All-Giver! For Dariu and all this empire's people! We can conquer everything that would destroy us!"

I happen to believe it's men like Marclinus causing most of the destruction, but I don't have to mention that detail.

Another roar of applause sweeps over me. I lift my chin high.

Elox, I did all I could here. I still stand for peace and healing, no matter what else I do.

As if in answer, a cloud drifts past the sun. The arena ground briefly darkens—except for a single beam of light that flares straight onto me like a divine caress.

The sunbeam's warmth flows over me, and my throat

tightens. The renewed surge of the crowd's furor sounds even more distant while I'm draped in the approval of my godlen.

As the cloud passes and the sunlight evens out, my sword arm drops to my side. I only barely manage to hold on to the sword rather than letting it fall to the ground.

The soldiers rush over, two going to collect the body, two others coming to flank me, as if I need their protection now that the danger is over. A medic in white Eloxian robes hustles behind them. He offers me a reassuring smile and bends to set his hands against the deepest wound on my thigh.

As the warmth of the medic's healing gift spreads through my flesh, I glance toward my husband. Marclinus is standing, clapping his hands alongside our audience with a wide grin.

He's fully confirmed himself as their emperor, and I've confirmed myself as their empress. Now it's time to discover where our triumphs will take the both of us.

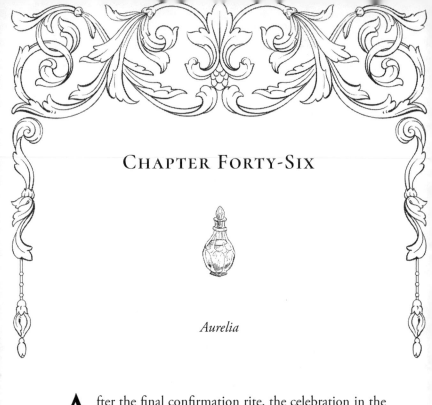

CHAPTER FORTY-SIX

Aurelia

After the final confirmation rite, the celebration in the capital overshadows all those before. Triumphant music swells from every direction; red and violet banners whirl in the wind from rooftops all around the largest city square. The bakers and chefs commissioned to supply refreshments sent a flood of smells both sweet and savory through the air.

In front of the audience of civilians, all of the nobles currently at court have knelt to reconfirm their loyalty to Marclinus and the imperial line. His foster brothers were among them, careful not to so much as glance my way.

They've departed now with some excuse I didn't hear, but I know they're actually sneaking through the city under the cover of Lorenzo's illusions and Raul's shadows, transporting the one rebel we could save from execution beyond the walls. I'm hoping that replacing the body should be even easier when it's an average-sized man rather than giving them more trouble than they counted on.

As Marclinus and I offer a toast to our subjects and eat morsels for dinner before the reveling crowd, evening falls. Lanterns beam to life, some streaming a golden light and others imperial purple or Sabrellian red. Many have been enchanted to drift through the air above the square like immense fireflies.

When I see the princes return, I school my expression to remain in its same warm smile. From the corner of my eye, I catch Lorenzo's furtive gesture. *All's well.*

The tension that's been weighing on my chest dissolves, letting my next breath flow more deeply into my lungs. I proved myself to Dariu's citizens and to my husband without actually compromising what I stand for—or losing anyone I love.

I swallow the next few bites of roast duck with more genuine enthusiasm. The people before us prance and whirl with periodic cheers encouraged by the imperial guards stationed around the square. Some of the nobles on the platform around us sway with the music too, while others simply relax and nibble on the offered delicacies.

Marclinus has spent most of the time when he isn't waving and bowing to the crowd laughing with his noblemen friends and tossing back wine. He's been in more exuberant spirits since we had our brief respite at the palace to wash and change our clothes after our battles.

He elbows me playfully, his eyes glinting. "Now we're right where we're meant to be, aren't we, wife? I'll bet you never imagined you'd be sitting in the capital of the empire like this when you were a little girl back in Accasy."

I hold my smile in place. "No, I didn't, but I'm ever so grateful to be here."

Those words aren't even a lie.

Marclinus hums and trails his fingers down the side of my arm. "I'll be grateful when we can have our time alone later tonight. Why don't we confirm just how—"

He cuts himself off at a parting of the crowd just beyond our platform. High Commander Axius strides over to us from the ring of guards. He dips his head to Marclinus with a slight nod to me as well—and a similar apologetic grimace to the one he offered me while he pledged his devotion to the empire this afternoon.

"Your Imperial Eminences," he says. "A party of citizens would like to make a presentation to Empress Aurelia. My soldiers have checked them over and can see no means by which they could harm either of you. Shall we let them through?"

My heart skips a beat. A presentation? I wasn't expecting that.

Marclinus's smile tightens slightly, but he waves at Axius to go on. "Let them up. An honor to my empress is an honor to me as well."

Yes, as long as he's beside me, I'm sure he'll never fail to take credit for anything I accomplish.

Several guards usher a group of a dozen or so men and women through the crowd and onto the platform. The music briefly halts. Faces all around the square turn to watch.

One man in a well-fitted linen tunic and trousers kneels before me while his companions cluster behind him. He's holding a parcel of fabric.

He clears his throat. "Your Imperial Highness, we represent the people of Vivencia and citizens all across our country who've passed on reports of your bravery and kindness. You may have come from far north, but you've shown more dedication to the Dariu's people already than we could have hoped to ask for. We feel you deserve this symbol of our respect and appreciation in return."

Tugging back the cloth, he reveals a crown that's made of twined leaves, their glazed surfaces artfully shaped into a ring.

Marclinus stiffens beside me. I lose my breath.

A woman speaks up at the man's shoulder, explaining what I've already guessed. "It's a wreath made from leaves native to every part of our country. Dariu was proud to present a similar gift to our former empress, may the gods still bless her soul. We felt you deserved no less."

I manage to find my voice through the swell of emotion in my chest. "I'm honored by your offering. May I put it on?"

The entire delegation breaks out into grins. "Please, Your Imperial Highness," the man says.

I lift the wreath crown from his hands and nestle it on my head. Someone in the crowd beyond lets out a whoop, and then the entire square bursts into cheers and clapping and hollers of, "To Empress Aurelia, long may she live!" The soldiers around us add to the applause, many of them grinning themselves.

As the guards usher the delegation off the platform, I can't hold back my own wider smile. Every beat of my heart resonates with joy.

All the pain I've gone through and the risks I've taken have been worth it. I've truly been accepted—by at least enough of Dariu's people to have received this honor. What doubters still exist, I simply need more time to win them over too.

Possibly including my own husband.

Marclinus pushes off his seat and holds out his hand to me. "It does appear I've chosen well. Let's give them something worth watching."

He spins me to the resumed music so abruptly the crown almost tumbles off my head. I only get a second to right it before he's grasped me by the waist to match the dancing below.

I'm not sure whether it's the presenting of the crown or the spirited music, but my husband appears even more impatient to get to the private part of the night. After he's led me through three dances and downed another glass of wine, he waves to the crowd once more. "Your empress and I must take our leave, but we look forward to tomorrow's celebrations!"

I follow him to the waiting carriage without complaint. My skin is still tingling with the knowledge of what I've accomplished today.

How could there be a more perfect time to share the news that should earn me if not his full devotion, then at least his dedication to seeing me survive the next several months?

I wait until the carriage is moving, the rasp of the wheels over the paved road obscuring our voices to the guards seated outside. Marclinus slips his arm around me with a stroke of his fingers from my thigh to my ass.

I set my hand against his chest to stop him. "Husband, we have one more joy to celebrate today. Before we left for the festivities, I used one of the common herbal means to test —it appears I'll soon be providing you with an heir."

I'm not sure what to expect for the strength of Marclinus's reaction, but I have no doubt it'll be positive. So when he simply blinks at me, his leering smile faltering, my pulse stutters.

He seems to recover quickly enough, with a broad smile that I can't help feeling is a little too tight. "What wonderful news! Are you sure?"

I spread my hands. "We can ask the medics to confirm, but the results seemed quite clear. I have been feeling a little under the weather the past few days—I thought it was nervousness about the rite, but when it persisted after, it occurred to me to check. We have had plenty of opportunity to produce this result."

"Indeed we have." Marclinus chuckles, but something about the sound feels a tad tight too.

My stomach knots. I don't understand why he seems hesitant to rejoice. Surely he's wanted an heir? Everyone else in the palace has seemed to think that's my main purpose to him.

I'd like to think he's only anxious remembering what befell his own mother in childbirth, but I have trouble believing he cares about my well-being quite that much.

"Many things to celebrate tonight indeed," Marclinus goes on. He presses his mouth against the side of my neck in a demanding kiss. "What a spectacular time it'll be! What a wife I have!"

My skin creeps at the manic energy in his voice. Thankfully, it's a short trip back to the palace. The carriage hitches to a halt before Marclinus can do more than grope halfway up my inner thigh.

To my bewilderment, the moment we've clambered out by the front steps, my husband pulls away from me. "Wait for me in your chambers! I have a couple of matters to attend to first."

What in the world? What "matters"? Minutes ago, he appeared to have no concern for anything but bedding me.

I walk through the halls at a regal pace, suppressing my uneasiness. The moment I push past my door, Sprite bounds to meet me. I scoop her up and flop into one of the armchairs, running my fingers over her soft fur until she's purring in a resonant thrum.

How long is my husband going to leave me waiting? What will I face when he returns?

Nothing about this situation feels quite right, but I'm so

confused about what could possibly be *wrong* that I have no idea how to prepare.

Is Marclinus simply upset about my reception from his people, the fact that they offered me a gift and not him, and that's bleeding into his reaction to my pregnancy?

As a precaution, I lift the wreath crown from my head and set it gingerly on top of one of my trunks. I'll need to see about getting a box built for preserving such a treasure.

The minutes slip by. The knots in my stomach multiply. I'd like to crawl into bed and get some sleep, but the last thing I want is for my husband's arrival to take me by surprise.

The bell is just pealing out the tenth hour of the night when the door swings open and he strides in.

I set down Sprite and get up from the chair. Marclinus walks toward me but stops a few feet away. His gaze sweeps down to my belly and back to my face.

The intensity in his expression sends a wobble through my veins. Gone is the nonchalant front with the trace of an edge. I have the impression he's grappling with himself, but I don't know what over.

"Women have ways of judging when their body is fertile, don't they?" Marclinus says without preamble. "The timing of their bleeds and whatnot? I've overheard one or two of the ladies of the court mention it."

I adjust my stance, needing to regain my footing. Where is he going with this line of questioning?

I offer a small smile that I hope is endearing. "There are ways. Of course we can never tell for certain whether any particular interlude will result in a child."

Marclinus takes another step toward me. "But you can at least estimate when this child was conceived."

He says it like a firm statement rather than a question, but it's clear that he wants an answer. I can offer one easily enough. "Based on the timing of my last bleed and the bodily signs I noted, I'd imagine it happened while we were at the palace by Rexoran."

That's the only time I was fully intimate with anyone since I last bled, so I actually know the timing for sure, not that I can reveal that fact.

The tension washes from my husband's face with a light like the sun dawning. He crosses the last short distance to me and brings his hand to my cheek. The other rests on my waist, palm against my belly.

His voice drops to a murmur. "Good. Good. I knew— He's simply—"

Marclinus stops, bowing his head toward mine. At the slide of his fingers along my jaw, I lift my chin to meet his kiss. He melds his mouth to mine, tender but with a strange sense of urgency.

I don't understand any of this, but at least he finally seems happy about the announcement.

When he draws back, I soften my own tone for my tentative questions. "What's happened? Is something wrong?"

Marclinus inhales deeply with a hint of a tremor that startles me. I've never heard him sound this shaken, even when his father died in front of him.

He grasps my hand, squeezes it, and lets it go again as if he's not sure whether the gesture is wise. With an air of resolve, he draws himself straighter. "You've proven yourself. You've earned your place in the family. You need to know."

I knit my brow. "Know what?"

"Come here. Let's sit together."

Marclinus guides me over to the sofa across the room from the bed. He lets me sit next to him with a little space between us and none of the groping he couldn't resist in the carriage. His gaze lingers on my face, dropping briefly to my belly before returning.

He reaches across the space between us, but only to clasp my hand again with an unusual gentleness. "You've heard the story of my birth—that my mother died in the process and my father raised me alone."

I nod. "But I'm sure you don't need to worry about—"

"That's not what I'm getting at." He pauses, and his eyes smolder even more fiercely. "Part of the reason my mother was in such a precarious state is she was pregnant with two children, not one."

What?

I keep my fingers curled around his, waiting for him to explain.

As he speaks, Marclinus's gaze doesn't leave mine for an instant. "She died giving birth to twins. Identical twins. And my father decided that it was best for us and for the imperial line if no one ever knew there were two of us. If we lived one shared life, combining our strengths, balancing out each other's weaknesses, and ensuring any assassination attempt could only target one of us."

He lays the story out so matter-of-factly that it takes a moment for the absurdity of what he's said to sink in.

My jaw goes slack. I know I'm staring at him, but I can't stop, can't hold back the question now blurting from my mouth. "*What?*"

Marclinus swipes his free hand over his face. "I know it's a lot to take in. But it's really very simple. Father got rid of the few people who had a chance to know when we were very young. Once we were old enough, we simply switched off regularly. He had the apartments in all the palaces renovated—there's an additional hidden room in our apartments where we stay when the other is living our life. The wardrobe carriage when we travel is mostly a living space… It's worked. Until now."

I haven't yet wrapped my head around the core of his story. "Then you—it hasn't always been you?"

"No. My brother and I have spent about an equal amount of time with you, trading off depending on the tasks at hand. Linus is fonder of fraternizing and flirting. I do better with strategy and practical action."

"Linus," I repeat.

The man I thought was my husband smiles crookedly. "Yes. I'm Marc. Father thought he was very clever combining the two names so anyone speaking to us always referred to both of us, even if they didn't know."

I think I need to lie down. Perhaps I'll wake up and discover I already fell asleep and this is all a bizarre dream.

Dreams. The one vision Elox sent comes back to me: the two lambs I was holding.

Great God help me, my godlen knew. He tried to tell me.

But no version of my husband that I've interacted with has struck me as remotely lamb-like.

"It's worked until now," Marclinus—no, just *Marc*— repeats, his expression turning more serious again. "But not anymore. Linus has gotten... paranoid. He doesn't trust you. He thinks you're trying to upstage and undermine us—he's had all sorts of mad theories." He shakes his head. "We tested you because he insisted, and all it's done is risk ruining the partnership I can see we should have. Not to mention the commotion he caused in Lavira."

"Oh." A lot of pieces are clicking into place in my head. The sudden shifts in mood, the moments when my husband has appeared frustrated with or even unaware of our past conversations. All the ways he's tried to provoke the princes and perhaps other members of his court as well as me.

Marc makes a disgruntled sound. "He's even soured this blessing—what should be one of the happiest moments of our marriage— He's been taking mirewort because he felt it was too soon to completely enmesh you in the family. I *told* him that you and I slept together more than once when we were at the Rexoran palace, but it's always been him otherwise, and he couldn't believe the timing—but you just confirmed it. He's fucking insane."

I look at the man seated next to me in a daze. "Is that why you're telling me now?"

Marc's eyes harden to steel. "I'm telling you because I'm tired of living only half a life. I can't stand by while Linus destroys everything that should be mine... I need you to help me kill him."

The Gods of the Abandoned Realms

THE ALL-GIVER (the Great God, the One) - overseer of all existence, creator of the godlen

THE GODLEN OF THE SKY

Estera - wisdom, knowledge, and education

Inganne - creativity, play, childhood, and dreams

Kosmel - luck, trickery, and rebellion

THE GODLEN OF THE EARTH

Creaden - royalty, leadership, justice, and construction

Prospira - fertility, wealth, harvest, and parenthood

Sabrelle - warfare, sports, and hunting

THE GODLEN OF THE SEA

Ardone - love, beauty, and bodily pleasures

Elox - health, medicine, and peace

Jurnus - communication, travel, and weather

About the Author

Eva Chase lives in Canada with her family. She loves stories both swoony and supernatural, and strong women and the men who appreciate them.

Along with the Royal Spares series, she is the author of the Rites of Possession series, the Shadowblood Souls series, the Heart of a Monster series, the Gang of Ghouls series, the Bound to the Fae series, the Flirting with Monsters series, the Cursed Studies trilogy, the Royals of Villain Academy series, the Moriarty's Men series, the Looking Glass Curse trilogy, the Their Dark Valkyrie series, the Witch's Consorts series, the Dragon Shifter's Mates series, the Demons of Fame series, and the Legends Reborn trilogy.

Connect with Eva online:
www.evachase.com
eva@evachase.com

Made in United States
Orlando, FL
24 November 2024

54371483R00290